Marks
of the
Forbidden

PRESS

Box 115, Superior, WI 54880 (715) 394-9513

Marks of the Forbidden

Olaf Danielson

To Abbe,
Best Wishes
@laf Daniel
"BRAD"

DEDICATION

To my great-great uncle, Arthur Vadelius, a Swedish-American who died in the trenches of the Argonne in World War I on October 3 of 1918 and is now buried near his friends and neighbors in Anscarius Lutheran Cemetery near Falun, Wisconsin. In many ways he inspired this book.

INTRODUCTION

Norse mythology and symbology play an integral role in the saga of the Defenders of the Earth. The shield on the front cover is the city emblem of Falun, Sweden. Across the top is the alchemic symbol for copper, the runic symbol for the Norse goddess Freyja, and the symbol for female. The bricks on the bottom portion of the shield represent the walls of Freyja's temple.

Near Falun, *Stora Kopparberg*, or Great Copper Mountain, supplied the world with copper beginning in the Nordic Bronze Age (1500-500 B.C.).

Freyja was the Norse goddess of love, sexuality, beauty, and magic. Her priestesses were called Volva, foreseers and trance workers with telepathic powers. Freyja was invincible in battle. In Norse myth, she and her Volva are credited with changing the weather, producing lightning, and changing one's fortune for better or for worse.

The "bricks" of Freyja's temple, though unproven at this time, are said to exist somewhere in the vicinity of Falun, perhaps on or near *Stora Kopparberg* itself.

As you will learn in this series of books, the Volva are the principal Defenders of the Earth who use the huge copper "Array" located in the center of their temple to stay in constant telepathic communication with their operatives throughout the world.

These goddesses, along with the Choosers and the Defenders of the Earth, have kept humanity safe from evil throughout the ages.

PROLOGUE

Gallipoli Peninsula, 1915.

Gunnar brought out his field glasses and watched as the British soldiers charged the summit. The first company went over the top of the ridge and promptly ran into the previously unseen main force of the advancing Turkish army. Gunnar watched as the men were quickly wiped out. The remaining companies, frozen by the initial shock of the enemy's appearance, finally started the retreat. They were overrun before making any real headway, two thousand British soldiers dying in a matter of minutes.

The Turks, invigorated by this preliminary victory, came down the hill like a swarm of locusts, chasing a few British stragglers who were now running for their lives. Gunnar realized that he was the only obstacle between the Turks and the British, and he didn't pose much of a threat; he was just an American military observer caught in the middle of a battle. Neutral or not, his fate would likely be worse than that of any captured British soldier. This was not his war; surrender could not be an option. Instinctively, he ran.

With heavy artillery raining down, he was the first to jump over the wall of the entrenchment. Instead of finding strength and safety, Gunnar found the units in the trench cowering under the lip of the freshly-dug ground.

"Get your asses up here and cover your retreating units!" he roared as the group seemed to perk up at his leadership. "Move or this will be our grave!" The young American officer didn't care that he was out of place. The British soldiers needed, even desired, leadership and his guidance seemed the only that was currently available. Finally, the men began to respond and ready themselves for action—all except for a cowardly colonel, who was running toward the beach and away from the oncoming action. Gunnar assumed command of the unit.

As things began to take shape, he saw that some of the first men down the hill had fallen to the incoming rounds of gun shots. He ran out to help them back to the relative his trench. The code of the U.S. Marine Corps is to leave no one behind. Many a battle had been inadvertently turned by Americans leathernecks throwing their lives on the line to reclaim a fallen comrade in arms, frequently when retreat would seem the only prudent course of action. Gunnar was no exception.

The first man that Gunnar saw had shrapnel in his legs. The major picked him up and dragged him limping back to the trench, then headed back for more. A second British enlisted man was unconscious after being grazed in the head by a bullet. A small band of Turks emerged, and Gunnar instinctively pulled his Colt .45 and executed the first two with single slugs. He shot a third and the man stumbled slightly. The remaining two he dispatched with shots to the chest. He grabbed the wounded man and carried him to the trench. The Turks had not yet arrived in full force, and the major ran to the rescue of a third wounded man crawling in agony near a clump of bushes.

He rounded the thicket only to find himself surrounded by at least ten enemy soldiers, their bayonets pointing at him. He raised his hands and dropped his Colt. He expected to be instantly shot but was prodded to move up the hill away from his men. Captured and soon to be infamous, Major Gunnar Nielstrom, USMC, was the first American POW of World War I.

A pair of muscular Turkish guards pulled him along, each one securely gripping one of his arms. A third guard aimed a handgun squarely into the prisoner's back as if looking for any excuse to fire and instantly solve their problem of a captured American officer. A door opened in front of the entourage and the two guards shoved the prisoner into a dimly lit and musty room. No matter how bad the room looked and smelled, it was infinitely better than the cell that had housed the Marine Corps major the night before. No word could describe the smell made from the combination of decaying flesh and feces mixed with urine.

As the major stumbled for one of the two chairs that dominated the room, a German colonel appeared from behind the door and summarily dismissed the guards, closing the door in their faces.

"You have created something of a political situation, Major Nelstrom," the German colonel started in perfect English, and using the correct Swedish name as opposed to the Americanized version of his last name. "The Americans aren't in this war yet, but here you are, a prisoner."

Gunnar replied in German. "I am a special military observer for the United States military. The Turks overran our position."

The colonel continued in English, sensing a bit of a game. "From what I hear, you're a crack shot with your pistol. Five Turks have now met Allah thanks to you. Most military observers stay out of the action; they watch, take notes, and report, but you organize, motivate, and kill. Were you commanding that brigade in the trench?"

After a sigh, Gunnar continued in German, "I did what I had to do. I was trying to save some men who had fallen."

To his amazement the colonel switched to Swedish, the language of his native soil. "So you have become a good American soldier, then? None to be left behind?"

Gunnar nodded involuntarily as the focus of the conversation changed and the colonel's voice grew softer, quieter, so that no one could hear him, let alone understand him. He continued in Swedish. "You have earned the right to choose, and each choice is as honorable as the other. The first choice is death. This death will spare you from your Turkish captors. They are planning a painfully slow execution by starvation. Here is your pistol; it has but one shell." He threw the pistol on the floor at the prisoner's feet. Gunnar didn't move or say anything.

"The second choice is life." The colonel paused and got up from his chair to look out the window. Artillery rounds exploded nearby. "Ah, but with life, you have responsibilities. You will pledge your heir's heir to us, your firstborn grandson. He will be a member of your family until the age of twenty-four. Then, he is ours." The colonel returned to his seat and asked, "So what is your choice?"

Gunnar was speechless.

The German officer interrupted him. "Choose!"

There would be no explanation, at least for now. Gunnar had been the bravest of the brave. He had shot men, many men. He had served in some of the bloodiest campaigns in the young history of the Marine Corps. But now he was feeling something new: fear.

"You have to make this choice right now, Major Nelstrom."

Gunnar kicked the loaded pistol back under the colonel's chair. "Scheißkerl!"

The colonel smiled, ignoring the epitaph. He holstered the weapon. "Life it is!"

CHAPTER 1: The Stockbroker "Present Day"

As the early summer sun appeared over the cloudless eastern horizon, the wind had already picked up to around twenty miles per hour. To the locals, this would be considered only a gentle morning breeze in this forgotten part of northeastern South Dakota. The rustling of the breeze in the cottonwood trees was broken by the warble of a meadowlark singing out joyously that June fourteenth was going to be an important day.

Daniel Nielstrom was twenty-four years old today. It had become his custom to get up with the sun on his birthday so he wouldn't miss a single daylight minute. Getting up early was nothing new; he had been raised on a small western Nebraska ranch with chores to finish before school. He spent those mornings alone with cattle, his dog Ranger, and a few horses. In contrast, he spent this morning with meadowlarks, bobolinks, sparrows, and an occasional hawk.

As Daniel sat on the back step of the farmhouse that he currently called home, his eyes focused on a red-tailed hawk perched on a dead cottonwood tree that partially made up the windbreak of trees lining the gravel driveway. But his mind was elsewhere. Daniel felt old. Although he'd had a typical childhood and young adulthood in rural America, he'd always felt different than the people he'd grown up with in Ogallala, Nebraska. For starters, he'd grown up in a Swedish home. Although he was a second-generation American, born at the local hospital, he and his two younger sisters were dual citizens of the U.S. and Sweden. His grandfather had immigrated to America over eighty years earlier and had always considered himself a Swede in a foreign land. Daniel's father, Dag, had maintained his Swedish citizenship and had actually married Daniel's mother, Ingrid, after tripping over her in the Stockholm train station on his first return to the homeland.

Daniel and his siblings were expected to act Swedish in custom and manner. They had to speak fluent Swedish, learn Swedish history, and visit their homeland as much as possible. Whenever the family discussed dating or marriage, it was assumed that every young Nielstrom would marry a Swede. Norwegians were acceptable too, both because Norway had once been part of Sweden, and because there was a precedence of such marriages within the family.

Daniel also felt he could bring a Finnish girl home without much complaint from his parents. Unfortunately, very few people in western Nebraska had kept their Scandinavian heritage intact. The pickings were better in Watertown, South Dakota, but he had dated only sporadically. Now at twenty-four, without any firm prospects on the social front, he was starting to feel both lonely and hopeless. He suspected he'd need to make a trip to Sweden to visit his relatives. He fervently hoped he would meet somebody special just as his dad had.

Daniel had always thought his last name a bit odd. The *Niels* was from a transcription error when his grandfather had immigrated through Ellis Island. The processor added an extra *i* that couldn't easily be removed. The *Nels* was actually from Nels, a great ancestor, and the strom came from the Swedish word for river. There was never a river where his ancestors had lived, though there was a small one near their summer cottage, but that one was the Sundborn strom, not the Nels strom. As the legend had it, his grandfather's grandfather had decided to forego the customary Nordic naming practice of changing surnames each generation. Instead, he decided one day to change the family name from Nelsson to Nelstrom because he liked rivers, and it made them different from their neighbors. It became Nielstrom in the United States seventy years later. Daniel's Swedish relatives from the old country still spelled it Nelstrom and chided his family about their Americanized spelling. Daniel's father had often thought about changing it.

Daniel was also raised under the rules of *lagom*, a Swedish word that defies translation but has come to stand for what is essentially the Swedish attitude toward life—"all things in moderation." His parents added, "Take responsibility for your actions and don't do anything you'll regret later," to this mantra. For example, Daniel had wine available for his consumption at an age much younger than the legal age in Nebraska. Yet, as was and is Swedish custom, drunkenness was thoroughly discouraged. He couldn't remember anyone, guest or family member, leaving to drive home after consuming alcohol. Even drinking a single glass of schnapps would require being driven home by a member of the family. With these attitudes in place, Daniel rarely drank in college.

Lagom didn't cover coffee. In Sweden, coffee is king, and the

Swedes have the highest per-capita consumption of coffee in all of Scandinavia. The Nielstroms were no exception to that rate. Daniel drank coffee since he was three or four years old, and it was his one true vice. In the winter he had a cup constantly in his hand as it quelled the melancholy that enveloped his race during the dismal months of January and February. He drank it iced, hot, and even slightly warm.

Daniel had also been instilled with a European attitude about sex and the human body. He remembered, as a teenager, his parents instructing him at length about sex. His mother and father described it in detail and gave him advice about positions and techniques. They also firmly encouraged contraception, reiterating the concepts of using moderation and good sense.

When he was sixteen, a French foreign exchange student had opened his eyes to the power of the male-female union one afternoon after school down on the banks of the Platte River. Discussing it that same evening at supper, his mother said that he should invite the girl over to get better acquainted. Although it never came up, he suspected that any of the Nielstrom children could probably have had overnight guests of the opposite sex without much family concern. His mother would have made them breakfast the next morning as if nothing unusual had happened. By and large, Daniel's sexual experiences were much like his drinking experiences—few and far between.

His lack of social relations weren't because of his appearance. Daniel was a good-looking young man with wavy blond hair. He was also thin and athletic, although he hadn't competed in sports since his senior year at Ogallala High School, where he'd lettered for the Indians in football and track. He excelled at neither sport, but in both he was an average participant on average teams. He was soft spoken, but not shy. He was funny and very open in conversation but not overbearing, much like the fictional residents of Lake Wobegon. He was above average in appearance, personality, and intellect.

His family also believed in long holidays per the European model. They would routinely take a month in the early summer and go exploring. Typically, they would go camping in the hot desert or deep forests.

As the sun rose and warmed his face, Daniel sipped his coffee and relaxed, reflecting on his life thus far. His father was fascinated with the desert. Every Nielstrom child was learned in the art of desert survival. It amazed Daniel that no one had ever been hurt, as deserts in June are very hostile places. The more extreme, the more his father and mother liked it. They had climbed outcroppings, scaled canyons, and generally lived like jackrabbits for weeks. West Texas and southern Utah were also favorite family destinations, and Daniel was no stranger to the deserts of Mexico, New Mexico, Arizona, southern California, and Nevada.

His feelings of being an outsider, though, seemed rooted in more than just cultural differences. Although he suspected that every young adult felt as though they were different from their peers, his feelings were more complicated. All his life he'd felt as though someone was watching him, and events of his life somehow seemed predestined—things just seemed to work out for him. He always got the right classes. He was invited to parties and social events that someone like him would typically be excluded from. Accidents never happened to him like they did with his friends. A few times he even swore he'd observed a shadowy figure keeping an eye on him. Was this the work of some guardian angel? Of course, he knew that most likely his concerns were just byproducts of an overactive imagination.

Daniel was currently living in a rented farmhouse set on forty acres about seven miles west of Watertown, South Dakota. The owner was a corporate executive who had been transferred to company headquarters in Wisconsin. The company had been unable to sell the property due to the post-9/11 recession and had offered it to Daniel for only four hundred dollars a month rent when he moved to Watertown from Sioux Falls.

Daniel was an investment advisor, the current politically correct term for a stockbroker, for clients to the local branch of the Far Western National Bank in Watertown. He had been promoted to this position after assisting and interning in a similar position in Sioux Falls. In the investment-banking world, Watertown was about as far away as a person could get from the glitz of Wall Street. The majority of his clients were conservative farmers and local business people. They traded little and avoided high-profit, high-risk activities like futures and options. He typically found himself talking for hours to a potential client about different investment options only to generate barely fifty dollars in commissions for a few hundred shares of a local utility. The truly big farmers in the area used professional grain-future and option-trading firms in Minneapolis or Omaha and avoided his services. Daniel understood cattle futures, having grown up on a Nebraska ranch. The intricacies of the grain trade were another matter and were barely in his lexicon. His boss, the branch president, had no illusions about Daniel being a profit center and seemed perfectly happy to pay him twenty-two thousand dollars a year to tend to the flock of elderly clients the bank served.

Despite the blustery wind, it was a serene morning in rural Watertown. And, in his favorite long-sleeved chambray shirt, the wind wasn't unpleasant. No cars passing, no planes overhead, no distractions during his birthday morning ritual, a typical central Codington County morning. As it neared seven-thirty, he stood up, gently touched the Swedish flag that hung from the porch, and went inside for breakfast. He didn't like to work on his birthday, but one of his clients, Martha Johnson, a retired seventy-four-year-old widow, had requested a personal investment interview this morning at ten. The meeting had been scheduled months ago and as a bonus for not taking the day off, the branch president had given him the afternoon off without taking half a vacation day. Mrs. Johnson had lots of money in the bank and liked to talk about it. Apparently she bugged the president all the time. She had just returned from Florida and wanted an update on her financial plan. Daniel figured he'd take a few phone calls, meet with her, and then slip out the back door for the rest of the day. Later he'd drive down to Ogallala to spend the weekend with his family for their customary birthday festivities.

Even though he was a young American male who'd had Swedish culture pushed on him since his birth, Daniel liked his Swedish heritage and culture. He was a first-born son and, following the tradition of his birth order, he did what was expected. Living alone, five hundred miles from his parents, he could eat anything he liked, but he still chose to eat traditional Swedish foods. His birthday breakfast consisted of *Wasabrod*, a crisp-bread topped with a spiced cheese called *Kryddost*. He inhaled a half-dozen pieces of pickled herring and washed it all down with a large glass of milk. *This is living*, he thought.

Heading for the front door, he observed the large set of family pictures sitting on the dining room cabinet. His mother had insisted on sending them with him when he left for college. She knew they would remind him of who he was and where he was from. She had always believed that he and his sisters would fulfill the hopes and dreams of previous generations. He needed to remember that he was part of something larger than himself. She had also hoped that the pictures would remind Daniel that no matter what, his family loved him.

At first, he had thought the pictures were silly and hid them in a box. But they were now among his prized possessions, always occupying a central position wherever he was living. They were irreplaceable heirlooms, and Daniel felt extremely honored that his mother had entrusted their safekeeping to him.

The graduation pictures of his two beautiful sisters, Erika and Hanna, sat on either end of the cabinet. In the middle were pictures of his mother, Ingrid, and his father, Dag. There were pictures of his mother's parents from Sweden, his aunt, and one of his dad's grandparents, Lars and Sonja Nelstrom. At the center of all the pictures was a wedding photo of Daniel's grandmother and grandfather, Erika and Gunnar Nielstrom. It was a stunning portrait, nearly two feet high and done in the finest professional caliber available in its day.

Daniel liked to gaze at this picture and wonder about the lives of these two ancestors. Both people had died around the time of his birth, so he had no conscious memory of them. Dag had always told him that we are mortal, and that memories and stories are our immortality.

Daniel looked at the regal man in the picture. Gunnar Nielstrom was all decked out in his Marine Corps uniform. Even though the portrait was black and white, Daniel could appreciate the colors. The gold oak leaves on the uniform seemed to have been highlighted by the flash of the camera. Gunner's blond hair was perfect. The most striking thing about his grandfather was his facial expression. Daniel had been to weddings where he had seen looks of shock, innocence, bewilderment, and even desperation in the faces of the married couples. But as he looked into his grandfather's eyes, he saw an expression of extreme contentment, as if he realized he had just fulfilled some portion of his life so perfectly that only happiness would follow.

His grandmother, Erika, was an extremely lovely woman with long blonde hair, perfect features, and an earthy appearance. Quite obviously, Daniel's sisters had Grandma to thank for their exceedingly good looks. Erika appeared confident and self-assured, despite having only met Daniel's grandfather a few days before the wedding. The picture went down only to her neckline, but it revealed the beginning of an ample cleavage. Daniel remembered the stories of the provocative dress his grandmother had worn on her wedding day. Apparently she didn't care—maybe that was why Grandpa looked so happy.

Daniel leaned closer to the photo, focusing on her jewelry. She wore long earrings, but because of the black and white picture, he couldn't tell for sure whether they were silver or gold. She also wore a necklace that ended in a depiction of two birds, possibly herons, just above her bosom. Their beaks were touching, perhaps kissing, and their craning necks made the shape of a heart. Daniel had never seen the figure anywhere besides in the picture. He had asked his mother and aunt about it, but neither had offered a reply. Most likely it had been lost. The symbol looked old and perhaps held historical significance. He had planned to research it while at Augustana College, but he never got around to it. It was just another mystery about the people in his life.

Daniel thought about his mother, who was undoubtedly already making his cake. Daniel had a great deal of respect for his mother. She was a good woman, and he had no regrets about her child rearing. Her only quirk was one of language. When Daniel was good, she spoke in Swedish. She spoke Swedish to him on the phone, wrote it in letters, and even decorated cakes using her native tongue. But if he was bad or needed discipline, she would speak to him in English. He learned to fear hearing, "Daniel, where are you?" or "Daniel, come here a minute." English was never good news. She would speak of bad events like a neighbor's death, an illness, or anything otherwise troubling in English. As far as he could tell, to her, Sweden represented everything good and America represented everything bad. Other than this quirk, however, she appeared content with her marriage and her new life on the prairie. She never mentioned moving back to the motherland and usually had to be prodded into returning even for a short visit. Daniel and his sisters used to laugh about it. It was just another mystery that he hadn't found the time to solve.

The drive to work was short. His office was located in the downtown office of the bank. Watertown was the fourth largest city in South Dakota with barely twenty thousand inhabitants. Unlike Sioux Falls, its larger sister two hours south, which always seemed more of a Midwestern city, Watertown had a decidedly western feel to it.

Watertown had a nice small zoo where Daniel liked to donate some of his time. It also had a small airport with two connections a day to Minneapolis. There was a significant shopping strip located on Highway 212, which boasted all the usual large national chains plus a few regional ones. There was also a small mall along the strip, which was a favorite hangout for teenagers.

Watertown had a large ethanol plant, a monumental grain elevator, a large and neatly-designed convent for nuns, a large art museum, and it was located just east of two large lakes. As he drove past one of these, Lake Kampeska, he decided he would have lunch today at the state park on the opposite side of the lake. Although he planned on leaving work early, he was in no hurry to drive all the way to Nebraska tonight. Maybe he would drive halfway. His birthday celebration wasn't until tomorrow afternoon. He parked in his usual spot behind the bank, which was already open for business.

The receptionist, Patti, greeted him as he walked by. "Good morning, Daniel. How about sharing some of that birthday cheer with me tonight?"

Patti was young, single, and not bad looking. She was quite forward for a Dakota girl. Daniel felt that he could have her any time he wanted. Somehow she seemed just too easy, so he had rebuffed her advances up until this point. Patti, being dark-haired and having an English surname, would not pass the family cultural requirements so he felt it would be better to not waste his or her time. If he needed a one-night stand, she would always be here. He had occasionally given in to his carnal desires in the past, and undoubtedly would in the future, but now, at twenty-four, he was beginning to realize there was more to life than sex. Having a relationship at work also seemed less than a good idea.

"How did you know it was my birthday?"

"I'm the receptionist; I run this place." She snickered. "I know everything. How about you letting me give you a birthday gift in person after work? I got a Victoria's Secret package yesterday." She winked.

Interacting with a sexually forward woman in a location that was generally sexually restrained felt weird. "Tell you what—you get me through this Martha Johnson meeting quickly, and I'll do just about anything."

Daniel felt the temptation. What the hell—everybody needs someone to spend a birthday with. He could leave early tomorrow morning and still make Ogallala with time to spare. He walked into his office and found a birthday balloon in the middle of his desk. *Tonight will be a birthday you'll always remember! Love, Patti.* How had she known he'd give in to her? It must have been just part of the game.

He settled down to work. The Dow was down twenty-four points and the NASDAQ down six. Daniel typed in Martha Johnson's name on his keyboard. After a second the account information appeared on the screen. Martha L. Johnson: 210 Third Street, Yankton, South Dakota, widow, and retired teacher. Savings account, checking account, and brokerage account all in order. Holdings: one hundred shares Ottertail Power, one hundred shares HF Financial, and two thousand shares of something called First National Bank of Belize B. V. I. The total value of all her accounts was sixty-six thousand dollars. That seems low, Daniel thought. The banking security had no ticker symbol. The computer listed no value to the stock. Daniel noted she'd purchased the bank shares seven months earlier for twenty-five thousand dollars.

His suspicions rose as he wrote the purchase date and price on a blank tablet. He had been to Belize for a Mayan Studies class in college and had not noticed any First National Bank. He remembered the Bank of Belize and Provident Bank but no others. Googling the bank, he found a cheaply designed one-page site stating the bank's excellent reputation and impressive credentials. He was not impressed. He switched to the Bank of Belize site and e-mailed the customer service representative:

My name is Daniel Nielstrom. I'm an investment advisor for Far Western National Bank in Watertown, South Dakota, U.S.A. I have a client needing offshore services. She has recently been approached by a bank I'm not familiar with, First National Bank of Belize B. V. I. Although I would rather use a bank with your excellent reputation, my client was offered impressive returns and safety. Please compare your capital strength to theirs and provide me with your rates, charges, etc. Thank you.

He hit "Send" and returned to the account screen.

"Martha V. Johnson, Sexy," came a voice from behind.

"What?" He was busy writing down the account number on the screen.

Patti smiled from the side of his desk. "You've punched up the wrong Martha Johnson. Our Martha lives in Watertown, not Yankton. See?" She pointed at the screen.

"Really? I thought she was worth more. I should have looked more carefully." Daniel punched in Martha V. Johnson. The computer screen image switched to Martha V. Johnson of Watertown, South Dakota. She had a checking account, a savings account, and a brokerage account. He clicked on the brokerage account. Holdings: cash, government bonds, money market funds, and corporate bonds in Sallie Mae and Wells Fargo. She held only two stock positions: one share of Berkshire Hathaway and fifty shares of Black Hills Corporation, a utility in western South Dakota. Total account value: $1.6 million. "Not a very risky portfolio."

"No," said Patti, sliding closer, "but you'd better brush up on your knowledge of those two stocks. She's owned them forever, and she micromanages each of them."

"Thanks," Daniel stood up abruptly and led Patti to the door. "I have research to do." An hour later Martha V. Johnson arrived, five minutes early. She was impeccably dressed and ready for business. The meeting was tense and lasted one hour and fifteen minutes. Mrs. Johnson grilled Daniel as to his knowledge of her holdings. He described in detail Berkshire, Warren Buffet, and numerous analysts' reports. Her fifteen-hundred-dollar investment in Black Hills Corporation took quite a while as he went over coal and oil prices with her. They even discussed the policy of electricity deregulation. After an in-depth look they decided she should rotate a few thousand dollars worth of money market funds into some nine percent bank bonds that were being offered by his bank, and rotate the rest into two-year treasuries. She also agreed to triple her position in Black Hills Corporation and allowed him to purchase one hundred more shares. She confided to him that he'd really sold her on that company's stock.

Her one share of Berkshire was now worth sixty-two thousand dollars, and he was astonished to learn that she had purchased it for just one hundred dollars as a lark to spite her husband some forty years earlier. She took great pride in the investment and had made the annual pilgrimage to Nebraska to see the Sage of Omaha, Berkshire's CEO, perform at the stockholders meeting. Just like the quirky CEO, she drank Coke, bought her jewelry and furniture at Berkshire-owned divisions, ate at McDonald's, and had dessert at Dairy Queen. She was truly a Berkshire believer.

The whole meeting had generated a total commission of ninety dollars, fifteen of which went to Daniel. When she finally left, he put his head on his desk as both an innate response to frustration and in relief from the ordeal. The sound of a coffee cup clunking on his desk woke him.

Patti had cornered her prey. She leaned closer, whispering, "Your massage starts tonight at eight. My hot tub is scheduled for seven-thirty, but my bathing suit is at the cleaners, so you won't need one either. You can come early for dinner, but we may not get a chance to eat." She winked again, then straightened and patted him gently on the back. "I've got to go to the branch office for the rest of the day; I've e-mailed you directions to my house."

Daniel tried to stand. "I need a trade slip." But she didn't move. She purposely moved closer to him and whispered something in his ear. Daniel blushed immediately, and without any further advances, she was gone.

Now besides coffee, he needed a cold shower. He'd be distracted for the rest of the day. He found himself warm, flushed, and sweaty. The thought of having the door answered by a semi-nude seductress was intriguing. Maybe one more episode of casual sex wouldn't be all that bad. It was his birthday after all.

His e-mail account contained three new messages. One from Patti, another from someone wanting him to buy a condo in Florida, and a third was from a Marlene Williams, Vice President of New Accounts, Bank of Belize, Belize City, Belize. He clicked the icon. It read:

Dear Mr. Nielstrom,

In regard to your e-mail requesting a comparison of service and quality of capital to First National Bank of Belize (B. V. I.), we appreciate your interest in our organization. We are always looking for international referrals from clients such as yours. Your e-mail has raised some concerns from our customer service staff.

Our organization is a two-hundred-million-dollar capital bank, able to handle all sizes of offshore accounts for both business and personal needs. We always strive to provide the utmost in integrity and give our clients honest answers and comparisons to other institutions of our stature. We believe our record of success and customer satisfaction speaks for itself. I have forwarded, by attachment, references that you may contact regarding our level of service.

Specifically, in regard to the organization called First National Bank of Belize (B. V. I.), we can find no history of such an organization in our country. I spoke with a contact at the Ministry of Finance, and he stated that no such organization has a banking license in this country. I also took the liberty of doing some research for you and your client. We have a sister bank in the Cayman Islands, and their office has significant records in the Caricom region. The B. V. I. nomenclature indicates this is a British Virgin Islands entity. On contacting their Ministry of Finance, I found that the First National Bank of Belize has only a Class B banking license. These are available

*for only a few thousand dollars and do not allow the organiza-
tion to function as a real bank in any sense. They are typically
used for captive companies and only for inter-company transactions. They cannot, by B. V. I. law, engage in securing and
maintaining any deposit accounts that one would typically associate with a bank. This specific company has been in existence for only eight months and does not have a real office in
the B. V. I. I suspect that a fraudulent company has contacted
your client. I recommend that you refer her to the banking authorities in the United States.*

*We appreciate your inquiry. I hope you or your client will
feel free to call me personally should our attached literature
produce any questions.*

*Sincerely,
Stephanie Windsor
Bank of Belize*

Daniel had almost forgotten about the weird stock in the other
Martha Johnson's account. He found the account number again
and jotted it down on a different notebook. *Fraud*, he thought. He
had never been part of a mystery, let alone discovered one. Turning
to the computer again, he typed First National Bank of Belize, to
see whether any other customers owned the stock. Eighty-five clients held the security in their portfolio, and all of the positions had
been purchased in the last six to seven months. Most of the transactions were relatively small, but some larger clients appeared to
have invested over two hundred thousand dollars in the bogus bank.

As his research continued, he noted some striking similarities in
the victims' accounts. They were all aged between seventy and
eighty-five. In most cases, the broker was authorized to make trades
for the clients, probably because they were in bad health or their
mental faculties were failing. Some owned a few, very conservative, income-producing stocks, and some didn't own any. All had
the same representative from the Yankton branch of the bank—
broker number YA-004. Daniel checked with the main office in
Sioux Falls and found out the broker, whose name was Greg Altorini,
had billed a standard commission on each of the transactions. Daniel

also found that a wire was sent to a Cayman Island bank for the purchase price on each transaction. What a good scam, he thought as he started to piece it together; set up a phony offshore bank and then funnel investments into the company from nearly dormant accounts. He speculated about the next phase of the scam. The bank then makes loans to people who never expect to pay them back. The bank fails, and the investors lose all of their money. The clients eventually die, and the heirs never know what happened. They just figure their mom or dad bought a bad investment. After all, banks fail every day. So the bank disappears, a new one is created, and the cycle repeats.

Daniel wondered just how big the scam might be. He quickly added the numbers. Over nine million dollars had been taken from Far Western clients alone. Was this more widespread? Were there other sham banks or companies? Were other brokerages involved? The answers would have to wait until after lunch. He was hungry. His stomach was growling. He should have had a few more herring for breakfast. Though he knew his boss was out of town for a couple of days, he quickly e-mailed him anyway:

Have found some inconsistencies with a number of accounts out of Yankton. Please look at these accounts. I think there are more. First National Bank of Belize is a fraud. Below is a copy of an e-mail I received from Belize. I would like to discuss this in person when you return. Daniel N.

Daniel peeked out of his office and saw that Patti was absent from her desk, so he darted out the side door. As he made the five-minute drive to the state park at Lake Kampeska, he thought of the name Altorini. It seemed familiar.

Traffic was slower than usual. The traffic lights on Highway 212 were uncooperative, their poor timing contributing to the stop-and-go traffic. The main drag in Watertown was clogged with summer tourists off to the Black Hills or Yellowstone National Park. He finally hit his horn in frustration. Soon Daniel could see the main cause of the holdup—a top-of-the-line John Deere tractor near the grain elevator pulling a full forty-foot-wide plow had blocked three of the four lanes and was stopped sideways in the road. Only in

South Dakota, he thought. He made a u-turn and went up a side street in order to avoid the obstruction. Suddenly, Daniel had an epiphany. He stopped the car as he finally recognized the surname of the criminal broker. Johnnie Altorini was the Omaha mob boss recently arrested for racketeering.

I'll bet this Altorini is related. A bad feeling crept into the pit of his stomach. He wished he hadn't been so stupid as to send that e-mail to his boss before doing more research. *Hell, the boss might even be involved. I should have contacted the FBI first.*

After lunch he'd have to go back to the office. At least his boss was off for a day or two, and he wouldn't read the e-mail right away. Daniel would call the FBI this afternoon. *The FBI will protect me*, he thought. *At least I hope they will. Organized crime in the Dakotas, what a scary thought!* He turned into the state park and parked next to a car carrier transport. No cars were on the rig, and no driver was in sight.

* * * * *

A shadowy figure sat at Daniel's keyboard. He wore sunglasses and a dark felt hat. A bandanna covered a large tattoo on his neck. The man first typed an e-mail to Patti:

Patti,

Thanks for the offer. It would have been a birthday gift I'd forever remember. Unfortunately, a close family member is ill, and I am resigning here to help run the family farm in Nebraska. I need to leave right away, as the situation is dire. I pray that you will have a wonderful life. Missing your touch will truly be my loss.

Daniel

Then he sent a second e-mail to Daniel's boss:

Sir,
I regret I must resign my position immediately. A member of

my family has taken ill, and I have to help out at the family farm. Please clear my bank account and forward it and my final check to my home address in Ogallala.

Please tender my apology to Mrs. Johnson and be assured that all of my other affairs are in order. I have no further information about the Belize banking affair, but again encourage you to look into that matter.

Finally, I want to thank Far Western and you personally for giving me an excellent experience in banking.

Daniel Nielstrom

As soon as he hit Send, the man scooped Daniel's desk items into a duffel bag and ducked out the same side door through which Daniel had escaped. The entire intrusion had taken less than five minutes. Simultaneously, a second man was driving a small truck down Daniel's road toward town. The truck was filled with clothes, furniture, and a box containing the Nielstrom family photos. The two men met at the UPS store in town. After filling out the paperwork, they sent ten large boxes to Dag Nielstrom in Ogallala, Nebraska, accompanied by a simple note:

Mom and Dad,

Odd as this will sound, I've left on a sailing trip to Sweden with a new friend. Maybe I'll meet a suitable girl there. I'll probably stop in and visit the relatives. Don't worry about me. I may even find a job over there. It may be some time before I call.

Daniel

The truck next stopped at the Goodwill store, where the men anonymously left several chairs, a couch, a table, a stereo, and a small TV. Then they drove off, but they didn't leave town.

* * * * *

Daniel sat on a bench overlooking the lake. Large waves crashed on the rocky shore. Rafts of white pelicans bobbed in the surf. This was one of his favorite places to sit and think. As was typical on a weekday, the park was empty. He liked the warm sun and considered stripping off his clothes for a quick swim. He ate his lunch and thought about the bank scam.

While he pondered the situation at the bank, he failed to notice the car carrier leaving the parking lot carrying his car. He also failed to notice another car pulling into the lot being driven by a shadowy figure with a bandanna around his neck.

With his stomach full and body warmed in the afternoon sun, Daniel began to doze. Meadowlarks sang in the distance, a song more mournful than usual. A red-tailed hawk soared high above as the pelicans bobbed in the waves. The branches of the cottonwoods rattled in the breeze. Then the breeze mysteriously paused, as if nature were creating a moment of silence for some tragic event. As his eyes closed, Daniel never noticed the man approaching from behind.

* * * * *

Six days later an express package arrived addressed to Mr. and Mrs. Dag Nielstrom, Ogallala, Nebraska. It was from the office of the Sheriff's Department of Suffolk County, New York. Mr. Nielstrom signed for it and took it inside. Ever since Daniel had left Watertown, Dag's wife, Ingrid, had taken to speaking only English. For some time they both had sensed that bad news was just over the horizon, and this package only added to that sense. Dag feared for his heart, so he thought he'd better open the package sitting down. As he opened the box, a sick feeling began in the pit of his stomach. The package contained a wallet, that appeared to have gone through a washing machine, and a letter. He read the letter.

Dear Mr. and Mrs. Nielstrom,

I regret to inform you that we believe your son, Daniel Nielstrom, has been involved in a tragic sea accident. We believe he was a passenger in a sailboat that was hit by a freighter in our jurisdiction. The sailboat was lost and no survivors have been found. The only personal effect that was recovered is the enclosed wallet. The identification in the wallet is that of your son. We have, to date, recovered no remains. We will keep the case open as a missing persons case. However, if no remains are found within three months, and we receive no contact from your son by the end of that time, we will issue you a death certificate from our county. Should he contact you, or if you have any information that he was not on this boat, please contact me immediately.

I sincerely regret the sense of loss you must be experiencing at this time.

John P. Smith
Missing Persons Investigator
Suffolk County Police Department

A large tear ran down the elder Nielstrom's cheek as he thumbed through the wallet. Looking at the picture on the blue-and-white State of South Dakota driver's license he found inside, Dag immediately recognized his eldest child, his only son. He was filled with tremendous grief as he thought of the waste of a life cut off in its prime. Daniel's father looked down at the picture again, then placed his head in his hands and wept.

CHAPTER 2: The Sands of Time

It was one of the largest funerals in recent memory. It always seems that a funeral for someone so young brings out the whole community to share in the tragic loss of so much potential. The First Lutheran Church had standing room only. The stores on Ogallala's historic Front Street were closed so everyone could attend the somber event. The Nielstroms had been residents of Ogallala for over eighty years. Everyone had liked Daniel. He was a member of the community who had made good. Now he was gone.

The day was hot and muggy with strong thunderstorms expected later in the afternoon. The funeral was unlike any other that the community had seen. Despite the lack of human remains, Dag and Ingrid had insisted on a casket. Everyone was invited to put a momento of Daniel into it so they would have something to lay to rest. The bottom of the casket was lined with the worn Swedish flag that had hung in his bedroom and, most recently, on the porch of his house in Watertown. The coffin also contained his favorite pillow, a toy from his youth, his favorite shirt, and his running shoes. His eldest cousin added a picture of the two of them together and a wedding card he had given her with a sweet message that she had saved. His youngest sister, Erika, added a large box of memorabilia, the contents of which only she and Daniel knew. His oldest sister, Hanna, was overcome with grief. She sat in front of his picture for a long time, just staring and sobbing quietly. Nobody had the heart to try to move her. Finally, after being filled with peace, she placed a folded note under the pillow and removed a small picture from her purse, kissed it and placed it in the same location.

Other members of the community added flowers, usually single roses, to the growing memorial. A classmate from college scribbled something on a page in an Augustana College yearbook and placed it in the coffin. Numerous relatives from Sweden had arrived and also paid their respects.

During the long visitation, Dag sat on a chair outside the rear entrance to the church and stared into the sky. He was seen shaking his head and appeared to be having an argument. No one dared interrupt him. Finally, after the pastor had deposited some papers from Daniel's confirmation studies eleven years earlier into the coffin, he went out to bring Dag in for the funeral.

Many songs were sung, some in Swedish and some in English. Hanna and Erika performed a duet, singing a somber sonnet in Swedish with such passion that even people unfamiliar with the language were brought to tears. Daniel's uncle George gave the eulogy. First he spoke in Swedish, then repeated the prose in English. His daughters, Daniel's cousins, followed the eulogy by performing a sweet duet on the piano and flute. As Pastor John Davis stood to give his sermon, Dag motioned for him to sit down. He had decided to deliver a eulogy of his own.

"Friends," he began. "I apologize for the change in the program, but I can't put my son to rest without saying something. I raised him; it's my responsibility to speak on his behalf."

He paused for a moment, choking back a tear, and then continued with a touching eulogy that lasted twenty-five minutes. He described a sickly baby, a joyful child, an irritating teen, and a responsible adult. His speech was sad at times. At other times laughter broke out. He concluded by looking at his son's picture and saying something in Swedish. The sentence caused all who understood, even the males, to be moved to tears. The Swedish women were overcome and sobbed openly. There was no translation.

Dag walked over to his wife, helped her up, and escorted her to the casket. They hugged each other and then placed Daniel's billfold on the pillow. Ingrid kissed something in her hand and placed it inside before Dag closed the casket forever.

Daniel's casket was buried at the Lutheran cemetery next to his grandparents, Gunnar and Erika Nielstrom. The family plot lay in the shade of a large cottonwood tree, whose leaves rattled in the breeze as the pastor read Psalm 23. The sky to the west looked ominous, as if even God himself was saddened by this tragic loss of life, and He was shedding tears. The women threw roses on the coffin as the men, including Dag, shoveled dirt into the hole.

Although it was rare to have alcohol in a Lutheran church, Dag had decided he was going to properly toast his son at the reception following the funeral. *Skåling* was a Swedish tradition and his son deserved no less. Dag had imported the finest aquavit from O. P. Anderson in Sweden. The schnapps was served chilled in small glasses and offered with pickled herring. The designated drivers were offered the finest mineral water from Sweden.

When everyone had a glass, Dag raised his in a toast. "To my wonderful son, Daniel—may he rest in peace and his life be remembered with happiness, not sorrow. SKÄL!" Everyone drank and Dag, looking at Daniel's picture, nodded thanks to his son for all the wonderful memories. He now felt Daniel had been properly buried and felt at ease with the world. Daniel was gone and nothing was going to bring him back.

* * * * *

Cobwebs began to clear from a mind that had been dormant for months. Much like a seed coming out of its over-winter stasis, Daniel lay on the ground being warmed by the sun, the giver of life. He was slowly becoming alert, but something was wrong—his mouth felt dry, as if he had just eaten a beach.

What a screwy dream! But when he opened his eyes, instead of looking out of his comfy bed topped with a goose-down comforter, he saw only sand. He tried to move but couldn't muster the effort. Feeling like he had the worst hangover ever, and like a cow had kicked him in the back, Daniel finally managed to roll over on his side. He opened his mouth and spit out sand. Rubbing his mouth and chin, he discovered at least a month's worth of stubble on his face. *What the hell? How long have I been asleep?* When his senses had cleared enough so he could sit up, Daniel stared in shock. Sand, sand, and more sand. He shook his head, closed his eyes, and looked again at the still endless desert. The shock started to subside and his thinking slowly returned. *What's going on?*

His last memory was of eating lunch on the shore of Lake Kampeska. *This definitely is not Lake Kampeska. This isn't even South Dakota.* According to the position of the mid-morning sun on the eastern horizon, he knew he was much farther south. He had been in every desert in the United States and several in Mexico, and he didn't remember any place that looked like this. This place had different vegetation, coarse sand, extremely flat terrain, and a ridge maybe thirty miles to the southwest, all under clear blue skies. The heat was his big concern. He estimated the temperature to be ninety degrees Fahrenheit. He was experienced in the desert and knew the temperature could break one hundred fifteen by afternoon, maybe more. *Where the hell am I?*

He looked around. Neither tire tracks nor footprints were evident. He checked his pockets but found nothing—no ID, no money, nothing. *How did I get here? How can there be no tracks? Why am I here?* Then it came to him. He muttered aloud, "That damn Belize thing! Altorini is trying to get rid of me, that Mafia bastard! This must be Mexico...."

He thought about how he had been found out so fast. Altorini was efficient, that was certain. Throw him out here, he dies, and the vultures leave no evidence. There would be no murder weapon, no body, no evidence, and therefore, no crime.

Daniel was angry, and he was determined to get out of this jam. Then he would find Altorini and.... But reality hit him like a train. He was without supplies. The nearest water, if there was water, would be in the hills, at least thirty miles away. He figured he had one chance in five to survive—then he noticed a canteen about fifteen feet away. To his amazement it was full. *Why did they leave me water? And who are they?*

Flipping up the collar of his rugged, long-sleeved chambray shirt to protect against sunburn, he started planning. It was hot, but the heavy fabric was better than sunscreen, and it would keep him warm at night. He would find shelter to get out of the sun, then sleep and conserve energy. In the evening, he'd head for the ridge. He estimated that he'd have ten to twelve hours of darkness and that he would need to average about one mile every twenty minutes. And of course, the ridge might be farther away than he thought.

He had spent a lot of nights on the move in the desert, so that would be the easiest part of the plan. He headed toward the ridge. About a mile-and-a-half away, just as the temperature was becoming fierce, he found a natural rock wall. It was three feet high on one side but deeper on the other, as a small depression had been carved out by the constant wind. He soon found a bunch of loose, smaller stones under a stable roof of rock. He dug and pulled at the smaller rocks, carving out a shelter to give himself some relief from the sun. The exposed earth was surprisingly cool, and Daniel fell asleep shortly.

As twilight descended, he awoke and took a long sip of water from the mystery canteen, sating his need. He estimated the temperature now at somewhere below a hundred degrees, so he headed for the ridge, still low on the horizon. As he walked, Daniel thought of his family, and he prayed. An almost full moon arose about an hour after darkness, providing light and allowing him to make better time than if it were a moonless night. He focused on a star set low above the horizon and kept to a fairly straight line of travel. He nicknamed it Altorini, the star of revenge.

Around midnight he took another drink of water. He could see the range ahead of him. In the moonlight, it didn't seem much closer than when he'd started, but he pressed on.

Exhaustion set in just before daybreak. Even after walking all night, stopping was not an option. Daniel estimated that the ridge was only about five miles away and was determined to make it that day. He could rest tomorrow.

The ridge was barren of vegetation and rose quickly a thousand feet above the desert floor. It was extremely rocky and in places had sheer cliffs hundreds of feet high. He headed for a point without visible cliffs, reaching the base of the ridge just as the sun had begun to warm the air. He sucked out the few remaining drops of water from his canteen and started the ascent.

The climb was easy; the firmer ground was a welcome change from the sand. Although it might have been only psychological, the shot of water from the bottom of the canteen seemed to invigorate him. The unforgiving sun beat down as he cleared the final rock and made the top, where he was rewarded with a cooling breeze. He had expended every bit of his energy. To his amazement, a shaded crevasse lay before him. His descent into the crevasse was more of a controlled fall, during which scraped both his legs. Deep in the structure he was well protected from the sun. He found a soft-looking spot and collapsed. Sleep enveloped him instantly.

The heat of the day awakened him, and despite the shade, it was still unbearably hot. Daniel realized that he had won the first battle, but the war was far from over. He was now out of water and hadn't urinated in at least twelve hours. It would be impossible to last long in this shelter. As he began to explore a few hundred feet from his resting place, Daniel was hit by a familiar scent he immediately recognized. Deep within a six-foot wide side crack he found the source—a water seep under a three-foot ledge. The extra shade protected the seep from instant evaporation and a few small, hardy plants sprang up from the edges.

Daniel and his father had once lived on such a seep deep in the Canyonlands Wilderness in eastern Utah for two weeks. This one was very small and in an awkward location, but at least he had something. It took nearly four hours to quench his thirst. The water was high in iron content and tasted metallic, but it sustained life. He laid back and dozed.

When Daniel awoke, it was already the next morning. The long, strenuous trek had taxed his muscles, and he was stiff and very hungry. In the early morning light, a movement caught his attention. A large cricket neared the seep. Slowly and steadily he moved his left hand toward the bug and grabbed it, then threw the bug into his mouth and crunched, swallowing fast.

He examined his surroundings. Not much new. The crevasse ended with a good view of the desert below. He could see the whole valley. Except for a few dunes, this side of the ridge seemed to mirror the side he had just left—another lifeless, hot pit. In the distance, he could barely make out another ridge, undoubtedly like this one. Unless he found something more than an odd bug to sustain him, he'd eventually starve and become too weak to even drink from the seep. That would be the end.

Daniel devised the best plan he could think of: he'd keep a vigil at the lookout any time he wasn't drinking at the seep. He hoped to see either a plane or somebody crossing the desert floor by vehicle. Then he'd yell for help, though the chances of anyone coming this way were slim. *Where the hell am I anyway?*

Day after day, he watched. His skin crawled under his shirt and his muscles ached. The scrapes on his legs burned in pain. During the vigils, he prayed a lot, preparing himself to die. On the whole he had lived a good life. He was happy, but he wished he'd been able to say good-bye to his parents and sisters. They deserved better than to just have him disappear. He hoped his mother wouldn't keep his room for years like he'd seen done by mothers in the movies. He also hoped Altorini would make a mistake and get caught, but not by the police; that would be too good for him. He wished one of his business contacts would get mad and that Altorini's death would be messy.

On the fifth day, his luck improved. He caught three bugs—two crickets and a big, hard-shelled, tank-like bug that tasted truly rancid. In the afternoon while on his lookout he saw something even better—a dust cloud on the valley floor heading his direction. He grabbed his canteen, which he had filled from the seep, and started down the hill.

The vehicle was at least five miles away. It would take a miracle for them to see him. Still, he feared that, by the time another vehicle came, it would be too late. The trip down the ridge was fast—in some places, too fast. He stumbled and fell repeatedly. When he finally hit the desert floor, the full heat of the day hit him and brought him to his knees. It was as hot as he'd ever experienced.

The half-mile trip to the crest of the first sand dune almost killed him. The sun, even at the late-afternoon hour, was doing its best to drive every molecule of moisture from his body. He drank from his canteen. Upon reaching the crest he could see the dust still rising and coming closer. About fifteen minutes later he could recognize the vehicle as a white pickup truck. He started jumping up and down, raising his arms and waving. Soon he noticed a change in the direction of the dust trail. He would be saved! He drank the rest of his water and descended the dune when he was sure they had seen him. He didn't have long to wait. As the vehicle stopped, three Arab men in simple tunics and sandals disembarked from the sandblasted white Toyota truck. He greeted them with a big smile.

"You Yankee?" they stammered in broken English.

Daniel had no idea how he'd gotten into the Middle East or even whether the men were indeed Arabic, but he felt uneasy announcing his true nationality. Since 9/11, it seemed as though America was at war with Islam, and all of Islam was at war with the U.S. He thought it would be better to be Swedish.

He spoke first in Swedish. "I'm Swedish. My name is Daniel. I've been stranded in the desert." He was greeted with a scowl. He repeated in the most broken English he could manage. "From Sweden. Stranded." He pointed to the truck. "Ride. Help."

There was a long pause. One man moved behind Daniel. The leader of the trio repeated, "American, no?"

Daniel pointed to himself. "No, no. Sweden—Swede."

"No. No, you American pig! Kill women and children! Martyr many of Islam."

"No, I'm from Sweden," he stated and then repeated this in Swedish. He held out his arms for mercy and understanding but was met with frowns. Without warning, he felt a sharp pain on the back of his head. His legs buckled and everything went dim. All three men spat on him as they dragged him to the truck and threw him into the back. They ripped off his shoes, then bound his hands and threw his empty water bottle at him.

"American pig!" the leader repeated, temporarily satisfied with the revenge he had inflicted upon the infidel. The three men happily piled into the front of the truck and drove away. The drive to see the sheik would take about three hours. They expected to arrive about an hour before dark. Their victim would be executed, and they would celebrate all night.

The ride to Uber and their reward took them across the Wahiba Sands, the local name of the Arabian Desert, which stretched along the border of Oman and Saudi Arabia. There was no road; they navigated by landmarks.

While they drove, Daniel moaned in pain. He head was bleeding from the blow he had received, and it took over an hour for him to be able to think clearly. His captors thought it would be bad for him to die before arriving at the sheik's compound, so they periodically allowed him a little water from their supply. They kicked him a few times with each drink to keep him softened up. As the drive of terror continued, Daniel began to feel hopeless about his situation. He prayed his death would be quick and painless.

* * * * *

Sheik Mohamed Al-Hamra lived in a compound on the edge of Uber. This part of the country was his to govern, and usually the Sultan left him alone. It was a long way from Uber to the palace in Muscat, and the sheik liked it that way. As long as this part of the country was quiet and ran efficiently, he had the power all to himself. As sheiks go, Al-Hamra lived in poverty, but Oman didn't have the wealth of their neighbors to the north, the Saudis, and Al-Hamra was a modest man. He had only two wives, he didn't have a fancy car, and although his house was large, it wasn't ornately decorated. Guards and a high wall surrounded his home, enclosing three acres. In this part of the world, however, the guards and walls were needed only to keep out the goats and sheep. The precautions weren't very effective, as the herd had attacked most of the shrubs in the compound, contributing to the spartan appearance of the exterior. To everyone in the region, however, Sheik Al-Hamra wielded unchallenged and unlimited power.

Al-Hamra was a cautious man. He felt that anything out of the ordinary could potentially be bad. Risk-taking meant change. He had a good thing going. If the Sultan began thinking about him, he might end up herding goats, or worse.

Al-Hamra had just finished his evening prayers when he heard the excitement outside his compound. One of his able captains interrupted him to announce that three men were bringing in an American spy. The captain was already brandishing a large knife, eagerly awaiting the opportunity to glorify Allah with the spilling of infidel blood. All were awaiting the sheik's blessing at his front step.

At the bottom of the steps, three men were removing a bound, shoeless man from the back of a truck. Al-Hamra's captain walked toward the man, the spy, and dug his large knife into the sand at his feet. Other guards fired shots into the air. The sheik caught sight of the strange markings on the blond man's face. The onlookers began to chant excitedly in Arabic.

The captain approached Daniel and spat on him, then grabbed his shirt and ripped it open. Daniel's head was spinning. He fell to his knees. The captain grabbed his hair and exposed Daniel's throat.

But Al-Hamra gasped and his smile turned to horror. He leapt down the steps and grabbed the captain's knife, barely preventing the beheading.

The man kneeling before them had large tattoos on his chest, face, and arms. As Al-Hamra could now clearly distinguish, the tattoo displayed prominently on the kneeling man's left breast was a large wild cat with its teeth bared and its claws outstretched. Beginning on his right shoulder was an arm that held a sword that extended across his nipple and continued below the man's belt line. Two small birds perched on his right cheek. The birds met at their beaks and formed the shape of a heart. Three small daggers deco-rated his neck and forehead. The tattoos were interwoven with a light background swirl. His final visible tattoo was on his right fore-arm—a pentagon with two points on each side, some sort of sun-burst. The mid-portion was open, and the points were randomly filled in. All the tattoos were jet-black.

Al-Hamra knew the story of these tattoos from his youth. They were the forbidden marks that represented the Modafea Danya, as such men were called in Persian or Farsi. In Arabic they were called Homat al Omma, the Protectors of the Country, the Defend-ers of the Earth. They were untouchables, emissaries from the forbidden temple. In his language, the name of these people was a word never to be spoken for fear of reprisal. To be allowed to show hospitality to one of these men was considered the ultimate bless-ing in life. His grandfather had received such an honor, and that was how his family had become leaders. It was always said that these people might return to again enjoy Al-Hamra hospitality.

Now, to the sheik's horror, one had returned and had been se-verely mistreated. He also remembered the curse. To harm or kill a Modafea Danya would mean a disproportionate reprisal. Death would be swift and sure. This would happen to the accused, his leader, their families, their livestock, and all who had contact with them. All would perish so that even their genetic line would be blotted from the earth.

The captain misunderstood Al-Hamra's reaction and thought that his master wanted to dispatch the infidel himself. That was the prerogative of power. To everyone's surprise, though, the sheik didn't strike the American. Instead, he sliced the throat of the leader of the trio who had captured Daniel. Blood sprayed from the sev-ered carotid. The man fell to his knees, and no one dared offer aid.

"How dare you subject my family to this curse!" the sheik screamed in Arabic. "We shall find your family and kill them also! I hope Allah curses you as well!" He thrust his dagger into the man's chest and abdomen until his breathing stopped.

The sheik ordered a group of his guards to bring the families of the three men who had mistreated the blond man. The families would be summarily executed. Al-Hamra next ordered other guards to tie the captain and the remaining two men to a pole in front of the compound. Maybe Allah would take them during the night. He then ordered the dead body to be hung upside down outside the main gate. At high noon tomorrow it would be thrown to the vultures.

He had his servants take Daniel inside and ordered them to nurse him to health and look after his wounds. Tonight would be a sleepless night for Al-Hamra. He considered suicide, but hoped that allowing the Defender to kill him would pacify his anger and cause him to spare his family. He prepared his will for such a scenario. *What a fool I am*, he thought, *to be surrounded by such incompetent swine!* He continued making preparations.

Daniel roused the next morning, still in a much-weakened condition. His head hurt, and he was dizzy and nauseated when he stood up. Moreover, all of his muscles hurt when he tried to move. He was summoned to the steps of the compound. He noticed he was wearing a white tunic with long sleeves. *Are these my execution clothes?*

He was invited to sit in the sheik's chair. The entire village was gathered in the courtyard. Three men were bound and staked in front of him—two of the men who had bushwhacked him and the one with the knife. The third bushwhacker was missing.

Al-Hamra knelt before him and spoke to him in English. Everyone else knelt as well. "Please, great man of the world, protector of the people, Defender of the Earth, please forgive me and my people. We have been put to the test, and we have failed. Do not show your wrath on us all. Please sacrifice me as leader. Take your wrath out on me and spare the rest. I plead for mercy on the masses and nothing more than an ugly, grisly death for myself."

What Al-Hamra said made no sense to Daniel. *My head must be addled. Why is this man bowing to me? I'm the one to be executed. I was just dragged out into the desert and left for dead by some Mafia jerk. Where the hell am I anyway?* When he opened his mouth, his first unprocessed thought came out. "They could have killed me!"

A sick feeling rose in the pit of Al-Hamra's stomach as Daniel's words hit him like a brick. In all his self-deprecation, he had forgotten about the real perpetrators. He had forgotten to mention to the Defender that they were also to be killed. Had he implied to this man of power and justice that he would sacrifice only himself for their crime? He ran the conversation through his mind. *My English is so bad that maybe I did*, he thought. Now everyone would die; he had blown his only chance. He motioned for everyone to fall prostrate and then approached Daniel. "Come, Great One. Let us avenge their crime first, as is the custom. I apologize for my ignorance. After they die, you can go on to your business with us."

Daniel heard the sentence differently as he rose. He perceived that it was the local custom for the harmed to mete out the punishment. He also thought he heard something about sacrificing himself to be killed if they weren't. That seemed weird. *If the harmed doesn't kill the accused, the harmed will be killed and the accused set free?* He wished his head didn't hurt so much, and he hoped he was hearing right. The sheik said something in Arabic to the first man from the desert, the one that had hit Daniel in the head and spat on him.

"What's to become of him?" Daniel asked, hoping his conclusion was wrong.

"You are going to avenge his crime. He will die." It was a dutiful reply. "You, Sir, can have the choice of killing him, or you can direct me, your eternal servant, and I shall do as directed." He offered Daniel a dagger.

It was clear, wherever this was, that they had strange customs. Some choice, kill or be killed. Those men had tried to kill him—that was evident, and they were guilty. They would go to prison in the States. Killing the men seemed extreme, but so would his own death. He grabbed the knife and pointed it at his tormentor. *Can I do this? It's him or me, I guess.*

Suddenly feeling light-headed, he lost his balance and fell forward, stabbing the man in the throat. Then Daniel heard the gurgling, gasping noise. The man with the dagger in his throat and windpipe was dying a miserable death of suffocation. It was the most horrendous thing Daniel had ever seen. He walked back to the chair. He needed to sit down. The still-conscious man continued to struggle for breath as the sheik urinated on him to humiliate him. Then the sheik pulled the knife out of the dying man's throat and thrust it into his chest, mercifully shortening the poor wretch's suffering.

The sheik now knew that this Defender was a great man. The

death was worthy to be described in legend. The villagers were filled with awe and fear and were turning away. Al-Hamra motioned for Daniel to take care of the second man. Daniel motioned with his hand; he wanted nothing more to do with it. The sheik read the gesture as: *You do it, and I'll critique you.*

Al-Hamra dispatched the second perpetrator in a slow and agonizingly painful fashion. Daniel thought the death would never end. With the third man, his captain, he tried to emulate the Defender's method but missed and got the carotid artery, making a huge mess. Blood was everywhere, even covering Al-Hamra.

"Enough of this killing. I need some water!" exclaimed Daniel.

The sheik was relieved. He must have done a good job with the executions. The Defender had tired of the whole process; hopefully, the villagers would be spared. He helped the weary figure into the house and offered him water. He would show this man the utmost in hospitality so he would forgive his mistreatment in the desert. *At least those idiot perpetrators are finished with!* Al-Hamra had their families executed privately, as was consistent with the law as mentioned in the legends of his grandfather. He wanted to cover all his bases. He fed their livestock to the vultures and wild animals. Their houses were destroyed and their belongings burned. All names were to be purged from the records of the village so that they no longer existed. To even mention one of their names would mean execution. He never told the Defender of these events. To tell him would mean that he had considering not doing it. The law was very clear.

Daniel was to be allowed to recuperate. Three of Al-Hamra's female servants were assigned to care for his every need. They were strictly instructed to comfort his aches, clean him, and give him whatever he wanted. When one asked shyly if he meant *everything*, the sheik tore her abaya and replied that of course it meant everything.

Al-Hamra was concerned that he still hadn't righted the wrong that had been done to the Defender, so he planned a big feast to be held when the Defender was better rested. The fact that one of the most powerful beings of the universe was exhausted and recuperating in the bedroom after several days in the desert never struck him as being odd. In fact Al-Hamra was a concrete man. He rarely thought objectively about a problem, a characteristic of his religion and culture.

Daniel, however, would soon experience one of the drawbacks of Western culture. Westerners tend to disbelieve things they cannot understand, scientifically test, or see for themselves. They have a difficult time accepting things by faith. Daniel would need a lot of faith in the next few weeks. He would be told and shown things that would be difficult for anyone to believe. He would heal and he would learn who and what he was and what he was to become.

CHAPTER 3: The Life of a Married Man

Daniel awoke the next day feeling better but still sporting a slight headache. He vaguely remembered a very scared young woman tending his wounds and giving him fluids. At times he wished he were in Nebraska submerged in the Platte River. He thought he could even drink the river dry. A large mug was next to the bed. He reached for it and drank the entire contents. The water tasted good. He was about to get up when two equally distressing observations hit him: He was naked in the bed, and a young boy was sitting beside a small pool in the room, waiting for him. *Is that my bath? Just where the hell am I anyway?*

The moment of hesitation passed when Al-Hamra burst into the room and bowed before him. "I see, my Lord, that you have awakened. The desert is harsh for all men, great and small. I see that you are recuperated. Your skin is fair, like the belly of a goat. Your pilgrimage, I hope, has been so far a successful one. Please accept my humble hospitality. What is mine is yours. Your people have blessed my family. I wish to repay you with anything that you deem appropriate. My servants are your servants. Tonight, we will have a great feast in your honor."

Daniel was very uncomfortable with two strangers in his room. He gazed at the boy, then back at Al-Hamra. The sheik caught Daniel's glance, and he also looked at the young male servant. His smile turned to a frown as he spoke in his own language to the boy, and then looked at Daniel again.

"I apologize for my servant. He is not used to a position of such importance. I can see your confusion. We are unfortunately not such an open people here; I assume Western men are much more used to receiving a bath from a woman. He will give you a bath and then, after you have relaxed, you can choose from among my new tunics." Al-Hamra gestured to a pile of cloth on a nearby chair. "Unfortunately your own clothes are unsuitable for the desert, and they were in such bad repair we had to throw them out." He glanced at the servant and said in Arabic, "Come help him to his bath!"

Daniel wrapped himself with the sheet and the servant boy helped him out of bed and into the bath water. It was just above body temperature and was very soothing. The servant was just starting to wash his back and hair when Daniel suddenly thought he was seeing things. He wasn't sure at first, but there it was on his right forearm—a large, strange tattoo. *What is this?* He pulled his arm out of the water and looked at it more closely. The tattoo was in a complex sunburst pattern with a five-sided, open pentagon at its center. The ten points, two to each side, were varied; some were filled in and others were not. The tattoo was as black as it could be. He gasped and released the sheet that he still clutched with his left hand. The servant gently removed the wet material from the water, giving neither it nor the tattoo a second thought.

Because there was no reaction in the ink when Daniel ran his hand over the tattoo, he surmised it had been present for some time. *Why haven't I noticed this before now? How did it get here? Who did this? When did it happen? I don't remember anything!* He suspected it had occurred sometime between that fateful birthday and waking up in the desert. *At least it isn't that large.* Then his gaze shifted lower, and he saw the other tattoos. A black arm stretched across his right shoulder to a point just above his nipple, where it grasped a sword. He stood up in the bath, his gaze tracing the blade, which crossed his abdomen and finally came to a point on his upper right thigh. It was also black and intricate. That tattoo had obviously taken some time to apply, as it was over three feet long. The servant, thinking this was an invitation, dutifully washed his backside and upper legs.

Daniel searched his body further, and he found an even larger, finely detailed impression of a wild cat on the left side of chest, extending around from his back. The cat was in attack mode, its fangs bared. He noticed the fine, pointed tufts of fur on its ears and motioned for the servant to get him a mirror. Using the mirror, Daniel saw that the cat's outstretched body extended around his body and crossed his spine. He recognized the cat as a lynx. Then he discovered three daggers graced his head and neck, one on his forehead, one just below his right eye, and one across his neck. The most obvious mark, though, was on Daniel's face—a heart-shaped mark on his left cheek. It was formed by two herons whose beaks met at the top of the heart. Their bodies, wings, and feet comprised the rest of the design. Daniel knew the symbol. It was the same as his grandmother's necklace.

Daniel was mortified about the disfigurement. Maybe they could be removed. If not, he would be marked for the rest of his life. He splashed back into the bath, trying to hide the markings from the world.

He considered his situation. He was now thinking of the possibility that the Altorini gang had not kidnapped him after all. In fact, they were probably still looking for him. If so, wherever he was, it might not be all that bad—at least he was still alive. He also reasoned that he probably hadn't been put out into the desert to die. Instead, it seemed like it had been some sort of test. Nobody would spend days applying intricate body art only to have the bearer die of exposure. But whoever it was hadn't made survival easy either.

Daniel was sure Al-Hamra wasn't part of the plot, but he was equally sure the sheik knew the meaning of the tattoos. His memory of his first day at the compound was blurry, but he remembered that Al-Hamra's disposition had changed when his shirt was ripped off. Undoubtedly the tattoos had saved his life. *But what are they? What do they mean? How could I have gotten them and not known it?*

The servant appeared with shaving equipment, but Daniel waved it away. Undoubtedly, he would be on the road for some time and having a beard could be prudent.

* * * * *

Al-Hamra was busy preparing for the feast. His daughters, his family, the community, and his servants were all working frantically. Everyone who was anyone in Uber would attend the party. Al-Hamra would expect no less. He was also going over all that he remembered and had heard about the Homat al Omma. He'd had a meeting with the village elders and the Moslem cleric about the visitor. Nobody wanted to further offend their powerful guest. One elder revealed that the Defenders despised telephones, so Al-Hamra had every telephone, cellular or otherwise, removed and hidden. They would reappear after the Defender had gone.

Another elder remembered something about the Defender's love of women. This seemed easy to solve as well. Al-Hamra had three beautiful, eligible daughters. He would offer all of them to the

Defender. If he refused, so be it. If he accepted, having a Homat al Omma as a son-in-law would have its advantages.

As they conferred, they remembered the Homat al Omma had a love of cats. The few cats in Uber would be treated as royalty. Killing a cat was made a capital offense. Any statues or images of the felines from throughout the village would be loaned to Al-Hamra. They would be displayed prominently.

* * * * *

Daniel probed every inch of his body, hoping to find more clues about what had happened to him. Other than the kissing herons, the only other clue was the lynx. It was a cat confined to the northern boreal forests of North America, Scandinavia, and Russia. His father had spoken of its sacred powers that were mentioned in Swedish mythology. It was usually depicted as leading the chariot of Freyja, the goddess of fertility. It had earned the name Bizhiw, loosely translated as a mythical hunter-warrior, in the Ojibwe and Cree Indian tribes in North America. *Am I supposed to be some kind of warrior, then? Is that what Al-Hamra fears?*

* * * * *

The sheik paid him a visit in the early afternoon. Daniel was still having difficulty communicating with the man. Although Al-Hamra spoke English well enough to understand, he hadn't mastered the verbs.

Daniel decided to be direct. "Do you have a phone here?"

"Absolutely not!" the sheik replied in a dutiful monotone, glad he'd had the forethought to banish the evil devices. *The Defenders really do hate phones*, he thought. "There are no phones in the entire village, Sir. None at all."

Surely the town has a phone. It doesn't seem that backward. This time he made hand motions, putting his thumb to his ear and his pinkie finger to his mouth. "Do... you... have... a telephone?"

"None, Sir, not even a little one." The sheik smiled. He had finally done something correctly.

Daniel wondered why the man was smiling so happily at him

for not having a phone. Must be some local custom or a religious thing. He had hoped to contact his parents and let them know where he was. He hoped they thought he was still alive, and he wished he could get a message out to them.

* * * * *

Word of a strange tattooed man was also spreading to Mecca, Tehran, and even Istanbul. Some who heard the tale were curious about the man. Others were fearful. A few were even frightened that he represented some American plot to conquer the Arabic people and that this was the start of another crusade. Many prayed to Allah, and clerics read and reread the Holy Scriptures. A great unrest began to build. Why had the Defender chosen Oman? It was a sleepy, dusty place of no significance.

Word of the Defender eventually found its way to a Turkish man of action living in refuge in Istanbul. He was muscular, well built, and never one to back away from a fight. He was a practicing Moslem, although not particularly religious, who had been educated at Oxford University. The report of a strange blond man with Homat al Omma markings in Oman amused him. He knew of the legends, their power, and their duty, but he also knew there were no blond Defenders. He prepared himself for a long journey, then left, heading east and then south toward Oman. He undoubtedly would hear more along the way to pinpoint the stranger's location.

* * * * *

The banquet started at five o'clock in the evening. It appeared to Daniel that everyone of any significance in the community was attending the event. Of course, all the guests were men.

In this society, women were afforded no respect. They kept mostly to themselves, ther were virtual objects to be bought and sold or married. By and large they were uneducated, not allowed to own property, and had no rights except those given to them by their husbands or fathers. They even had a separate place to pray away from the men.

The event started with a formal introduction. Because Daniel couldn't understand what was being said, Al-Hamra translated, and Daniel suspected he wasn't being told everything. One or another of the guests would ramble on and on and his translator would simple say, "This is Barkart, a merchant from the town." The people he met, however, seemed genuine, and he was starting to feel most welcome.

Although Daniel was hoping to be served some good wine, there were no alcoholic beverages. The beverage of choice was a strong, spicy, cold drink that tasted truly vile. It burned the palate, but with patience it seemed to go down. After suffering through a cup just to be polite, he accepted and drank a diluted tea.

Entertainment came next. Women danced, accompanied by traditional music. Daniel was impressed and wondered how often these people had such celebrations. The men lounged in various positions on a series of pillows. During interludes, servants brought out various food items, always serving Daniel first. He sampled each dish and soon realized he was dictating the menu for the evening. If he liked something and ate more, everyone else ate that. When the servants offered him large, savory pieces of goat meat, he tried a small piece, but didn't appreciate its strong flavor and declined a larger helping. Goat meat was then removed from the event. The owner of the goat was very much ashamed, but some good came of the decision. The servants and women had wonderful goat meat to eat that evening, and not a morsel was wasted.

Next, Al-Hamra's daughters performed a seductive dance. They teased Daniel with silk scarves and moved gracefully with the music. It was a pleasing performance. Colored silk scarves covered their faces.

After the dance, some type of fowl was offered. Daniel suspected it had been the scrubby chickens he'd observed roaming the village streets. The meat, however, was fine, and the spices used to highlight the bird put a slight bite on his lips.

Toward the end of the feast, Al-Hamra finally rose to speak. It had been nearly three hours since the event had started, and Daniel welcomed the change. He hoped his host would wrap up the evening so he could go to bed.

Al-Hamra called his daughters out again and looked at Daniel.

"I will have them dance for you again, Great One. Then you shall choose."

"Choose?"

Al-Hamra laughed. "Of course, you will choose which of my daughters will be yours."

Before Daniel had time to object, the women began dancing, and Al-Hamra took his seat. They paraded themselves in front of him, still with their faces covered. *What will happen if I say no thanks?* As the tempo of the music increased, the women's sensuality intensified. Finally they stopped and each young woman knelt in front of him, her head bowed.

"Now, Great Warrior, Protector of the People," began Al-Hamra, "which of the fairest of our town will you choose, as is our custom?"

Daniel was trying to figure a way out of the dilemma. *Maybe this was something that was offered to all visitors? Would they figure out he was just a sham, a farm boy from Nebraska?* He decided to stall, hoping the situation would just quietly go away. "I'm not sure I could choose one; they all danced well."

"I promise you, any of the three would make you happy. If you need more time to choose, I understand. You have been given only a superficial look. I will present the whole package." He instructed the women to dance again, and this time they removed their veils. They danced around Daniel, showing their smiling faces, clear brown eyes, and fair complexions, using their scarves to dramatic effect.

Daniel decided to choose the oldest woman. She wasn't that bad looking. The music stopped, and all three women knelt at his feet. As Al-Hamra approached each daughter, she looked up and smiled at Daniel.

Al-Hamra looked at Daniel and smiled. "My great and powerful ally, which do you choose?"

Daniel paused for effect, then got up and walked around. He touched the head, finally, of the eldest daughter, Mashira, and sat back down. A beaming smile crossed both her face and her father's. The men of the community spontaneously voiced their loud approval. Al-Hamra joined his daughter's hand to Daniel's, and the couple was escorted out of the room to his chamber.

The ritual celebration was over. Daniel had pleased his hosts, at least for now. But how long would it last? He desperately needed to contact someone.

Al-Hamra, his fellow tribesmen, and elders of the region felt their efforts had succeeded. The Homat al Omma seemed pacified. The party continued as a victory party. As the night went on, the marriage would be consummated, and their community would be spared further destruction. All rejoiced and looked to Al-Hamra with reverence.

Unfortunately for Al-Hamra, not all was well. Two of his daughters had been forced to remove their veils in public, so now they could never marry. They would have to hide from the world for the rest of their lives as single, barren women. But he did have a Homat al Omma as a son-in-law. That would definitely be an asset. All in all, he was happy for Mashira.

The marriage, however, remained unconsummated as Daniel fell asleep with a naked, willing woman at his side. Daniel's indifference confused her. She felt that he still must be weak after his ordeal in the desert and would wait patiently for him to be ready for her. It was her duty as his wife.

* * * * *

A surprise visitor appeared before the court of the powerful Sultan of Oman. He was received without hesitation, as his power and stature were great. The Turkish man had followed news of Daniel into Oman and had decided not to proceed without further guidance. Time was becoming a problem. The longer the tattooed man remained alone, the more anxious the Turk's associates were becoming. There was no telling what kinds of problems the man was causing, and these were problems the Turk would have to fix. He had to secure the man soon.

The Turk was offered food and drink, but he accepted none. He just wanted information.

"He is in Uber," announced the Sultan. "He is at the home of my regional sheik, Al-Hamra. My personal vehicle will transport you to the province. The journey is long. We will give you ample fuel and water for the desert crossing."

That was all the Turk needed. He went outside and climbed

aboard an almost-new six-passenger Mitsubishi four-wheel drive vehicle. The back was stuffed with water supplies and extra fuel. He pointed the vehicle toward the southwest and was off.

* * * * *

The stalemate in the bedroom continued. Daniel ignored Mashira, lost in his own reality. A servant brought in food for each meal as they remained in the room. It was forbidden for a new bride to emerge from the bedroom until after the marriage was consummated. By the third day Mashira was becoming concerned.

In her culture if the marriage remained unconsummated she would be held responsible. He had chosen her, but unfortunately that was where it had ended. If she didn't get him interested, she would be stoned and her father would be disgraced. Even though it was against custom for her to question her husband, she felt she had to. Maybe his culture was different, or maybe he had been injured and was unable to perform his duty. If that was the case, maybe she could help. She waited for the right time.

Daniel wallowed in self-pity. He felt that his life was stuck in a time warp, like Bill Murray in *Groundhog Day*. He couldn't leave and he couldn't call for help. *Why aren't there phones in this place?* He planned on not defiling this woman no matter what. In fact, he paid her no attention. In the mid-afternoon, he lay on the bed, staring at the ceiling and thinking of home.

Mashira saw her opportunity and lay beside him, gently tracing his tattoos with a soft touch. "My lord," she began softly in surprisingly good English. "I have not spoken because it is not my place. But I fear that I must, in order to protect my family. We have been joined before all of the community. It has been three days since our marriage and we have yet to unite. I fear that I have somehow caused this. For the sake of my family, kill me now; our servant is bringing a knife. That will be the only way to save my family's honor. If it is not me, please tell me what the matter is. Maybe I can help. I am proud to be your wife, and I was happy you chose me."

Daniel was shocked. "My wife?" he yelled. He'd chosen this woman as the best dancer, not his wife.

Mashira said, "You do not understand. I was given to you in

marriage. You chose me. I can never marry another man. You defile me by not taking me. To leave this room without consummation would mean that I have displeased you. I would be stoned, and my father would be a laughingstock. Considering your stature, he would probably be stoned too." As she spoke, she continued touching his chest and abdomen. "My lord, I am the wife of a Homat al Omma, and even if I could remarry, no man would dare have me. I am perfectly willing to be yours in any way you desire."

Daniel leaned up on one elbow. "What does Homat al Omma mean in your language?"

"Protector of the People."

Daniel closed his eyes.

To Mashira's delight, he began fondling and kissing her. She was now a woman—a valued member of the community, an asset to her family, and the wife of a Homat al Omma.

* * * * *

Later that day a strange man arrived in Uber driving the Sultan's Mitsubishi Raider.

CHAPTER 4: Omar

Daniel needed some time alone to think, and he dismissed the servant. He needed a long bath, and the water was pleasant. It was hard to believe he was married. His parents would have a hard time accepting this. As he was just starting to relax and was passing into a trance-like state, Daniel heard a commotion outside. Heavy footsteps came in his direction. The door burst open, and a stranger entered; he was a man who appeared to have an agenda. The man was large and dark-skinned, wearing a white tunic and a turban that cast shadows over his face. He stopped in front of Daniel who stood up, unashamed of his nakedness.

The stranger gazed at Daniel's entire body. He showed no fear and did not bow as everyone else had. Daniel feared that this man knew what he really was, an impostor. The man continued to stare, motionless, and Daniel sensed impending doom.

Under the turban, and beneath the swaddling cloth around the man's face, all Daniel could see was a set of fiercely penetrating eyes. *Is this one of Altorini's men? Is this the guy who deposited me in the desert? Is he back to finish the job?*

The man started forward and—just when Daniel suspected he was to meet his maker—the man surrounded him with the largest bear hug he had ever experienced.

"I have finally found you, my boy!" He smiled broadly and spoke with a slight British accent. "I worried that these savages would have killed you by now. You are an Infidel, you know." Releasing Daniel, the man began unwrapping his turban, then stopped. "I have forgotten my manners. I am Omar the Turk, the son of Ramula." He had removed his turban and was pulling off his tunic.

Daniel was shocked. Before him stood a naked man with the same body markings he had! The lynx, the kissing herons, the sword and daggers; they were all exactly the same.

"I am not what you think I am," started Daniel. "I am an impostor. I don't know how I got these markings. Everyone here bows and calls me Homat al Omma. I am not sure I even know what it means. I just want to go home." He held up one hand. "And I mean you no harm. Please don't hurt me."

Omar looked confused for a moment, then laughed heartily.

"My boy, I couldn't hurt you if I wanted to! It is forbidden to harm another of our Order. You have much to learn, much to learn about who and what you are. Daniel, your markings do not lie. Your humility has given you away. You cannot be a false initiate. You are as I am. You are Homat al Omma. But let's keep to the English—you are a Defender."

"How can I be something I know nothing of? And how, Sir, do you know my name?"

"It is by my powers of thought that I can tell your name. I also know that you are from America, have a fondness for Swedish, and hmmm—that's not good."

"What's not good?" *Is he reading my mind?*

"Tell me exactly how you came to be married," Omar insisted. "I need details."

"The sheik threw me a big celebration. Everything was going fine. There was food and a lot of entertainment. Then he said I had to choose the best dancer from among three young women, his daughters. The women danced and I stalled; then they danced again. I relented and chose one. Then she told me she was my wife."

"Is she happy?"

"She left this morning beaming."

"Good! Now, tell me more about the dancers."

"They danced to music, twirling about, and they seemed interested only in me."

"Were they veiled?"

"The first dance, yes," he replied. "But during the second dance their father stripped the veils off of them so I could see their faces. The girls didn't seem to mind, and I thought it was just part of the production."

Omar looked displeased. "Do you know what you did? Do you not know where you are?"

"If I wanted to hazard a guess, I'd say Morocco."

Omar shook his head. "Why did you not take all three of them as wives?"

"Okay, that's a strange idea. I mean, I didn't want even one. Besides, the sheik asked which I wanted, and I took that to mean only one. I took Mashira only to keep them quiet. I really didn't know what I was doing."

Omar shook his head again, then pulled his tunic on but left the turban off. He found a chair and sat down. Daniel used the interlude to dry off and find his own tunic, then sat opposite his visitor. Omar continued. "You are in Oman in a small city called Uber on the Arabian Peninsula. Here, it is not uncommon to have up to four wives. Your actions will have grave consequences for the women you refused. They are defiled. They have bared their faces to someone that is not their family or husband. They will be sub-citizens in a land where women already have little status. I must try to fix this situation." He paused, thoughtfully. "What other problems have you caused since you awoke in the desert?"

"I killed a man, and I think I had some others killed," he admitted. "They beat me up in the desert and brought me here to be executed."

"That is no problem," reassured Omar. "They deserved to die. It is written that any who do not show proper hospitality to a Defender shall die by the sword. Even the seed of the guilty shall be cut up, as well as the family that brought him into the world. Let them never be seen again on this earth. Have no regrets for your actions. You are lucky to have lived."

"I'm still confused, Omar." Daniel looked at him. "Why was I left in the desert? Did you leave me there? The last thing I remember was eating a sandwich on a lake in South Dakota. I woke up in the desert, thousands of miles away, and I nearly died of exposure. Thank God I've had some experience in the desert. It was lucky that I found water."

"Only the strong inherit their birthright, Daniel." Omar smiled. "Those from whom much is expected are tested harder. You still could have died. Your test sounds very harsh. The Choosers must expect great things of you."

"What birthright? Choosers? Who are they? Am I still being tested?"

Omar was growing tired of talk. "Now you are safe. You have survived a very dangerous time. I will look after you and take you to the temple. There is much to learn and much to see. We will have time to discuss your questions. Have faith, my boy; you are a very lucky man, and you have been given a wonderful gift. I have been on the road a long time and I need food and drink. Tonight will

53

be a night of much rejoicing. I have found a new associate, and our Order will add a great new Defender to our ranks. We will leave for the temple in the morning. Until then eat, drink, and be merry. Tonight you should ravish your wife. It may be a long time before you return to this wonderful place." He smiled. "Give her a night to remember for life. She may never again be with a man."

"Do you mean she can't come with us?"

"No, but have no worry. She will be treated like a queen. She is the wife of a Homat al Omma. For another man to hurt her or defile her would bring your wrath upon the whole village. She will eat with the men and she will be treated as if she were the richest woman in the whole province. Why do you think she seems so happy? When you are here she has to serve you and provide you her body without shame or remorse, but when you are gone, she answers to no man. They all fear you. I will remind them of the wrath of the Homat al Omma. If you ever need someplace to spend a night when you're in the area, she will always be here. If by some chance you do show up again, you will find a most willing mate and a supportive community. I need to find your father-in-law. We need to plan a shotgun wedding; I need to regain some respect for the women you rejected. Hopefully they haven't already been stoned."

"You mean you're going to marry them, sleep with them, and then leave, never to be seen again?"

"Unless you have a better idea." Omar called for a servant and summoned Al-Hamra, and then turned back to Daniel. "After tonight they will be treated with respect. You caused this. You should have married them." He grinned. "Now you have to share."

"Can I contact my family, Omar? They must think I'm dead. I never got to say good-bye."

"At some point you will get a chance to contact them. They will be okay. Every Defender's family seems to handle losing a son better than regular people handle it." He placed one hand on Daniel's shoulder. "Daniel, you are part of the Defender family now. You have much work ahead of you. We have a long way to go and little time. Tonight we will eat the only decent meal we'll get for some time. We won't see any women for over four weeks either, so go and enjoy your wife's company."

The sheik arrived promptly after hearing that he now had two

Defenders in his home. "What can I do for you, my Lords?"

"Prepare a large banquet for us tonight. There will be much celebration," ordered Omar. "I want to marry your other two daughters. They are beautiful, and I need the services of a wife. I cannot choose, so I will marry both."

Al-Hamra questioned this last order. "But my Lord, they have been defiled! They are not eligible to be married!"

Suddenly the ground began to shake, and dust filtered down from the ceiling. It looked to Daniel like Omar was causing the geologic event. *How can this be? Who or what is this man?*

The shaking stopped, and Al-Hamra was filled with fear. "You will find, Al-Hamra, that I am a patient and fair man. You have listened but have not heard. I understand the problems of your daughters. They are not defiled in my eyes, and I will marry them promptly. They are to be my wives. We will leave in the morning, and I expect you to treat our wives with as much respect as you would give us. If we hear that you have harmed them or insulted them, we will consider that you have insulted Daniel and you have insulted me. One of us will return at once and with great care eliminate you and this fair city from existence." He smiled. "But I will expect your full cooperation. Now, we would like goat tonight. Your women will also eat goat, and we will dine with our wives. Where is my room?"

As Omar left, he winked at Daniel, proud of his conquest. Daniel was shocked by what was going on around him. He needed to take a walk, needed to think. His situation was changing too fast, and tomorrow he would start a new adventure.

The celebration started that evening. Omar celebrated his discovery of Daniel. Daniel celebrated his impending departure. Their wives celebrated their new status in the community, a status unlike that of any woman before. Al-Hamra celebrated the elevation of his daughters, especially the two married to Omar. Their marriages were already consummated. The townsfolk celebrated the impending exodus of the Defenders, wanting life to return to normal.

Despite his previous dislike of goat meat, Daniel ate heartily. Omar had warned him that it might be some time before they would enjoy another decent meal. There was enthusiastic music and dancing. All were happy. During the whole evening, Omar's wives beamed with pride—he had changed their lives. Daniel understood the situation better now. The women were certainly better off as Omar's wives. Such was the evening, and the last stragglers went home from the party around midnight.

As Omar woke Daniel, handing over a roasted goat leg, he laughed. "Breakfast!"

Cold goat didn't taste any better than hot goat. Daniel would have to acquire a taste for the strong-smelling meat.

"Is not Arabian goat the best?" said a cheerful, well-fed Omar.

"The terms 'best' and 'goat' should not be used in the same sentence," Daniel grumbled.

"That from a man whose cultural food is a smelly fish. Which is the better cuisine, reconstituted cod or pickled herring?" retorted Omar. "You need to widen your horizons."

"I'll stick with herring, if you please." They both laughed.

"Come. The car is ready. We must leave immediately," Omar said.

After driving through the village of Makinat Shihan, the pair finally reached the border of Oman and crossed into Yemen on a route used by trucks carrying goods from Dubai.

Local traders carrying incense from the groves in Oman to Egypt and Rome had first used the route thousands of years earlier. Ancient ruins of forts and many mysterious megaliths lined the route.

Daniel was nervous as they approached the border. He had no identification and feared the Yemeni officials would give them a difficult time. However, as they slowed for the border, the guard lifted the gate, and they sped through. It was as if he never even saw them.

"What was that all about?" asked Daniel. "I thought crossing the Yemeni border would be a big deal."

"The first thing you have to realize, my boy, is that we are different from everyone else. We have special powers." Omar looked at Daniel and saw total confusion. It was obvious the boy had no idea what he was. "The border guards didn't stop us because I filled their thoughts with other things. They didn't even see us." They were now driving in a wadi, a desert valley between two low mountain ranges, an area of stark beauty with scant vegetation. As the road neared a rock outcropping, Omar stopped. "It's time you learn of our powers."

Omar got out of the car. Daniel followed. Oma gestured Daniel to the front of the car. "See that large rock on that cliff?"

Daniel nodded.

Omar closed his eyes and raised his arms. A large, low-pitched rumble filled the valley. The rock moved and then rolled from its ancient perch, bringing other rocks down with it as it sped down the slope. The small avalanche crashed to the valley floor with a thunderous roar. Daniel instinctively ran to a position behind the Mitsubishi.

"What the hell was that?"

Omar smiled. "A small demonstration of a Defender's power."

"You mean you did that?"

Omar laughed. "You have much to learn, my boy. First, you must believe and accept what you are."

Kidnapping of foreigners is a cottage industry in Yemen. While Omar was giving his demonstration, neither he nor Daniel noticed a pair of white Toyota pickups nearing them. When Omar finally noticed them, the trucks were accelerating toward them and only about a hundred and fifty yards away. Riders in the back of both vehicles pointed rifles at them.

"Don't these people ever learn?" Omar said, frustrated. But there was no fear in his eyes or his manner. He calmly opened his arms and both trucks disappeared in a cloud of sand, spinning end over end until they lost momentum. Omar turned and walked calmly toward his own truck, then opened the door and climbed in. "Come on, Daniel; the break and the lesson are over." They sped off, neither man paying any concern to the occupants now staggering out of the two trucks.

They drove toward the mid-afternoon sun in the Wadi Masila and passed through the villages of Husn al-Urr, Qasam, and Inat before they reached the city of Tarim. Omar started a travel narrative. "These long valleys—wadis—are weird, geologic formations. I always found it odd that these valleys formed the roads here. None of the roads are graded; we're driving on old river bottoms. This is the city of Tarim. Here the Wadi Masila joins the larger Wadi Hadramawt. Tarim is an educational center of the Sunni sect of Islam. Although most cities and villages in Yemen have historical mosques, the one in Tarim has special significance."

The vehicle entered the city of brown multi-story mud brick buildings. Daniel was impressed by the architecture, which resembled that of the adobe buildings found in the American Southwest. "How do they make the buildings here?"

"They make bricks using molds during the dry season," he explained. "They mix mud and straw and then arrange the blocks. On larger buildings and mosques they smooth out the bricks to form a smooth wall. They have been doing it this way for thousands of years. They use larger blocks for the bottom with gradually tapered, smaller blocks toward the top."

"How come you know so much about Yemen?"

"This is my region," came his delayed answer. "I was here during the unification war between 1990 and 1994 and also before then when Yemen became independent of the West in 1967. We kept a close eye on the area back then. One portion, South Yemen, the area around here, was extremely leftist and Marxist. The northern portion was very pro-Western and was supported by your friends in America. The Russians had naval bases here and on a Yemeni island. We suspected we needed to keep a close eye on this region in case a war broke out. World War III could develop, and the use of nuclear weapons seemed all too possible. The animosity between Yemen and the Saudis goes very far back and includes the Saudi's attempt to steal the northern Yemeni oil fields back in the sixties. I have been to Yemen quite a few times over the years but have not been here since the unification war."

This seemed like a good opening for Daniel to pry more information out of Omar. "So who are the 'we' you are referring to?"

"Our Order, of course," he said.

"How many of our Order are there?"

"Eleven women and nine men," he replied. "Ten with you. One man, Tanoka, the Japanese Defender, is very old. He will die soon."

Daniel studied Omar. "You were here in 1967? You don't look over forty years old, and that was thirty-five years ago."

"You are indeed smart, my son." Omar laughed. "A Defender's life span is different than normal people."

"So when were you born?"

"I do not think you're ready for the answer to that, and I suspect you would not believe me even if I told you." He glanced at

Daniel. "Let's just say I am older than I appear. You will find out how and why in due time."

"These powers you have," Daniel asked. "Were you born with them, or do you somehow acquire them?"

"You will acquire your powers when you are initiated at the temple."

"Will it hurt?"

Omar laughed. "Only with Marta. Don't worry, my son. Your transformation will happen without pain. The women at the temple will take good care of you. Did you have any pain when you received the markings of the Defender?"

"Not that I know of, but I almost died in the desert."

"That was a test, my young friend. The Choosers needed to know whether you were worthy of your calling. You made a choice in the desert to live and fulfill your destiny. It would have been easier to have curled up and died, but you chose to fight. Nothing in life is free; you have to earn respect as a man and as a Defender. You did very well. You survived, and now I am bringing you to the temple. There you will receive your birthright."

"Where is this temple?"

Omar was momentarily distracted by something ahead of him. "In the hills of Ethiopia."

What looked like a restaurant lay ahead at the main square of the town. Omar stopped the vehicle in front. He paid no attention to the vehicles he was blocking as he jumped out of the car. "This is the Rest House Qasr al-Qubba. Here we eat."

Daniel hoped that they would serve something besides goat. Omar spoke with the owner and beckoned Daniel to sit. Daniel sat and looked at Omar. "Have you been here before? It looked like the owner knew you."

"I have never been here before."

"How do you know his name? We did just sort of barge in."

"The owner told me they have good fish. I know you like fish."

"I don't have any money, Omar—do you?"

"A Defender never needs money, and he never has to pay. We always—" Omar's lecture was cut short as a waiter served Omar a large piece of goat and Daniel a plate of fish and rice. Both men were served tea.

Omar didn't speak while he ate except to comment about the particular quality of his food or to ask Daniel to pass him something. He truly enjoyed his gustatory delights.

After finishing their meal and taking a stroll around the city square, Omar started becoming impatient, so they returned to the vehicle. They filled the gas tank and headed west. The road improved greatly on the west end of town and was actually paved. The valley also became much greener, with trees and some agriculture. The reddish brown edifices of the canyon walls impressed Daniel. The plateau outside soared several hundred feet above the valley. The whole scene reminded Daniel of northern Arizona's Canyon de Chelly.

They drove through many large and small towns along the wadi, completing the thirty-kilometer journey to Shabwah with two hours of daylight remaining.

"We have to leave the wadi here and head south toward Ataq." Omar seemed to enjoy talking like a tour guide. However, it was apparent to Daniel that this was no road that a tour guide would ever see. It was little more than a trail across the desert. "The local government has little control here, so few people ever journey across this high desert plateau. The nomads will stop buses, trucks—just about anyone. Keep vigilant. Some of the locals carry rocket-propelled grenades. We have no extra time to fix our vehicle."

They drove over hills and sand and saw nothing for the first fifty kilometers or so. Suddenly up ahead, a dark truck blocked the road. Two more vehicles sat on the rise overlooking the road. "Daniel, take the wheel. I need my hands."

Daniel did as he was told, and Omar raised his hands, looking first in the direction of the vehicles on the rise. The vehicles disappeared in a cloud of sand. Omar shifted his attention to the truck in the road. A large dust devil appeared from nowhere and picked up the vehicle, depositing it a hundred meters away on its side. Omar retook the wheel. As they neared the site, most of the men were running away, but two raised rifles toward the Defenders' truck.

"Big mistake, my boy, big mistake." Daniel again took the wheel as Omar pointed a finger at the first man, who immediately collapsed. Then the second clutched his head and hit the sand hard. "I don't know what those two were thinking. Remember this, Daniel:

Never let your opponent have an opening. We have much power, but we are not immortal. Some people know when to run, but some just seem to want to die foolishly. Always think of the big picture. That's why the legends about us are so terrible and scary. Old Al-Hamra was afraid you'd wipe out the entire village after those men beat you and tried to execute you. And he was right to be scared. Sometimes you need to make an example of a situation so others will give you respect. We are an important Order and are respected for a reason. If I had found you dead, I would have leveled the whole district."

Daniel was horrified by all the death he had witnessed in the last few days. "But don't you have any remorse for the death and destruction you cause?"

"Yes, to an extent." He glanced at Daniel. "But we are few, and we have a bigger purpose; one that you will soon understand. I kill to protect a greater good. Even some innocents die, but we are a fragile race, and the needs of the many outweigh the needs of the few. We rarely have a new initiate. We take great care to protect our initiates." He jerked one thumb over his shoulder. "Those men chose to die. They could have run with their friends, but they did not, so they died. One is always given a choice. Sometimes, though, either you do not realize you have a choice, or you make the wrong one. They made the wrong choice."

A few hours later, they arrived in Ataq. It had been an amazingly long day, and they had driven many kilometers in a hot, dry desert. Both men looked forward to a rest. Omar announced that most of Ataq had been built during the oil boom and that it had only a minimal history compared to some of the previous towns they had visited. They pulled into the modern-looking Gulf Hotel. Both were happy to be given a double room with a private bath. Daniel took the opportunity to get cleaned up. He'd planned to ask Omar many questions but was disappointed to find Omar sound asleep when he emerged from the bathroom, clean and relaxed. His questions would have to wait. Undoubtedly Omar had had a long night previously with his two wives and was recouping his strength.

Daniel quickly descended into the first deep sleep of his adventure. He had no idea what lay ahead of him, but he felt secure in the company of Omar. There was much to understand, and he would soon be taught what he needed to learn. He dreamed of cows—acres of cows, fields of cows—and of endless prairies.

Morning came quickly, and the teacher awakened the young Defender. Their journey on this day would be equally long but uneventful. The scenery astonished Daniel. They first traveled the two hundred kilometers through Nuqub to Harib, and then drove southwest on a terrible road, climbing toward a distant group of mountains.

Omar drove fast and hard, cursing the road and anyone or anything in his path. Daniel had never seen such aggressive driving. He enjoyed watching. They soon approached the town of Rada.

Daniel noticed that this town was different than the others. The mud brick houses were gray instead of brown, and there was a mixture of old and new buildings. The old part was still surrounded by a nearly intact stone wall. He saw several finely decorated tower houses, many with double- and triple-arched fanlights with huge alabaster frames around the windows. The road had also improved; they were driving on a paved highway.

Omar always seemed to know what Daniel was thinking. "The Dutch paved the road after the reunification, as part of a larger development project. The smooth mud on the outside is replaced every year. It takes a lot of work to keep up a home here."

They continued past a still-smoking volcano that, oddly, had a communication tower on one side. Forty minutes later, they were in Dhamãr, a town on the high plains. They stopped at a roadside restaurant and ate a filling meal of rice and meat.

Afterward, Omar continued his tour guide narrative. "Dhamãr is an ancient town. A Himyarite king, Dhamãr Ali, who was known for restoring the famous dam of Ma'rib, founded it. This is the only town in Northern Yemen without a protective wall. There was also a large Jewish settlement here, but they are gone now. The unification war of 1994 broke out here. I always thought this was a strange place for a war to break out."

Daniel agreed and enjoyed the remaining sips of his tea without replying. Omar announced they still had a ways to go to reach the sea. They refueled and left the city. Daniel continued to be amazed that no one had asked them to pay for anything.

When they arrived in Yarim, Omar pointed. "Those low, flat

buildings with cupolas on them are bath houses. The people here enjoy hot baths in the springs. The whole area is geologically active. You saw the volcano as we came into Dhamãr. I think this town is about the highest in the country. We must be close to three thousand meters above the sea, but it is all downhill from here." Omar laughed at his own joke.

Daniel could tell the air was thinning, and their vehicle was struggling. They were both happy to start the descent. As they approached Ibb, Omar was surprised to find that a new road bypassed the sprawling provincial capital. The plateau, and what used to be a fertile valley floor, was now urban sprawl. "This city has doubled in size in the last ten years. This road is new. It used to take forever to bump and grind through the city center."

Their next stop was Ta'izz, a city of a third of a million people that looked more European than Yemeni. This stop was not entirely planned. As they drove around the hilly city, Daniel admired a series of beautiful mosques. Then he noticed that they had passed the same mosque twice. They decided to stop for fuel, and although Omar said he was going to relieve himself, Daniel suspected he went in to ask for directions. Upon his return, Omar handed Daniel a copy of preprinted directions to leave the city heading south.

As they pulled away from the gas station, Omar went back to his travelogue. "This town was a center of the Turkish occupation during the Ottoman period." As Daniel listened, he looked at the fortresses around the town and the large mountain looming to the east. Finally, they put the highlands in their rear view mirror and were off toward the Red Sea.

"Where are we going to cross?" Daniel longed for the cool ocean breezes.

"At Al-Makha," Omar replied. "It is an old coffee port. From there we can catch a boat to Assab, Eritrea. It used to be part of Ethiopia, but now they have become independent. Did you know that the first coffee came from Yemen? All the coffee imported into Europe came from here until the demand outstripped the supply, and the coffee industry developed elsewhere. Although some is still grown in the hills, the major agricultural product now is qat, a mild, stimulant narcotic that is widely popular in Yemen. The people here have parties with the stuff. Sometimes there are so many parties going on, by mid-afternoon all the streets are bare. They chew the fresh leaves from the trees or make a tea out of the dried plants."

"Seems like a real problem."

"I do not know—you Americans are funny about drugs. You view that anything in excess is bad. The productivity seems to wane during these parties, but there does not seem to be the same criminal element associated with qat that there is with marijuana or cocaine. Anyway, the government tolerates it. They used to even have certain days you could use it and certain days you could not, but they finally gave up enforcing any restrictions. Many righteous-minded Europeans want Yemen to try and torch the qat groves and increase coffee production. Needless to say, they were unsuccessful. However, farmers make much more money from qat than from coffee.

"By the way, Daniel, did you know the word mocha comes from makha and this village? Coffee beans were smuggled out of Yemen, and the plants were started in Java and Cyprus. Al-Makha is just a little tourist village now, although there is still a large smuggling faction in existence. In fact, most of the liquor consumed in Yemen is smuggled through the small port here."

All the talk of coffee made Daniel thirsty. The thought of a large cup of java filled his mind with pleasure. Coffee was his drug of choice. He felt less damning of the qat use when he thought of it that way. He settled for one of the last bottles of water from the back seat.

"We're almost out of water."

"Don't worry, my boy. We are almost to the port, and this vehicle will be history."

Al-Makha was a small town of barely a few hundred people located on the Red Sea. All around there were piles of dirt that had been old buildings. The town was in decline, as was the port. Only a handful of small cargo boats were docked opposite the city center. Omar stopped the vehicle near a dock. Darkness would fall in an hour or so, and they needed to locate transportation for crossing the strait to Africa. Daniel hoped they could catch a boat tonight. He longed for his destiny and didn't want to stay in the seedy little seaport.

Omar began arguing in Arabic with a ship's captain. He returned looking disgusted and angry.

"Well, at least you didn't kill anyone." Daniel laughed at his friend.

"I offered to, but the man only encouraged me." He scowled. "Since the war has escalated between Eritrea and Ethiopia, no sea captain will go across to Assab. He would even allow me to destroy his ship with him in it instead of going. There was no discussion on that point. He will not go to Assab. But he will go to Djibouti."

"What is Djibouti like?"

"We are leaving in thirty minutes." He still looked unhappy. "It will be a twenty-hour boat ride instead of the five it would take to get to Assab, and I hate ships. The delay will be costly. Now we have absolutely no extra time in the schedule. There is an old trail that we can cross back toward the main road from Assab, but we will have to drive all night. We will also need to get the best possible vehicle in Djibouti as that road is historically bad."

"I've never heard of Djibouti."

"It is an old French colony—French Somaliland," he answered. "Not much of a place. It's just a port in a very small country. It has more French people than natives. The captain needed to go anyway—apparently their biggest export is alcohol to the Moslems here in Arabia. Moslems aren't allowed to drink, so alcohol is more illegal than qat in Yemen."

"Do we have a cabin?"

"No, just a deck." Omar walked off toward the captain.

Daniel grabbed the remaining water from the truck and climbed aboard the ship, *al-Mandab*, an ancient, hundred-and-fifty-foot steamer, with more rust than paint. It was early evening when they headed out to sea a few minutes later. Soon the monotony of the engine and the gentle rocking of the boat with the waves caused Daniel to yawn and fall asleep.

* * * * *

First light caused the heavily tattooed blond man to stir. His mouth felt like cotton as he awoke, and he immediately grabbed for the water bottle he'd been holding when he fell asleep. It was gone. He struggled to his feet and shook himself to get the blood flowing. Still dizzy, Daniel almost fell over the rail and out of the boat. He looked around and saw no one.

The canvases on the deck were covered in dew, and a small haze sat over a calm ocean. Daniel began to search for Omar and was soon in a slight panic that his guide had somehow left him. A few moments later, he was relieved to find Omar under the canvas of a lifeboat, still asleep, with an empty water bottle in one hand and a half-empty bottle leaning next to him. Daniel helped himself to the remaining water, then moved to the bow of the boat and watched the ocean roll by.

He watched as porpoises followed the wake of the ship for a time. Sea birds flew above as a warm breeze occasionally stirred the tarps. A continent he had never visited came closer and closer. Africa had always been a mystery in his mind.

A few hours later the ship turned south by southwest, and by mid-morning it was heading into a small gulf. Still there was no sign of Omar arising. Daniel thought he should get some sleep as well, but he wasn't tired. Besides, he expected they'd take turns driving tonight. He suspected that was why Omar continued to sleep.

Soon he could see a city ahead, and surmised it was their destination. He noticed a volcanic cone that seemed to rise out of the sea on the northern shore of the bay and stared at it for some time.

"That is the Ardoukoba volcano," came Omar's voice. "It last erupted in the late seventies. It was very frightening to everyone. It was feared that the flow would block the port. It is said that the volcano had not erupted in three thousand years. Just between you and me, I think the geologists' timelines are a bit inaccurate. Let us get some food in Djibouti before we head off. Do you speak French?"

Daniel nodded. "I can get by."

"Good," he said rather smugly. "I hate the language. You can order the food, and I will just provide backup."

When they arrived in port, they thanked their captain for such a smooth ride. It was early afternoon, so, after lunch, they had a chance to begin their drive before darkness set in, but their plan deteriorated as they had trouble locating decent transportation. After what seemed like an eternity, they found an older Land Rover

Defender model. It had two seats with a box in the back. The ceiling over the passenger compartment was covered by a canvas tarp, standard issue for the desert.

"Hey, a Defender for a couple of Defenders." Daniel laughed at his little joke. Omar wasn't amused. He walked away to look for the owner. Daniel followed. They were met by a contingent of French soldiers who were on leave and itching for some action.

As the soldiers approached the duo, Omar muttered, "I have no time for these men." He waved his right arm from left to right, and all six men fell to the ground. "They will be okay; I hit them with only a small amount of energy."

Daniel heard their moans as he and Omar walked past.

At a bistro on the waterfront, they located the owner of the Land Rover. Omar described his situation, and the man gave them the keys. Either Omar had helped him make up his mind, or the Djibouti tribal elder had recognized their tattoos. Daniel approached the owner of the café and explained in French their need for food. A half-hour later they collected a large package and bottles of water. After they stowed supper, they went to a gas station and requisitioned extra fuel and gas cans. Daniel drove as they left the station. Omar located a map in the back seat and provided the necessary navigational aid.

Daniel was nervous about driving in a strange country at night and was relieved that they drove on the right in Djibouti. As he drove out of the capital, Omar gorged on the now-cold food. Daniel ate with one hand as he juggled the frequent shifting, steering, and swerving that encompassed driving in a developing country. Pedestrians were constantly crossing in front of the British vehicle, and more than once Daniel had to slam on the brakes. All the while Omar kept eating the chicken and all but inhaling the rice.

"Omar, don't eat my half of the food!" scolded Daniel as Omar threw a well-abused chicken bone out the window. "I can't eat as fast as you can because I'm driving."

"I am not eating your food, my boy," reassured Omar. "I was counting your chicken pieces to make sure they were divided evenly." He laughed as Daniel swerved to avoid a pothole.

"Yeah, right." Daniel enjoyed driving and being in control for a change, but the going was slow.

Omar studied the map closely. "Stop the truck, Daniel. I must show you the route before I fall asleep." When Daniel pulled over, Omar quickly outlined a route with his finger. "Do you see? We will go here."

"Why is that road a dotted line?"

"It is probably not much of a road.... This country had a civil war in 1994, and they had to bring the French back in to restore order. This whole of the Horn of Africa and Yemen seemed to be at war back then. Do you remember the U.S. being in Somalia? Ethiopia fought Eritrea, Djibouti fought Eritrea and the Somali-backed rebels, Yemen fought for unification, and Somalia fought a civil war. And all the while the entire region was gripped in the biggest drought of the century. Famine was everywhere. What a waste. This place has been a hotbed of unrest for thousands of years."

Daniel kept driving and gnawing on his chicken. Omar fell asleep. Daniel continued along the dark, soon desolate road, occasionally swerving to avoid camels and large potholes. The road began to deteriorate further into large rocks with an occasional bit of road somewhere underneath. Daniel inched the Land Rover along, trying not to kill himself or Omar. He said a prayer and was thankful he had finished his meal.

After two hours, he made the required left turn onto the dotted line indicated on the map. At first the trail seemed surprisingly smooth as he crossed a dry lakebed marked Asal on the map. It was flat and free of rocks. Fifteen kilometers later the interlude ended. He was now following a rut in the desert that was filled with sand, holes, rocks, and about every geological oddity in between. He drove cautiously as Omar snored.

He felt he was on the road to oblivion, and he was too scared to be tired. Bumps frequently knocked the truck out of gear, and in other places the trail suddenly veered to the right or left, and Daniel would bounce the truck off a pile of dirt on one side or the other. He wasn't impressed with Omar's shortcut.

As Omar slept, oblivious even to the jarring bumps, Daniel took advantage of the silence to consider his adventure. He knew he had a lot to learn, and he was also scared at what he would become. He was slowly being initiated into a secret society, joining an organization he had not chosen to join and one. He was also afraid of controlling the power Omar apparently had. Somehow, deep in his consciousness, he still doubted what he had seen. *It has to be a trick. It defies the laws of physics! How could anyone do what Omar can do? How could a group of people I've never even read about possess such power and apply such influence on the world?*

He looked in the rear-view mirror and marveled at the large moon centered there. It was almost full, and it illuminated the desert floor. He thanked the moon for helping to light the way and continued bouncing up the desert plateau.

His travel companion was starting to stir. Daniel hoped that Omar would want to drive so he could rest.

Omar awoke and told Daniel to pull over. Daniel had survived his first driving experience on the continent of Africa. Omar threw the remaining scraps of chicken out the door and headed toward the back of the Defenders' Defender.

CHAPTER 5: The Temple of the Defenders

Daniel stepped out from behind the wheel and stretched quickly as Omar refueled the vehicle. Then he slid into the passenger seat, and Omar threw the Defender into gear.

"Ah! Now you are going to see some real driving!"

If Daniel replied, it wasn't audible over the loud rumble of the truck, which bounced along the rough road more like a basketball than a vehicle. He thought that only someone from the third world could truly enjoy this kind of road. Whereas he had driven in fear of every bounce, Omar seemed to take the bumps personally, as if each were an insult directed at him from the road. He was steering with two hands, shifting with another, and gesturing with a fourth. It wasn't long until the constant jarring had lulled Daniel into a passenger coma, not really sleep, during which his head alternated bobbing about or striking the side window. This was followed by an expletive after which the whole cycle was repeated. Daniel finally wised up to the fact that a serious head injury was going to ensue if he didn't take some preventative action, so he announced to Omar that he was going to crawl into the back seat and catch some Zs.

"What is a Z?" Omar had been amused watching Daniel's head bounce off the side window, and he reluctantly agreed that the back seat would be safer.

A bright light interrupted Daniel's sleep. The Land Rover was stopped. He heard Omar barking orders in a language he couldn't understand. He opened one eye to see a uniformed man dropping his weapon and falling to the ground. Omar threw the Land Rover into gear, and the vehicle lurched back to life. "What was that about?"

Omar was putting his shirt back on while shifting gears and steering. "Ethiopia, a backwards land. I had to show him my marks before he would obey. You had better get some sleep; tomorrow is going to be a long day."

"So, will we get to the temple tomorrow?" Daniel asked, still trying to clear his throbbing head.

Omar looked irritated. "The moon is full tomorrow, so we either enter tomorrow night, or we wait four more weeks. Now sleep boy, sleep. I will talk no more. Sleep!"

* * * * *

As the sun rose, the heat of the day filtered into the vehicle, and Daniel slowly stirred to life. "Where are we, Omar?" They were still traveling through the rough terrain. He carefully negotiated the distance to the front passenger seat without catching a bump the wrong way and hitting the ceiling. Ahead was what looked like an arid highland plateau surrounded by hills. "Ethiopia looks like Oman, which looks a lot like west Texas."

"Texas? I understand that the ladies in Texas have big breasts! Ah, I would like to visit Texas someday. I remember seeing a Hollywood movie about The Best Little Prostitute in Texas. This sounds like a place for a man with my tastes!"

"That's, *The Best Little Whorehouse in Texas.*"

"Whores . . . my English is no good sometimes." He laughed, purposely highlighting his English/ Turkish accent. "You Americans are very locked up sexually. You have sex on the television, and yet you cover up your sexuality in public. A man needs a place to sow his oats without breaking the law. You Americans are even afraid to be naked in your own house. Modesty is a misguided thing, you know. Are the Europeans who lie topless on the beach or at the pool more immoral than the Brits or the Yanks? Are the Finns who take a family sauna naked together immoral?"

"But what about the Arabs completely covering their women from head to toe?"

Omar answered. "You speak of the abaya—yes, it is a prison for our women." He paused. "Some Moslems seem to want to lock up their women so they can go play with the boys. Culture and religion are strange bedfellows. I am sometimes surprised anyone gets along at all."

"Are you a Moslem, Omar, or a Christian?"

Omar smiled. "Religion . . . what is religion? Is there a God? Most certainly, I grew up a Moslem and learned the prayers. I fasted, did the Haj, and visited Mecca. After receiving the call of our Order, my view changed. In fact, learning the truth about our history has strengthened my belief in God, and I have also realized some of the truths taught to us by our religious leaders are based on nothing. Religion is like politics or business—usually nothing but a power play where men are trying to use religion to get ahead or to gain control of the masses. The religious leaders want to keep the masses in the dark and prey on their ignorance. It has been like this for centuries and probably will be forever."

"What is our Order about?" Daniel asked, trying to capitalize on Omar's talkative mood.

The reply came quickly, almost like it was the core of his being. "World order, protecting the species from itself." He paused. "Humans were made with a flaw. To put it simply, we were made with egos. We cannot get along, no matter how civilized we become. Everything we do potentially leads to our extinction. The Order tried to stop the development of the atomic bomb. Then, after realizing that wouldn't work, we allowed the Americans to build it, but prevented the Nazis and the Japanese from obtaining it. The Japanese were very close to creating one and almost succeeded despite our efforts. We came to the conclusion that the Americans were the lesser of three evils. Then we gave it to the Russians just to make things even.

"Tell me one thing, my boy: You are a college boy. What good ever came of developing something like the bomb?" After there was no answer, he continued. "We lost a few Defenders in that war. That was undoubtedly the closest the human race came to oblivion in the last few centuries, and probably ever. I wish I had been there in all the action. I would like to have seen those Nazi bastards fry at the temple."

"Nazis at the temple? How could we control what was going on during that war?"

Omar looked at him. "You are like a baby with mother's milk. You know so little about what has really been going on all these years," he said. "The Nazis were into the occult—artifacts, religious power, archeology, and other similar aspects. They had an entire SS unit scouring the planet for anything they thought could be used to legitimize their existence: Thor's helmet, the Ark of the Covenant, anything."

"You mean like *Raiders of the Lost Ark*?"

"Boy, did you not study? Hollywood is not history! Where did you study? Harvard? Yale? I thought those were good schools!"

"Augustana," Daniel said, looking almost embarrassed. "My family couldn't afford anything else."

"Well, an Oxford education was a lucky thing for a Turk like me. Anyway, the Nazis in the mid-nineteen-thirties were in Ethiopia looking for the Ark." He gestured to the right. "The Ark, incidentally, is hidden in a Jewish synagogue that is in a village just over those hills. Someone told the SS about the village and the temple of the Defenders. When they learned of the Defenders, they forgot about the Ark. Instead, they did extensive research into us. The trouble was that the records and manuscripts they could find were very sketchy. Information about a secret society . . . well, it is secret.

"Early on the Nazis did not seem so bad to us, and initially we thought Stalin and his cronies were the ones we had to watch out for. As we were focusing on watching the Russians, we were given free rein to come and go in Germany. But the Germans were watching the Defenders in Germany quite closely. They came up with a plan that involved an attempt to infiltrate us. They captured a young Defender in Austria by the name of Heinrich. They tortured him for information about us and eventually killed him. Then one of their SS agents copied our tattoos and traveled out here to our temple."

"That seems pretty much like the Nazis I read about."

"Those bastards didn't know very much at all about us." He continued. "They did not realize that if they killed a telepath, he would alert everyone else. The Nazi impostor presented himself at the door of our temple. He removed his clothes as is customary when entering the temple and walked into the temple as if he belonged. He thought he was going to become a Defender and use his new powers to aid his comrades. He was met by the temple high priestess, the eldest Volva. He pointed his finger at her and said, 'I am a Defender; give me the rewards and power I deserve.' Those were his last words. The fool.

"The priestess looked at him and said, 'The penalty for entering here is death for you and all that you stand for. Your entire genetic strain will be blotted from this earth.' She then set him on fire, a slow melt that grew from his toes upward to his imitation tattoo. As he screamed in horror, she grabbed him by the neck and physically ejected him from the temple. He landed at the feet of his Nazi comrades, thirty meters outside. Undaunted, the Nazis then attempted to storm the temple. An entire division of soldiers fried in much the same manner outside the temple. Those who retreated were blocked from escape by our female colleagues and later hunted down by the two Defenders who had been resting in the temple. The Nazis called in two squadrons of fighters and Stukka dive-bombers from nearby bases. All were destroyed when they crossed over the valley walls. A now much-angered male Defender named Manfred met a larger, second wave of ground forces of mixed Italian and SS troops at the entrance of the valley. As legend has it, Manfred had been a tutor to Heinrich and was about to enjoy a great deal of satisfaction in avenging his death. But he was pushed aside by Marta, one of our female colleagues. Although it was rare for a woman of our Order to lead an attack outside the temple, she said the Germans were her people, and it was her responsibility to correct their wrong.

"She began by surrounding the infantry with fire. She unmercifully melted the few supporting Panzer units into metal boulders. Creating a storm, she used lightning to electrocute every man except one. That man, a young German officer, was caught up in the air and thrown to the ground at her feet. She melted the clothing from him and made him look into her fiery red eyes, then instructed him to report the outcome directly to Berlin. The Germans were to have the impostor's family executed immediately, or they would face a retribution that could blot out Germany forever. Marta told him to tell his superiors that the mere hint of any more activity against us would not be wise. With his report, the Nazis lost interest in us. They had the capacity to learn from their error."

Daniel was amazed. "That's a great story!"

Omar pointed out the window at some odd looking rocks. "Try to imagine those as former Panzer Mark IV tanks. Perhaps you are beginning to understand what you are to become."

Daniel looked with disbelief.

Omar slowed the truck, then stopped and opened his door. "Now we walk." Omar noticed Daniel was still gazing at the desert monuments. "Yes, those were tanks."

Daniel was suddenly overwhelmed with a strange feeling in the pit of his stomach—anticipation and dread of what lay ahead of him up the narrow trail.

"Hurry up, boy, this is no nature hike," Omar barked. "We have a long way to go, and I am not waiting another month." Daniel ran to catch up.

The trail followed a fold in the hillside and soon turned up a narrow, barren valley along a dry creek bed. About a mile up the trail, Daniel stopped to look back and noted they had been gaining elevation. "Did we pack water?"

Omar shook his head no. "That is why we need to hurry, boy, and cover ground before the sun has fully heated up. The gate to the forbidden valley is near. We can rest and drink there."

Daniel forced his quickly-tiring legs to push on. As he walked, he thought of the heat, the unknown mysteries, and the answers that were waiting for him on top of the hill. He also thought of his constantly throbbing head.

The valley walls became increasingly steep and narrow, the valley itself becoming more of a canyon. At some points, the trail was so narrow that both Omar and Daniel had to hold on to the wall to avoid falling. All of a sudden the trail ended against a hundred-foot-high wall. *I've been duped after all. He's gotten us lost. We'll probably die of thirst.* "You've gotten us lost in a blind canyon!" an exhausted, desperate Daniel exclaimed. "What are we going to do now?"

"My boy, you must believe. How could I be lost when I have eleven women in my head calling me home? How could I become lost going to a place that is more a part of me than even my own arms?" He pointed out small steps in the wall. They were so expertly camouflaged that only after Daniel saw them could he appreciate the ingenuity of their design. The steps were scattered, but Omar made quick and easy work of the climb. Daniel followed. At the top of the wall the trail reappeared and curved around a large boulder. On the other side was a gate. Strangely hewn figures flanked an opening twenty feet high by only about three feet wide.

Daniel asked, "What are these figures?"

Omar pointed at the marks and read, "Beware to those who go forth from here. What lies beyond is forbidden. Death awaits any trespasser. A prudent man will turn around and consider himself lucky to live." He pointed to the other wall. "And look over here: The waters of the bitter river that is devoured by a rock will cause all that drink of it to perish a horrible death. Even the plants of the valley will melt the flesh that touches them."

"Harsh words!" Daniel said, startled. "What are we going to drink?"

Omar reached over, ripped Daniel's shirt open and pointed to the heavily-tattooed chest. "Do you need a bigger invitation? Do you think I would go to all this trouble and then hike seven kilometers just to kill you? Walk through there and drink some water!"

A short way through the gate Daniel heard running water. He noticed a small stream ending at a rock. "This is weird! The stream just ends!" He looked at Omar. "I've only seen something like this once before." Daniel knelt and drank, then sat back. "It isn't bitter; it's actually very sweet. In the Guadalupe Mountains in west Texas there's a place called McKittrick Canyon. There's a river there that starts on the mountaintop and flows down a valley. It forms a genuine oasis and then just ends, right in the middle of nowhere. The whole oasis is so hidden that it was a secret lair of the Native Americans. It's the only fresh water for many miles. The stream even has fish in it." He glanced at the stream again. "What's at the other end?"

"Home, my friend, home," offered Omar between drinks. "Tell me more about Texas. Do the women lie topless along this mysterious river?"

Daniel smiled. "Omar, you've got boobs on the brain. I thought you were educated."

"When you have been in the desert at length, and you have got eleven lovely ladies in your mind, it is hard not to think about women. I am a Defender, but I am also a man." Omar had moved up the bank a little and was removing his clothes.

"What's this women-in-your-mind stuff?" Daniel asked as he followed Omar to a perfectly round water hole. Omar waded in. Daniel stripped down and followed him.

Omar immersed himself, and then came up. "Telepathy. We are linked to our women by telepathy. It is the source of our power, our strength. They sit in the temple with all this energy, which they harness and then transmit to us. We focus it for specific purposes. We can change the weather or cause someone to be healed or to die. We put thoughts in people's heads, create fire, lightning—all sorts of things. The link is always there. I can tell what they are doing and they can see what I'm doing. It takes awhile to get used to it. If they get . . . what is the English slang, horny? . . . I get horny thinking about it. If I get hurt, they can heal my injuries. It's a symbiotic relationship; we need each other. Without the bond, the whole fifteen thousand-year-old system would fail, and humanity would soon destroy itself."

"Do I get the bond? How?"

"Sex, my boy, sex," laughed Omar. "It is what makes the world go 'round. Are you man enough to even handle a woman? I hear you Americans are all talk and no action. We Turks are real animals, even tigers!" He grabbed his scrotum and continued to laugh as he quickly put on his clothing and sandals.

"Sex? What do you mean by that?" Daniel stepped out of the water, realizing Omar's propensity to not wait for him.

"You will find out soon enough." He turned up the trail, already back up to full speed.

Daniel quickly caught up. "What if I don't want to have sex? What if I refuse? I didn't volunteer for this, you know."

Omar stopped and looked hard at him. "That would be stupid—sheer insanity." He glanced at the ground, then back at Daniel. His voice grew quiet. "No, you did not volunteer. Your grandfather volunteered you. It is your birthright, and you are paying back a debt he owed." He clapped Daniel on the shoulder and then turned away. "Now, no more talking. We must concentrate on our journey."

Daniel was puzzled. *My grandfather? I never even met my grandfather. What did my grandfather have to do with anything that's happened to me?*

The duo soon found themselves before a pair of fearsome-looking guards toting WWII-era German rifles. The guards approached Omar with determination until Omar opened his shirt to reveal his markings. Daniel followed suit. The guards immediately fell to the ground, lying on their stomachs and looking away. Omar placed his hand over one's head and whispered something. The man's body relaxed as the pair moved on.

"What was that about?"

"He thought he had pointed his gun at me. He expected to be

killed. I reassured him. The people in this village owe their very existence to us. They are cut off from everywhere. They are given the ultimate in protection and success in exchange for providing us with food. The relationship has been in existence since four thousand years ago when a Hebrew group settled in the valley and filled a void needed by the temple."

"The whole village is Jewish then?" Daniel pressed. Ahead, stone structures flanked the trail. The valley had opened up and looked to be at least two miles wide with steep walls on the sides.

"Yes, one of the lost tribes." Omar seemed more interested in talking now. "There are many Ethiopian Jews. This group has been isolated for so long that their language has evolved uniquely. Four thousand years of isolation can do a great deal linguistically. There is no immigration into or out of this valley. They are given perfect weather and protection. There are no natural disasters, and the people are protected from war, disease, and religious persecution. This is Nirvana. Unfortunately, it tends to only work on a small scale. These people have everything a person would ever want."

"How many people live in the valley?"

"About twenty-five hundred. If we were not Defenders, and if the guards had not recognized us, they would have killed us on sight and thrown our bodies back over the wall—assuming those old Nazi rifles still work. These people have a huge interest in keeping us happy. They would all die out here in the desert on their own. The rebels, the Moslems, or even other Jews would kill them for sport. Every man, woman, and child here knows they have a good thing going. They all remember those Nazi bastards. They saw, they remember, and they learned. Try to be nice to them and be understanding, because they are still far too sensitive."

Word had already spread of their arrival. As they walked through the heart of the village, every person turned away or fell to the ground. Omar approached the biggest building in the village. The village elder knelt and beckoned to the duo to come in.

"A hearty meal!" exclaimed Omar. "Let us eat!" He touched the elder on the head, walked in, and sat down to a table covered with all sorts of food. Daniel followed him.

"Do not talk to them," Omar whispered. "Eating their food will be thanks enough. Remember, they only have goats here, so they have only goat cheese or goat-milk yogurt. The naturally-leavened bread is not bad with the goat butter. The figs and wine are quite standard. Get used to the food. This will be your fare for quite a few months." He lifted his mug of wine. "To us!"

Daniel liked the wine and was too hungry to talk. As something was devoured on the table, the elder replaced it with a new portion without making a sound. The man didn't make eye contact. Daniel liked this new food in a strange sort of way, but as he ate, a phrase kept running through his head: *Eat, drink, and be merry, for to-morrow you shall die.*

He was apprehensive about his arrival at the temple. Omar was eating hastily, packing away what appeared to be a whole pound of a salty, soft cheese. *Do what Omar does*, he thought, and he kept eating. At last, when he could eat no more, he stopped. He was feeling good. He had eaten lots of food and drank just the right amount of wine. *Maybe this life isn't so bad after all.*

Omar got up and headed out the door, and Daniel followed. It was just starting to get dark when Daniel first saw the temple, a low pyramid surrounded by a wall. The pyramid appeared to straddle the small creek in the middle of the valley. The flora in the court-yard around the pyramid was lush. As they approached the wall, Daniel saw a beautiful, naked woman with long hair standing on a small stage halfway up the pyramid. She was making gentle arm gestures and, even from this distance, he could see her breasts outlined by the declining light. She also was marked with a large tattoo, but Daniel couldn't tell if it was the same as his. He felt a great attraction to her and hoped this would be his woman. It was a pleasing thought.

"Tonight is a rain night; we need to get under the overhang," said Omar as he quickened his pace. Clouds suddenly rolled over the wall on the north side of the valley. The rain started just before they reached an overhang at the front of the temple. Omar sat down on the step. "Here we wait until the full moon is above the wall. We cannot enter until the moon rises over the valley and is fully visible. While we wait, I will teach you some things about us, before the wine wears off. Ah, the wine was good! I have been purposely vague, as I have been deciding your worth—your mettle, so to speak. It appears the Choosers have acted wisely."

"Who are the Choosers?" asked Daniel as he leaned back against the side of the temple.

"We know very little about them. We do not know where they live, who they are, how one becomes a Chooser, or what powers they might have. They are the ultimate secret society. I assume they must be leaders or influential people of some type. The legend states that if a Chooser is identified, he must kill himself. We know they wear a mark. Their mark is said to be only on one arm. It must be covered and only revealed to others in the society. I have heard of one man who, on his deathbed, asked his son to help him remove the mark, burning the skin off his arm before he died. The son had to do this blindfolded. Many men in ancient times were found dead in large groups with large pieces of skin missing from their arms. We know that they keep track of us because, on the twenty-fourth anniversary of our birth, they claim us and give us our marks."

"They sound pretty mysterious," sighed Daniel, not sure whether he could really believe the tale. "These guys select us, follow us around for twenty-four years, kidnap us, bring us to some secret location, tattoo us without our ever realizing it, and drop us in the desert?"

"It is indeed mysterious," assured Omar. "However, they did not choose you, they chose your grandfather. My grandfather and your grandfather were given this gift to bestow on their first-born grandson. The generational lag was built in to protect the system from being abused."

"But my grandfather died right after I was born," uttered Daniel, now really suspicious. "I'm confused."

"The legends, my boy, the legends," muttered Omar. "It is stated that the Chooser will give the gift to an unmarried male of noble character, pure heart, and steadfast beliefs to bestow on his heir's heir. Then, after proper education, and moral teachings, the heir's heir shall give up his life after his twenty-fourth birthday for the protection of mankind. If the receiver of the gift tells of the gift or fails to provide the heir, or if the heir is found unprepared or lacking, the bestower of the gift shall repay the dishonor by removing all that has been bequeathed. The choice has been given, life or death. If it shall not be life, then death will ensue." He indicated the temple walls. "That is the translation of the writings on this temple wall."

Omar indicated a series of symbols on the wall that were partially visible in the advancing dusk.

"So are we to die then? Are we some kind of sacrifice?"

"No, that is not it at all. We give up our previous life for a life with this Order. It is not a bad trade, if I do say so. But then again, I am already a part of it." He paused, looking closely at Daniel. "And I am sure you think that I am just a drunk, telling you garbage."

"You have to admit this is pretty damn weird." Daniel again assumed a suspicious tone. "How could anyone really believe all this stuff? It seems to contradict everything I've known."

"It is a paradigm shift. To be perfectly honest, I have kept some of the less believable stuff from you so far. You will have plenty of time to learn our way. The women make better teachers anyway."

The valley was now completely dark. The men were sitting at the main entrance to the temple on a set of ten steps covered by a flat rock supported by a pillar. The rain continued outside. The only sound other than the rain that could be heard was the gentle babble of the stream in the midst of the valley.

"With the coming of the full moon, the lights in the village will be extinguished. The villagers will be praying silently. They take their animals to the opposite side of the valley in preparation of the moon phase.

"Daniel, you must remember a few rules. You do not get second chances here, so hear and learn. A male can enter the temple only on the full moon. Tonight when we begin our rituals, you must follow what I do exactly. There is no hurry. The same rituals have been followed forever, and tradition is important to us. None of our secrets can be revealed to non-Defenders, ever. The penalties can go back to your grandfather and all his descendants. Dishonor is an unforgivable sin. These women are in our heads; they know everything we do."

Daniel was hoping Omar wouldn't see his bewilderment in the darkness. "Explain this women-in-the-head thing again please."

"We have telepathic links. The women are able to pass the power from the temple to us. Once we have been united, we can communicate, share experiences, share pleasure, pain, and even transmit the power of healing. At first, all the thoughts and voices are a confusing mess, but as you get used to it, it is like having multiple television screens in your brain. We keep no secrets. We work to a common purpose. Every Defender has to return here every four to five years, or the link will decay and your power will weaken. Letting that happen is not good for your health, either. You can always visit sooner. We have the ultimate in intimate relations with these women. No matter where I am, I am never alone, though much of what we do out in the world is done without the physical presence of others like us. When our Order was created, I think telepathy was a very important adaptation. We have instantaneous communication." Omar paused. "I know what you are thinking: telepathy is impossible."

Daniel had a thought and laughed. "What are the ladies thinking about right now?"

"They are curious about what you look like in person, and about your mannerisms," Omar answered. "It is like talking to someone on the phone or seeing them on the television for a long time. When you finally meet them in person, you know a great deal about them but you still have much to learn." The rain had stopped. "The women make it rain in the valley for one and a half hours every third night at nightfall—that is why the valley is so fertile—and that is what Anna was doing when we arrived. She is a gorgeous creature, as they all are. She is also from America.

"The Defenders are represented by all races. Chinese, Turks, Africans, Polynesian...people from everywhere. We have all been developed as one. We all must be prepared to protect our race."

"Omar, to be honest, I'm pretty nervous," Daniel confided. "I feel as though my destiny lies inside this building. My gut says run, and my head says pinch yourself and you'll wake up. I don't know if I can go through with all this. It's so overwhelming it defies all description."

"Son, we must all face our destiny sooner or later," reassured Omar. "The receiving of the gift does not hurt." He smirked. "And I will tell the ladies to be gentle with you."

"Gentle?"

"The gift is shared with all members of the Order, freely. The women are stronger than us because of their biology, but they need to be close to the temple, the source of power. Our creators originally designed this system. They decided that males would be better at traveling the world. Members need to be spread all over so that we know what is going on everywhere."

Daniel said, "But how do I get this telepathy thing?"

Omar was slightly exasperated. "I think you knocked something loose when you hit your head. As I told you earlier, you have to be united with the lady-Defenders. Do they speak English in Montana or wherever you are from? Sex, boy! Sex!"

Daniel nodded to indicate that he was starting to grasp the concept.

Omar stared at Daniel, still unable to believe his young associate's daft questions. "They have had sex with all of us. Just like you will have sex with all of them. Any cultural prudishness you might have needs to stay out here in the valley. And do not give me that ridiculous look—this is the way things are done here. What is wrong with having sex with beautiful women, then sharing your power to help save the world?"

"I'm Swedish, and sex is no big deal with us. So how exactly is the power transmitted? Magically?"

"We do not do magic. Magic does not exist," Omar replied. "The power transfers biologically by some bug, a virus, using genetics. It is quite complex. The women will explain it much better. Magic is the common term used by ignorant people to explain things they do not understand."

Daniel realized that he was now part of a world that operated under a different reality, a different morality, and had different values.

"Who created us, Omar? I mean way back? Who created the Defenders, the Choosers, and all the rest?"

Omar glanced at him. "The answer to that question is something you are not quite ready to handle, something you would not believe right now." He looked in the direction of the valley wall, then back at Daniel. "The moon is almost up. Now remember, when we enter the temple, follow my lead. There are no directions and the process has to be done correctly. This is the only time you will be able to go through the purification process while following someone else's lead.

"We will be separated from the outside world for one full moon cycle. Our days will be spent getting our mind, body, and spirit back to peak performance. We need to get right with the world and ourselves. This will not be social time. We will be at the mercy of the women. We will pray to our God. We will strengthen our bodies. We will purify our souls. It is a time to renew our commitment to what we are and what we are to become, and we need to solidify our core beliefs.

"The daily ritual will be long but not difficult. Talking interrupts contemplation. I will talk only enough so that you understand what must be done. After entering tonight we will pray and meditate until we fall asleep. The routine begins in the morning." He paused. "You belong with us, Daniel, and you will be a very good addition to our team. Just do not let your personal hang-ups interfere with accepting what you have become. Any questions?"

"Questions? It's like the first day of school." He glanced toward the valley wall. "There's the moon — let's get this over with before I chicken out." He jumped to his feet and walked up the stairs. Omar followed, and then took the lead at the entrance. The initial opening led to a small entryway with no visible door. The far wall contained writing in the same strange language he had seen earlier and a six-inch starburst shape—the same shape that was tattooed on his right forearm. The moonlight illuminated the room through the doorway.

Omar looked at the starburst and read the marks: "Enter here, Defender of the Earth and protector of men. Be free of the world. Enter, kneel, give thanks for your great gifts, and be welcomed home." Omar removed his clothes and put them in the corner. He stretched, waiting for Daniel to do the same. Daniel obliged. Now both men stood naked before the sunburst. Omar raised his arm, pointing to the points of the starburst; some were blackened in and some were not. "Daniel, start at six o'clock and, going counterclockwise, first touch the dark points in order, then the light ones, following the pattern of your tattoo. If you make a mistake, hit the middle of the starburst twice and start again. You may have only two tries. You will not live through a third. Stand in the doorway when the light stops, step forward and kneel, then pray to God for forgiveness, saying loudly 'I am Daniel the Defender, requesting to enter my temple. I come without malice in my heart.' Count to ten with your face on the floor. Then get up and walk to me. We go through the doorway one at a time. Do you have any questions?"

"No."

Omar began pressing the points in the order of his tattoo, first black and then white. Then he motioned Daniel to stand back. The wall slid open, and Omar took a half step forward and was enveloped in a blue light. Omar then took another half step forward and knelt. The wall slid shut, and Daniel was alone.

After a small prayer and a large sigh, Daniel approached the symbol. "Counterclockwise, start at six, black then white," he muttered. Daniel began black, black, black, and black, black, white . . . he hit a black point that he had already hit. *Shit! I've got to be more careful!* Daniel hit the middle twice as instructed. Carefully this time, he followed his tattoo, first black and then white.

The wall opened. Daniel took a half-step forward and held his breath. The blue light enveloped his body and he was filled with a sense of warmth. The light seemed to be exploring every contour of his body and the outline of his entire tattoo from his upper thigh to his face. It was a good feeling.

When the blue light stopped, he took another half-step forward and the wall closed behind him. The room was dark. He knelt and prayed to God for forgiveness of his sins; then, not knowing what else to pray, he prayed the Lord's Prayer. Then he placed his face on the ground and said aloud, "I am Daniel the Defender, requesting to enter my temple. I come without malice in my heart." He counted to ten slowly. While he counted he felt a wind blowing above his head, like being close to a moving fan. *Will I be accepted?* After a brief moment the room was illuminated. Daniel stood up and walked to Omar, who had been watching the entire process. Omar warmly greeted Daniel, "Welcome to the purification chamber."

The room was about thirty by forty feet. No windows or lamps were visible, yet the room was lit. On either side of where Daniel was standing were two wooden beds covered with what looked like zebra skins. On the other side of the bed to his left was a stone stairway that ascended through the ceiling. Directly across the room from Daniel were three hot tub-sized pools of water. Omar pointed to the pools. "We will use each of these during our ritual purification. The pool on the left is cool and salty, the pool in the middle is very cold, and the pool on the right is very hot. We will use them soon. Notice that the middle pool has a small basin where water enters from the river, then cascades into the pool below. The water is continuously flowing in this pool. The basin is used for drinking water." Though the stone walls were barren, the room was warm and Daniel felt comfortable.

Omar pointed toward the beds. "Pray!" Omar knelt beside one of the beds.

Daniel followed, taking the other one. He knelt and started clearing his mind, then began to concentrate on all that Omar had revealed to him. Following Omar's lead, he climbed into the bed and began to think of the woman on the temple stage, her long hair and enticing body; of the inviting blue light and the moon; of the warmth that enveloped his body, of his childhood and his grandfather. He even thought of west Texas. Daniel was soon asleep, his pleasant thoughts changing to pleasant dreams.

* * * * *

A bright light awakened Daniel. After clearing his head, he sat up and looked around the room. Omar was doing exercises on the floor nearby. There were small holes in the ceiling; one was creating a sunbeam right in his face. Interesting alarm system.

He asked quietly about a bathroom and Omar pointed to a small closet almost under the stairs. It appeared to be an outhouse with a rock base. On closer inspection it contained a flushing mechanism that was based on weight. After Daniel stepped off the rock, it shifted up and water washed the area clean. Cool—a thousand-year-old flushing system.

Daniel ran in place, did sit-ups, stretched, did push-ups, and lifted a rock he found by one of the pools. Daniel and Omar exercised for over an hour until they were covered in sweat. Next they stepped into the salty pool. The water was cool but not cold, with a high mineral content that felt odd on Daniel's skin. After just a few minutes, Omar stepped out of the pool and bounded up the small stairs that led through the ceiling to the roof. Daniel followed.

The roof was essentially a garden of plants that had been arranged along the walls to form a c-shape. Two flat platforms, slabs of rock, opened onto the stage that Daniel had seen the woman standing on the night before. The stage looked directly down on this roof from about forty yards away.

Omar broke a meaty stem from a yucca plant and went back downstairs. Daniel did likewise.

Back on the main floor, Omar broke the yucca stem lengthwise and started rubbing the exposed interior on his skin. He performed the task with great care, being sure to cover all his skin. Daniel did the same.

Next was a quick dip in the same pool, then back up to the roof. This time, however, Omar motioned for Daniel to lie face down on one of the slabs. Daniel could feel the heat from the mid-morning sun beginning to sear into his back. Just when he was starting to feel like fried bacon, Omar flipped over and Daniel copied the action. He could feel his stomach rumbling and hoped a meal would soon be a part of the program.

When Daniel had again started to feel as though he was having too much sun, Omar slapped him on the chest and was down the stairs before Daniel could react. Daniel stumbled to his feet and followed Omar, whom he found at the drinking pool. *Just the ticket*, he thought. After a long drink, he noticed that there were two meals on a small, newly-exposed shelf.

"The village elder is the only person allowed to bring up the daily rations. It is impossible to have both doors open at the same time. When you close this door, the outside one opens. It is a ten thousand-year-old mechanism. This is your daily ration. It contains your exact caloric and nutritional needs, so eat it all."

Daniel noticed that Omar had more food. Omar outweighed Daniel by perhaps thirty pounds and was at least three inches taller. The meal for each man was a piece of goat cheese, a fig, some gritty paste, and a very chewy, large loaf of bread. There was also a sour-tasting substance that defied description. This was no gourmet lunch. The Defenders, obviously, didn't believe in gustatory pleasures.

Next on the agenda was quiet meditation while sitting on the beds. Daniel was on the verge of sleep when he sensed Omar stirring and looked up. Omar was heading to the bathroom. *Good idea*, thought Daniel, and he did the same. When Daniel emerged from the bathroom, he noticed Omar was now in the hot pool. Only Omar's head was above the water. Daniel placed one foot into the water and immediately pulled it back. The water was hotter than he expected. He eased himself into the water, and just about the time he was getting sleepy again, Omar yanked him up and out of the water.

Omar smiled and whispered, "Be careful, friend. Not too long or you will drown."

Omar released Daniel and threw himself into the middle pool, letting out a primordial gasp. Daniel followed and soon understood the reason for the gasp. This pool was cold, damn cold, just above freezing. Daniel was now so awake he felt he could sense everything. He was shivering when he stumbled out of the pool.

"Good! Push yourself!" Omar said, pleased. He jumped back into the hot pool, eventually repeating the cycle three more times. Daniel was getting dizzy and exhausted after these sensory challenges. An hour of meditation followed.

Daniel thought again of his grandfather, Gunnar Nielstrom....

* * * * *

His grandfather, Gunnar, had been rumored to be a wild man in bed. He showed up in Ogallala by train one day. As legend had it, he happened to meet Daniel's future grandmother, Erika, on Front Street while getting off the train in his Marine uniform. He had lunch with her, and they were married the following Sunday after the regular church service. It was the quickest courtship in the history of the county.

Gunnar bought a ranch just north of town, and the newlyweds moved out there for the honeymoon. Nobody saw much of them for the better part of a year. The townsfolk thought it was a Swedish thing. It was said that Erika would give her husband a lascivious wink after church and the couple would speed off home in their Model A Ford, forgoing most after-church functions. His grandparents' ardor continued after the birth of their two children, his dad and his Aunt Hilda. Nobody ever saw Erika unhappy.

Grandpa Gunnar made some money at their ranch but not a lot. Daniel's dad had said that Gunnar did well during the Depression because he was the only one who had spent ten full years storing and saving in anticipation of hard times. Gunnar also took other measures to protect the family finances and resources. For example, he was the first person to practice careful overgrazing control. He built a large cistern and water collection system at the ranch to store water. He built a special storage shed for coal six years before the bad winters of 1933 and 1935, and he built four underground cellars for food storage. Everybody in town thought he was crazy. That belief changed during the Depression and Dust Bowl years. After the war he was heralded as some sort of weather sage for the county. What he planted, everyone planted. When he thinned his herd, the neighbors did likewise. Now Daniel knew why he had done so well during the Depression: Gunnar had known about it long before it happened....

* * * * *

The meditation period ended. Exercise followed again and the whole morning routine was repeated in the afternoon. Daniel enjoyed the ritual, and the hot tub reminded him of the family sauna.

By the time he had finished the second trip through the routine, darkness was creeping up outside the small room. Omar and Daniel both hurried upstairs with their zebra blankets. *Good*, thought Daniel. *That stone slab is hard; the blanket will cushion it somewhat.* But Omar folded his in half and spread it on the roof, then sat on it. Daniel quickly followed suit.

"When the Volva, the woman Defender appears, close your eyes and pray—pray to your God for guidance, forgiveness, strength, and judgment. Tonight will be the first night of purification. You did a good job, Daniel, a very good job. Do not fight the energy. Accept it. With a penitent heart, you will enjoy it much more. Your cells need to be cleansed of the old you so you can be reborn. It will not hurt."

Daniel was confused but said nothing. They had been sitting for some time when the Volva appeared on the stage. It was a different woman than from the previous night. She was a shorter brunette with shoulder-length hair. She had a dark complexion and looked Greek or Italian. She bore a tattoo on her face and upper body. Despite the distance, Daniel could tell that her tattoo was different from his, but he couldn't tell the exact nature of the difference. She was pleasant to look at, but Daniel closed his eyes and prayed as Omar had instructed.

He felt his entire body becoming warm. A tingling began on his ears and quickly spread through his body. Although he'd felt a similar sensation in the doorway light the night before, this experience was decidedly different. The tingling came in waves, pulsating throughout his body. The warmth continued and intensified. He prayed hard for strength and protection. His thoughts began to drift to warm beaches, then to a strange, singular thought: *Don't sleep here; the coconuts may fall on you.*

Daniel's next awareness was of feeling warm on only half his body. *Why is this process going on so long?* he thought, and then he brashly opened his eyes. It was morning, and he had slept through the night on the roof. The sun was just beginning to warm the morning air. Omar was starting to stir next to him.

After a morning bathroom stop, exercising began in earnest. Day two was a carbon copy of the first day. For the first week, the only variation was that a different woman came to the stage each night for the first week, as if on a rotating schedule. Despite the rain every third night, the two Defenders slept outdoors without awakening. Each day was the same routine, the same food, the same pools, and the same exercise. Daniel felt as though the preparations would never end.

With each day, Daniel's thoughts became clearer and clearer. On the twenty-third day, the whole purpose of the preparation became clear to him. This was a quarantine period, set up from antiquity. He had to purge his body of old thoughts and new-world bacteria and viruses. He noted a slight change in the food. The extra supplement was becoming tarter. He also noted his body becoming more fit, his skin more taut.

As the final week wore on, Daniel became more accepting of his fate and even believed the strange stories Omar had told him. Could he really be a person capable of protecting humanity? He felt the long wait for information would soon be over. The moon had gone through a full phase. The next phase of his journey was about to begin.

Day twenty-eight arrived. The pair hadn't uttered a word in several days. As they ate their daily rations, Omar finally broke the silence. "We enter the main compound at sunset. It is always hardest the first time. I have the ladies to keep me company. You have only your thoughts and God. Telepathy has a downside. You can never be alone. You need to make your mind strong. Try to create a place where they cannot go or it will drive you crazy."

"Can they control us?"

"Not us. Most regular men can be swayed." He paused. "We believe in free will among the Defenders. Mind control is out of bounds. I hope your language skills are good. You are going to have to learn a new language fast. We call it the Old Language. It is the language of the beginning. You have seen its written form on the walls here. It is the only way we can communicate telepathically. The women will talk to you in English until you learn it. You must have a gift of languages or you would not be here. The Choosers would not have approached your grandfather. How many languages do you know?"

"I know two very well, not counting Norwegian, which someone who speaks Swedish can usually understand. I also know enough French to communicate pretty well." Daniel confided, "It must be in my genes, though. My grandfather knew at least ten. He even picked up Mandarin Chinese so he could order more knowledgeably at a restaurant."

The afternoon session was more relaxed: light stretching, hot soaks, and a very good nap. As the evening approached, Daniel became increasingly uneasy. He would meet his destiny tonight.

Darkness set in. As Omar waited by the wall opposite the door they'd originally entered, a portion of the wall suddenly swung open to the courtyard of the temple. They headed down a trail through a lush garden that led to the main pyramid. As they entered the main entrance, Daniel saw a hall that turned immediately to the right and opened into a well-lit larger space. The women were waiting in this main room of the temple. Ten of the eleven were standing in a semi-circle, an assortment of Caucasians, Blacks, Asians, and one who looked Polynesian, all nude. All bore an identical large, single tattoo that Daniel could now better identify. It was made to look like a black cloth with folds and wrinkles. It was intricately done, beginning on the bridge of the nose and running under the right eye and across the cheek. The tattoo wrapped behind the neck, reappearing over the left collarbone. It gently caressed the left breast and nipple so as to mostly darken the left gland but leave the right side completely unaffected. Then it widened down the left flank with many pleats and undulations before curving to the back, where it swung around the right buttock, reappeared on the right vulva, followed the crease of the groin, and tapered off by circling the leg twice.

A one-foot-long dagger extended from each woman's right abdomen down onto her upper thigh. Each woman also sported the same star-like pattern with randomly filled-in points that Daniel bore. Theirs were on the left forearm, though, instead of the right. On their left cheek, each bore a tattoo resembling Daniel's, with two birds kissing in the shape of a heart.

Omar knelt. "Omar the Turk, Defender of the people, requests entry into the temple. I wish to strengthen our bonds and unite as one. I have fasted and purified myself."

Omar stood up, and each woman in a turn gave him a sensual hug and a kiss, welcoming home a friend they had not seen in some time. One of the women, a beautiful Greek goddess, took Omar's hand and they wandered off.

Now it was Daniel's turn. He knelt. "I am Daniel, an American-born Swede and new to the Order. I have fasted and purified myself, and I present myself with a humble heart for whatever is to befall me." He was afraid to look up or to move.

He stayed motionless for only a moment before a woman spoke in broken English. "My name is Irena. I am Georgian. You look so afraid. You are now one of us. It makes me sad to think that you believe we are some sort of monsters. It is rare we have a new member to greet. Please rise and let us greet you as our friend. We have been longing to meet you."

Two women helped Daniel to his feet and they all shared long, deep hugs. Each woman whispered her name to him as they embraced. Daniel was so overwhelmed that after the last had greeted him, he sat down and began to cry. It had been four months since his kidnapping. He had been left for dead, shot at, tortured, and then treated like royalty. He had accompanied a strange man a thousand miles across a desert. He had fasted for twenty-eight days in what was basically a cave. And right this moment he felt more accepted than he had in all of his life. The women were not just being polite; they truly welcomed him. A few wandered off but most of the women sat down around him.

"I feel as though I have been on a long journey for many years just to make it here," he said, and then apologized for being so emotional.

Irena smiled. "You are a lucky one; most do not succeed. We were made with a 'survival of the fittest' plan. It is good that Omar found you. Our numbers will be thinning shortly. Our Japanese Defender will die soon after many decades of fine work. It will be good for your training to get to know him; he has much to share. Omar is not the best at instruction and I am sure you have many questions. You have twenty-four years of false teaching to unlearn. Do not fear us, Daniel, we are your refuge. This temple is your home and we are your family. We support and nurture our own. We do not destroy them."

"I have so many questions," he confided, still sobbing. "I can't even properly ask them. Does my family know I am all right?"

"I suspect your parents knew you would leave them after your twenty-fourth birthday. They will not expect to see you again," she replied. "Your grandfather was told of your selection and should have passed information along to your parents in some fashion. You were chosen many years ago to be one of us. But you will be able to visit them again—do not worry. The Choosers bless Defenders' families; they will do well.

"We will show you to your room. Sleep well. Tomorrow will be a new day and you will need your strength. We have much to share and you have much to learn."

One of the women led Daniel out of the room and down a few stairs to an ancient bedroom, the middle of which contained a canopied bed. His guide showed him the toilet receptacle, told him that the garden was just down the hall, and left him alone.

No union tonight then, he thought. The lights in the room went off as he lay on the soft bed. He even had a pillow. A simple thing such as a pillow was just what he needed. The mere thought of it caused his apprehension to subside. The bed seemed to swallow him up, and he was out in seconds.

CHAPTER 6: Anna

The garden air in the middle of the temple was surprisingly humid. Daniel couldn't quite figure out why the climate here seemed so much different from the semi–arid desert valley outside the temple. Most likely it was a combination of the rain, the creek, and all the lush vegetation. He was surrounded by a tropical paradise. Flowers of all colors, fruit trees, running water, and beautiful shade trees filled the space, and if there were no path, it would be difficult for Daniel to find his way out. He had awakened in a new day and had meandered out to this spot to contemplate his situation. Unfortunately, his botany training in high school and college had focused on corn and soybeans. All these tropical plants were new sights for the young man from the Nebraska prairie. As he sat staring at a particularly tall specimen, a feminine voice pierced the stillness.

"That's a date palm," she said.

Daniel recognized the beautiful American blonde, Anna, whom he had first met the day before but who had filled his imagination for the past four weeks. She walked with a confidence and grace that Daniel had scarcely seen in his twenty-four years. Her long blonde hair swayed over her hips and gently caressed her supple breasts.

"I wish I'd studied more in college," Daniel said. "Somehow I think all those business and finance classes that I suffered through are not going to help me much anymore."

"I studied psychology and always thought I'd be some kind of social worker," replied Anna. "This is a long way from Ohio, but I've no regrets. Not everyone gets to save the world." She paused, studying him. "You look like a guy who's daydreaming about a lost life. No boo-hooing here, my friend. Everyone has been dealt cards in life; some have aces and some deuces or treys. This isn't cancer, you know."

Daniel hadn't realized his inner uncertainty about his new life was so obvious. "What about free will? Shouldn't I have a say in what I've become? What right do you have to take me away against my will and throw me into a desert, mark my body with these tattoos without me even realizing it, and tell me I've joined a group of naked spiritualists? Does everyone just expect me to be all right with all this? Hell, this whole ordeal seems like a nightmare at times. One that won't end."

"You're not in Kansas anymore, Daniel." She laughed, proud of her little joke.

"I'm from Nebraska," he replied, appearing less than amused at hearing the same tired joke.

"Nebraska, Kansas, the Dakotas—they're all the same to me." She giggled again, and then grew more serious. "Daniel, like it or not, you're a Defender. Obviously your grandfather made a bargain with a Chooser. During the Great War either his life was spared or he was rewarded for some heroic deed by promising you as a Defender. That, to me, seems like free will. We all have family obligations and expectations to uphold. Queen Elizabeth was born to be queen and you were born to be part of us. This isn't the worst thing to happen, you know. Where else do you get to save the world, have supernatural powers, hang out and have sex with beautiful women, and live in luxury wherever you go? It seems to me people might even pay for a job like this, and you get it free."

"Yeah, the fringe benefits aren't that bad, are they?" He began to look more positive. "But it all still seems a bit farfetched to me. The more Omar talked about it, the more improbable it seemed. I'm still waiting for someone with a camera to jump out from behind a bush and say 'Got you!' Shouldn't a group this powerful be mentioned somewhere in a history book or something?"

"Rule number one is that history is bunk. American history, or at least the history we were taught, is just a bunch of myths. My former perception of world history was so out of whack with reality that to this day, I'm still shocked that some people dare to call themselves historians. I'm also amazed that I could have been so gullible. For example, Americans like to think they were responsible for ending World War II. We grew up in an ethnocentric world with America at the center. The real history of North America is so very different than what I thought I knew, I re-read the archival texts here at the temple many times to make sure I wasn't misinterpreting them."

"There are archives here?"

"Yes. Over the centuries, the Defenders have chronicled the entire history of the world," she replied. "It is very detailed, with maps, charts, and descriptions that I find remarkable. I've just finished my tour as chief historian, and I found the process extremely enlightening."

"What language is it written in?"

"We call it the Old Language. It's the original text of the culture that came before us. The letters look like a cross between Chinese characters and hieroglyphics. Once you learn to read it and write it, you'll hate to use Roman text again. You'll learn it soon enough, don't worry. But until you can go down into the archives and read them for yourself, you can ask me any questions you may have. We also the Old Language to communicate telepathically."

Daniel thought for a moment. "Okay, when were the pyramids made?"

"The pyramids had multiple purposes. They were made as sort of a time marker and also were an energy source used to communicate with Mars. They were built long before conventional theory holds that they were built. The pyramids on the Giza plateau mimic the stars in Orion's belt. What everyone misses is that shafts were used to align the stars due to the wobble in the earth. When the shaft points at its representative star, it signifies a date. The pyramids were built about twelve thousand five hundred years ago so that everyone of that era would be remembered. Underneath the pyramids was placed all the history of the world for safekeeping. The sphinx was constructed then as well. In Egyptian mythology, 10,500 BC was the beginning of time, the birth of the god Osiris. In reality, this was the time of a great calamity on the earth.

"Only bits and pieces of your concept of human history are correct. Human history is more complex than the hypothesis of Darwinian development. To put it simply, we were helped. In fact we were helped a lot."

"You mean God?"

"No. There is definitely a God," she continued. "God made life possible, but where our thinking and scientific theories lapse is in how we get from life to us. We assume that no force below God had a hand in developing things. You need to think about developmental evolution like being a rancher or farmer. Farmers raise animals and crops with certain traits that they like best, be it redder tomatoes, larger ears of corn, or fatter cattle. Some modifications work and some do not. After many years of selective breeding, all of the crops or animals have these traits. In a sense, farmers developed the Defenders. Those farmers modified our ancestors so we could become who we are.

"About sixty thousand years ago, long before Defenders existed, the earth was populated with almost-human creatures. One group was the Neanderthals. There were others. They lived in loose family groups in mountain caves, and generally were hunter-gatherers. They developed some tools, but by and large had an undeveloped society and culture. At that time the earth was a very wild place. Life on earth has always been a sort of genetic laboratory. There were dinosaurs, nasty mammals, big birds, and so on. Who controlled this genetic laboratory, I think, has always been open to debate, but I suspect the truth is much stranger than anything you've ever hypothesized. Dinosaurs didn't live all that many years ago. Primitive humans came in contact with these creatures. They are the monsters and dragons of our dreams and fears, sort of a genetic memory, an innate fear stamped into our genome to help us survive. Being a humanoid then wasn't good. You had to basically hide or be eaten.

"Prior to that, over a period of thousands and thousands of years, the earth was used, like I said, as a genetic laboratory. New species were created. These either replaced older, established species or they were wiped out themselves. There were genetic mistakes, some genetic breakthroughs, and some events that changed nothing. In fact, I suspect the whole dinosaur family was an experiment that failed."

"So who or what was doing these experiments?"

"By and large they came from beings on our sister planet, Mars. It wasn't the lifeless desert that it is now," she said carefully, understanding his difficulty at grasping alien life. "The beings of Mars had a complex, advanced society. They had cities, canals, marvelous technology, and space flight. However, Mars was ecologically dreary. They did not have the diversity of life that was found here on Earth. Their atmosphere was thinner than Earth's, and they didn't have as many ecological buffers. As their society developed, pollution and selective pressures slowly killed off all the other species on the planet until there was only one remaining life form."

"That seems an extraordinary tale. Then again, everything I've learned so far has seemed extraordinary." He looked more bewildered than ever. "Let me get this straight—we were developed by Martians?"

Anna, realizing this was going to be a long conversation, sat down opposite Daniel, stretching her long legs so her feet were just touching Daniel's lower left leg. "Is this okay?" Daniel nodded and she continued. "Yes, in a word, we were. They were called the Old Ones, but for lack of a better word, Martian is correct. These Martians couldn't live here on Earth. The gravity and oxygen levels on Earth were too great and the carbon dioxide level was too low. They had a few outposts here in specially-constructed chambers. They couldn't reproduce their species here either, due to both the gas levels in the atmosphere and high amounts of trace elements like selenium. Also, their immune system couldn't handle our bacteria. They were basically bubble-beings.

"Sixty-five thousand years ago, a large caldron-type volcano in what is now Indonesia erupted, emitting well over five thousand times the amount of ash produced by the Mount St. Helens eruption in 1980. It was the largest eruption in human history. The hole left by this eruption is a lake, many miles across and thousands of feet deep. The discharged sulfuric acid and ash caused the average global temperature to drop at least ten degrees Celsius for ten to twenty years. Most plants died, the dinosaurs became extinct, and just about every living thing disappeared. Even the Martians living here perished. The ash disrupted their energy and communication systems so that they were unable to communicate with Mars to ask for help; they died of exposure to our elements. Only a few humanoids, something like six hundred, lived. The humanoids were scattered around the planet—not enough people to support a viable population. We would have soon gone extinct."

"Noah?"

"No, more like Genesis," continued Anna. "After the dust and ash settled, a massive Ice Age started. On Mars, the Martians had a long discussion about the ethics of all these experiments and concluded that thousands of years of genetic experimentation on this planet had been ruined. Shortly afterwards, in an unrelated incident, a large asteroid narrowly missed hitting their planet. After careful evaluation, their astronomers calculated that although it would be a while, the asteroid would hit Mars directly on its next pass. Finally, reality set in that Martian society would end in a terrible cataclysm.

"The Martians decided to leave a legacy, using their genetic superiority to create a new race of beings on Earth to serve as the intelligent creatures in the galaxy, or at least this part of the galaxy. The only creatures left with enough starting intelligence were mammoths, monkey-humanoids, and dolphins. Since the humanoids were headed for extinction, they tried to improve that genome first. So the Martians gathered up a few pairs of humanoids and brought them to Mars. Sadly, the remaining humanoids died out during the Ice Age.

"The Martians reconstructed the human genome, making us who we are today. They introduced us back to Earth in stages, upgrading the genome with successive reintroductions. When things were going well, they decided to send back the last pair, their masterpieces, whom they had kept on Mars in case something went wrong on Earth. Biblically they are called Adam and Eve, but those weren't their real names. All of this took many, many years.

"The final pair had the perfect genome; they were referred to in the Bible as the sons of God, with the earlier humans who had been reintroduced referred to by Moses as sons of Men. In Greek mythology, the offspring of the pre-Adam and Eve humans were called heroes. The two groups were similar and eventually, when they intermarried, any distinctions were lost. If you remember, one bible passage reads, 'The sons of God married the daughters of Men.'

"Humans now were smarter than before, and all the nasty creatures like dinosaurs were dead, so we thrived. There was one small difference, however, that turned out to be a flaw in humans according to the Martian thinking. The humans of this era lived a lot longer than we do now—six hundred or more years—not as long as the Martians, though. As society developed, the Martians gave the early humans technology, and a complex society developed. In some respects the early humans were much more advanced than we are today. Soon the Martians observed another flaw. Humans had a propensity to destroy themselves. They were beset with violent tendencies—greed, the need for power, and so on. They were filled with perversions and all sorts of bad societal behavior. The Martians thought about starting over with a different species, such as the dolphins, but never had a chance to pursue that idea."

"I remember hearing in my biology studies about that volcano," Daniel said. "They deduced that very few humans lived around fifty to seventy-five thousand years ago due to random mutations in mitochondrial DNA. It was postulated that there were fewer than a thousand individuals alive at any one time during that period. The only event that could be found to be a likely cause was an asteroid hitting or that volcano exploding in Java. I'm beginning to believe this wild tale of yours isn't so different than what science can prove."

Anna smiled at Daniel and rested her head on his left thigh. She flipped back her long hair, which covered Daniel's manhood and most of his lower abdomen. Daniel didn't mind; he enjoyed the female attention. He smiled back, trying to remain composed. He was aware of the blood flow to the part of his anatomy now covered with beautiful, silky blonde hair.

"We know all of our history, if we put all the pieces together," she continued. "The twenty-mile-wide asteroid hit Mars squarely, just above the equator. It ruptured the planet's crust and almost ripped the planet in two. The atmosphere was blown away entirely. The whole planet was enveloped in massive volcanic activity. The now-airless planet cooled down and all life on Mars was lost. A few Martian spaceships took off before the cataclysm and some of the ships made it here to Earth carrying the Martians we call the Old Ones. Others just floated around in space for thousands of years, carrying long-dead aliens.

"The problems of the humans remained. Humans were bad, we lived too long, and our Neanderthal-like tendency for violence would eventually cause us to self-destruct. The Old Ones didn't have time to find a new species to develop and refine, but they could try to modify a few of the existing humans, and then kill off the rest. They had time left for only one more chance to further improve the human situation, as all the Martians would die out in a few thousand years.

"They first needed to solve the problem of longevity. Humans had originally been given a Martian gene. The protein complex that made it was extremely good at reading and repairing the genetic code. It was so good that, because of it, we didn't age very fast, cancer didn't exist, and there wasn't much genetic change or mutation in humans. This is why we lived much longer and were generally free of disease at that time. Earth was paradise.

"The Martians spliced the genetic information for two modulator proteins into our genetic code, both of which succeeded in blocking the expression of a specific 'fixer gene' and thus production of certain 'fixer proteins.' The codes for both of the modulator proteins are located on our X chromosomes. A few of the fixer proteins get out, enough so that we live to our current age. Since women have two X chromosomes, they have more anti-aging genes and generally live longer then men. The whole process is very complex and involves expression caused by our sex hormones." She paused. "I don't want to get too detailed here. My genetics courses from college are coming through; I hope you're still following all of this."

Daniel nodded as he thought of Genesis 6: The sons of God saw that the daughters of men were fair; and they took to wife such of them as they chose. Then the Lord said, "My spirit shall not abide in man forever, for he is flesh, but his days shall be a hundred and twenty years." The Nephilim were on the earth in those days, and also afterwards, when the sons of God came to the daughters of men, and they bore children to them. These were the mighty men of old, the men of renown. The Lord saw that the wickedness of man was great in the earth, and that every imagination of the thoughts of his heart was only evil continually. And the Lord was sorry that he had made man on the earth, and it grieved him to his heart. So the Lord said, "I will blot out man whom I have created from the face of the ground, man and beast and creeping things and birds of the air, for I am sorry that I have made them."

Anna repositioned her head, ever so slightly, higher up Daniel's leg, and then continued. "The Martians were successful in trimming our life expectancy. They next needed to cripple the existing society before it got out of hand, so our Martian forefathers came up with a ruse.

"They told the leaders of society that another asteroid was heading toward Earth, and that it would take only one generation to get here. It was expected that most people would perish. Everyone believed the Martians. The Martians then convinced the humans to build a series of monuments to memorialize and record the twenty thousand years of human history. This process consumed the planet for decades. According to Martian direction, the Giza pyramids were constructed first as the principal repository of human knowledge. Unbeknownst to the humans, the Martians installed energy generators inside the pyramids for the purpose of sending out messages to the stars to guide any Martian ships back to Earth.

"The entire human population was gripped in an apocalyptic frenzy focused on erecting monuments throughout the world—in the Americas, Asia, Africa, and Europe. These monuments still exist, although some are now under water. The Martians also convinced humans to build this temple and others like it to hold Martian history records. Once the temples were built, humans took no further interest in them—these belonged to the Martians. Humans were blindly immersed in their own concerns.

"Meanwhile, another great part of the plan to improve humans was underway. Certain individuals with the new genetic modifications were told to build ships, arks if you will. They were told to store food, be prepared to gather animals, and that, in general, they would need to be afloat for a long while if they were to survive. These people were ridiculed as survivalists and were considered unable to face the truth. As the end drew near, the people of the earth were having one big drunken orgy. What the Martians had actually built at Giza and here with our temples was a large conductor system that they could use to harness the intrinsic power of the earth.

"In those days, Antarctica was not at the bottom of the planet. It was about thirty degrees up off the pole and had weather a lot like Iceland has today. There were even large cities there. North America, by contrast, was rotated farther north and mostly covered in ice. Europe and Asia were ice-covered as well. The Old Ones planned to use their conductor system to invert the poles and cause the Earth's crust to slip. The people in the southern hemisphere were told to go to Antarctica—that it would be the safest place. They packed up, moved, and waited. One hot day, twelve thousand six hundred fifty years ago, the Old Ones executed their secret plan. Fortunately or unfortunately, they never warned the masses and everyone was taken completely by surprise. The shift of the poles and slippage of the crust caused massive earthquakes and volcanoes. Everything that wasn't made of hard rock on solid, stable bedrock was destroyed. The Ice Age caps were warmed up by twenty to thirty degrees overnight. The Martians had even installed direct heaters to warm the ice caps more quickly and produce a faster melt. The landmasses moved until the Giza pyramids were lined up with the stars of Orion's belt. That was where the Martian leader rode out the event.

"The rapid melting of the glaciers caused a massive fog. There was a hard rain for months, and the millions of people who weren't killed initially were stranded in Antarctica, which was now located at the South Pole. They froze to death in the first eighty-degree-below-zero winter. The summer in the northern hemisphere wasn't much better. Up to fifty inches of rain fell every day for months. The oceans rose four hundred feet in a little over a year and the flooding inland was truly massive. Very few people who were not in arks survived."

Daniel was nodding his head with a new understanding of things he had read in his youth. "They talked about this Glacial Lake Missoula, formed after melt water backed up in Montana due to a natural dam. The lake covered two-thirds of the state. Then suddenly it blew the dam. Water that was miles high rushed down the Colorado River system, carving out the canyons. They always said that the Grand Canyon was made over millions of years, but that contradicted the whole Lake Missoula history and geology. It amazes me how geologists accept some ideas and not others as evidence. And they never adjust older theories to fit all the newer evidence. That lake must have been impressive. I'll bet it cut the canyon in only a few weeks."

"I'm glad to see you're accepting this so well, Daniel," Anna observed. "For me it was a farfetched story. I thought it was all some sort of brainwashing or something. Not until I read the archives did I finally believe." She smiled. "Anyway, once the water receded, humans were allowed to restart society. However, only three Martians lived through the event, and they were on their last legs. They feared humanity would eventually destroy themselves without protectors, as we still had the flaw of self-destruction in our genome. That was when they dreamed up the Defenders. Before they died, they set up a few checks and balances in case humanity became too perverted, and they created our Order.

"To create Defenders, the Martians created a retrovirus, much like the AIDS virus you're familiar with. The virus carried a self-replicating mechanism and a foreign genetic code. Once it was in the human body, it would get into cells, replicate itself, and finally splice itself into our genome. The Martians originally left a viral attachment point on one of the genes that turned off our aging process. That gene would be made ineffective after spliced from the retrovirus, and the new gene would be in its place. The new gene contained coding to make a protein that causes our neurons to be maximally efficient, allowing them to transmit thought energy to other neurons that then concentrate the energy. Once concentrated, the energy could be transmitted to affect other organisms, people, and objects. The whole process needed a central source of energy for really big events. The old temples with their conductor systems were used to further power us.

"Women have two X chromosomes, so we make more of this protein than do males. The extra protein enables us to take the energy from static sources, like the conductors here, and convert it into telepathic energy and transmit it to you or any other male. The protein also has the effect of heightening and modifying our secondary sexual characteristics in appropriate organs. Our breasts are fuller but not too much bigger, our hips wider, our legs longer. It also affects males causing some change in muscle mass, but nothing too extreme.

"For the women to harness and transmit the energy, we need to be very close to the energy source. It diminishes rapidly as we get farther from the temple, until eventually we are like you. Then we can only have it transmitted to us from another female. One of us must always be on the Conduction Array transferring the energy to our colleagues in the field."

"Does the virus cause any long-term health problems?"

"No, it doesn't. Initially, you'll experience a flu-like illness." Anna was pleased that Daniel wasn't too shocked. "The virus stays in us and concentrates in bodily fluids just like HIV. Semen and vaginal fluid have a very high concentration. After a few years the virus stops replicating itself and is gradually shed from the body. The genetic code spliced into our DNA is stable, but after about five years it starts to degrade and the fragments are removed. So we all need to get new virus loads every so often, at least every four to five years for males. The virus coat seems to stimulate the virus levels to rise and cause the genetic splicing. That is why the system requires us to be openly sexual with all members of the Order. If we let our virus loads fall, the energy that runs through us could harm us. It's like having a short circuit. Males who lose the virus will simply lose contact with us."

"Omar has sex with all sorts of women," Daniel asked further. "Why doesn't that give them this power?"

"There is something in our tattoos, a chemical or something, that activates the virus," she responded. "The exact way in which this activation happens is neither known nor written anywhere." She gently took Daniel's hand and placed it on her shoulder. "If you don't have a tattoo, the virus has no effect on you. The virus becomes inactive and is shed. We have been taught that it is dangerous for us to have sex with non-Order males, but I have found no evidence of any reason for that. On the other hand, we rarely leave the temple, so it doesn't come up much." She laughed. "Most of us have enough sex anyway."

"The Martians really created an elaborate system."

"They wanted a system that was secret. They took the power of recruiting away from the current members of the Order by using the Choosers. However, they gave the Choosers neither significant power nor access to our temple. In fact, one of the basic rules that we live by is for us to kill, on sight, any person we believe is a Chooser. That rule understandably keeps our worlds apart. We have the virus and they have the tattoo chemical.

"The Old Ones required multicultural recruitment so the Defenders wouldn't promote certain ethnic groups. They needed us to have long-range communication with little or no technology, so they gave us telepathy. They thought females should have more power than males because they felt women would be more stable and less willing to cause unnecessary violence. They felt the men would be better able to travel to potential trouble spots. The men may also need to have sexual relations on the road without fear of giving the power to the uninitiated. Finally, they needed us to be able to live longer than normal people because of the two generations necessary for recruiting the males. We needed to be able to change minds, the fortunes of war, and the performance of technology. I think the system was designed very well. In fact, it has run without a problem for twelve thousand years."

"What finally happened to the Martians?"

"They died off a few hundred years after this system started."

"Are we visited by aliens anymore?"

"No, there are no aliens that we know of in this part of the galaxy." She'd almost expected the question. "During the Martian days and the pre-flood civilization, many spacecrafts were made. The Roswell incident was due to a spacecraft that had left Mars just before the asteroid impact. The aliens died in the spacecraft and it drifted around on autopilot for a long time before finally getting caught in the earth's gravity and crash-landing in New Mexico. Some of these spacecraft have preset autopilot rituals and are unmanned. Some have been coming here for water for thousands of years. They still come from Mars, despite the demise of life on the planet. They hover over a lake, load water, fly back to Mars, unload, and start over again. These are most of the UFOs that are sighted."

"Does our government know about this? I mean, are they covering it up?"

"Yes," she said. "But it's because of us. The stuff they find is stored out in the Nevada desert. Back in the fifties we approached the U.S. government and told them what was up. We told them they could have anything that was found, but that if we caught them using the Martian technology, they could expect a swift and nasty retribution. We didn't want the technology to be developed unchecked and used unilaterally. They could easily use it to destroy everybody, including themselves."

Daniel instinctively stroked Anna's upper arm. After a short moment of contemplation, he summarized, "Let me see if I have all this. We were created from a genetic experiment designed by Martians. We were inferior creatures at the core and had to be almost exterminated so that a few changes could be introduced to keep us from destroying everything. All the Martians died. The Defenders were invented to provide a sort of check and balance so that maybe the human species wouldn't all die out. My grandfather pledged me to be part of this Order. I grew up a normal kid, but my life was predestined so that on my twenty-fourth birthday, the Choosers would kidnap me. They would mark me with these tattoos without me even being aware of what was happening or of having any sense of time, and then they would dump me in the desert and hope that I'd survive long enough to get here. Here at the temple, I'm to have sex with the lady Defenders, be passed an HIV-like virus, and once infected I will develop supernatural powers to complete my appointed destiny. Am I missing anything?"

"You have it right, my love. No more big secrets," she confided. "The term I like for lady-Defenders is from Norse mythology where we are called Volva." She sighed and a note of sadness crept into her voice. "This is no small thing. We give up our families, our chance for children, and our normal lives for this singular purpose. There are tremendous responsibilities. We have to like each other, both to live here for two hundred years and also to be in each other's minds, day in and day out. My thoughts are yours, and your thoughts are mine. There are no secrets—none. I don't know how the male mind works or, to be quite frank, how you can live with all the thoughts you guys have. The male mind is a place of non-stop sexuality. How can a man get anything done?"

She moved his hand closer to her breast. He obliged. "One important thing—although it is very rare, we can conceive and get pregnant. Although we live longer, women still have only so many eggs to ovulate. Due to all the genetic manipulation, the best chance for me to get pregnant is to mate with a young male whose ethnic genome is as close to my own as possible. The few times it has happened before, the parents were young Defenders. One pair was of Chinese descent, and two other pairs were of African heritage, but that was thousands of years ago. The best chance for me to bear children would be with a Scandinavian male, young, blue eyes, fair skin, and blond hair. When I saw you in Omar's mind, I gasped. I'm only in my mid-thirties, and to even have a chance to bear a temple child would be my greatest dream. These special children have a stable, virus-free genome. They have all of our powers. Unfortunately, only three have ever been born, but none at the same time. This infertility prevents a new permanent race of people from being developed. The only unfulfilled dream I have is of bearing a child."

"Well, I gasped the first time I saw you too," he admitted. "I got an erection and felt warm and tingly when I saw you in the darkness making the rain that first night." He gently caressed the side of her breast.

She laughed at his openness. "You aren't like most Americans. You are comfortable with nudity. Most Americans I've met can't handle group nudity. I have never seen a male look at me as a person when I'm naked and not focus on my breasts or—"

Daniel interrupted her. "Even with all the Defender stuff aside, I'm not a typical American. I grew up in a European household that just happened to be located in Nebraska," he said, feeling proud that all his hard work in keeping his cool was being noticed and appreciated. "My sisters, mother, female cousins, and aunts were always naked around my house. We took saunas together, nude. My female relatives would strip down on the beach whenever nobody was looking. I've also spent a lot of time in Sweden. You learn to think of something awful to keep your hormones in check. I think of skinning animals and processing meat." He laughed. "I have to admit, though, I've had a lot of difficulty controlling things since I met you. I've processed a lot of meat, and I'm afraid I'll have to find a new awful thought as meat cutting isn't working so well anymore."

She smiled, but seemed a bit troubled. "You do have a choice here, Daniel," she said softly. "You didn't have a choice to be marked, but you are perfectly free to refuse the final gift. I can't use any powers against you; it's forbidden. You may enter here anytime— the tattoo allows entry—and you can stay as long as you want. I can't force you to have sex with me, nor can any Volva. We absolutely cannot hurt or harm a bearer of the forbidden tattoo." She paused. "I'm sorry to have shared my intimate thoughts about babies; that really was over the top."

"Don't worry, I like your openness and honesty," he said reassuringly. "I'm also cool with fast romances. My family has a history of quick courtships: my Grandfather dated for three days, my

father for a week, and my great-grandfather supposedly had a courtship of only a few hours. If I have to have sex with the others, I'll
do it. I understand my role here, I think. I also understand that you
need to have sex with all of the men, but I already consider you my
soul mate here, and I think I always will. Hell, sex is fun, but making love with your soul mate is in a whole different dimension. I
think I can exist here and be free of jealousy, but I'm only human,
so please be patient with me. We are what we are. If I'm a Defender, who am I to fight the system of which I am now a part?"

Anna smiled at his confessions. She loved him, too. She closed
her eyes, thinking it was all a dream. She reopened them and he
was still there. Despite her needing to have sex with the other
Defenders, she was sure this was her man. She felt the gentle
touch of his hands. They were getting closer to her nipple. She
could feel his breathing becoming more labored. She was starting
to smell the slightly acrid odor of his nervous sweat. *How sweet!
she thought. He can have me in any way and at any time he
desires and he's waiting for me to make the first move. He wants
to be sure this is what I want. I have fallen in love with a gentleman—a man more worried about my needs than his own.*

Daniel was focusing on Anna's nipples, which were becoming
increasingly erect, and he noticed her breasts were heaving with
every breath. He also noticed she was subtly spreading her legs.
He was trying to control pressure that was increasing in his organ.

Finally she broke the silence. "Follow me," she said softly.
"There is a hot pool over here that will help you relax." She took his
hand, then rose and led him to a twelve foot by twelve goot pool.
He stepped in after her and sat on a small ledge just under the
water. She motioned for him to stay, then hopped out and approached
him from the rear. "You need a massage. Close your eyes and
relax." She began tenderly rubbing his shoulders, his temples, and
his arms. Daniel was in ecstasy. Anna carefully placed her legs on
the ledge while massaging his shoulders, arms, and chest. She moved
around him to sit on his lap, astride him, her knees on the ledge. He
opened his eyes and was about to speak when she placed a single
finger over his lips, then gently touched his eyelids until they closed.

She resumed her massage, first rubbing his chest, then his flanks
and abdomen. Her kneading hands slid to his back, then around to

his upper thighs. She could feel the passion welling up inside her. She hadn't known that she could feel so much passion. The big moment was at hand, literally. She ever so carefully caressed him. She could feel that he was already excited and tense as if he were about to burst. She sighed as his arms came around her. She had been ready for him the moment she saw him, and her femininity swallowed him without further foreplay. At the same instant, her lips met his in a long, passionate kiss. Her rhythmic movements enraptured his body. She started slowly and tenderly, but with each ensuing thrust she gradually increased the tempo of her movements until it was barely noticeable when one thrust ended and a new one began.

She took his right hand and interlocked her fingers with his, then fully extended her arm so their starburst tattoos met.

Daniel opened his eyes to see blue energy leaping the distance from her arm to his. Daniel had never felt a woman want him like she wanted him. He felt absolute acceptance from her, even hunger. Even though she was swollen around him, her hips were flexed back in the most passive and surrendering manner possible. Their passion had grown intense. He could feel energy welling up inside him, wanting to leap the gap to her. With one more thrust, he obliged his need to give in to his sensations and felt the energy burst from his body and into hers. He hugged her tightly as the transfer occurred, kissing her deeply. She was likewise shuddering and experiencing ecstatic spasms of her own. They embraced and remained locked together for some time as they basked in the joy of the moment.

Daniel was disappointed in himself. He hadn't lasted very long. The combination of not having been with a woman since his exploits in Uber, and a month of fantasizing about Anna, had left him overly sensitive and too easily excitable.

Anna whispered in his ear. "That was everything I hoped for."

Daniel had expected himself to relax after the big release. This, however, did not happen. He was again tense, firm, and ready. He was filled with a vigor he had rarely experienced. This is love, he thought, then sat up and gently pushed her toward the opposite side of the pool, caressing and kissing her gently. She returned the affection readily. He lifted her onto the side of the pool, her buttocks resting on soft sand, her legs spread and her feet in the water. They continued to embrace each other hungrily.

Daniel noticed that the way Anna was sitting made her hips the same height as his. She noticed it, too, and rotated her pelvis up to a maximally accepting position, then lay back on the sand and pulled him to her, wrapping her legs around him. "I'm yours, love, forever yours."

The most beautiful woman he had ever seen had her legs wrapped around him and was receiving him with such a feeling of mutual love and desire that he thought for a moment he was in heaven. He slid one hand under her buttocks and began to rhythmically glide into her. She arched her back. Her femininity surrounded him, grabbing him, releasing, grabbing and releasing until he could take it no longer. He was being filled with love, and with one mighty thrust, the feeling was released back to her. The mighty sharing of their love caused them both to smile and sigh with joy. He would enjoy trying to impregnate her.

He slid out of her and fell back into the water with a soft cry of joy. She joined him in the water, washing the sand off her back.

"Wow!" Daniel tried to stand but was having difficulty because the blood still hadn't shifted correctly and his legs were twitching. Anna just smiled, her blue eyes clear and shining, her upper torso a bright red. Her nipples were the color of cherries.

"Follow me," she beckoned. She left the pool quietly and headed down the trail, leading him through the garden and back into the main temple. When he set foot in the temple, he suddenly hesitated, feeling self-conscious. Seeing Daniel looking unsure of himself, Anna went back to him.

"Come on, my love." She took his hand and led him down a hall toward the sleeping chambers. "You were pretty sure of yourself back there in the pool." She giggled and gently pushed him onto her bed. "My bed is softer than yours."

A tray of beverages with a bunch of grapes and other fruits sat on the bedside next to him. He smiled. "We even have room service here?"

"Our friends figured we'd have more on our minds than eating," she replied with a smirk. "I think they were worried that a big sexy man like you would wear me out and I'd need my strength."

Before Daniel could reply, she placed a grape in his mouth. "I've been waiting for you, Daniel, dreaming about you and wanting you for the past five weeks." She slid down along his body and looked deeply into his eyes. Her voice grew even softer. "In fact, I feel like I've been waiting for you for my entire life. Your personality fits mine so well. Although I realize I must share you, it arouses me to know that, emotionally, you will always be mine."

Just then an equally beautiful, darker-skinned, dark-haired French Polynesian woman slid into bed on the other side of him. "This is Monique," Anna continued without changing her voice as she gently rubbed his stomach. "This soft bed is much better than the ground. I figured it was about time I introduced you to some of the others."

Daniel noticed Monique's striking brown eyes as she started gently kissing his right nipple. Neither woman appeared at all bothered that they were now a threesome. They just went to work. To his surprise, he was up to the challenge. Anna began kissing him passionately. He closed his eyes in ecstasy. She climbed on top of him, kissing him and again accepting what his body had to offer. He opened his eyes in pleasure, wanting desperately to caress her breasts, and saw that it was Monique.

Anna was still kissing him and touching his stomach softly. "It's okay Daniel," she whispered. "Just enjoy yourself." She returned to kissing him. The kisses became more passionate, and she soon matched her cadence to Monique's thrusts, embracing his tongue and lips after exploring his mouth.

Monique grabbed Daniel's hands, bringing them to her breasts. She was in control and he obeyed her wishes, gently kneading her breasts as she thrust harder and harder down onto him. As he felt her opening wider to take him in, Daniel could only think of the woman now kissing him and whispering in his ear. He found himself at the point of maximal energy, and he prayed for a release as he felt he couldn't take it any longer. Finally, Monique's body was cajoling him with such an invitation that his body consented and, with pulsations of his own, he shared himself with the brown-eyed French woman on top of him.

Anna introduced him to Irena and Marta, the elder, with more of the same activity. Daniel lasted through the day, performing his duty with a vigor he scarcely believed possible until, finally, he was completely exhausted and unable to go any further. He fell asleep in Anna's arms as she gently massaged his temples. He was a very happy, very satisfied man. Anna was extremely satisfied as well. He would be an asset to the Order. The Choosers had chosen well.

Daniel awoke the next morning to the gentle caresses of two entirely different women. His muscles were sore, especially his lower back and thighs. He wasn't used to the physical exertion he'd experienced the day before. The pair were applying oils to his skin that brought him tremendous relief. They seemed to know just how he'd feel. He tried to sit up but moaned in discomfort. The ladies pushed him back down and told him to roll over. These women were different, yet both were strikingly beautiful. Daniel had never seen an Indian or Latino female nude before.

"Where's Anna?" he asked.

"My name is Darna," said one woman. "I'm a Hindu from India. I was trained as a physician. It is Anna's turn to be on duty, so she left earlier. She will help take care of you when she is finished. This is Maria. She is from Uruguay. She does not speak English. You need to eat and drink as much as possible." With their assistance, he ate and drank as much as he could stand. He was very tired and he felt feverish. After he finished eating, the women helped him to the bathroom receptacle. The short trip exhausted him. He was definitely under the weather, and he remembered Anna saying that the virus would make him feel he had the flu.

Their stroking and massaging was assuming a sexual overtone when Darna asked, "Do you think you feel up to it? It would be better to do this now than later." Daniel nodded. She started kissing him and whispered into his ear. "We will do the work. You lie back, relax, and enjoy." He did as he was told. Both women took their turn, and despite the growing pain in his muscles, he was up to the situation with both. This wasn't the worst job he'd ever had, that was for sure.

He ate another large meal, then fell asleep. He didn't notice Anna's arrival early the following day because the virus and his body were now locked in a mortal struggle. He was extremely feverish and was unable to become aroused. The Volva were constantly at his side. They massaged his muscles with special herbal oils to eliminate his pains, and they dripped fluids into his mouth in an attempt to keep him hydrated. All he could muster was an occasional moan. Daniel was now in the throes of a severe illness.

Omar was shocked at Daniel's condition. "Is it always this bad the first time, Marta?" Omar asked in the Old Language. Although most women preferred to be silent and communicate telepathically, Omar liked to talk and be talked to. "I have never had the experience of watching someone's first reaction to the virus before. Of course, I do not remember much from my own experience."

Marta was the oldest of the women at the temple. She looked to be in her early forties and was a strikingly handsome woman. Her real age undoubtedly was much older. Her wisdom from experience was second to none, and she had seen much in her life. She replied to Omar. "I picked up a quote from a European archeologist that sums it all up: To sleep within the Goddess' womb is to die and come to life anew." She paused for a minute, looking at Daniel, then resumed. "Omar, you were unconscious for days and not worth much for many more days. As far as I have experienced and heard, nobody has ever died from the exposure. However, sometimes they look like they could. The women can exhibit even worse symptoms, but they seem to bounce back more quickly." She poked Omar in the ribs. He responded with an obvious snarl and she continued. "It is odd. We can cure and comfort an array of illnesses and injuries, but we are forbidden from interfering with the process of virus integration. We can use only traditional methods—oil and aloe, massage, and various herbal remedies Darna has made from the garden. We can use our telepathic powers, however, to soothe Daniel's mind. Anna has been singing telepathically to him almost around the clock, and he has remained unusually calm. Most initiates have such severe delusions from their fevers that we have a difficult time keeping them in bed."

"Marta, exactly how old are you?" Omar asked sheepishly. "I know that is a personal question," he quickly added.

"Sometimes I feel like I've been around forever." She shook her head. "I was born in Prussia, Königsberg on the Baltic Sea on the seventeenth of March, 1801. Germany as it is was not even a state. For that matter, Königsberg, is now part of Russia and is not even a German city anymore. I am a woman without a homeland."

"That is sad—to have no roots left, nobody to have contact with in the real world," sympathized Omar. "I suppose I will feel the same when I have been around for as long as you."

"Unfortunately, we Volva do not age as gracefully as you men," she sighed. "Typically, after we feel comfortable that we have trained our replacement, we take ourselves out to pasture, like old Inuit women on icebergs. I am now basically a woman in her early forties. I have fought battles, initiated many new male Defenders, satisfied many existing ones, and controlled power beyond anyone's wildest imagination. I do not want to have this power in my head forever. I look forward to ending it someday. You think more about it as you age. Maybe twenty years more for me, I suppose.

"I still like the wonder of a new member. I remember when Anna came to us." She smiled at her young associate, caring over Daniel's nearly lifeless body. "She was absolutely astounded by the whole process. She thought we were some demented cult. The first time she and I spoke telepathically, she giggled like a schoolgirl who had just received a secret note. That was the moment she actually believed we were real. That is why I keep going, training our younger members in the correct ways, seeing them grow and mature. It will be exciting to share our secrets with Daniel. He will be a very powerful member of our kind. The Norse males always are. Their genes seem to focus the power better. It is the same with any person who is chosen from an ethnic group that has resided near one of our temples. Tanoka was the same way."

Omar changed the topic to his more immediate concern. "When do you think Daniel will regain consciousness?"

"I am sure it will be a few more days," she replied. "I know you would like to leave the temple and I am sure Daniel will understand. With the Middle East having so much turmoil right now, it will be good to have our eyes and ears back out in the field."

Omar agreed. Besides, he'd had enough female company for now. "When he awakes, tell him we will have a laugh together sometime after he has trained and happens through the Middle East. Have him use the usual links. And tell him he owes me for saving him from that sheik and his daughter."

Omar hugged all the Volva, then left the temple and exited the compound through a secret door in the outside wall. He reclaimed his tunic from the front door. The local villagers had cleaned it, and it was hanging next to Daniel's tunic. He smiled, thinking of Daniel's innocence to the whole process, the real order of life. He hiked down the trail toward the waiting Land Rover and his trip back to the world, having enjoyed his first experience with a newcomer. He hoped that sometime he would help initiate another.

* * * * *

Dag Nielstrom was in town running errands. He was heading over to the bank from an earlier stop at the hardware store. As he was fuming over the fact that the hardware store didn't have the size of PVC pipe that he needed, Dag almost ran into Jonathon Smith, a local lawyer.

Smith was nearing retirement. He had been a lawyer in Ogallala for a long time. He had been Dag's father's attorney and had handled the estate after Gunnar had died. Dag thought Smith wasn't very bright, which is probably why he was in Ogallala in the first place.

"Whoa, Dag, what's up? You seem to be thinking and not looking. Is Mr. Mason at the hardware store out of toggle screws again?" Smith laughed.

"No, Smith, it's PVC pipe this time, if you must know," he replied, still vexed at the local merchant. "How can you be out of one-inch PVC pipe in the summer? All the ranchers need it. I could run that place better myself."

Smith's tone changed to sympathy. "Hey, sorry about your son. Mine's in the Marines in Afghanistan, and I worry about him constantly. Did you ever find out anything more?"

"No. That person in New York never followed up with me. Those damn city people are so impersonal."

"Oh, I just remembered, Dag, your father left me a package before he died."

Dag glared at him. "What?"

Smith put his hands up in a defensive manner and forced a smile. "He left strict instructions to not deliver it to you until sometime this year. He even had me include a note in my will so that if something happened to me, you'd still get it this year from my attorney. He even made a trust for payment of some of my services that

I couldn't touch until I made the delivery. I'll be glad to get the thing
out of my safe and get paid. I think he also has a letter to the state
bar association, ready to go with another lawyer if I fail to complete
the task. Gunnar always had his strange ways about things. The
package is in my office. I was supposed to give it to you a month
ago, but with Daniel's death and all, I figured it could wait."

Dag decided he had spent enough time thinking about PVC
pipe and followed Smith to his office. What had his father sent
from the grave? It was just like Gunnar to do something like this.

At the office, Dag had to sign a waiver addressed to a lawyer
in Denver that the package had been delivered with the seal unbro-
ken. Smith slipped the waiver into an envelope and placed it in the
outgoing mail bin. Dag next had to sign a release allowing Smith to
cash out a trust that contained some shares of Nokia and Volvo,
two familiar Nordic companies. The thousand-dollar trust had grown
to be worth over twenty-seven thousand dollars in the twenty-five
years since it had been formed. Smith was getting well paid for the
wait. In the fine print, however, Dag noticed that any monies over
ten thousand dollars would be given to the church. He also signed a
receipt letter, with multiple copies for the record, in case Gunnar
had left any other security measures that required proof of delivery. Finally, Smith handed over a large manila envelope addressed
to Dag Nielstrom or a direct descendant. It was to be opened twenty-
four years later, on a typical day for a Nielstrom family gathering.
Unfortunately, Gunnar had no way to know that his grandson would
be buried two days before that date. Dag thanked Smith, took the
envelope, and left.

Later that afternoon while he was listening to a baseball game
on the radio, Dag inspected the package more closely. He had not
yet mentioned anything about this to his wife as he wanted to see
what it contained. A message on the package was handwritten in
Swedish. It was a common practice for the Nielstrom family to use
Swedish as a code so the rest of Nebraska wouldn't be able to read
important communications.

*To the Nielstrom descendant, hopefully Dag, who reads this:
DO NOT OPEN UNTIL AFTER TWENTY-FOURTH BIRTHDAY
OF MY GRANDSON. After that, break the seal and remove the
instructions and the second envelope. DO NOT OPEN THE*

SECOND ENVELOPE UNTIL CAREFULLY FOLLOWING THE INSTRUCTIONS.

Gunnar Nielstrom.

Gunnar had written the note just a few weeks before he died. Obviously he wanted to share something with his family, but why this year? Twenty-four years is not a number you'd think of: ten, twenty, or twenty-five maybe, but not twenty-four. Dag broke the seal. The envelope contained a letter, laminated to prevent moisture damage, and a second watertight envelope with a wax seal on it. Dag laughed at the precautions. Senility and paranoia had obviously set in by the time Gunnar had prepared this. Dag dutifully opened the instructions:

Dag, if you honor me as your father and grandfather, please follow the instructions below carefully, as I would not have presented them in this manner unless it was absolutely necessary. I am carrying to the grave some information that will affect the family many years into the future. After much deliberation, I have decided on this method to inform you of the situation. If not everyone is in agreement or if they do not think they can follow the instructions precisely, please destroy this letter and the enclosed envelope, unopened and unread. I will not think any less of you. Everyone must hear it or nobody can hear it. I wish Erika could have been a part of this letter as well; unfortunately it is entirely of my doing and she passed away and I never shared this information with her.

Arrange a gathering of all of the direct descendants of Erika and myself along with their spouses. Have a Sunday meal and find a bottle of that A. P. Anderson schnapps you like and then deliver a toast to all of our family.

Make a large fire outside for use later on.

Have an afternoon sauna. Only direct descendants over twelve years of age can participate, along with your wife, Ingrid. The other spouses need to stay in the house. What is contained in the second letter is not for their ears. This is nothing against them. Blood is blood and that is what binds us.

Ingrid is invited because she has been a part of this.

Outside the sauna, read this letter aloud; if anyone has any doubts, do not proceed further. Everyone must be in agreement to handle the second letter, and everyone must agree to follow the instructions precisely and completely. Forces are at work driving the level of precautions I have initiated—forces that you do not want to experience.

Take a sauna and read the sealed letter out loud, then let everyone examine it.

Discuss the contents in the sauna only. After leaving, you are never to speak of the contents again with anyone—not with spouses, not even with each other. Burn both letters and the envelopes in the fire you started earlier.

Keep the knowledge I have given you in your hearts, and know that certain things have been done for reasons with a larger focus. This knowledge will undoubtedly cause happiness and contentment. Let that feeling be enough and keep it to yourselves. Our family has been blessed, but if anyone repeats any of my messages, it would cause that blessing to end and cause certain horrors to unfold on everyone. Again, either everyone is told or no one is told. I have kept this secret for sixty-three years and so can you. If any cannot follow these parameters, not knowing the message would be better than the consequences of sharing it.

Gunnar Nielstrom

The envelope also contained five thousand dollars in cash for airfare to bring any grandchildren from Sweden. He had covered all the bases. Dag was bewildered. He showed the letter to Ingrid. After much pondering, they decided to fly Hanna back from the Old Country in two weeks. Erika would already be back from Sweden by then. One of their two nieces lived in town, and the other, according to Dag's sister, would be available on the chosen weekend. He and his sister completed the list of invitees for the special reading of Gunnar's mysterious letter.

The fateful Sunday finally arrived. It was a cool day, as the searing heat of summer was starting to abate. The sermon in the

Lutheran church was about respecting your parents. The pastor didn't realize the irony of his subject to the Nielstrom family's situation. Lunch was grilled salmon prepared with onions and served with the last sweet corn of the season. After dinner, a spouses' championship game of Risk started after Uncle George had summoned his two sons-in-law to battle. The invited headed quietly for the sauna.

After everyone was ready outside the sauna, Dag read the opening letter aloud. Many questions were asked and the instructions were discussed at length. Finally, everyone agreed that they could keep the big secret, whatever it might be. All the precautions seemed silly to the younger generation, but it was not silly to Dag and his sister. They knew their father and had seen him at work before. Prophecy was not a new experience to them. They all filed into the sauna. Dag had kept the temperature down a little because they might need time to digest the contents of the second letter. He didn't want anyone to pass out from the heat. He opened the letter and started reading aloud:

To my beloved family:

I understand that the mystery surrounding this letter has seemed extreme and you are, without a doubt, curious about the contents. This letter is the final thing that I will write in this life. I would like to thank my wonderful family for making Erika and me truly proud and happy. I died a happy man, knowing that I had two wonderful children. By now you have raised five wonderful grandchildren, four young women and one young man, who are, undoubtedly, sound citizens beginning to start families of their own.

Dag paused for a question from Erika. "How does Grandpa know he has five grandchildren? I hadn't even been born when he died." Dag just looked at his daughter and went on:

As you are reading this letter, you have by now experienced a great loss of one of these progeny, my only grandson, Daniel. Exactly how and why I know this I will explain.

I was told certain things when I was still with the Marines.

This knowledge was, under no circumstance, to be shared with anyone, even my wife or children. If I had told anyone, everything that I have created and all my descendants—my entire seed—would have been eliminated from existence as a penalty for transgression. I have never revealed to any living soul any of what I am telling you. Erika at times wondered about things, but she always had a special belief and accepted the fact that certain knowledge would be left unshared.

While I was in Gallipoli in the Great War, I was captured and was going to be tortured and executed. I was unaware that, as a boy back in Falun, Sweden, I had previously assisted a man who was part of an important group known as the Choosers, and would at this time reappear. Because I had assisted him all those years earlier, when I was captured in Gallipoli I was rewarded with a choice: I could save myself and escape or I could take my own life and be spared from the torture. If I chose the former I would have to live right, raise a good family, and meet the high expectations of the man's group. The group would, however, take my first-born grandchild on his twenty-fourth birthday to be one of their own. Obviously, I chose this option. I apologize to Ingrid, especially, for predetermining her son's life so that he would be taken from her. Ingrid, you were to be blessed with a third child, so you could have two children to look after you.

The one thing I feel incomplete about is not being able to meet this beautiful young woman, and I have no way of knowing what your name is. I hope Dag and Ingrid chose a wonderful Swedish name for you. The Chooser told me you would have a special closeness with your mom and that you would be a lot like your grandmother, Erika. You must therefore be a truly beautiful and intelligent young woman. Use whatever special gifts you have been granted to the fullest.

Because of my pledge, our family has been blessed with love, an identity, a rich cultural heritage, and certain knowledge that helped us prosper and survive when other families suffered and died. That is why I always kept us apart from everyone and why I knew certain things before they happened.

The Choosers are good people. They have taken Daniel,

but do not lose heart. Know that he is alive somewhere. You may or may not see him again, but rest well in the knowledge that he is in good hands. I truly believe he has been granted a special destiny in this world, but I was never told anything more about what he was to do. The Chooser said only that my "heir's heir" would be pledged to them, and that "he is to be a special person in this world." That is all I know.

Although I was forbidden to share this knowledge, I could not die knowing the sadness I have caused everyone without sharing the hope that I know. Sometimes I have wished I had taken the pistol when I was given the choice of death. I have undoubtedly caused much sorrow; you have had to bury a son, brother, cousin, and nephew. I hope I have lifted your hearts a little by letting you know that Daniel is still alive. Now in my twilight, I know that if I had chosen the latter option, four beautiful young women would not be in existence and I would not have had such a wonderful son and daughter. I would not have had the opportunity to marry such a wonderful woman, and Daniel would not have been blessed.

Remember, nothing you have learned here can ever leave your hearts. Never repeat the contents of this letter. Remember Daniel and sleep well knowing he is fulfilling his destiny. Re-read the letter, ask questions, and do whatever else you need to do, then leave the sauna and burn both letters. Let your smiles be enough to remind each other of what I have written.

Your loving father and grandfather, Gunnar.

Dag handed the letter to his sister and there was a brief moment of silence.

Ingrid broke the silence. "Can we believe this? I don't know if I'm ready to believe that my son is still alive."

Dag's sister looked at her. "But Dad gave so much detail in the letter about the current make-up of the family, the year Daniel would disappear . . . everything. We never buried a body, Ingrid." She paused. "We just buried a memory. Why would he go to the trouble to send us this letter?"

Ingrid looked at her husband. "What are you thinking, Dag?"

"I don't know what to think. Papa always seem to know a lot about things before they happened. He told me once that he wasn't going to be able to die until I got married and had a son. He gave me some money and sent me to his sister's in Sweden and I met you." He smiled at her. "And remember? When you were pregnant, he said if it was a boy, he and Mom would pass on, and if it was a girl, he'd live another year or two. All that depression planning stuff is still legendary around here." He paused. "I guess I have to believe that if he says it's so, it must be true. I still have three children alive and nobody is going to tell me different."

Erika looked at him. "So what do we say to everyone, Dad?"

"Nothing—absolutely nothing. Life goes on as before. We keep Daniel's marker in the cemetery as a place to remember him. Nobody will ever hear of this again. Dad wouldn't have gone to such elaborate measures to warn us if we weren't at a significant risk."

They all agreed that nobody would ever mention anything about the letter or about Daniel being alive ever again, not even to each other or their spouses. They walked from the sauna to the house happier, knowing that Daniel was still alive and that they might see him again someday.

As to how and why old Gunnar Nielstrom had known of these events, the family only knew what he'd revealed in the letter. Gunnar had always seemed beyond their comprehension. He was a mysterious man with a mysterious past that he rarely shared with anyone. But despite his shortcomings and unorthodox ways, he was a devoted family man with the utmost integrity.

CHAPTER 7: The Awakening

On the fifth day Daniel's fever broke. The Volva had started to become concerned, as they had rarely seen anyone react to the virus so severely. Shortly thereafter, he began to stir from his comatose condition. First with moans and then with words, the young Defender slowly came back to the world. Darna and Anna took turns massaging his muscles and giving him fluids, drop by drop. By that evening he was able to drink on his own and ask the most simple questions.

"Where am I?" he asked wearily.

Anna smiled and hugged her awakening friend. "You're with friends," she whispered. "We thought we'd lost you."

Daniel still looked confused and dazed. He looked at Anna. "Erika? Where am I?"

"I'm Anna, and you're at the temple," she said. "You need to rest." She began humming a soothing tune to relax him. She had hummed the same tune to him almost continually since he had taken ill. Daniel smiled in recognition and appeared to understand that he was safe. He soon went back to sleep.

The worried women remained by his side to give him constant attention.

By the next morning he was slightly more coherent and, with some assistance, he was able to eat and drink. He was still confused and frequently called Anna by his sisters' or his mother's name. If another Volva was at his bedside, Daniel appeared to become depressed and despondent and refused to eat or even make eye contact. They all agreed that until he had fully regained his faculties, Anna would be relieved of her other duties and devote her full attention to him. She continued humming quiet lullabies to soothe his mind and give his confusing tangle of thoughts some order.

It was a full three days before he actually called Anna by her name consistently. He was still too weak to even sit up, but with continual fluids and food he was gradually regaining his color and vigor. Marta spent some time in the archives in search of any historical reference to such a severe reaction to the virus. As far as she could determine, his reaction indicated that he had a very close genetic match to the original carrier of the virus. Obviously his Scandinavian heritage had something to do with it. She suspected his ancestors must have come from an area near one of the original temples. This ideal match meant that Daniel would undoubtedly form a strong link with the Volva and he probably would have stronger powers than most males of the Order. He could never have power approaching that of a Volva, but he would be a very powerful male. She was pleased with these findings. They needed a strong young Defender. It had been many years since the last successful initiation. New blood lines would strengthen them all.

Daniel's mind slowly cleared, and he gradually remembered who and where he was. Although it all seemed like a dream to him, he remembered Omar, Al-Hamra, the purification, the desert, and even Altorini. Finally, after more than a week of this living confusion, he felt strong enough to sit up and walk to a chair by himself. Anna had gone to get some food, and she returned to find him out of bed for the first time.

"Where's Omar?" he asked, much clearer now.

"He left while you were ill." Anna looked surprised at his progress. "He came and looked in on you, but he had completed his duties here and needed to get back to the Middle East."

"I hope somebody told him thank you for looking out for me and rescuing me from the Arabs."

"You can tell him yourself in a few weeks." She bent to hug him. "We should start your training."

"Training?" He looked confused again. "I'd like to thank you, too, for helping me during this illness. I still feel like I have the hangover of a lifetime. My head has never hurt this bad."

Anna offered him a preparation of plant material that contained a natural, non-steroidal aspirin-like compound. His headache began to abate.

"You know, some of what I remember doesn't seem real—like this whole Defender system. But I remember our conversations, and I remember some damn good sex. Am I dreaming?"

"No, Daniel, you're not." She smiled as she hugged him again. "I'm glad you're finally back with us. Marta said you've had the roughest conversion she's ever seen. Being the eldest, you know; she's seen quite a lot."

Daniel wept. His mind was filled with fear. Just as the emotional outburst peaked, he heard a familiar tune. He wasn't hearing it with his ears, but in his mind. He had heard it many times in the last few days. It immediately calmed him. He looked at the smiling, nude, heavily-tattooed blonde woman sitting next to him. The song switched from his brain to coming from her voice without changing a beat. In a state of epiphany he said, "You're the source of that lovely song."

"Yes," she said, her smile unwavering. "I'm telepathic, remember? Soon you'll have this skill as well." Daniel nodded and she continued. "Your neurons must reconfigure before you can sense it. You also need to learn the Old Language. That is the language we use; you must learn to think in the Old Language. Right now, you think in English and Swedish. I understand English, so I can read and convert your thoughts directly. I do not understand the thoughts that are in Swedish, so I have to share my link with Marta. Even her knowledge is imperfect, though. I think in the Old Language. We wield our powers through this language base. Singing and music is natural and doesn't need to be converted.

"You will soon start to hear voices or noises in your head. Do not be afraid; you are not going crazy. As the transmittal protein builds up, your neurons will begin to detect the natural telepathic link that we all share. It starts as noises and then voices. I hear all the Volva's thoughts all the time. In the temple we are in constant contact. If one stubs her foot, we all feel the pain. If I have an orgasm with you, they all share the pleasure. With work, you will learn to separate these links and organize your thoughts.

"When you are away from the temple, the most prominent voice you will hear is that of the Volva on duty on the Conduction Array. She will always be in your mind. She also serves to filter out inter-Volva and inter-Defender traffic. We serve as sort of a routing station. It is complicated, but I'll take you to the heart of the temple tomorrow after I rest from my turn on duty. I have been fully devoted to caring for you. Since you are better, I need to resume my duties. I think you can handle being alone for a few hours."

"How often are you on duty?"

"Every eight hours we switch. Following our turn we are truly exhausted. The experience is difficult to explain. On one hand it is ecstasy, and on another it is like running a marathon. It is joy and fear all wrapped up in one. The energy that we focus and control is very powerful; after eight hours, our neurons need a rest. During the war, we were sometimes providing two Volva on the Array at the same time and we changed shifts every six hours, but that was before my time.

"I was trained for a year by my mentor before I was even allowed to share the Array with her. The initial rush caused me to scream in terror. It was a week before I tried it again." She laughed. "I was such a naïve young woman back then. After more than two years of shared experiences, I was able to tolerate the energy and assume my full duty independently. That is probably why we were allowed to live longer when the system was designed. It is very time consuming and intensive to train one of us."

"I look forward to seeing this machine of yours."

"You should stay in your room and rest until I get back. Xu Li will be looking after you. I don't think you've met her yet."

"Am I a prisoner?"

"Daniel! This is your temple now as much as mine. You can go anywhere and do anything you want. You can start to tear down the walls; you can have your way with the Volva . . . anything. You can even leave if you want. That would sadden me though. You have very few limitations. You can even go on to the Array, but the energy would kill you, so that would not be a good thing to do. We are here of our free will. I hope you stay though; it would be lonely around here without you." Daniel looked more at ease. "Now, Xu Li is here and I have to go. She will keep you warm tonight." She smiled. "Don't do anything with her that you wouldn't do with me." She winked, kissed him, caressed him suggestively, and was off.

It soon became apparent to Daniel that Xu Li spoke nary a word of English. She was a bouncy, petite Chinese woman who appeared to be in her late twenties. Like Anna and the rest of her Volva sisters, she bore the same tattoos. Her hair was dark and short, and her female endowments were smaller as is typical of Asian women. She smiled at Daniel and laughed at him often. She also liked to giggle and did so frequently.

The evening meal was the usual fare: goat cheese, goat yogurt, and bread washed down with wine. He was happy the alcohol content was low because he suspected he couldn't handle much. He also found himself very thirsty, so he drank some water. Following the meal, Xu Li motioned for him to lie down. Daniel was worried that he may be expected to do more, but such an opportunity never presented itself. She was giving him a lovely back, leg, arm, and foot massage. After a brief interlude, she made a motion that at first confused him, but he soon recognized that he needed a bath. She led him out of the room to an open area.

She led him to a pool in the garden. The garden was dark so Daniel deduced that it must be evening. His sense of time had abandoned him while he was ill. This was a different pool than the one in which he and Anna had first made love. It was larger and filled with rocks. It appeared to be part of the main stream leading out of the temple and into the valley. Daniel, still lightheaded, carefully crawled in. Xu Li followed carrying some fleshy leaves, which she placed on a rock nearby. The water was very warm in general, but there were pockets where it was quite cool. He found a warm spot and leaned against one of the rocks, then stretched, enjoying the feeling of water on his skin. He had not bathed like this for quite some time. Anna had been giving him daily sponge baths while he was too ill to move.

Two more Volva entered the pool. He hadn't met either of them. He suspected that this pool was the communal bath. Christina was of Mediterranean heritage and strikingly beautiful. She was the one who'd left with Omar that first night. Ushenna was black, and although in many ways she was the opposite of the blonde-haired, fair-skinned Anna, she was also exceedingly beautiful. Before they started their own baths, they greeted Daniel properly with long, deep, sensual kisses. He was both surprised and uncomfortable with their advances. They must have sensed this feeling, and each looked at him strangely. He then remembered his place and repeated the greeting and they all laughed. To these women, he was still an unknown new member of the Order, a situation that would soon be rectified.

Xu Li went to work on Daniel, washing him with one of the fleshy leaves as thoroughly as she'd washed herself. He was aroused by the naked, bathing women but did not know what was expected of him at this moment. He tried to quell any passionate feelings. The women, thankfully, seemed focused on getting clean. Other than occasionally splashing him, they paid him little attention.

Eventually Xu Li led him into the coldest part of the pool, which caused every exposed muscle to contract. Then they exited the pool on the opposite side. There were no towels and Daniel suspected he would have to dry off in the air. Xu Li pointed to a square hole in the temple wall. It was almost as high as his head, but he could see no opening to the outside. She motioned for him to stand in front of it, and then she walked over to a lever a few yards away. She pulled the lever and Daniel was hit with a rush of warm air. After he was dry he repeated the process for Xu Li.

Back in his room, Daniel was starting to get sleepy as Xu Li began massaging him again. He liked the attention; the Volva were good at their craft. He was feeling nicely relaxed when she motioned for him to flip over. Her gentle, caressing hands soon found their way to a much firmer object and, without objection from Daniel, she helped herself to his manhood. He was so relaxed that it seemed a natural release. When they were finished she cuddled him and they slept soundly.

By morning, Daniel was starting to feel guilty about his weak willpower. Anna surely wouldn't be pleased that he had given in to such temptation. But it was a new day; Daniel felt better and stronger, and life was good.

Xu Li took no note of any problems. In her mind, the previous day's events were a simple progression—a male gets clean and relaxes, he needs sex, you have a mutual release, and then you go to sleep. It was just the way things were done. She would have awakened him the same way, but she suspected he hadn't yet regained his strength.

Daniel ate and drank well, and later Anna arrived looking refreshed. She thanked Xu Li. The Chinese Volva passionately kissed Daniel and left.

Anna stared at Daniel. He was obviously in some sort of trouble. Then she laughed. "Daniel, you don't get it. Why do you feel guilty? You spent the night with one of us. You should always spend the night with one of us. As a male, why would you ever desire to sleep alone here?"

"I know, Anna. I just was raised with different values. I'll learn."

She shook her head. "Today we begin your lessons. First we are going to go over some of our basic rules. You'll get a tour, and then we'll start language training. We'll keep today light, but we'll work harder each day. Every seventh day is a day of self-purification and religious prayer. Feel free to question every point. You need to learn quickly but correctly."

Daniel nodded. He was going to start a crash course in a field he knew nothing about; in fact in a field he previously hadn't even known existed.

"First, let's cover Defender life and etiquette. It seems to me that Americans want to make religions out of things. They think runes have some hidden religious purpose, for example. They look at fiction and make it into something more than just a story. First off, we are not gods. We are not divine. We have been singled out and given special powers, but the powers are not from God. They are from the Martians.

"Our mystical powers have nothing to do with religion. We have no power over life but we do have power over death. Life has never been created, apart from the divine creation. We have no further insight to the supernatural world than anyone else does. On our death our spirits go to a different place. Almost everything you believe from your Christian background is still valid. For example, some of the people in the Bible were Defenders, but that changes nothing. I will enjoy worshipping the Almighty with you on purification days. All the so-called New Age stuff is mixing humanism with creationism, fiction with non-fiction. Some of these religions are actually trying to worship us, or stories about us. They try to make me into some sort of goddess and you into a god. Do not let anyone worship you. Humans and Defenders all end up in the same place. Our bodies become part of the earth and our spirits become part of a higher plane."

Daniel stopped her. "Everyone here worships in their own way?"

"Yes. We have two Hindus, two Buddhists, two Moslems, and five Christians." Seeing that Daniel understood this basic point, she went on to the next subject. "Hygiene is a good next topic. The Volva are passionate about cleanliness. Xu Li showed you the communal bathing pool. We all bathe in the evening after dark. The water is let into the pools during the rain, and the water is naturally replaced. The products of our bathing are washed downstream. The pool we made love in is for soaking and relaxing. The water doesn't flow through as well so we like to keep the cleaning plants out of there. Typically we wash each other, so don't be surprised if someone wants to wash you. I'd be truly surprised if you ever bathe alone here. Sex in the bathing pool is expected and is no problem even if others are in the pool. Water is an aphrodisiac to us. I wish I knew the origins behind this effect.

"The drying vent is connected to an underground cave system that fills with hot air during the day. It blows out only at night. Don't open it during the day as the vent blows the other way and could suck something, even you, down the hole. It is one of my favorite inventions here.

"All the plants in the garden have a purpose. I'll be teaching you about each plant and how it is used.

"Toileting is another issue. You've seen our ten thousand-year-old sewage system. The waste is sent out through a different system from the river. We have our own natural drain field that processes our waste and organically leaches the nutrients into the garden. The system is designed to work forever, and so far it has, thanks to the Martian engineers.

"Bodily grooming puzzled me when I first came here. The Volva need to have limited body hair, especially below the waist. We sit on the Conduction Array and hair could potentially interfere with the signal. So we keep our female hair in check." She pointed toward her Venus' mound, which was neatly trimmed. "We wear the hair on our heads any way we want. I like mine long, for example, but it cannot be longer than my hips as it cannot touch the Array when I'm sitting. We use our power to trim our hair. The men tend to let the hair on their heads grow out but they usually keep their facial hair short. I will help you get it to your specifications until you learn the technique. You'll find that your chest and facial hair has been adversely affected by the tattoo process and will grow sparsely and lightly around the tattoos."

Being of Swedish descent, Daniel had never expected to have a hairy chest, so this was no difficulty for him to endure. "I'll think about my hair, I guess. I've always been short-haired and cleanly shaven until this recent desert trip."

Anna smiled and continued. "Eating is simple. We eat twice a day. I'll show you where the food is available. Eating isn't a social event with us. We just eat and go on with our activities. The food here is ordinary and monotonous. The locals provide it for us every day. We have some fruits in the garden that are available to all of us. I'll show you which ones are edible, as some have medicinal properties only.

"You will not have your own room while you're here. We have only one extra bedroom and that one is being used by another Defender, the ancient one named Tanoka."

"I heard from Omar that he hasn't long to live," Daniel said. "I'd like to meet him."

"You will. He won't die until he meets you. Unfortunately, he doesn't speak anymore. He uses only telepathy, so until you've mastered the Old Language, meeting him will not be beneficial to either of you. You'll just stir him up. He is well attended by us as we take care of all the old Defenders who come here when they've finished their duties.

"The Volva have no use for personal possessions. Even our individual sleeping rooms are identical. Typically we sleep alone, although after being on duty we sometimes sleep with one of our sisters. The process of being linked is taxing and the togetherness helps in the recovery. Most males like to sleep with one or two of us. As I said before, why would a male ever desire to sleep alone here? Sleeping together is both a sexual and a bonding event. And by the way, you are expected to share a bed with one of us each night. No one will ever ask you to share her bed. On the other hand, no one will ever refuse you either. It's just part of life with us. Typically, after the communal bath, a male just follows one of us to her room. To ask is to imply that you believe one of us might consider saying no. As none of us would ever refuse you, to ask is a redundancy."

Daniel was looking confused. Although he was more open-minded than most Westerners, she needed to reinforce this point. "Daniel, I reflected your hesitancy with Xu Li last evening. She thought it was great fun. She is always looking for a reason to laugh, and you playing hard to get was a new joke for her—but I suspect there was more to your reaction than just playing hard to get." She paused. "You and I consider each other soul mates, for lack of a better term, but we need to think of the larger picture. We have to share ourselves with the other members of our Order. This is the only way the Order can survive. We cannot afford jealousy, nor can we impose any worldly morality that was not meant for us. To refuse to be with one of my sisters would be a refusal of me and everything of which I am part."

"Can I at least think of you while I'm making love with one of them? It isn't that I want to refuse any of them; it's just that I don't want anyone other than you."

Anna smiled. "We need to accept each other for what we are and what we represent. We are all human and have human needs, but we are also Defenders and have certain responsibilities. All cultures and beliefs here are melded into one. Can you accept this?"

When he nodded, she went on to a different topic. "As you will see, the temple here is very basic. Besides the twelve personal rooms, we have an expansive garden. There is also the isolation room you spent twenty-eight days in, as well as a central meeting room, an eating chamber, two meditation rooms, an exercise area, the expansive archival area and, of course, the Conduction Array. It is a place of hard stone, open air, natural lighting, and flowing water. You will learn that the life of a Volva is equally simple. We eat, sleep, take our turns on the Array, and work with the historical archives. We spend most of our free time living in the minds of the male Defenders. Our few sources of personal pleasure are bathing, exercise, massage, and music. We get to leave the temple only once or twice in our lifetime. We are on duty every fourth day. Our few physical diversions from this routine are personal intimacy with the occasional visiting Defender, training a new male once or twice in our lifetimes, and finally training our replacement."

"It isn't exactly the life of paradise," Daniel observed. "Is it worth it?"

"We are given a wonderful gift." She looked thankful. "I wouldn't want my old self back, ever. The telepathy we share is both addictive and stimulating. Being part of a sisterhood is something all of us desired in our youth. We were all women and girls without homes—orphans would be the general term. I believe that is why we were chosen."

"You mean the choosing of the Volva is different than the choosing of the men?"

She nodded. "We are not pledged by our grandfathers as were you. My parents died when I was a baby. My mother's only sister began raising me, but she and her husband were killed in a car accident when I was four. I was then placed under the care of the State of Ohio and lived in foster homes. When I was five, a kindly older gentleman who introduced himself as Uncle Albert visited me. He told me to not worry and that he would look after me from afar. I would go to all the good schools and he expected nothing of me except to do my best. For the rest of my school years, Uncle Albert sent me letters congratulating me on my successes, giving me advice on my concerns, and always encouraging me. I never saw him again after that first meeting, but I knew he was there, always around, always watching me.

"I went to the best elementary and boarding schools in Ohio, and when I was fourteen, I was told in a letter that if I wanted to, and if I succeeded at my schooling, I might be selected for membership in the ultimate sisterhood. I graduated high school and then attended a small private college in Wisconsin where I majored in history. I had normal youthful experiences but I never allowed myself to have any lasting affairs. Upon graduation, I was informed in a final letter from Uncle Albert that I had exceeded his expectations. He gave me a check for fifty thousand dollars and wished me well. He also stated that I'd been selected for a secret society and that I should enjoy myself and do whatever I wanted to do for two years. I could travel, go to graduate school, buy a car, take a job, or just take the money and forget the whole thing; it was up to me.

"The letter also said if I presented myself for five consecutive nights at the steps of my college library starting three nights before my twenty-fourth birthday, I would be contacted and initiated. The third night, the night of my birth, I suddenly fell asleep. I woke up at the entrance to the temple, tattooed, naked, and bewildered, in the arms of the Volva I was to replace. I later learned that I had been brought to this place by the elder of the local people after being left at the foot of the trail."

"That is a much different system," Daniel said. "Do you have any family left?"

"No, I only have my Volva sisters and you Defenders. But that's all I need now. I belong here; this is my home."

She decided it was time to take Daniel on a tour of the temple. After showing him the upper living quarters, the eating and receiving areas, and the meditation and exercise areas, she proceeded to the heart of the temple, the Conduction Array.

Daniel didn't know what to expect. What he saw was straight out of a science fiction novel. The vast room was dimly lit with an eerie blue glow coming from Ushenna's ebony body, the same glow Daniel had experienced when he'd first entered the temple. Anna waved her hands and the room filled with light. Daniel could now see the room in great detail. Ushenna was sitting on a tremendous bridge of pure copper. The bridge was approximately twenty feet long, four feet wide, and two feet thick. It was highly polished. She sat cross-legged with her palms on the copper bridge. Her eyes were closed, and Daniel couldn't tell whether she even knew they were present.

The ends of the bridge were anchored in a grayish metal that formed the boundary of a great lake of shimmering liquid mercury the size of a motel swimming pool. The room was otherwise empty except for some copper rods on the walls. Daniel had seen them in most of the rooms. The stone walls also contained a few symbols that he suspected were of the Old Language. Anna motioned for him to sit down. A strange hum began to fill his thoughts.

Anna spoke in her normal voice, as if they were the only ones in the room. "The large copper bar conducts energy from deep in the earth. The rods you see extend down perhaps five hundred yards and connect with a whole web of similar rods. We believe some sort of super-conductive material is also involved. The web collects intrinsic earth energy and funnels it up to Ushenna. There is an alloy of gallium and platinum around the lake of mercury that serves as a safety switch to protect us. It is complicated to explain, but the conductive characteristics of the alloy and mercury act to siphon off surges and thus keep a constant level of energy available to the Volva at all times.

"The energy then flows at a fixed wavelength from her mind to all of ours. That humming you hear comes from the neurons in your brain starting to tune with our telepathic link. When Ushenna is done, her replacement, Marta, will sit next to her. Using telepathy, Marta will connect to Ushenna's thoughts, find the energy frequency, resume the global telepathic link, and two of us will help Ushenna off the Array to rest. In this way the link is never broken. It has not been broken for twelve thousand years. We fear that if the link is lost, we will be unable to find the correct frequency again.

"You're always welcome to watch, but you must never touch the metal surrounding the pool or the bridge itself. Only females have the ability to handle the energy and even for us, it takes much training. If you touch it, you will die or, at best, lose your sanity. I would also suggest that you don't come here until you've mastered the Old Language—coming here will only make the voices or humming in your head grow louder. The garden will probably be the quietest place for you until you've learned to control the voices."

Daniel pointed to the stone wall. "What are those smaller copper rods?"

"Those conduct heat throughout the temple," Anna replied. "The temperature in here is always the same. Those copper rods take some of the extra energy that goes through the Array and convert it into heat. There are even heating rods under the garden to warm the soil. Some of the rods are also connected to other structures, causing them to glow, thus giving us the light we have here. It is all part of the Martian technology and to be honest, the exact mechanism is poorly recorded and not well understood."

Daniel nodded and followed her up the stairs to the main greeting room, then down another set of stairs into a multi-level library. A few Volva were diligently looking over texts and apparently using their powers to copy or correct them.

"This is the history of the Earth as it truly is," Anna said proudly. "Our second charge is to keep records of what happens in the world. We write everything down on parchment. Then, every three hundred years or so we copy and replace it. This is how we know so much about history. We read and write about it all day."

Daniel thought suddenly about a paper he'd written in school about the strange earthen pyramids found along the river valleys of North America. A truly massive one near St. Louis was now called Cahokia. There had always been a mystery about who'd lived there and why it was there in the first place.

Anna read his thought and headed over to a section of the parchments, pulling one from its location. She opened it without touching it, using only her powers, found what she was looking for and returned the scroll. Then she walked down a long set of stairs and quickly returned, smiling. "Here, my love. The answer to a mystery of your youth." She opened the scroll and read, "The Egyptians set up a series of trading fortresses in the far off continent along numerous rivers that were tributaries of the main river of the land mass. Some of the fortresses were many days' journey up the great rivers. This land was to be later known as North America and the large river was the Mississippi. The forts were used for trading, mostly for metals such as copper and silver, which were found in abundance around the mighty lakes just to the north. The Romans later used the forts after they had conquered Egypt, but they rarely were present themselves and allowed Aztecs to occupy the areas. With the fall of the Romans, the area gradually lost its importance and contact from Europe to the area was eventually lost. Most of the slaves became primitive peoples living in their former areas. The Mongols invaded the area around 720 A.D., the result of which was interbreeding. The forts were abandoned and the people of North America became a primitive, generally nomadic people who remained intact until Europe and Asia made contact again a few centuries later."

Daniel grinned. "I thought some of that pottery looked Egyptian. I always wondered where all that copper from Michigan and Wisconsin went. Those pyramids extended north. Spiro Mound in Oklahoma is near an ancient silver mine." Daniel stopped, noting that Anna was not interested in his academic discussion. He had just gotten a taste of correct factual information. "Thanks Anna. You've helped me more than you can ever know."

She smiled and continued the tour, eventually returning to where they had started. After they paused for some water, she began instructing him in the Old Language. It was unlike any he had ever seen, but he seemed to instinctively recognize it. It was a very formal language that gave Daniel pleasure when he heard it spoken. He plowed into the coursework with a devotion that impressed not only Anna but all of the Volva.

The second night after beginning his studies, Anna took Daniel to the bathing pool. He needed to be properly introduced to the enjoyment of a good group wash. She also wanted to share him with her sisters, not only as part of her communal thinking but of the communal need. She formally introduced him to Ushenna, the Nigerian whose name meant "God's will." With Anna's encouragement he allowed Ushenna to bathe him. Later, he allowed himself the pleasure of sharing himself with the ebony beauty. Anna was glad her man was becoming freer with himself and sharing himself with her sisters.

Daniel's days became very simple. He soon learned the language in which he would think and converse night and day. He felt the rapid learning was a good thing because with each day the hum in his head grew louder. It later became almost distinct voices that he suspected were the voices of other Defenders, but he was unable to even partially understand them. He had initially felt like he was going mad, but Anna kept reassuring him and repeatedly explained the process of his neurons melding with the viral protein.

After his daily studies, they would exercise together. Anna and the other Volva also entertained him with music. Unfortunately, Daniel had never mastered musical skills so he couldn't return the favor. He spent his evenings relaxing in the bathing pool, soon becoming more comfortable with his lady friends. Despite not being able to communicate fully with most of them, he had no trouble performing his duty for the female Defenders. He could think of a lot of things worse than making love to eleven beautiful women, although he typically slept with Anna, unless she was on duty. During those nights, he would just see whom he was attracted to at the pool and follow her back to her room, then share her bed.

He always felt odd being with Marta as she was the elder of the group and, he deduced, the most powerful of the Order. Marta, however, always rebuked such talk. She claimed that Christina was probably the most powerful. Power was based on genetics, with Norse women or ones of Japanese, Mediterranean, or even East African descent having the most potential. They were the daughters of Freyja, and the virus had been designed using their genome types. She also said Anna would have tremendous power as she honed her skills with experience. Daniel felt she was just being humble. He also communicated mostly to her in basic German, as that was her native tongue. Daniel's bad German was better than Marta's bad English or Swedish.

Being with a two hundred-year-old woman was, to say the least, different. Despite her chronological age, she was a handsome Nordic woman who appeared at most to be in her early forties. She was also very tender with Daniel, and she once even confided in him that if she had been younger, he would have been her special male. Her soul mate was the German Defender who had been killed by the Nazis. He had been dead for over sixty years, and it appeared that she was biding her time until her end.

He soon became aware of how truly sexually excited the women would become if he turned the tables at the pool and washed them. He later discovered that the male Defenders didn't usually do this activity. It often turned them on so much that he wouldn't have time to leave the pool before being enveloped by the woman on whom he had bestowed the pleasure.

Anna also loved being washed and being caressed by his tender hands and wouldn't let him leave the pool without coming into her. This he did with great eagerness as if it was their first time every time, and he soon developed a reputation as a mighty lover.

With each passing day, his mastery of the Old Language grew until, after four intensive weeks of study, Daniel was able to fully communicate verbally with Anna. It was at this point that he stopped speaking English or German in the temple. He knew it would take some time before he could actually think in the language, but he was making excellent progress. He was pleasantly surprised to be actually talking with the Volva. Most of them were not used to verbal communication and they welcomed the change.

Daniel found all the Volva to be interesting, intelligent women. He was impressed by Ushenna's depth of spirituality. Xu Li was better suited to be a stand-up comedian. Both Darna and Maria had a very deep intelligence. They had IQs far exceeding his own and both were very well read. Christina was the prime botanist and she was always upgrading the garden. Daniel liked smart women and his Volva had the best of all combinations; brains and beauty. All in all, now that he could communicate with his hostesses, the experience at the temple enriched him more than anything he had ever been a part of.

One morning, Anna took his studies a step further. She had noted that he wasn't controlling the voices in his head very well, even though he understood them better. She worried that this budding telepathy might still lead him to go mad as she remembered her own early experiences with the voices.

"You must identify and isolate our individual thought waves," she instructed. "As mine is the one you are most familiar with, it will be the easiest to identify. Marta is on the Array so her signal will be the strongest."

Daniel spent the rest of the week in deep meditation with Anna as she helped him identify her thoughts and the thoughts of her sisters. One evening, while she was resting after her turn on duty, and long after Christina, his companion for the evening, had fallen asleep, Daniel found himself isolating a quiet, sweet signal. It was Anna's dream. She was dreaming of school and of a family she'd never had. Daniel was so excited he almost burst right out of his skin. He then drew his attention toward Christina. He was unfamiliar with her thought stream, but once he found what he was looking for, he had begun to master his powers.

Finally, in the early morning, he decided to try something truly daring. He concentrated on the large, amorphous signal coming off the Array. The signal was frightening at first, but as he searched for something he could concentrate on, he found what he believed to be the individual thought signal of the Volva on duty, Minh. As soon as he focused on her thought stream, the voices that had been plaguing him disappeared. He first embraced the pattern and felt it warm him all over, then decided to be more than a passive observer. He sent a message to Minh.

Minh was doing her usual routine, monitoring the thoughts of the Defenders in the field. Her fellow Volva were asleep and, although she occasionally allowed herself to drift in and out of their dreams, she was at this moment in a lull of cerebral activity. Suddenly, she was filled with a strange message. *Hi Minh, how is your night going?*

Who is sending this strange message? she thought. Finally, it dawned on her—she was telepathically communicating with Daniel! He had found the link and was now part of the Defenders' collective consciousness.

Welcome, Daniel! she exclaimed. *I did not expect you to be part of us so soon.*

Well, I could not sleep tonight so I just sort of figured it out, he communicated cheerily. *This is a weird experience, like walking through a tunnel and experiencing a new, tremendous view when you walk out through the other side. I'm having quite a rush.*

They communicated for a little while until Minh became concerned and warned him not to overdo it. What amazed Daniel the most was his ability to even see through her eyes. Exhausted, he fell asleep in Christina's arms.

Daniel was allowed to sleep in and awoke with Marta straddling him. At first, he thought she was in the mood to enjoy him physically. Then, with a large smile, she hugged him and telepathically shared the message that she was pleased with his progress. *You have become one of us. Anna has proven to be a good teacher. How does being part of our collective consciousness make you feel?*

Daniel had hoped to surprise his associates with his new powers, but as he now realized, what one knows, all know. *I feel as though I have been plugged into an electrical circuit. At least the voices have improved. Now, as I have identified each thought pattern, the voices seem controllable. For a while I thought I was going mad. Anna warned me of this, but until I truly experienced it, it was hard to imagine.*

In reality, you have now become plugged in, Marta explained. *Once you have become connected, you cannot disconnect. You must continue to identify all of us and then spend your energy sorting and controlling our signals in your mind. It can be a great deal of work. We will all do something to help you. I will show you and then you can visit each of us today and tomorrow. I think it would be better for you not to be with Anna until you are finished, as you already know her signal very well.*

With Daniel's consent she put her hands on the sides of his head and then held his hands so their starburst tattoos touched. Daniel closed his eyes. Suddenly his mind was filled with blackness and then with light as he was enveloped with Marta's thought energy. First he was in his mind, then in her mind. He felt her arms, her innermost female parts, everything, as if her feelings were his feelings.

Then he felt himself going back into his thoughts. It seemed the cerebral equivalence of sexual intercourse. Marta allowed him access to her most personal thoughts. All her memories suddenly became his memories, and he reciprocated. They shared passion, fear, childhood, warmth, and even experiences Daniel couldn't understand. By the time their telepathic ecstasy neared its end, Daniel had become imprinted on Marta's thought pattern.

"Wow! That was intense!" Daniel sighed out loud, feeling spent.

Marta repositioned herself so she was no longer straddling him. She was using a cloth to clean herself up. "I was glad to be able to share that with you. You now will have open access to everything I feel and think."

Daniel realized he must have become over-excited while they were communicating telepathically. He apologized for his bodily response to the mental excitement.

"Daniel." She paused and kissed him. "Why would you apologize for doing something natural? Your body desired the release. Nobody said life is not without a little messiness." She giggled. "Come and eat. You will need your strength today. The Volva are all eager to complete their mental bonds with you."

Daniel ate and then spent the rest of the day sharing his mind with Christina, Xu Li, Maria, Darna, and Ushenna. The next day he finished with Monique, Minh, Irena, and Astria. The experiences were similar to the one he'd had with Marta, and each left him with a strong telepathic bond. He soon felt as though he had twelve sets of thoughts instead of one.

Finally, Anna arrived and took him to bathe. It was obvious to Daniel that he would be spending the night with his woman. She already had a special bond with her male and soon after the bath, they entered each other's mind. But unlike the other Volva, she shared her body with him as well during the experience. For the first time Daniel was allowed to experience a female orgasm as well as his own. It was as intense an experience as he could imagine. Afterward, Daniel wanted more and Anna, in the Volva fashion, was all too willing to comply. Neither of them would sleep that night. Daniel found being in Anna's mind highly erotic, and Anna found it erotic that Daniel liked her thoughts and feelings so much.

This obviously had been Marta's plan. She knew as Daniel experienced Anna's telepathic bond, he would be too preoccupied with her to learn the others' thought patterns. Because he'd melded with the others first, he was now firmly embedded in the collective consciousness and a full-fledged member of the small band with a tremendous global responsibility. He had finished the circle of what he was to become. He still had much training ahead, learning to harness his powers, but he had made the jump from mere human to Defender and had crossed a one-way bridge. He was now fully subject to a different set of rules, ethics, language, history, and responsibilities.

As Daniel continued his training, other events were beginning to unfold. Taken individually they were seemingly unimportant and of no particular significance in the overall future of humanity. As such, they went unnoticed by the ever-observant members of Daniel's new Order. But they represented the tip of a potential iceberg. And like the iceberg that sank the Titanic, if this one was not averted, it could present a similar problem and sink humanity. The first noticeable manifestations of something suspicious became apparent in, of all places, Tortola.

CHAPTER 8: A Tiger in the Bushes

A hundred miles east of the island of Puerto Rico, located in the curve of the Lesser Antilles, are the fifty or so islands, islets, and cays that make up the British Virgin Islands. These volcanic remnants closely resemble their American namesakes but are much less populous; a quiet outpost of the British Empire. They are mountainous, covered with thick foliage, ringed by barrier reefs, blessed with fine, white-sand beaches, and surrounded by clear, azure-turquoise water. The license plates of the British Virgin Islands proclaim them Nature's Little Secrets.

The largest island, Tortola, has a population of twenty thousand people and contains the capital, Road Town. Tortola is named after the turtle dove and is the liveliest of the isles. There is special emphasis on sailing and water sports, although nature is the true star. The island is circled with narrow, steep roads with intermittent speed bumps to remind the residents to keep the pace of life slow.

Road Town is by far the least impressive port city in the Caribbean. It has all the traditional, Caribbean-style, brightly-colored shops, but it also hosts many large banks, the number of which is disproportionate to the amount of industry and people on the island. It is also the home to over two hundred fifty thousand international business companies. On a per-capita basis, that's more than ten companies per resident. Because of special laws enacted in the territory since 1984, the British Virgin Islands have become a favorite location of offshore finance, tax avoidance and, in some cases, more suspicious activities. The government fees alone from these companies represent fifty percent of the annual budget of the whole territory. This, along with banking, property management, and extra business visitation, represents a substantial part of the economy.

One of these international business companies is named Aracari Holding Company, something of an oddity since it actually has an office located in the territory. The second story office is located in a weathered yellow building between the post office and the folk museum on the narrow Main Street. Most of the traffic moving through Road Town was long ago re-routed onto Waterfront Drive, located one block to the east. Other than the rare delivery vehicle, Main Street is generally a pedestrian affair, mostly traversed by tourists on day trips into the city from cruise ships docked a few blocks away. The cruise ships can be seen from the only window of the five-by-eight-meter Aracari Holding Company office space.

AHC is in the ship chartering business. It operates through a subsidiary based in Barbados and other locations that receive orders for shipments, some large and some small. The company arranges for a ship to pick up and deliver cargo at the desired ports. AHC has a wide range of international contracts and no shortage of business.

Its president, a local forty-two-year-old named John Williams, manages Aracari. He lives with his wife and three children in a modest house on the other side of Road Town and drives a small Daewoo SUV. Otherwise he lives like most of the islanders he grew up with. He went to college across the Sir Francis Drake Channel in St. Thomas in the U.S. Virgin Islands. At the University of the Virgin Islands, he majored in finance, then began his working career as an accountant.

The AHC office is conservative. It contains two desks, two computers, a pair of fax machines, and has posters of important-looking places covering the walls. The occupant of the other desk is the company treasurer, Clive Edwards. He's in charge of keeping the company's books. Both are paid handsomely for their duties. Mr. Williams is paid one hundred twenty thousand dollars per year and Mr. Edwards is paid sixty thousand dollars per year.

Both men know the finances of the company intimately. AHC has a tremendous turnover for such a spartan operation. Their fax machines and e-mails cough up a surprisingly large number of orders. Despite the heavy volume, the company's margins are tight, showing a very meager profit after expenses. Somewhat surprising to Mr. Williams, he receives no complaints from the owner of the company.

The attorney representing the owner is Mr. Li of Macao. Macao is a former Portuguese colony just off Hong Kong that has recently been returned to China. Mr. Li has just given the pair of AHC managers a slight raise and a three-year contract renewal.

John Williams takes pride as the president of the operation. He had worked an extra hour each day for the past three weeks to try and secure inter-island business in the Caribbean basin to bolster the company's finances. He had been surprisingly lucky and had secured three small contracts that were more profitable than all the rest of the company's contracts. In their monthly phone conference with Macao, Li had been surprised at this revelation and had awarded the men a large bonus that matched the profit of the combined contracts. Mr. Williams was slowly becoming suspicious that profit was not the sole motive of Aracari Holding Company.

Who was its owner? And who was this mysterious Mr. Li? The pair had never met their boss, and as far as they knew he had never visited the island. The stock in the company was twenty thousand American dollars' worth of bearer shares. The shares weren't issued to any specific owner, just to whoever held the certificates. The company was formed over the telephone through Tom Jenkins, the lawyer who had the office downstairs, and Williams and Edwards had been hired over the phone through ads in the local paper, *The Bee*. Jenkins had drawn up the required paperwork as he was instructed. He knew nothing about the company either, but in Tortola, it was rare for anyone to ask too many questions. For the majority of people doing business here, secrecy was the prime concern. Loose lips lost jobs, and word traveled fast in such a small place. Williams and Edwards were too ingrained in this belief and had much too good of a deal going to think anything about it. Williams' wife wanted him to buy a new Toyota, and the extra bonus money would come in handy.

But Williams and Edwards also had a secret they hadn't shared with Li. As was typical with a society initially based on piracy, both men had answered a second ad in the local paper. Only a limited number of qualified people were available in Road Town, so a second international company was based out of the same office, International Pharma Research Limited. In the official corporate documents, the company listed its president as Clive Edwards, and its treasurer was none other than John Williams. When the phone rarely rang for either company, Williams would answer for IPRL and Edwards would answer for AHC. Their involvement with the second company wasn't free either. Edwards charged a salary of one hundred thousand dollars a year and Williams drew a little over sixty thousand dollars. They definitely had a good thing going. Jenkins even got in the act and charged both companies full rent for the same office. He called one Suite 2A and the other 2B. They all were profiting due to the lack of oversight from the lax ownership of the companies. The men treated it all as part of the service they provided.

IPRL was an even larger enterprise than Aracari Holding Company. They received government research grants and monies to develop various vaccines and drugs. Countries as diverse as Syria, Iraq, Iran, Yemen, Ethiopia, Eritrea, Albania, Myanmar, Afghanistan, Liberia, and even Libya frequently used the company to do their state microbiological and virology research. IPRL, in turn, subcontracted the research to other companies located all over the globe. Although neither Williams nor Edwards knew anything about the success of the company, they figured the continual receipt of grant monies was proof enough of the stability of the enterprise and concluded that IPRL had extensive expertise in research. They believed the research director, Professor Mohamed Khan, was a Pakistani. He talked to them rarely and drew a research salary that they wired to various international banks. He was frequently on the road, supervising research experiments. Khan had never visited Road Town, and they suspected he had no immediate intention to do so. Their secret of double dipping was safe.

The sign on the door said Aracari Holdings Limited, but a sign for International Pharma Research Ltd. was stashed in the closet. Despite the self-serving nature of their management, the pair did a good job and both were exceedingly honest with their company's money. There was an old saying on the island that one should aspire to be an honest thief, and honest thieves they were. They even switched the signs every other week or so in an attempt to give each business equal billing.

Life in the little office was relatively easy. The morning started at nine o'clock sharp. Each day, they brokered a few charters, the majority of which were prearranged. Faxes were sent between offices to seal the deal. Each day one of the men made a trip to the local banks while the other went to the post office. They alternated the duties every other day. They usually ate lunch at the restaurant near the marina, more often than not, with their landlord, Jenkins. They kept a running tab for the usual hour-and-a-half affair. Friday was office supply and cleaning day. Both men liked walking into a well-supplied, clean office on Monday morning. They never wavered from their unhurried, unstructured pace.

November brought a sense of calm to the island due to the end of the hurricane season. No major storms had found their way to terrorize any of the islands lining the Sir Francis Drake Channel.

Tourism projections had been dire, but so far the arrivals were better than expected and cruise ships were still frequenting the port. Much-anticipated reforms of offshore banking had been announced, but the British Virgin Islands were left unscathed by the watchful eyes of the American tax authorities. Little terrorism money was found in the large local banks, so the CIA had turned their attention toward other jurisdictions, such as the micro-republic of Nauru in the South Pacific. Everyone on the island expected a wonderful Christmas and an even better new year.

November fifth was a relatively slow day at the office. The evening produced a lone fax, so there was little to do. Edwards was ill, so Williams had given him the day off. The orders on the fax were simple, and as Williams had performed the task many times in the past, he knew the routine. The fax read:

Client: Frozen Arrow Exporting, Ltd.
Cargo: Cement, packaged, 22,000 metric tonnes
Shipment date: December 7th from Hamhüng, North Korea
Destination: Sana'a, Yemen
Specifications: Ship to self-unload the cargo at port
Preferred Shipper: Golden Yangtze Shipping, Ltd.
Terms: Usual plus 5% for late request

These were all familiar terms to Williams. Frozen Arrow was a frequent client; a Bahamas-based company that they used occasionally for pre-packaged cement. Williams suspected aggregates were not their main business, but he had only communicated with them via fax. He thumbed through the Golden Yangtze information. They had a Nauru return number and probably were part of a larger organization, with each ship owned by a separate company. Williams was unsure of where exactly Nauru was, but he assumed it was near Asia as many of his shipments to Asia used banks and companies registered out of that jurisdiction. Maybe he would take his family there on his next vacation. He thought he could call it a business trip, but any thought of vacation would have to wait until his kids were out of school for the summer break.

He made the required fax to Golden Yangtze and received a reply in a half-hour, telling him the So San would be available and that the spot rate was quoted as the price. Williams faxed back the official request. The confirmation returned in ten minutes. The promptness of the replies didn't bother him, considering it was nearing midnight in Nauru at the time of the request. He simply assumed that people worked longer hours in the mysterious republic.

His booking arrangement with Frozen Arrow required two sets of faxes with releases, contracts, contingencies, and other paperwork. With the paperwork complete, he faxed a copy of the contract to Nauru and the deal was sealed. His morning's work completed, he went out to get a new supply of coffee. Edwards had forgotten to replenish the supply during his trip on Friday.

* * * * *

It was early December and Captain José Maria Flores de Santiago was at the bridge of the *Navarro*, a one hundred thirty-eight-meter frigate of the Armada Española, the Spanish Navy. The day was beginning to break and Captain Santiago had just sent his first officer to bed. The *Navarro* had entered the Gulf of Aden after steaming all night through the Red Sea to replace the *Victoria*, which had been on duty in the area for the last six months. The crew of the *Navarro*, two hundred twenty-five sailors and Marines, had left their home port of Rota, Spain, just four days earlier, and Captain Santiago had welcomed numerous new sailors who would gather needed experience during the coming assignment.

The world was at peace, but the tensions in the Persian Gulf were high. America was threatening Iraq with an invasion, and concerns over terrorism had mobilized the various navies of NATO to patrol strategic areas in search of weapons of mass destruction. The *Victoria* had inspected a few ships, but so far nothing of substance had been turned up. It was the stance of the Spanish high command to avoid any rude interference in legal commerce and intended the *Navarro* to be on more of a training voyage than a proxy for American aggression toward Iraq.

The *Navarro* passed the Yemeni trading ship, the al-Mandab, a small ferry and supply ship that traded between Al-Marka, Yemen, and Djibouti. Captain Santiago slowed to allow two of his crew to scan the ship. They observed nothing out of the ordinary, so he ordered the seaman at the helm to steer the *Navarro* out into the open ocean. They would soon be in the main shipping lanes. The captain had decided that they would practice charting and intercepting ships by sight and radar.

It was just a little after high noon. Santiago's radar operator, navigator, and helmsman were all raw seamen. Other than the captain, none of the sailors on the bridge had any significant experience at sea. Suddenly a blip appeared on the radar screen—a freighter slightly larger than the *Navarro*. The captain ordered a mock attack run and powered the twin LM 2500 GE/Bazán gas turbines up to full speed. She was soon doing close to thirty knots.

"What's she doing, Hernandez?" the captain asked his radar operator.

Hernandez had spent a lot of time in a simulator and was proficient at this task. "Nineteen knots, Sir, heading due north, range thirty-two point four kilometers."

Santiago then ordered his navigator to start plotting the *Navarro's* course in relation to the freighter's course. "Our heading?"

Sanchez was busy cleaning the map and was late in his reply. "Five degrees east of south."

Santiago ordered them to maintain the current heading until they were just about even with the ship. Then he would turn his ship ninety-five degrees and close the range. Correct procedure would be for him to approach a slower ship from the rear. If this were a real encounter, a freighter's only offensive capability would be ramming, and by the time it would be able to turn around, he could disable the pilothouse from this approach. But it was all going to be just navigational training anyway, so he wasn't as concerned about procedure as he would be normally.

At the captain's mark they made the big turn to starboard and headed toward the phantom ship. Since she was still twenty-two kilometers off, they still couldn't see their quarry on the high seas. Five minutes later, the phantom ship turned a full one hundred sixty degrees astern and was now heading away from the *Navarro*. Hernandez was off getting some coffee and wasn't paying close attention to the radar screen.

The range had grown to over thirty kilometers before he notified Santiago. "She's reversed course, sir. She's heading perpendicularly away from us."

The captain scolded his seaman's inattention and ordered a ninety-degree turn to port. The frigate was soon gaining ground on their quarry again. It seemed odd to him that a cargo ship would change course so radically in the open ocean.

Five minutes later, Hernandez interrupted his thinking. "She's turned ninety degrees to starboard again."

Santiago matched the change and an odd feeling appeared in the pit of his stomach. He grabbed the intercom. "First and second officers to the bridge. Ensign Ramirez to the bridge, on the double!"

The crew on the bridge was momentarily stunned. Had they done something wrong? Nobody had suspected anything odd from their phantom quarry.

"Helmsman, match that ship turn for turn. I want her in my sights within a half-hour."

His officers arrived running and unkempt—they had been sleeping. After the captain briefed the officers, he sent the ensign to the crow's nest to get a look at their quarry. It still might be nothing, but he wanted his top men on watch in case something developed.

At eighteen kilometers, Ramirez's voice filled the two-way radio. "She's a freighter all right. Nothing looks out of place. I'll keep an eye on her."

The captain planned to pass the freighter a few hundred yards to port to get a good look at her and see what was up. The distance closed, and at one kilometer Ramirez's voice again filled the bridge. "We've got a problem, Sir. She doesn't have a flag. In fact, it looks as though the name has been removed from her stern and bow."

Santiago took the inter-ship radio and turned the frequency to the maritime setting. "SNS *Navarro* to the unflagged cargo ship in the Gulf of Aden, please identify yourself." No answer. He repeated the message two more times in English as well as Spanish. No reply. He grabbed his binoculars and looked the ship over. There was much activity on deck—too much activity. He even saw two men trying to hoist a flag. He watched as they fumbled and accidentally threw a Cambodian flag overboard, and then he saw a whole pile of different flags. They were trying to look legit. He was closing fast, too fast. The freighter suddenly turned away from its pursuer and the captain became more alarmed. He had an unflagged, unnamed ship only five hundred meters to starboard. It was probably a pirated vessel, and at this range even a shoulder-fired missile could be dangerous to him. He had to take action.

Santiago ordered his helmsman to turn away and he grabbed the intercom. "Battle stations, all hands! Battle stations! This is not a drill!" The sleepy ship lurched to life. He ordered boarding parties of Marines to the Sikorsky SH-60B helicopters on the aft deck. The teams were quickly assembled, wearing assault black complete with Kevlar vests and assault rifles. As soon as the twin choppers had cleared the ship, he turned again toward the freighter. The choppers would await his orders. He didn't want his aircraft hurt in an exchange of fire.

He had the radio operator transmit a message to both the Spanish admiralty and NATO command:

SNS Navarro, 400 miles off the Horn of Africa in international waters. Have encountered a suspected pirated freighter with suspicious activity. They have refused orders to stop and identify themselves. We are taking action to engage and board the vessel. If she shows hostile action, we will disable her.

Capt. Santiago

As the distance closed he ordered a shot fired over the bow of the freighter. The freighter again turned away. Santiago got back on the radio. "SNS *Navarro* to unflagged, unnamed vessel. Stop and be boarded!" No reply. The sixty-two-millimeter cannon fired another warning. Again Santiago called to the ship, and again received no reply.

Finally, Santiago, now angry, radioed the ship. "Unflagged vessel, if you are not dead in the water in thirty seconds, we will take out your pilothouse and I will not be responsible for casualties."

For an instant, nothing changed. The guns on the *Navarro* fixed on their target. Just when Santiago was about to back up his threat, wisdom prevailed and the mystery ship slowed to a halt. The choppers were called forward and the Marines were deployed onto the cargo deck of the ship.

Despite some tense moments, no shots were fired. Crewmen on the cargo ship scurried like cockroaches being chased with a light. Nobody was armed, and a captain, a first officer, and twenty-two crewmen were soon held at gunpoint. The Spanish captain went over personally to check out the situation. Why hadn't the ship stopped? What was the precious cargo?

In moments, Santiago was getting answers; all kinds of answers. The captain of the phantom ship had a North Korean passport. The first officer spoke broken English and babbled something about cement, Yemen, and an illegal search. The ship was identified as the *So San*. The ship's manifest and log were located and then located again as there were two sets. In fact, Santiago suspected they also had a third set, the real one. It had probably been thrown over the side during the chase. Were they carrying weapons of mass destruction or nuclear material? With North Korea involved and with them developing nuclear arms, Santiago decided he would let the Americans be the heroes. They could come and inspect the ship so it could then be their international incident. He would prefer training exercises to this kind of action.

Santiago held the ship until an American frigate joined the intervention. A hazardous inspection team began to search the ship. Both navies moved their valuable property a safe distance away from the captured ship in case there might be some sort of trap. No trap was found, but under bags of cement was some interesting contraband—fourteen North Korean SCUD missiles along with highly explosive chemicals that could be used as warheads. Had the *So San* been flying a flag, any flag, the *Navarro* would have just steamed by.

As it turned out, the SCUDs were not bound for Iraq and were not to be implements of terrorism. They had been legally sold to the army of Yemen. The ship was released and the cargo unloaded at Sana'a, Yemen, the next day. This ship did, however, reveal something of importance. It provided an interesting clue to the Americans, a clue which was passed on to the San Juan office of the

CIA. The captain had forgotten to remove a fax—a shipbroker's request for a cement transport dated November fifth from an outfit named Aracari Shipping Ltd. out of Barbados. The return fax number indicated a British Virgin Islands exchange. Obviously, the Barbados connection was a dead end. A CIA agent, Tim Spires, was dispatched to the tiny Caribbean island of Tortola.

* * * * *

Spires had been with the Agency for only fourteen months, and since everyone was preoccupied with other, more pressing targets, he had been chosen for this, his first field assignment. As an expert in banking fraud and money laundering, he had been on the phone many times with members of the British Virgin Islands and British authorities, so his superior had assumed he was an expert on the small island territory. He would meet a member of the British government and they would poke around for clues.

Just as Spires suspected might happen, the government travel office made a mistake and his flight went to St. Thomas. He had learned before that in cases such as this it would be better for him just to take the flight and wing it from there, because he might not get reimbursed for out-of-pocket expenses otherwise. His flight to St. Thomas was only a thirty-minute hop. At the airport he grabbed a taxi that would take him to the ferry terminal at Red Hook. It would cost him thirty dollars and take almost forty minutes to traverse the narrow, hilly roads to the other side of the island. The ferry to West End, Tortola would cost him another fifty dollars, and to his surprise he realized he would only have four hours on the island before he needed to return. The Agency hadn't budgeted for overnight accommodations, so he needed to get his job done quickly. If he missed the return trip, the hotel bill would be his responsibility. At least his British contact would expedite customs.

The trip to Tortola was beautiful. He was able to see the whole expanse of St. John's. He saw the numerous rocks and cays that made up the archipelago. It seemed like it would make a good vacation spot. He noted the azure blue color of the water as the ferry neared the small British port called West End. Unfortunately he was wearing a gray suit and tie on a ninety-degree day, and he was on business. He ignored the stares from the few tourists and native islanders. They all agreed that he was either a cop or a member of the IRS. No white man traveled to Tortola wearing a business suit.

The boat turned into the colorful ferry terminal. Spires disembarked on a cement pier and entered the yellow and brown customs station. He waved his diplomatic pass and passport, and the blue uniformed customs officer waved him through. The customs officer pointed to another man who looked just as out of place chatting with a luggage inspection agent.

Jim Hilliary introduced himself to Spires as the British agent in charge of fraudulent activity. They boarded a Mitsubishi truck and drove along the coast toward Road Town.

"I took the liberty of doing some of your homework for you, old boy," Hilliary said. "This Aracari Company has been around for about four years. They actually have an office here. A very trustworthy chap named Williams runs it. I don't know who the owners are, as they use bearer shares. The three directors are Williams, the treasurer—a fellow named Edwards, and one of our barristers named Jenkins. We've never had a reason to suspect them before. I fear we're barking up the wrong tree here as I think they were just unwitting dupes in the whole SCUD affair."

"How much information can we force them to give us?" Spires asked.

"Not much. We have no probable cause and no intent to deceive. Even with the SCUDs involved, since this was a legal shipment with legal buyers, I can't force them to divulge much of anything. They are honest, hard-working chaps; I suspect they'll cooperate. In fact, you'll find the British Virgin Islands are filled with honest, hard-working people. We are not a land of tax cheaters like your IRS believes."

They drove into Road Town, parked the car, crossed a ditch, and ducked under a bunch of tropical bushes, exiting onto Main Street. They found the address and climbed a set of stairs to an office bearing the sign Aracari Holding Company. A second sign stated Out to Lunch—Back at 1:30.

"Looks like we're off to lunch, Spires." Hilliary seemed unfazed. "I know a nice place on top of the old Fort Burt. Consider it a treat of our government. We have a standing reservation and it has a wonderful view."

The food was a welcome change from the usual Spanish fare Spires had been eating since his arrival in San Juan. They returned to the Main Street office at 1:45, but the door was still locked. Such was island time. Spires was starting to grow concerned that his time was running short. At 2:05, two well-dressed black men joined them at the office door.

"I'm John Williams. Can I help you?"

Spires introduced himself; the men already knew Hilliary. They had also heard of the arrival of Spires when they were at lunch. He had been fingered as a U.S. banking agent, and word of such arrivals traveled fast in such a small place. They hadn't expected him to be at their door since they were not a bank. They rarely did business through any U.S. bank or with any U.S. company, so they had little to hide from the U.S. agent.

"Come in and sit down," Williams offered. "I'll have Edwards find you some coffee, or would you prefer tea?" They both asked for coffee, so Edwards brought four coffees.

"Now, how can I help the American government?" Williams said.

"You chartered a ship last month, Hamhüng to Yemen," Spires said. He showed them the copy of the fax. "The ship was carrying a hidden cargo of SCUD missiles."

Williams paused and checked his records. "We brokered the charter. I have the same fax—yes, that's ours. Cement . . . no record of SCUDs . . . I guess they added some extra cargo. We should have charged them more for the hazardous cargo." Everyone laughed. "Saw that whole deal in the news. But I thought the entire shipment was legal. What's the beef?"

"Just following up," Spires said quietly. "Who ordered the charter? We've also been trying to track the payment for those missiles. You'd think that at half a million dollars per missile, you could track seven million dollars."

"You know, I don't have to tell you," said a cool Williams. "But it's nothing sinister. It's a company based out of the Bahamas. They ship packaged cement through us all the time. It's called Frozen Arrow Shipping. In fact, we received another request today." He held up the fax. "Eighteen thousand tons from Russia to Iran. I think someone borrowed some space. I'd check with the ship owner, Golden Yangtze."

"Already did," revealed Spires. "They don't exist anymore. The ship was leased. It was basically abandoned in Yemen, and the crew disappeared. The real owner turned out to be a Japanese bank. Yemen is allowing them to retrieve it."

Spires looked at his watch. He needed to go or he'd never make the ferry back to the U.S. Virgin Islands. He thanked his hosts and had Hilliary drive him back to West End.

The only relevant conversation about the matter on the way back was a simple comment by Hilliary. "Seems to have been a waste of your day. It was a good lunch though, a bloody good lunch. I hope I'll have the opportunity to see you again over here. We always love to help the Americans. Maybe I can be of more help next time."

The official investigation of the affair was over.

On the third of January, an apparently unrelated event occurred in the accounts of Williams' other company. A seven point four million dollar grant for research was received from the government of Yemen. Any possible correlation between Yemen and the seven million dollars and the Spires investigation went unnoticed. Edwards just logged the revenue into the books and wired five million dollars to a Belize bank account under the title of the "Vaccine Research Center, Ltd., a division of Western Caribbean Pharmaceuticals" as he had done many times before. He was late for lunch and had to get this done before he could leave. It was going to be another lazy day in Road Town, Tortola, British Virgin Islands.

* * * * *

January third was also a nice day in Pyongyang, North Korea. This city was not a major center for banking, commerce, or power. On top of one of the city's largest buildings was the spacious penthouse office of a sinister and powerful fellow. The man was not a political leader. He liked to work in the background, and he was largely unknown outside his universe. He carried the rank of general but he wore no uniform. In fact, he wore a simple two-hundred-dollar suit and fifty-dollar shoes. He rarely even wore a hat. He was called by his trade name, Tiger.

Tiger looked out across the city. From his office he could see all the buildings, the mountains, the airport, the seat of government—everything in this small, seemingly insignificant country was literally under his watchful eye and control. He was the judge and benefactor, and whatever he wanted, he got.

The man was no giant at only about five-foot-four and weighing maybe one hundred forty pounds. His hair was graying slightly. He had a tattoo of an attacking tiger on his shoulder. Very few people still alive knew of its existence. It was from his former army days, and he never showed it to anyone.

He was well read and educated in both Eastern and Western traditions. He was a concrete man, so he believed in what he could see. He didn't believe in luck or fate. Things were as he made them. He believed in work, study, and preparedness. He trusted his enemies more than his friends; therefore, he had few of the latter as most of them had been killed. He believed in his own theory of society, which he had tested in his domain for the last twenty years. It was a theory that had proven surprisingly effective, and in due time, the world would see what he had created. Meanwhile, he looked forward to watching CNN's account of the upcoming war in Iraq. He also looked forward to furthering his education, and he firmly believed real history was the best teacher.

Tiger wasn't a businessman either, at least in the true sense. Nor was he wealthy, although he was never in want. He ate what he desired. He slept with any resident, male or female, that he chose. He even possessed the power to choose who lived and who died. He seemed to have almost divine powers, yet he was no god. He had no religious affiliation whatsoever. He felt that religion was a waste of resources and of his and his people's energy. Ostentatious appearances were also wasteful. His office contained his only known material possessions, a small collection of models.

He marveled at his successes of the past years as he watched the beautiful sunrise. He had big plans and anticipated the complete success of his master plan, although its full potential was still a couple of years away. The world would be his. He had begun a chain of events that would ensure his ultimate success.

Olaf Danielson

He looked at his collection of models, which he had assembled on the table. They comprised an eclectic, seemingly unrelated collage of technology and architecture. He picked up a model of a 747 with a TWA logo. He smiled at a model of a modern-looking U.S. warship and another of an oil tanker with a small French flag. The table also contained models of four U.S. fighter planes, two identical, each with differing tail markings, and one C-130 cargo plane. There were architectural models each about three feet in height. One depicted the World Trade Center towers. He ran his fingers over the top few stories and, after enjoying the tactile feeling, moved two of four small 757 models in front of the buildings. One was a United plane and the other was an American Airlines plane. He also placed one near the model of the Pentagon. The other he placed near a Swiss Air 747 model. He also had models of what looked like a U.S. embassy, a postal building, an unknown hotel, and a multitude of Middle Eastern buildings.

He walked along the interior wall of his office, the only one without windows. On this wall, he had hung many certificates and pictures. The individuals pictured were all once-famous people who were now deceased. Some had been killed and some had died of natural or unknown causes. He also had electron micrographs of numerous microorganisms labeled anthrax, West Nile virus, and monkeypox. One was not labeled. Upon looking at that one, he smiled before walking back to his desk. The desk was mahogany and contained nothing but a statue of a single, multicolored bird. The statue was over eighteen inches tall and dominated the otherwise barren desktop. The black, yellow, and red tropical bird seemed out of place on the desk of a man whose office was located in a decidedly non-tropical location. The bottom of the statue contained a single word. It was the name of a beautiful bird with the stout, toucan-like bill: Aracari.

CHAPTER 9: Tanoka

Daniel had learned the Old Language well enough so he could browse through the archives without assistance. The hardest thing he had to do to read the archives was turn on the cerebrally-controlled lighting. Of late, however, thanks to help from Anna, he had even mastered that skill. It was his first real use of his new connection to the Conduction Array. Truly, the lighting and heating of the temple was a marvel of technology. Deep inside the temple, underneath the Array, was a sort of generator. Daniel had found the schematics of the complex machine and learned that it used a technology that had since been lost. It had been the main source of electrical energy for the Martians.

The generator used multiple Helmholtz Resonators; round, hollow spheres that were tuned to the same frequency as the natural vibrations of the earth. These allowed the amplification of natural vibrations to produce more energy. The excess energy was then sent into separate copper filaments deep in the walls of the temple, which were connected to phosphorescent chambers in rocks in the ceiling. These stones, once excited by the electricity, illuminated the room or hallway. The lighted rocks had thus far lasted for twelve thousand years. The reactors were also the power source that the Martians used to power the massive earth shift that had resulted in the great cataclysm leading to the end of the last Ice Age.

While looking into the history of the generators, Daniel came across something truly interesting: these reactors had been used in other locations as well. One location seemed obvious. The Martians had used a large system based in the Great Pyramid in Giza. Daniel was no expert in physics, but it seemed to him that the energy output of that system was much larger than that of a traditional power plant. The tremendous energy was used to communicate with the Red Planet, to supply the energy needs for the massive construction of the Defenders' temples, and possibly even to protect the earth from incoming asteroids. It was apparent that the full potential of the three pyramids had never been realized.

What astonished him most was the location of the Defenders' temple in North America. As he read, he learned that it was the final one of the four that had been constructed. He had supposed that a temple might exist in Central America or Mexico, but this temple was located off the Florida coast on the island of what was now called Bimini. The temple was originally built to be the greatest of all the temples, but unfortunately its usefulness lasted less than four thousand years. It was built too close to the ocean, and as the glaciers melted, the sea rose over three hundred feet, and the entire temple went under water. It had been abandoned long before its end and all the inhabitants had relocated to the temple where he now was. The Bimini temple had a rectangular enclosure with a stone pyramid at its center. Stone roads had led from a protected harbor to the temple. Numerous people had lived near the temple, just like in Ethiopia, and helped support the ancient Volva.

Anna informed Daniel that the temple had been left mostly intact and that, even though it was covered by sand and many feet of water, news of any exploration in the area should be watched closely so that neither it nor its technology fell into non-Defender hands. The archives stated specifically that the penalty for tampering with the temple would be immediate death. The site was still marked by a pavement of flat rectangular and square stones on the west side of the north island of Bimini. At one end of the path a stone obelisk served as both a warning and a marker; the pyramid stood at the other end.

Even though the text was thousands of years old and even though the beaches near the site were frequented by thousands of tourists, nobody had yet discovered that the geological offshore oddity marked a significant archeological remnant of an earlier time. All of this history lay just fifty miles east of Miami. Daniel knew they didn't have to worry about the site being discovered. Nobody would believe it was anything important even if it was found since it didn't fit the current archeological model.

The temple's demise also suggested why North and South America had been thrown into the dark ages for thousands of years until the Incans, Mayans, and Aztecs reawakened civilization in the western hemisphere. The Defenders purposely put the area into disarray because it would be difficult for them to adequately observe the region. Once they left, they knew it might be some time before they could comfortably come back. Primitive people didn't cause significant problems. It would be over five thousand years before any significant Defender presence would grace the western hemisphere.

Daniel was also progressing with learning how to harness power from the Conduction Array and think telepathically. He spent his days practicing this power and in meditation to try to organize his mind so as to handle all the Volvas' thoughts that were now so much a part of him.

Anna approached him one morning while he was sitting in the garden. "Daniel, I think today would be a good day for you to meet Tanoka. I think your ability is now good enough to communicate with him. I fear he hasn't long in this life, and he has extensive knowledge to share with you."

They walked to a room at the end of the hall of personal sleep rooms. A silk curtain covered the doorway. Anna drew back the curtain and Daniel entered the room. Sitting up on the bed was an ancient man. He had gray hair and extremely wrinkled skin. He looked as old as any human Daniel had ever met. He was of east Asian descent and in many ways was a much different sort of man than Daniel, but he bore the same markings and, despite his outward appearance, carried an air of dignity.

Daniel could tell that Tanoka was aware of his entrance. He was nearly blind, but his connection was strong and so was his telepathic awareness. Daniel sat next to him and Anna placed Tanoka's weathered hands on Daniel. Tanoka moved his hands over Daniel's face. He was seeing him with his fingers and using Anna's eyes to study his newest partner. Without talking, Anna told Daniel she would be back later. She wanted to give them plenty of time alone.

It was some time before Daniel and Tanoka communicated. Finally Tanoka broke the silence of thought. *Mensooree, Daniel. In my language that means welcome, come in and relax. I have been monitoring your progress. It has been some time since we've welcomed someone new to our ranks. I think you will make a fine addition. You have characteristics that will serve us well.*

Thank you, sir, thought a reverent Daniel. *I will try my best to uphold to ideals of the Order.*

First of all, Daniel, I am just as you. Please speak to me as

*an equal. I am not your superior. We both have slept with the
Volva. We share the same virus, the same marks, and ultimately
the same fate: death. Our only difference is perspective. I am
looking into the past and you are looking to the future. Call me
Tanoka.*

I appreciate you accepting me as I am, thought Daniel.

That is all any of us can hope to be. Tanoka had never been
a man for pleasantries and he had much to share. *I see in your
thoughts that you have been researching our origins, our roots.
That is very good, as we cannot know where to go unless we
know where we have been.*

*I found the history of the old temple in North America fas-
cinating. I have also been marveling at the unique design of
our generators.*

*Who would guess at such a powerful archeological site
under the water of the Bahamas? You know, I know a lot about
the Asian temple.* Tanoka paused. *Where do you think I am from?*

You are Japanese.

*No. I would be Japanese now, but I am from the small is-
land of Yonaguni, between Formosa and Okinawa. That region was not part of the Japanese empire until 1889. We had
our own kingdom, even our own emperor. It was called the
Ryukyu kingdom. I was born in 1856 and I came here to the
temple to be initiated in 1880, well before the Japanese swallowed up my homeland. My family was mostly peasant fisher-
men. That is what I was trained to be. We caught gurakun, the
banana fish, and the staple of our diet. My native language is
Shuri, which compares to Japanese much like Norwegian compares to Swedish, but it is not probably as closely related. The
languages separated about fourteen hundred years ago. My
homeland was a powerful shipping center between China, Japan, Maori-Polynesians, and India. Okinawa was the business center of Asia, and for hundreds of years we had the
wealth of a merchant class.*

He paused for a moment. *That is why the Old Ones, the
Martians, chose my home island as the site of one of the temples.
Coincidentally, both of our homelands were the sites of an-
cient temples of the Defenders. As Anna originally shared with*

you, the Martians set a trap where the people over twelve thousand years ago built the Yonaguni temple. It was originally built as a monument that would be easily seen from the ocean so that anyone in the area sailing by would see it. It was part of the system that used the Earth's energy to cause a cataclysm that wiped out all but a few of us. It was used as one of the homes for the special people, us, the Defenders who would protect the rest of the people when the Old Ones died away.

Unfortunately, that temple met a similar fate to the temple in the Bahamas. It was built at nearly sea level. With the melting of the glaciers, and then with all the rain that followed, the ocean eventually rose over four hundred feet. The temple is now under a hundred feet of water. It has only recently been discovered. As is typical, nobody believes it is important. Again, he paused.

Daniel looked surprised. *I am equally surprised by a temple being on an island off Japan as a temple being on an island off Florida.*

The old man continued with the history of his homeland. *My culture has a current oral history of the old people. It was told to me as a child. This story concerns the Big Straw Sandals. My folklore has it that big straw sandals were set adrift on the sea in order to make pirates and enemies believe that giants lived on my island. These enemies would be scared away and would not invade us. For four thousand years nobody invaded the island.*

Daniel smiled. *Yours were a resourceful people.*

Tanoka went on. *Unfortunately, most of our historical structures were destroyed during World War II and the first forty years of Japanese rule, as my people tried to assimilate and become Japanese. When I die soon, I think seeing my home as it was in 1860 will be my goal for the afterlife.*

Daniel touched the man's hand. *Tanoka, I am sure you have been a treasure of wisdom in your old age.*

No, Daniel. There is no use for an old, worn-out Defender. We are people, you and I, designed for action. It may seem weird to you now, but your genetic makeup leaves you with a thirst to get in the middle of things. You will kill men. You will cause chaos, and you will create order to replace chaos. Just to sit here and rot the last few years is not something I would recommend, my friend. I came back here fifteen years ago to share the company of the women of my mind for the last time. Then I got a feeling that my replacement would be coming soon. So I allowed the women to continue to share the virus with me.

Daniel smiled as the old man continued. *You will see that the Volva will make sure you are always able to perform your duty. The ladies have spent these many years taking care of me and using their bodies to pleasure me and keep me happy. Pleasuring a woman at my age is like a miracle, you know. Now you are here and my journey in this world is nearing an end.*

Daniel was in awe of the great man. *I am sure you have much to share with me. You are so learned and experienced that I do not even know what to ask.*

My goal in seeing you was to impart to you some of my experiences, Tanoka said, getting to the meat of the day's lesson. *Remember who you are and where you came from, Daniel. In our society, the male and female roles are reversed. The Volva are creatures based on absolute power. They cannot lie or hide their feelings and they tend to look at things in a very black and white way. They also have been in isolation for most of their lives and have lost some of their ability to relate to the common person. You will understand more when you continue your training outside the temple. Your Volva guide will not react to people as you might expect. Any transgression toward the Volva will mean death, usually quick and painful. That is how they think. They are very concrete.*

We men, on the other hand, serve to soften their hard edges. We need to remember our humanity. Look out for the common man. Heal the sick and the infirm. You should protect the unprotected. By all means, we must find evil and corruption and stomp them out without mercy.

Should I fear our sisterhood?

No. The Volva simply are what they are. There is no sinister plot and there is nothing you have not been told. The Volva cannot harm us, nor we them. They are more powerful than us, but they have a difficult time functioning away from the sister-

hood. They have become used to collective thinking, and you will soon see that talking to one is like talking to the whole group. You never need to assemble them for a conference. They are constantly in each other's thoughts. With practice we learn to isolate their individual thoughts and continue with external input. They break their barriers so that each is part of a much larger consciousness.

Also, their love and affection for us is real. They have a great capacity to share emotions with us, their equals, but sometimes they have a little or no capacity for putting up with mere humans. They will make you very happy over the years, and I suspect you will die in Anna's arms after many glorious experiences. You will make the world a safer place and will be a fine member of our team. Of that I am certain.

What glorious experiences can you share, Tanoka? asked Daniel. He was becoming more comfortable with calling his elder by his first name.

To Daniel's surprised, Tanoka spoke aloud. "My life has been a busy one." He paused, thinking of some of his experiences. Daniel quickly absorbed these and Tanoka continued. "I have seen many wars that almost spelled the end of our society. The Russian-Japanese War early in the century proved to be a strange little confrontation. We suspected it would have spilled into Europe had Russia won or even if they had kept it close. We purposely dragged the battle on into a long, frustrating stalemate that cost the Russians plenty. The downside was that it gave the Japanese too much self-confidence, but their only real gain ended up being the southern half of Sakhalin Island. World War I was actually a good release for everyone. There was never any real danger of it leading to extinction or of one side taking over the world. The technology for real destruction had not yet been invented. The biggest problem initially was to keep the losses high enough in Europe to keep the risk of war on a grand scale lower later on. In that sense we were not at all successful.

"Early on we also needed to keep the Japanese and the Americans out of World War I. The Japanese almost caused a war when they sent their battle fleet into the Gulf of California in the spring of 1914. We used our powers to mask their ships, and I filled the

Japanese admiralty with doubt. They withdrew before anyone realized they were there. The Americans had already invaded Mexico, and with Germany on Mexico's side, adding the Japanese would have created a bigger, nastier conflict. I hate to say that twenty-one million deaths are insignificant, but it could have been forty or fifty million had war spread into Asia or the Americas.

We failed in the first war because we wrongly thought that with a big confrontation, the eagerness for death and destruction would subside. We read human nature wrong, and it only got worse. The Old Ones even sprung a viral trap, and with the close of the war the Spanish Influenza outbreak wiped out another twenty million. Even after all this death, World War II began anyway.

"In this war, all of the Defenders were busy—I spent the war in Japan. I confused a Japanese fleet in the Indian Ocean so they ended up not attacking Madagascar. I passed some information about the Japanese Midway campaign to the Americans. The Japanese had a tremendous problem during that period as they seemed to have a fatalistic way of looking at life. They did not believe in surrender, held no remorse for the tremendous loss of life, and held a seemingly skewed view of the rest of the world that made us all very nervous. They had developed a tremendous jet program and had an almost workable nuclear device. Despite the Japanese being backed into a corner, had the war progressed into 1946, it would have meant a nuclear holocaust and the loss of billions of lives. We allowed the Americans to bomb them, but we will not tolerate any more nuclear detonations after Nagasaki. I had to watch my homeland bombed, my relatives tortured and killed, and my old palace in Okinawa destroyed during the battle. It all still saddens me.

"During the Korean War, I was also busy. I stalled the North Korean advance and then stalled the American advance into China. I helped create the stalemate that is still going on today. I will say to you, Daniel, beware of the North Koreans. Everybody worries about the Americans, Chinese, or Moslem extremists starting something big. If they start something, however, it will be by accident. The Americans deserve our mistrust. Try to be objective in evaluating your homeland, but they seem more preoccupied with money than true imperialism. The Chinese too have found both imperialism and capitalism and they are becoming much too open to be plotting anything sinister. The Moslem extremists have money from oil and religious zealotry, but if the West gets smart and starts cutting off their money, the rulers in these places will respond to greed and crack down on the terrorists. That will keep them disorganized.

"The North Koreans, however, have a fifty-year-old plan for reunification. Everyone thinks they are starving, but I never trust a closed society. They could be planning something huge. If so, we won't know about it until it happens. I think the Russians used to rein them in somewhat, but 'Mother Russia' has been out of the loop these past ten years. I speak Korean, and I am the only Defender who does. For the next few days I want to impart to you this knowledge in case we ever need it. None of the other language skills I have are of much value. My native tongue will not help you. Japanese and Mandarin are known by others."

"How can I learn a language so fast?"

"Telepathy is a strange and powerful thing. Near our death we can impart certain memories, including languages, to a successor. That is why I wanted to meet you before I died. In this way we can be remembered and know that we will continue to be part of this great responsibility. To have someone care for your thoughts is, in a way, immortality."

Daniel bowed. *That is a great honor, Tanoka. There has been so much that I have been taught and shown, I am overwhelmed. How is this process done?*

It is nothing too complex or painful, but now I am tired. We will start the process tomorrow. Tanoka finished and Daniel's mind became silent.

Anna entered the room and gently kissed the old man, then tucked him back under the blankets. Daniel focused on Tanoka and saw that he looked pale and tired. The long conversation had taken a lot out of him. Anna dimmed the lights and signaled Daniel to leave with her. He followed her to the garden and into the hot pool where they had initially made love. Anna was still in a talkative mood and didn't look interested in anything else at the moment.

"Anna," Daniel said. "What did Tanoka mean by imparting memories?"

"I suspect he was describing what we can do near our death. It doesn't happen all that often with males because most males don't die in the company of another male Defender. We Volva often do it. We are selected to replace someone. After our training, we are given the gift of our predecessor's thoughts and memories. It has to be male-male or female-female. You can also select the memories and knowledge given to your successor. A lot of our thoughts are just junk, but certain experiences—your first kiss, your mom's face, your favorite dog, everything that makes you who you are— are passed on. It is a kind of immortality here on Earth. Part of me is Fareda, the Volva I replaced. I have some of her memories, her spirit so to speak, in me. You are lucky to have Tanoka here. I have always felt honored to have a little part of my teacher in me."

Daniel agreed and shared some of Tanoka's past with her, then summarized his mindset. "It scares me a little, I suppose, to have his thoughts in me. I'm getting used to carrying someone else's thoughts, but it scares me to look ahead. I look and see a life of responsibility, awesome responsibility. I had planned to live life as a western Nebraska rancher or maybe a businessman. I planned to marry a blonde-haired Swedish girl, have two children, and sit next to them in my modern sauna. I expected to grow old with my wife and eventually die in her arms. I wasn't born to be a hero or somebody important in the world. I was just born to be a nobody to the masses and important only to my family."

"Daniel," Anna interjected. "You are somebody and you were born to be a hero. We don't always have the luxury of planning who we are or what we are to become. A prince didn't choose to be born a prince, but someday he might become king."

"I know all that," Daniel replied. "But hearing Tanoka's stories, especially about the war, just overwhelmed me. I hope I can live up to the expectations everyone has in me."

Anna decided that Daniel needed to be reassured that he was a man and that she had faith in him. He was soon lost in the rapture of the spasms of her muscles, the embrace of her lips, and her wet, heaving chest. It was hard not to feel confident in her arms. She accepted him with such openness that soon Daniel was ready to take on the world. At least he felt ready that afternoon in her entangled embrace in the safety of a pool in the garden in the middle of the temple of the Defenders.

During the next few days, Daniel spent much time with Tanoka.

They shared thoughts, Tanoka gave advice, and they finished each day with their minds interlocked to exchange important bits of knowledge. Daniel had never experienced anything so easy, yet so complex. It was like downloading files on a computer. With each day, pieces of Tanoka's thoughts and experiences became Daniel's memories. He soon found himself enriched with another perspective on life. He began to understand how the Volva, even a young one like Anna, seemed to have so much wisdom.

Daniel also enjoyed the prepackaged training in Korean. It was a language type he had not yet experienced and, although he couldn't say for sure that he knew the language, he seemed to understand every word and phrase that Tanoka shared with him. He hoped he'd have a chance to use it.

On day five he found Tanoka full of life to a point that he hadn't previously seen. Daniel was spending the day with Irena since Anna was currently on duty. The old man desired to walk. With Daniel and Irena's help, he went on a little stroll. Although Tanoka couldn't see with his eyes, he was able to fully experience his surroundings by looking through Irena and Daniel's eyes. Tanoka asked Irena if she could take care of the preparations for a victory feast for that evening. Daniel realized today would probably be Tanoka's last in this world.

The threesome worked their way through the garden and back to the main greeting area. Then Tanoka communicated to both of them that he wanted to watch the Conduction Array for a while. They worked their way down the stairs and sat opposite Anna. Tanoka wanted the lights lowered for effect. Anna had her eyes closed and was sitting cross-legged on the copper bridge. Her palms were down, also making contact with the brown metal. She was bathed in the typical, now-familiar blue glow. Despite her apparent lack of attention, she was totally aware of the presence of three individuals in her chamber, but she was busy aiding a translation of a Chinese text between Xu Li and Carlos, the Brazilian member of the Order.

I would like to sit here for a while and watch, Tanoka telepathically told the pair. *Then I would like to have my victory feast. I think I would next like to have a fine bath with all the Volva, and finally I would like to request one of Minh's special massages. I have always thought it would be best to leave this life while being in the saddle.* He smiled. *That is, assuming Minh's powers are such to get a one hundred fifty-year-old man up and running.*

Tanoka, the local people are giving us a fine goat for the occasion, Irena replied. *I do not think Minh has ever failed in such a mission and with you concerned, I know she will be as sultry as ever.*

Daniel, observed Tanoka. *You have a fine Volva in Anna. She will be a blessing for you during those lonely days on the road. She will no doubt conceive. My dying prophecy will be that she will bear you a child. You two are the closest genetic and emotional match I have seen. She will also train you to be powerful and fair-handed.*

At that moment Marta came down the stairs to join the small group watching Anna. Tanoka continued his telepathic discussion. *I would like to talk with Marta now. Daniel, you should take Irena and enjoy each other. I will be here when you are done, and then we can have a long talk before the dinner this evening.*

Irena took Daniel by the hand and led him upstairs and toward her room. Daniel had no intention of making love with Tanoka's death at hand, but Irena had thoughts to the contrary. She was a dark-eyed beauty. Her Georgian descent and long limbs made her pleasing to the eye, and her skin was soft to the touch. It didn't take her much time to get Daniel up for his duty. He liked being with her and had learned certain activities that she especially enjoyed. After fulfilling their needs, the pair relaxed next to each other on the bed. Sex had become as much a telepathic exercise as a physical one, a fact that made the climaxes stronger and the releases greater. His difficulty with immediate post-coital movement allowed time for reflective conversation.

"What's a victory feast?" he asked aloud.

"A celebration of the life of one who is about to pass on to the next life," Irena said in the Old Language, still breathing heavily. "The villagers prepare their best food, and everyone eats. We toast the victor on his or her accomplishments, drink the best wine, and enjoy our last meal together in this life. Afterwards, he or she inspects the funeral pyre and then imparts his or her last wish. One of us assists in the quiet passage while we wait with the rest of the villagers outside the temple. Tonight it will not rain, and when the full moon is high overhead, Marta will lead in the funeral of Tanoka."

"How does he know he will die tonight?"

Anna answered for her sister. *Daniel, Tanoka's life is fulfilled. He has reached the conclusion of a wonderful and productive life. He has chosen tonight. Minh has been given the ultimate honor of assisting and comforting him. You will know when it is your time as well.*

"If one of you dies in battle or away from the temple, we have a victory feast in your honor, funeral pyre and all," Irena added. "It was a tradition that started with Freyja and Thor and has continued ever since."

The culture of the Defenders was shown again to be different than what Daniel was brought up with. He decided he had to think about the whole concept of euthanasia before he could accept it without question.

Wait until afterwards before you judge, concluded Anna. *Just appreciate the love and finality of it all before you make up your mind.*

Irena was soon distracting Daniel with her hands and tongue. They would complete another round of relations before Daniel could think further. Such was the level of passion they'd created. Anna seemed to be in Daniel's mind while Irena worked him over. This was a part of the culture that Daniel had accepted. This time when they finished, Irena kissed him gently and left. Daniel later stumbled down to rejoin Tanoka.

Tanoka was still sitting near the Conduction Array, as was Marta. She left on Daniel's arrival. The two men talked for almost two hours. It was going to be their last time alone together and both wanted it to be a fitting conclusion to their new friendship. Tanoka reassured Daniel about his upcoming victory. They talked about Defender strategy and about the Volva. They talked about Daniel's ongoing training and the use of his newfound power. They talked about politics, and Tanoka warned Daniel again to be wary of America, that he should be suspicious of his homeland most of all. Daniel was reminded that he was a Defender and no longer an American. Tanoka quizzed Daniel about his mastery of Korean until he was satisfied that his pupil was up to any challenge. They talked about life and finally they talked about death.

They watched as the changeover at the Conductor Array occurred. The strikingly beautiful East African, Astria, joined Anna on the Array. Anna, looking unconscious, was helped off the bridge and to her room for a much-needed rest by the loving hands of Maria and Darna. This was the one event where the men were not welcome, and through Daniel's eyes, they watched exactly as it had happened uninterrupted every eight hours every day for the past twelve thousand years. Tanoka added a narrative, reflecting on his final vision of the exchange. "I always thought the changeover would be a bigger deal than it is. I guess the Volva are so alike that the transition is smooth."

Finally, now that all of Daniel's questions were answered, Ushenna came and announced that it was early evening and the feast was ready. Tanoka's worn face showed a happy smile. Ushenna and Daniel helped the old warrior to the seat of honor at the victory celebration.

They sat in a circle on mats on the floor, and the food was laid out in front of them. Marta, being the eldest Volva, had the honor of serving all of her fellow Volva along with the two Defenders. The meal was a wonderfully prepared young goat, served with some native vegetables that Daniel hadn't tasted before. They were like sweet potatoes but somehow different. The finest fruits from the garden were also served, and each member of the banquet had a choice of their favorites from a large bowl that was passed around. They washed down the food with the finest wine Daniel had tasted outside of Europe.

During the meal, he watched Tanoka, who looked perfectly ecstatic. He dug at his goat like a man who hadn't eaten in years. Daniel learned from Maria's thoughts that all the fruits were Tanoka's favorites. After the feast, everyone took turns toasting Tanoka. When it was Daniel's turn he reviewed the highlights of his mentor's life, including his tributes, his trials, and his thoughts of the future. It was a happy and joyous celebration.

After the meal the gathering wandered down to the bathing pool. Daniel looked on while the women alternated seductively washing the old man. During this exercise, the Volva not currently involved in the bathing activities played musical instruments. The joyful tunes and the pleasant giggles of the Volva attending Tanoka had a powerful, soothing effect on Daniel's spirit, and he was starting to come around to this cultural celebration of death. Soon he was invited into the frolic as the women also took turns bathing him. The sensuality in the water was invigorating to his spirit. The women were playful and did not keep their hands to themselves.

Slowly, one by one, the women each spent some time with Tanoka. Daniel peered into their thoughts and noted each were sharing times previously enjoyed and saying their last good-byes to the noble man. He turned his cerebral attention elsewhere, because he viewed these parting good-byes as a purely private matter. Each Volva seductively washed Tanoka during the telepathy and each concluded her private session with a prolonged embrace. Daniel almost felt out of place as he realized most of these women had known Tanoka for over a hundred years and had known him carnally countless times as well. He watched the process repeat nine times, with all the Volva involved except Anna and Astria, the latter on duty and the former resting from duty.

Darna was carefully lathering Daniel's back when she read his thoughts. "Anna and Astria bid their farewells yesterday."

"Darna?" Daniel asked as he enjoyed her soft and gentle touch. "I've never asked you . . . what does your name mean?"

Darna hadn't thought about herself in some time. "I was given the name by the Chooser who befriended me at an orphanage. I do not remember whether I had another name. He said I would be a goddess someday so he chose the name Darna for me. I later learned that Darna was the name of the Hindu goddess of peace and love. A beautiful statue of her with six arms and a sword stands in a park in Delhi. I was told that she had the sword to indicate that if you crossed her she would destroy you; otherwise, she would fill you with passion and peace."

"Sort of sounds like the Volva," Daniel said. They both laughed. "It is a beautiful name for a wonderful woman." He turned his attention again to the women individually sharing time with Tanoka. "I can't help but feel like I'm interfering with your celebration and farewell to Tanoka."

She finally responded to his lack of self-confidence, having finished carefully scrubbing his blond hair. "Daniel, you are as much a part of this as any of us, so do not feel out of place. You are a special part of the celebration of his life. You are carrying on with his memories. He thinks more of you than of any member of the Order. You will also be given the high honor of lighting his funeral pyre. Now, it is your turn to pay your final respects to our beloved Tanoka."

Reluctantly at first, Daniel worked his way over to the old man, who was sitting on a rock slightly under the water. His eyes were as opaque as ever, but he was anything but unaware. Daniel sensed that he was having a great time. Daniel was looking at a content man approaching his terminus of life.

Tanoka communicated first, speaking aloud in Korean. His message was simple. "Daniel, take good care of yourself. If you are lucky, you will have a victory celebration as grand as I have had. It is my hope that you will have one that you can attend. That will mean you have been a successful member of our little band, and that humanity will be safe for another one hundred fifty years. Trust in yourself, my friend, and you will live long and prosper."

Daniel's final words to his mentor were likewise simple and also spoken in Korean. "I will always remember you, Tanoka. I will guard your memories with my life and hope I can live up to your and our group's expectations. I will uphold my duties with the integrity you have shown me. I hope the next life treats you well, my friend."

As the two men, old and young, embraced, Daniel could tell that the old man had no fear of death. He hoped he would approach his end with such a calm, contented heart after a fulfilling and complete life.

Shortly after their meeting, Minh took her fellow Defender to her room. Daniel was somewhat introspective, but that soon changed, as the remaining eight women's frolicking turned decidedly sexual. He was beginning to understand that the end of life was also a celebration of their present lives. In their experiences, the ultimate celebration of life was their freedom of sharing their bodies through the most openly living experience they knew, their sexuality. The obvious object of this part of the celebration was Daniel.

While Marta generally laughed and watched, her sisters took

turns rubbing, stroking, enveloping, and embracing their male. Daniel gave in to his partners in the pool and was allowed to relieve his sexual tension in whomever he wished. It was unabashed mutual ecstasy of a like that Daniel hadn't experienced before. His mind was filled with the thoughts of happy, sexual women. He couldn't satisfy them all, but he did the best he could, and they all shared the experiences. Ecstasy with one was ecstasy with all.

After the episode in the pool, they all dried themselves with the air blower and went into the main room where Daniel had first entered the temple. The eight women sat in a circle, leaving an open space for Daniel between Maria and Monique. He took his place and they all held hands. They began in unison to telepathically meditate on thoughts of peace, happiness, and joy. Daniel's mind was filled with such a multitude of relaxing thoughts that he was unable to think of anything independently. The meditation continued for roughly thirty minutes.

They were interrupted with what felt like an electrical shock. The two Volva who were holding Daniel's hands squeezed them tightly and his mind was filled with thoughts of an island paradise, Yonaguni, Tanoka's home. He visualized faces, events, and memories of a place Daniel was familiar with but had never seen in person. The women in the circle were also experiencing the vision of their newly departed comrade from Daniel's mind. As Tanoka passed, Daniel was free to release the memories Tanoka had given him.

The eight women and Daniel broke the circle and went outside to the platform where Daniel had first seen Anna make the rain when he'd entered the temple many months earlier. A two-by-one-meter wooden platform had been newly erected on the stone platform. The base of the platform had been filled with wood. This would be the funeral pyre. The members of the Order filed past until they were halfway up the pyramid, where they formed a line on the same level and sat down. At this spot they overlooked the platform, facing the village. The full moon was now well above the canyon walls and the dry, warm air hit the ensemble with a slight breeze. The village was dark and quiet.

Marta left her spot in line and climbed toward the top of the pyramid. In the moonlight he could see her grab a piece of wood. He felt her create fire to light what was actually a torch. She placed it on the top of the pyramid in a special alcove so that the firelight illuminated the highest point of the structure. In the darkness, the light accentuated her beautiful, naked torso as she walked down the five steps and stopped just above her previous spot in the line. Daniel turned and noticed numerous torches being lit in rows outside the temple. The torches were approximately two meters off the ground and lit the entire area in front of the temple for approximately two hundred meters. He could see that the area was filled with people, the villagers, and that they were sitting silently with a full view of the wooden platform. Daniel was given the thought from someone that they had also had a feast of celebration that evening.

The pause was filled with Minh levitating Tanoka's motionless form through the doorway. She gently laid the body on the platform, then quietly kissed his forehead and took Marta's former spot in the line above the pyre. Suddenly the air was filled with lightning bolts striking the canyon walls and flashing into the sky, illuminating the entire valley. The display lasted several minutes and concluded with an intense aurora borealis display. The sky danced with vivid colors for over ten minutes. During this period, no audible voice was heard anywhere in the valley. The gathered crowd sat motionless.

Marta filled Daniel's mind with instruction. "Daniel, it is now your turn. You have the honor of lighting the funeral pyre of our beloved, departed friend."

Without thinking, Daniel rose and walked up the stairs to the peak. Marta watched him approvingly as he removed the torch and began the slow descent to Tanoka's body. He passed the line of Volva, all of whom stood as he passed them, then continued to the platform and paused. He looked at the worn out, heavily-tattooed male that he had come to know so intimately. His wise, coarse featured face was full of contentment. His face bore a slight smile. Daniel hoped that he too would die in such a manner.

The wood in the funeral pyre was covered with straw, and when Daniel touched the dry material with the end of the torch, it immediately caught fire. The flames quickly grew and soon began consuming Tanoka's body. Daniel threw the torch into the inferno and backed away, rejoining his friends in the line. He looked out and saw that the villagers were also standing, watching the funeral pyre. As the fire consumed Tanoka, the torches in front of the temple were extinguished. The process continued until the only light in the valley was the funeral pyre and the ever-present moon. Marta also rejoined the line of Defenders and Daniel found himself again holding hands with the women, who were forming a semi-circle open toward the pyre, signifying the loss of one of their own, the great Tanoka.

Everyone watched, motionless, speechless, and relatively free of thought until the last of the flames had died out. Then, without a word, the occupants of the temple filed back inside, and the villagers walked silently back to their homes. In tribute, the village would remain dark at night for three full days. The sky would also darken each evening, but it would not rain until the mourning period was over. In some ways the celebration seemed almost insignificant, but any variation in this valley was a significant event. The lack of rain and the darkening of the sky were small changes to an ancient routine that signified the death of a good man and someone who had given his life so humanity could exist a little longer.

Monique took Daniel's hand. Tonight he would sleep with her. It was a good night not to sleep alone, and he appreciated her gesture. They cuddled together without any added physical exertion. This night they would just appreciate each other's warmth and the comfort of each other's spirit. They fell asleep together, their minds filled with visions of Yonaguni, banana fish, and huge, strange sandals made with straw.

CHAPTER 10: The Master Plan

On a quiet day in early February, Tiger was busy in his office studying plans that looked complicated and were known only to him. The weather outside the penthouse suite was chilly. A light snow fell, but he took no notice of it.This year would mark the fortieth year of a project started by his predecessor, the Ferret, the man who had taken the initiative and assumed the absolute power given to him by the Great Leader.

Forty years ago, the dictator of this country of twenty-two million souls, a man called the Great Leader, had endured a world war, an invasion by America, the communists, and internal strife. He had not only survived but had prospered. However, he was a man of intense vision and keen intellect, and he looked over his little country and quickly grasped the scope of where the world was heading and how his country could reach its goals. The Great Leader organized a meeting of all of the powerful people of his land. They would formulate a grand plan with absolute agreement and dedication to the ultimate objective. If they all agreed, he reasoned, their land would prosper; if any dissented, they were on the road to oblivion.

A handpicked cadre of two hundred six men attended the meeting at the central governmental assembly chambers. There were no press, no photographers, and no minutes of the meeting. The dignitaries included party leaders, diplomats, generals, admirals, and other leaders of the masses. There were no aides or secretaries, and no outside observers. All the members in attendance were considered one hundred percent loyal to the Great Leader. Dissenters and spies had been purged through the previous years and were now not even memories. The Great Leader believed in a unified voice and unified thought.

He opened the meeting with a few ground rules. Nobody was allowed to talk to anyone outside the meeting. Whatever the outcome of the meeting, discussion of anything pertinent was not permitted even between the delegates afterwards. On a table in front, the leader placed a loaded handgun, a bag of cyanide tablets, and a long knife. He announced that whatever the final plan—and to be certain, he himself wasn't exactly sure what he wanted at that moment—it had to be unanimous. Any dissenters after this final outcome would be expected to come to the table and choose his method of suicide. It would be all or none. If they could agree on no plan of action, they would all take their turns at the table, including him. To take your life here would mean saving your family from a brutal end. Each member, in turn, expressed his loyalty openly to this ground rule—all except one. This man, an army colonel, walked forward and took a cyanide capsule. The Great Leader himself dragged the body to the outside hallway. The ensemble praised the man's loyalty.

An assistant, the leader of the underground police, presented the current world situation. In 1961, the Great Leader had signed the Treaty of Mutual Assistance and Military Cooperation with the U.S.S.R. This, along with other agreements, allowed for the sharing of military technology and training with the Soviets. However, their trust of the Communist Bloc had waned recently due to Khrushchev's spineless concessions to the Americans with regards to missiles in Cuba. The Great Leader knew of the Cuban and Soviet preparations in the Caribbean nation and had expected a U.S. invasion similar to the Inchon invasion ten years earlier in Korea. In Cuba, they had set a trap for the Americans and, instead of leading the prey into it, Khrushchev had allowed the Americans to escape. Due to this act of cowardice, the Soviets were not, under any circumstances, to be trusted. The Great Leader said the Soviets were self-serving, and added that he suspected the entire Eastern Bloc would in time crumble. The Americans would continue to focus on areas of the world that benefited them economically—lands rich in oil and minerals, or valuable as buyers for their products. Their happy little country had none of these and, as long as the Americans remained distracted, their interest would be focused elsewhere. The Great Leader also proposed that China would eventually accept and even embrace capitalism. In time they, too, would not be able to be trusted. The one variable that bothered the Great Leader was China's excessive population. He feared China would take drastic action to limit the number of children. Eventually, a severe male-female imbalance would develop. Would China provoke a war just to thin their male population? Only time would tell.

The remainder of the first day of the great summit went on with open discussions of where the country stood—its natural resources, its economic strengths and weaknesses, what it lacked in technology, and where any deficiencies could be made up. It was a surprisingly open meeting for a closed society.

Early on the second day, the delegates discussed the goals of their society and their ambitions as a nation. Everyone agreed to the first principal goal, unification of their homeland. They lived in a land that had been occupied and split for so long that unification had become an idealistic dream. This would be Phase One. They also talked of self-sufficiency, independence from vassal state status, and of being a regional powerhouse. Maybe even someday they could export their superior world order to other countries and create a new, better system of human living that would actually change society to their way of thinking. Realizing that these goals would take a lot of time, the delegates recognized the need for patience.

They needed a long-range plan that would allow them to sneak up on the world so that when they were ready, they could strike hard. Before the Soviets, the West, or the even the Chinese knew what was up, they would have already secured their objectives and be on to Phase Two of their activities.

In the early afternoon, the Great Leader himself proposed an idea so radical that at first the delegates thought he was just testing them. He proposed to marginalize his power and the power of his successor. As he had no confidence in his son anyway, this didn't seem very radical. The body would elect a secret leader, a man who would be molded after the American Mafia. This underground boss would head all the preparations of the state. He would initiate the vision to achieve the goals dictated by this meeting. All the while, the Great Leader would act as a figurehead. They would close their society to the outside world so that the world would focus only on what the Great Leader was doing. When he died, his son and family would continue acting like the ultimate authority, whereas as the actual power would be secretly brokered elsewhere. Keeping the real leader's identity secret was so important that they would never even refer to him by name. Only a code word or nickname would be used. Once elected, the man would have absolute, unquestioned authority. On his sixtieth birthday, a successor would be elected. The successor would then learn and wait until the boss died or became incapacitated.

These underground leadership positions could go only to unmarried, unattached men. Their zealotry to the cause and dedication to the nation's goals would have to be sworn in an oath to this body, which would become a secret society dedicated to the master plan. Strict criteria would be introduced. The privileges would be lavish, but the penalty for dishonor would be so extreme that no amount of money from anyone would be able to turn the members to the other side.

The group broke for lunch and afterward the society agreed that the Great Leader's plan was excellent. Without much more discussion, everyone knew the correct person for the boss position. He was a forty-five-year-old general, a ruthless political ideologue, and a zealot for the causes of the People's Republic. As he strode forward to accept the position and the trust of his countrymen, the membership chanted his new nickname, the Ferret.

The Great Leader shouted, "I give you the Ferret!" The hall erupted into cheers. The Ferret never used his own name again.

With the advice and consent of the delegates, the Ferret dictated the start of a system to undermine the world. It would be the ultimate stealth attack. The country would model itself after 1930s and 40s Germany. They would move most of their economy into bombproof tunnels, out of sight of spy planes and outer space observatories. They would stockpile everything from food to arms to oil. A powerful spy network would steal ideas and technology from the West and the East alike. The society would undergo a complete militarization. Everyone, male and female, would become part of the military machine. Those poor souls who were unfit or too old to contribute would simply not be tolerated, as the small country had no resources to waste on non-productivity. A law legalizing euthanasia was passed with a wholehearted cheer.

The Ferret would mold their military into an elite fighting unit. He believed in a Spartan model of soldiery, coupled with the modern ideals of the German SS, the American Navy SEALs, and the Marine Corps. The regimen would be so tough that they would crush all opponents that came before them. They would structure the country's education and social behavior to what best suited their ultimate objectives. The Ferret suspected it would take one or two generations to develop, but when the time was right, the People's Army would be unstoppable.

It was with these goals that this experiment in social evolution began. Eventually the Great Leader died and was replaced, as prescribed, by the Dear Leader, his son. The Ferret, too, in 1977 was given his successor, the aptly nicknamed Tiger, for he was the one they believed would strike from the bushes in one mortal blow. Five years later, the Ferret died of a sudden stroke. He was buried without fanfare in a grave that bore only his given name. No casual observer would know the man's true position in this new Spartanesque society.

Tiger was thirty-eight years old when he was given ultimate authority over his twenty-two million subjects, and he threw himself into the task with every ounce of his being. To an outsider, the man showed no signs of his position. He left vanity to the Dear Leader. He had no intention of altering the plan or the world's perception of his little country. He was a simple man who lived simply. He expected the same from his lieutenants and they too shunned most material possessions.

By 2003, the rules of the society had been fully developed. Everything was dictated by the state, including daily meals, future spouses, and time of marriage. The society preached conformity without question. Problem citizens were identified and dealt with at an early age. There was no room for error and since their resources were few, the needs of the many outweighed the needs of the one. School started at age five. Every child was taught Japanese, English, Russian, and Chinese as well as mathematics and science. Military training and fitness also began immediately. Complete dedication to the program was required. At age ten, children were screened and assigned career tracks. Some were labeled scientists, others identified as laborers, and the truly resourceful individuals were marked for leadership or espionage activities. Every able-bodied person under the age of fifty was a member of the military and assigned to a unit.

Even factories were organized like the military. The manager was a major or colonel, depending on the size of the company, and beginning laborers carried the rank of private. It was an efficient system. Everyone knew their place and promotions were based on a simple military system.

The Ferret also had a novel idea that hadn't been fully utilized since the time of the Greeks—a unisexual society. Training only men to fight was a waste of his other resources. As had the Spartans, he designed a system that trained the women to be as effective soldiers as the men. They were skilled in the use of the rifle, hand grenades, and knives, and they all had to complete the equivalent of a black belt in some form of martial arts. He also had instilled a mindset that their bodies were designed for the purposes of the state. This made the women even more powerful weapons. They were trained to seduce members of a potential invading force. The Ferret had never known a male soldier to refuse a willing, conquered female. While these women were performing their civic duty, they would execute their foreign love makers, thereby crippling the invasion force. It was a tactic he hoped he would never need, but the female citizens of his country embraced the strategy and would be willing accomplices.

After reaching fifteen years old, both men and women were assigned into various subdivisions that included training in elite attack divisions, special forces units, or secondary reserve units. All of this was done while they completed their basic education. The Ferret had thought of everything, even the details of social arrangements. Although children were cherished in a land trying to grow in population, childbearing was strictly limited to those over the age of twenty-two. The secret leader had realized a key to keeping his men and women happy and focused. If he kept them fed, sexually fulfilled, fully occupied in their free time, and kept their attention focused on a higher purpose, they would be enthusiastic followers.

From the ages of fifteen to sixteen, men and women were introduced to each other during weekend social events involving athletic activities, games, and just plain socializing. After age seventeen the events were frequently staged as overnighters. Sexual training manuals were passed out and the young adults were instructed to follow the steps from a to z for maximum enjoyment. Each relationship had to be approved by the social coordinator, typically a junior officer from the young women's school. These activities were designed to train people for spousal relations, but they also served to train the young women in ways to use their bodies for the defense of the motherland. Occasionally, they would even have a mock war game during an evening exercise to see how many young males they could kill. So that partners would not develop bonds, a strict rotation schedule was used until the age of twenty-one, when applications for permanent relationships were accepted.

At this age the government either approved of or assigned a person's future mate. Marriage licenses were assigned on the first of June every year. Divorces were rare and granted only in the case of disloyalty to the state or for other treasonous activities. Otherwise the citizens made do with the partner to whom they were assigned.

Second marriages were encouraged after the death of a spouse, or after one of the rare divorces, and were assigned during the same period as for those not otherwise matched. This was also a strictly heterosexual society, as homosexual behavior served no purpose for the growth of the State. Homosexuals, if identified, would be immediately executed.

By and large, the twenty-two million-odd citizens of this forgotten land were happy. They made very few decisions on their own, and the State made sure they had just enough pleasure in their orderly, controlled existence that nobody had reason to complain. Even while closed societies from Yugoslavia to the Soviet Union were crumbling, this society remained healthy and strong. There were no demonstrations, activities of unrest or social upheavals. In fact, the internal dynamics of the society were strengthening as Tiger took full control. Despite this happiness, Tiger made sure his propaganda machine spread rumors to the outside world of mass starvation, food shortages, and fuel problems. Even though this was far from the truth, it was all part of his ruse to keep the rest of the world from giving any attention to his country.

Nobody knew he had an army of five million elite troops supported by nine million regulars. He also had three million Chinese mercenaries at his command, camped just outside his border. Selling these soldiers to him seemed to temporarily satisfy Beijing's problems of having thirty million more men than women, a disparity caused by the one-child policy and the infanticide of young girls.

They were cheap soldiers. For the payment of one woman, usually a Cambodian, Indian, or Indonesian, he demanded and received three years of service. His "decrepit" military had two thousand eight hundred jet fighters and bombers. He had amassed fifty-two thousand tanks designed after a Russian prototype. Using depleted-uranium, armor-piercing rounds, they could easily knock out their American counterparts. The rough terrain of the mountainous countryside would negate the added mobility of the American tanks anyway. This would not be a desert war, and he didn't think the West would be able to change tactics so easily from their last two Iraqi campaigns. As an added bonus, he had developed enough chemical weapons to kill the world many times over and did not fear using them. In fact he planned to use them during the first few hours of an attack to slow his enemies by forcing them to fight in the summer wearing hot, taxing, chemical battle suits. If it came to nuclear warheads, his missile program had developed a superior attack vehicle that could deliver warheads to the mainland of the United States as well as to their allies and regional economic powers. His nuclear arsenal was small, but within a year he would have one hundred warheads, and with its extensive underground defense network, his country was better capable of withstanding a nuclear war than anyone else. Besides, the Americans wouldn't use their weapons. He would threaten and they would appease him by letting him keep any territorial prizes he had won. The passive Europeans would support him in a verbal confrontation with the Americans. He had done a great job of hiding his military potential.

The Ferret and Tiger had also successfully veiled the state of their economy. They had built huge underground storage chambers for oil, weapons, and foodstuffs. The storage capacity was so vast that there were reserves for at least two years of all essential items. As the surface façade decayed to the delight of their enemies, a modern industrial mega force was being devised and built underground. Under the tree-lined mountains there existed a network of bomb-proof, gas-proof, totally self-sufficient tunnels and chambers. You could walk from one end of the country to the other entirely beneath the earth.

Tiger read reports of his country's imminent collapse and civil unrest with delight, knowing he had bamboozled the rest of the world. His country even received over four million dollars a year in donations from do-gooders, mostly Americans, to feed his starving people. He kept this money in a special place, his terrorist account. In time he planned to repay the favor to the hapless Americans through some act of kindness much like 9/11.

Tiger was now deep into Phase Two of the master plan, using his extensive espionage wing to subvert and distract other governments. He loved terrorist organizations, whether the I.R.A., Hamas, Al Qaeda, or the Chechen rebels. These organizations were all pawns and so blinded by their narrow-minded focus that they didn't realize how they were being used. Tiger especially had become fond of Osama bin Laden. The Al Qaeda leader had grown almost mythical in stature and had an uncanny knack for staying alive. Osama bin Laden was called the terrorist super mastermind and was public enemy number one of the powerful Americans, yet the Americans had proven unable to kill him.

Tiger would have his agents plan some atrocity and then find some terrorist Moslem extremists to do the dirty work. His agents knew exactly what the West was looking for, so he would send out fake messages, and when an embassy blew up, bin Laden's crew would get all the credit. He would even release a tape of bin Laden's ramblings or some other evidence of him being alive. The Arab nations would suck it up and maybe even create a little turmoil for the Americans on their own. While Osama bin Laden was making the Americans' lives miserable, the Americans wouldn't have time to worry about Tiger.

The level of stupidity and incompetence of the American anti-espionage service still amazed him. Right after 9/11 Tiger had orchestrated an anthrax letter campaign designed to cripple the American mail system. It was largely a test developed by Tiger's bacteriological warfare specialist, a man he would see later today. His code name was Professor Khan. The Americans were so stupid they never even suspected that the anthrax threat was from a foreign government. Just like 9/11, how could a project so massive and complicated be accomplished without the aid of a foreign government?

Tiger enjoyed all of the inertia in the American government caused by political power plays. The Americans would oppose truly insignificant things like sex with an intern, the wife of the president making a few thousand dollars with a book deal, or something pathetic like the rising price of postage stamps. Hell, in his country, the interns were expected to have sex with the president, as he knew was the expectation everywhere else around the world. His president, the man known affectionately as the Dear Leader, had sex with just about every female he met. It would be much more newsworthy if a world leader didn't have sexual relations with his secretaries and interns.

February marked the beginning of a new campaign. Today he would meet some of the instruments of his team. First he would wait for the Americans to attack the Iraqis. He had set up enough misinformation to lead the Americans to suspect the Iraqis had massive nuclear and chemical stockpiles. If he were lucky, they would take heavy losses.

The Americans, likewise, had drawn a line in the sand and had to press forward with the battle because elections in the Yankee nation were not far off. He looked forward to the upcoming battle and he had just had a big screen television installed so he could watch the invasion real-time on CNN. His spies in Washington, D.C., suggested a mid-March invasion. In the meantime, he had more sinister aspirations to plan.

* * * * *

Dr. Khan was a member of Tiger's inner circle of operatives. The pair had known each other for over thirty years. Khan had pledged himself for Tiger's use when the secret leader had saved his life during a skirmish between Pakistan and India.

Khan was not, however, a member of the privileged secret society that ran the country. In fact, he wasn't even a citizen. He knew little of the land's military prowess and nothing about the master plan set in motion in early 1963. His whole interest in the matter was one of personal loyalty to Tiger, and his reward was carte blanche, enabling him to travel and research what he loved best, population epidemiology and microbiology.

Khan entered Tiger's office at the prescribed time, eleven sharp. He had learned the value of punctuality. Tiger was a busy man with a country to run. Khan was razor thin and slight, barely five foot six inches tall and exactly the same age as Tiger.

"Good to see you, Khan," said Tiger. He was looking out through his window and, although he seemed uninterested, he was in fact deeply interested in his chief bioterrorism officer's report.

Khan started the report. Despite their long-term relationship, he knew Tiger didn't like small talk. "It looks as though our experiments with animal vectors are proceeding nicely. The corona virus we started in China has now begun to spread outside of China. It looks very promising for terrorist activities as it has proven to be lethal and, as we expected, the Chinese have so far been covering up all instances of outbreaks."

"How is it being spread?"

"We introduced it on some of the exotic animals the Chinese like to eat. But to our amazement, it now travels easily from human to human. Our studies predicted a five percent mortality rate, but it looks like it may be closer to ten percent. The World Health Organization is now starting to investigate, but the Chinese are blocking their attempts."

"Good! What other distractions are in the works?"

"We are planning to check on the American resolve with quarantines. We have found a way to introduce a smallpox look-alike into their country. We have found that the monkeypox virus can be carried by certain exotic pets, such as the North American prairie dog. The little rascals show no ill effects and they are quite popular in America and Japan. We also hope to introduce the virus into Japan. We are all set to introduce the virus into the Chicago area by early May. The symptoms look so much like smallpox that we hope to create mass hysteria. I think May will be just about right, as the outbreak will appear to be in retaliation for the Iraqi invasion."

Tiger nodded. "That sounds promising. How is our biological attack plan going?"

"Unless these last experiments change things, we will have enough hoof-and-mouth disease virus stashed in Canada for the mules to spread to the cattle of the central plains of the Americas. North America has not had an outbreak of this disease in the last seventy years, so they will have tremendous difficulty keeping the virus from wiping out their entire beef industry. They will have to close down transportation and tourism, and invariably their economy will go into a recession. Then, two weeks later, we will resume the anthrax mail program we started after 9/11. These should keep the Americans distracted enough so you can go ahead with your other objectives."

"How will the Americans respond when the hoof-and-mouth outbreak occurs?"

"Their plan, as we have read it, is incomplete," replied the professor. "We suspect they will restrict interstate and perhaps even rural transportation in the Midwest. They will close their borders with Canada and Mexico for imports and they will slaughter all ungulates. It will be bad news. They have not known sacrifice since the end of World War II."

"How will our mules spread the virus?"

"The virus spreads easily on shoes, hay, tires—just about anything. I think as few as ten men slipping across the border can trigger widespread transmission in just a week's time. I am surprised no one has used it before. It is the worst virus imaginable for agriculture with the exception of a wheat fungus, and it has no cure or vaccine. Best of all, the Americans will blame the Canadians, or at worst Moslem terrorists."

Finished with his report, Khan was dismissed as Tiger pondered his bigger plan. He would start the epidemic in the West and stir up unrest in Russia, the Middle East, and Europe. While all the major powers were looking the other way, he would strike for the heart of the country south of his border with his five-million-strong elite first-strike units coordinated with over two hundred thousand troops already infiltrated south of his border. He would have absolute control of his southern neighbor within one week, and his country would be unified after over seventy years. After the unification, he could turn his might toward other, larger objectives. He wasn't practicing imperialism so much as exporting a solution to the ills of mankind in that he had developed the perfect society and he intended to implement it everywhere.

For the last twenty years, Tiger had wished that America would be foolhardy enough to try to invade his fair land. An invasion would have given him an excuse to declare all-out war. He realized, however, that the détente in existence for the last sixty years was still in effect. His small country didn't matter to America, and their ignorance of his homeland was irrelevant now that he had almost completed his plan.

Thinking about the upcoming conquest made Tiger yearn for a sexual release. He decided to have one of his secretaries for lunch. His secretaries considered their minds, bodies, and souls to be part of a bigger purpose, and providing carnal recreation for their leader was an honor.

* * * * *

Daniel was developing his powers for purposes other than mind reading. Anna began to bring him out to the temple platform every evening to learn how to create weather. Within two weeks, he was starting to grasp the concepts required to make rain and thus water the valley. Anna was also teaching him how to channel the energy of the Array to move small objects. Oddly, despite the level of difficulty, the entire process seemed second nature to him.

A few weeks after Tanoka's death, Anna announced to Daniel that he would soon finish his training at the temple. In seven days they would depart together. She would accompany him to provide protection while his skill levels were low enough for him to be vulnerable to attack.

Anna looked forward to having time alone with him. Since she'd arrived thirteen years earlier, she hadn't left the temple confines. She also wished to see her homeland one last time. Anna had always felt something was missing in her life, and she hoped that the upcoming journey abroad would provide the means to find that elusive something.

The week before the departure gave all the women one more chance to share their bodies and their viruses with Daniel. Anna made herself scarce after each evening meal, and Daniel found himself being invited to one of her sisters' beds. Anna would have plenty of time alone with Daniel later. The women made life so pleasurable for Daniel that he never thought twice about it.

The evening before their departure he spent with Marta, the Queen of the Volva. She was always soft and gentle with her much younger lover, and he could tell that she harbored great affection for him and yearned to go in Anna's place. But her duty was here at the temple, not on the road in a strange, far-off land.

"Take care of yourself, Daniel," she said as they lay in a state of post-coital relaxation on the morning of the departure. "Anna can take care of herself, but look after her anyway. She seems to be searching for something. Hopefully, together with you, she can find it. I hope we've welcomed you sufficiently to our little group." She smiled. "Don't be a stranger. We expect you to visit us as frequently as you can as we've all grown quite fond of you."

"Thanks, Marta, for your kindness and love. I will do the best I can."

She raised herself up onto one elbow. "Daniel, there is one favor I ask of you. I need you to notify the Choosers for me. It is time they start looking for my replacement. It will probably be many years before she comes and it will take a long while to train her. I am getting old, and I am sure a few more years will be enough. Seeing you with Anna has made me believe that my generation has long since passed. Do not be sad though; we will still have many visits together."

Daniel was sad at first and moved to kiss her. She returned the embrace. "If that is what you want, I am in no position to refuse. How do I signal the Choosers?"

"You need only lay a yellow and red cloth on one of the world heritage sites, such as the top of the temple in Tikal, Guatemala, or the Temple of the Moon in Mexico City, on any structure in Giza, or at the Parthenon in Greece. There are others, but these should be enough. That color combination means a Volva is ready to retire. It signals them to start the replacement process. They watch these sites closely. They may also observe your activities, but none of us know for sure. They know the penalty for exposing themselves to one of us. They are good at blending into the background. There is no hurry, but when you have a chance, leave the signal. I really would feel better if it came from you."

"It is sad to think of this place without you someday, Marta. But I suspect everyone needs to know when their time is ending, and I will do what you ask when I am near one of these locations."

"Thank you, Daniel." She kissed him one last time. At that moment, Anna entered the chamber, her long hair braided to ease her travel. Otherwise she looked the same as usual. She had just awakened from a refreshing rest after duty on the Conduction Array. She was full of energy and ready to begin the journey to America. She bounded playfully on top of Daniel and allowed him to roll her off. She smiled gleefully, as happy as Daniel had ever seen her. She kissed Marta on the lips and hugged her while Daniel began collecting himself.

"I will miss you, Marta," Anna said to her Volva sister as she released her. "I am looking forward to better appreciating the perspective of our men. I hope you gave Daniel an appropriate farewell." She smirked and poked Daniel in the ribs.

The trio ambled down to the main meeting room where they were met by the other Volva. Anna and Daniel exchanged hugs with all of them and then made their way to the exit point of the temple in a wall not far from the bathing pool. Anna approached the wall first and pointed to the star pattern matching her arm tattoo. She touched the colored points in sequence and the door opened. She went outside. The door closed behind her as Daniel approached the symbol.

Daniel turned and looked behind him. Nobody was now within visual range. He heard the gentle rumbling of water, but no human sounds. His mind, however, was filled with the thoughts of the Volva. He had grown accustomed to these women and this place, and he looked forward to his return. But for now, just as a baby bird has to leave the nest and fly, he had to leave the temple. His future lay on the outside and he yearned for private time with Anna. He touched the symbol matching the pattern on his arm. The door stirred and opened, and he walked out onto the other side.

"What took you so long?" asked an impatient Anna. "The French are picking us up by helicopter in a little over six hours." She had already covered herself with a low-cut, white, flowing tunic and had slipped on a pair of sandals that looked like something out of a Greek play. A similar white tunic and accessories lay next to her. Daniel put them on and, while he was fastening his shoes, Anna fastened his long hair into a ponytail with a leather strap.

"Where did we get the clothing?" he asked as he strapped a water bottle to his side.

"The elders were notified of our departure. They burn our old clothes when we go in and provide new ones when we leave."

Daniel asked no further questions while he followed Anna down the trail into the village. As before, the citizens fell to their faces when the Defenders went past to the main trail leading down through the valley and out to where Daniel and Omar had abandoned their vehicle. Neither spoke as they followed the winding trail until they came to the pool just above the gate. They were still connected by thought, and speaking was a waste of energy. Without warning, just as Omar had done, Anna shed her clothes and waded into the pool. Daniel followed.

"It is good to be on the outside for a change," Anna observed. She was still filled with excess energy. "This water feels good after the long walk."

Daniel agreed and they sat at the edge of the water for some time before they resumed their walk. Anna didn't replace her robe but walked naked, allowing her skin to air dry. She continued in this fashion until she reached the bottom of the valley near the wider plain. As they approached the meeting place, she stopped and re-clothed herself, although Daniel could tell by her thoughts that she wished she didn't have to.

The French military helicopter was prompt and flew the pair back to an American military base in Djibouti where a transport plane was waiting on the runway, and a French officer escorted them from the chopper to the waiting plane without comment. Daniel could tell by his thoughts that he was a confused by the presence of the VIP passengers but did his duty without hesitation. The plane headed toward Spain, and then toward Washington, D.C.

* * * * *

One of Tiger's overseas agents, a man code named Mr. Li, was escorted into his office. As he came through the door he saw his leader buttoning his pants. On the couch lounged a stretching, naked woman. She smiled at him as his gaze caught hers, then casually picked up her clothes, put them over her shoulder, and left the room.

"I decided to deliver my report of the So San personally," Li began. "It appears the Spanish just got lucky. The ship's owner has been dealt with and the company has been dissolved. The crew has also been retired, permanently, and the ship has been abandoned. The Americans and British looked into it but lost interest with all the shell companies that are set up. We have made three shipments since and nothing has happened. Nobody seems to have noticed."

"Good! We have no time for errors. We need the arms sales and drug money so we can fund our other ventures without the world knowing the source of the funds."

Li nodded. "I anticipate increasing the number of shipments. We have a shipment of explosives heading to the Sudan later in the spring, plus four more arms sales, and numerous drug shipments upcoming. We will triple the cash flow this year, maybe even more."

"Good. Anything else?" Tiger looked impatient.

"Yes, I have brought you a gift from a contact I have in Vladivostok. The man's father was an officer at a Siberian work camp. They had a German World War II prisoner that they could not kill. He lived to a ripe old age and died only a few years ago. The prisoner had become a favorite of the guards, a mascot of sorts. As a reward, he wrote the commandant, my contact's father, a narrative of his war experiences. Since I knew one of your favorite pastimes is collecting and reading obscure war history, I thought you would like to have the document.

"I took the liberty of reading it myself, as it is written in German. The man was a young SS officer, and he was involved in some interesting encounters. He was captured during the battle for Warsaw. He described the Polish nationalists' desperate attack on the Nazi positions while the Russian troops took a vacation outside the city, allowing their allies to fight alone. His SS troops chewed up the Polish resistance while the Russians waited. Three weeks later the Russians entered the city and shot more Poles than Nazis."

Tiger looked uninterested, as he already knew the story.

Li continued, trying to garner his interest. "It also chronicles, in some detail I might add, the entire Nazi program to collect spiritual and religious artifacts. Among other things, it describes a battle in Northeast Africa where this young officer was the only survivor of an invasion force of nearly three divisions of mixed Panzer and Italian forces supported by over fifty aircraft. This battle near the Eritrea-Ethiopian border was very strange. It occurred prior to the actual war and was caused by a Nazi attempt to infiltrate a temple harboring something called the Order of the Defenders. According to this German soldier, women and men bearing strange tattoos used supernatural powers to destroy the entire force. He was left alive and was told to warn the Nazi command that any more incursions into the valley would be met with an even more deadly response. Hitler soon canceled the program as other operations distracted his attention. It seems like fanciful imagination, but the guards at the camp said he was never one to boast." He laid the book on Tiger's desk next to a colorful statue of a tropical bird. "I hope you enjoy it, my leader." With that, Mr. Li turned and left the room.

Tiger was indeed interested. He enjoyed reading about secret conflicts or forgotten engagements, and the thought of some sort of mystical battle piqued his curiosity. He had the added knowledge of several volumes of original Nazi war history at his disposal. His predecessor had acquired all the captured Nazi paperwork from the Russian occupiers over a friendly wager. These Nazi documents were kept in a large room downstairs.

* * * * *

The American plane landed at an air force base located just outside of the capital city. A waiting limo took Daniel and Anna to the U.S. State Department where the secretary to the Assistant Secretary of State greeted them warmly. She escorted them into the large office of Milton C. Andrews. Andrews was a self-confident man who had labored in obscurity under the president's father. He had now risen to this position of authority under the new Republican administration.

The Defenders read that Andrews harbored very few concrete thoughts other than those that supported his fanatical ambition. He desired higher office and would do whatever it took to achieve that goal—his dream was a simple one.

"How can I help you?" he said.

Daniel spoke, but it was Anna's thoughts that he shared. "We have come to reclaim the embassy of the Defenders that was offered to us in the past. My name is Daniel. I will be the new liaison to North America. Our mission here was abandoned many years ago due the death of our ambassador. President Truman personally guaranteed our position, and we were offered arrangements befitting our status, compliments of your fine government. My tattooed body will serve as my credentials. We bear the forbidden tattoos."

Andrews looked over the pair. He had never encountered anyone like them or anyone so bold. He surmised they were from some insignificant place or that they were trying to bamboozle him into something. He was careful in his reply. "I do not know to what treaty you refer, but I can assure you, we do not typically support foreign missions here. It is customary for the referring country to fund such operations, and I'm not even sure I can grant you diplomatic authority as I don't recognize your country."

Daniel was unfazed, due mostly to his links with Anna and Astria, who was currently on duty. "I suggest you call your superior. I don't think you would want to alienate us." Daniel removed his shirt. "I would especially describe my lynx and sword tattoos carefully to Secretary Powell. I would hate for you, a man who has advanced so far in his career, to jeopardize that career so hastily."

Andrews thought about throwing the pair out of his office, but as he was about to push the security button under his top drawer, he decided he'd better call Secretary Powell. He didn't wish to create an international incident if the pair had some actual treaty with his government.

The Secretary was not in a cheerful mood. Secretary Powell thought Andrews was wasting his time until he described the man's markings. Powell had remembered those markings from his days in the Pentagon and now worried that his assistant had somehow offended the mighty Warrior and Defender of the peace. He had heard stories of these people from the war, and he had heard what they could do. He had even met one, an older fellow named Henri. He was shown the man's odd tattoos and was told by his superiors to respect him. He also remembered that he was to give the man anything he wanted. These people were not ones to make angry. That old man, Henri, had likely died long ago. As far as he knew, no one had occupied the embassy building since his departure. The man in Andrews's office was obviously the long-overdue replacement. He told Andrews to wait and he would run right over.

Secretary Powell walked into the office without knocking and shook hands with each Defender. "Welcome to the United States of America," he said with gusto. "It has been some time since we've had the pleasure of your representation, but we expect that we will be under the same agreement as before. Andrews here will be your personal contact. He will make you comfortable and will make available whatever you desire. We will provide a full-time cook and a maid, and a car will be put at your disposal. For any travel or other needs you will need only to contact Andrews. I apologize for not having your residence ready, as we were not informed in advance of your arrival. If I can be of any further assistance, please contact me personally any time of the day or night."

"Thank you, Sir," Daniel replied. "I'm sure Mr. Andrews will do a fine job."

"I'm sure he will," the secretary said, then turned and left.

Andrews immediately called to make all the necessary arrangements, and then he personally escorted the pair to a waiting car. He gave them a satellite phone that they could use to contact him twenty-four hours a day. He feared he would need to do a good job with these people or he would be posted to an embassy in some forgotten wasteland. He was glad at least that he hadn't pushed the security alert button. If he had, he would have already been on a flight to the Faeroe Islands or some other out-of-the-way spot.

The embassy building was a small, fenced structure that contained a pool, a sauna, a hot tub, a sitting area, maid and cook's quarters, and two extra bedrooms. It was a Victorian building located near the Swiss embassy. It was small because the Defenders never needed much room, so they never desired anything larger. To Daniel, it was luxurious. Their secretary was named Darlene. She introduced them to the cook, Mildred, and the maid, Dayle. As they toured the house, Anna removed her top. She was hot and the clothing was starting to make her itch. She was soon wearing nothing but her sandals and her tattoos. Darlene was at first startled at the foreign woman's brazenness but dismissed it as a cultural difference. She figured the woolen top would make her itch as well in the Washington, D.C. heat. She had been assigned to foreign diplomats before and had seen some pretty strange sights. At least the Nordic beauty was easy on the eyes, and the man, she expected, would look equally good in the buff. As long as they didn't expect her to bare all, she didn't see any problem with the embassy being clothing-optional.

"Could I go out and buy anything for you?" Darlene asked. "You appear to be traveling light."

Anna blurted out a small list, mainly toiletries, some German sandals, and some basic clothing. Darlene agreed to have the items by morning. She left them in the bedroom, assuming correctly that they would be sleeping together, and gave them her twenty-four-hour number.

Daniel was exhausted and, after the maid had left, he disrobed and spread out on the satin sheets of the soft, king-sized bed. He hadn't slept on something so soft in so long that he'd almost forgotten what comfort felt like. He hoped to just slip off to sleep, but Anna interrupted him.

"Aren't you forgetting something, love?"

He looked up to see her moving over him in a position that would allow her to slide down onto him. Her smile was seductive, and he felt himself stirring. She didn't even wait for him to become fully aroused before she enveloped him.

"I've been waiting for you to take me ever since we left the temple," she said with a heavy breath between deep thrusts. "I wanted you to take me at the pool back in Ethiopia, but I think you didn't notice my signals." She filled his mind with her pleasure until he begged her to come. At the moment of climax they experienced each other's pleasures until they had released their pent-up sexual energy. Afterwards, they fell asleep in each other's arms.

Over the next few days, Anna and Daniel got used to their new surroundings and allowed their bodies to get reacquainted with Western food. Anna showed surprising resiliency for someone whose diet for the past thirteen years had been goat cheese, goat yogurt, and grain mush, intermingled with wine and the occasional roasted goat. Although they both frequently were nude while at the embassy, Anna experimented with Western clothing that she thought might feel better. Her favorite outfit was a pair of loose shorts and a button-up shirt worn as open as the culture would permit.

She started Daniel's training immediately. She led him to a place near Georgetown University, and they started reading the minds of people in the park. She demonstrated how to quickly peel off external thoughts and get to the depth of their thinking.

During the first day she taught him a valuable lesson. He was watching a beautiful blonde coed walk by when the young woman suddenly turned and approached him. She smiled at him, then grabbed his hand and placed it under her shirt and on her ample bosom. Daniel was unsure of what to do as the woman rubbed her whole body on his and groped him, her thoughts on passionate sex. Anna just watched and laughed, and the coed paid her no attention. Daniel was able to break off the encounter by promising to visit the woman at home.

After the coed left, Anna confided that he could uncontrollably send out thoughts to anyone near him. If he thought of sex, as men typically did when they looked at a female, the thought would make the woman become aroused. Anna was surprised the woman hadn't tried to go further with him. If he were hungry, his thought transference would cause people near him to be hungry—it was the same with all basic emotions. He would need to exercise substantial mental control to be safe in public. Anna used her powers to help her novice loose-cannon male mask some of his thought transference while he gradually took control of his random thoughts.

As a test Anna decided to unmask her man's raw thoughts as a very pretty woman approached them as they sat on the front porch of their embassy. Daniel couldn't help himself as he gazed at the five-foot-ten bombshell who worked in the Swiss embassy nearby. She smiled at the pair and stopped right in front of their entrance, then turned and walked toward them, still smiling. Without warning she lifted her skirt and was lap dancing Daniel. Anna was enjoying Daniel's thoughts of fear mixed with pleasure and purposely blocked his attempt to cool the Swiss woman's passion. Anna stood, opened the door, and pulled the half-naked woman into their greeting room. She also had become aroused at her male's passion and was kissing any body part she could find, male or female. The Swiss woman found Daniel and quickly pulled him into her. He instinctively thrust into her. She was screaming in orgasm almost immediately. He flipped her onto her knees and finished in that position as he had become incredibly aroused. It took no time for him to finish as well.

Later the Swiss woman continued her journey to work, flushed and somewhat undone. She wore a sly smile all day, not really sure what had come over her to be so forthright with the man and woman at the other embassy. She hadn't even gotten their names. Perhaps that was better, considering the spontaneity of it all.

* * * * *

Tiger had finished the German prisoner's narrative. He was fascinated with the strange, tattooed people. At first he found the stories hard to believe, so he searched his Nazi database. The prisoner's details were precise. The units mentioned were all sent to Africa. What had happened there was not apparent. He figured they'd eventually found their way to Rommel's Afrikaans Corps. However, no record of them was mentioned in the command's reports. It was as if they had vanished into thin air. He had no way to cross check the Italian units that were referenced, but he suspected they'd been lost at about the same time.

Thirty thousand German and Italian elite troops didn't just disappear; it was an intriguing postulate of the German prisoner that a few people used powers strong enough to melt Mark IV tanks into metal rocks. And these were SS units no less. Obviously something must have happened to them. He had been through Ethiopia and knew of no military capabilities there that could cause such an incident, but obviously the old German's diatribe was no mere fantasy. The tattooed people had existed, and he doubted that they'd just faded away. They must still be around somewhere.

It quickly dawned on him that these people had power superior to anything he possessed. He needed to know more about them. He needed to find them, and if they still existed, he had to find a way to neutralize them. He concluded that they represented a significant threat to the master plan. These tattooed warriors were an unknown, and Tiger had always been wary of the unknown. He was a prudent man who assessed all possible moves before acting.

He assigned his best men to research the beings from the Horn of Africa. He wanted to find out everything about them: who or what they were, what they'd done in the past, whom they'd defeated, and whether they'd ever been defeated. If any reference to them existed, his crack historians would find it. Knowledge was power, and he needed all the knowledge he could get.

CHAPTER 11: The Flight of the Merlin

It was early summer and Daniel had just celebrated his twenty-fifth birthday. Anna had allowed him to sleep late. Since their arrival in Washington D.C., he had been involved in a very busy schedule of training. He found the intense mental activity exhausting.

They typically started the day early with Anna arousing Daniel. After this morning exercise, they showered and ate. By morning rush hour, Daniel was practicing mind reading, mind control, and using his powers of suggestion to mildly interfere with random people around the nation's capital. Sometimes he practiced at the airport, and other times at the mall, the Smithsonian, or anyplace else where a lot of people had gathered.

Anna's initial goal was for Daniel to learn to control his own thoughts that could inadvertently affect people around him. Daniel remembered his first day in public and didn't want the embarrassment or resulting problems from having strange women come on to him. Just about any random thought that Daniel might develop had the potential for doing harm, so his training had been intensive. He and Anna usually worked together over twelve hours a day. Only on Sunday would they lessen the pace; they would have a light workout and then do something athletic together.

They had been inseparable since leaving the temple, both because Anna was afraid to leave Daniel alone in his raw form for fear of potential trouble and because they truly enjoyed each other's company. Both were happier together than either was alone.

Of late, the training had progressed well, and Daniel was showing mastery of the skills that he would need for his new life. The long days, however, were taxing, and he would typically arrive home exhausted. It would take some time for his brain to get used to all the energy being directed through it. Anna, however, showed no ill effects. Daniel concluded that she just needed less sleep than he.

Each evening after she had massaged Daniel and he had fallen asleep, she would sit on the balcony and watch the city. At other times she would meditate, have long interactions with fellow Volva, or enjoy soaking in the Jacuzzi. By and large, she was enjoying her time away from the temple and especially took great pride in her pupil and his progress.

Today was Sunday and Daniel had just completed his fourth week of field training. He awoke with a smile as Anna gently stroked his chest. "Good morning, gorgeous," he said, looking into her lovely blue eyes. He would never tire of seeing this woman in the morning. "You are always so ready to go in the morning, but today is my rest day." He was being bold, but he knew his place and always let Anna control the agenda.

"I have been thinking that we need to work on your other skills," she said, continuing her massage with more gusto. She motioned for him to turn over and he obliged. Anna liked giving and receiving massages, and they helped Daniel relax during the heavy training. "A Defender must learn three types of skills. First, you have to master the control of telepathic communication, basically between fellow Defenders. You learned the Old Language, and you learned to rearrange the order of your thoughts so you could allow yourself to get plugged in to our network. That is a passive process, and you learned it well while you were still at the temple." She was working hard on the knots in his lower legs.

"The second set of skills involves mind reading and suggestion. We use our energy to first listen to the non-Defenders' thoughts and later to transfer our thoughts into them to make them behave differently. This is a more active process and is what we've been doing for the last month.

"Thirdly, you must learn to control nature. We can channel the forces of earth, as you saw back at the temple when we made rain in the evenings. You participated in that process, although we were confined significantly by the geography. Controlling nature will be the next step in your field training. I believe we should begin your lessons immediately."

Daniel was moaning in pleasure, much to his teacher's delight. "So what limits do we have in our powers?"

"Our powers are limited only by the laws of physics. Since we use the natural energy of the earth, we can do pretty much anything the earth can do. We can create weather, lightning, or even tornadoes. We can part water, ala Moses. We have the power to heat or to take heat away. We can interrupt gravity in certain locations, remembering that somewhere else gravity will become stronger. We also can use earth energy to affect the perception of time, especially to slow it down. We cannot beam ourselves from place to place or anything like that. We cannot fly. But we can levitate. Although levitation is possible for short distances, it would consume too much energy for anything over a few hundred yards. All of these skills were discovered by our predecessors and have been added to the collective experience and passed down from generation to generation. We are continually discovering new ways to use our gifts, and when we do, it is shared with all."

"Moses' powers seemed like those of a Defender, didn't they?" pondered a very relaxed Daniel.

"That is because he was one of us." She liked providing her star pupil with revelations that contradicted history. "The parting of the Red Sea, the miracles, making hail and whirlwinds of fire—that was all Defender stuff. Remember the scripture describing him at a young age going out to the wilderness, seeing the burning bush, and later returning as a changed man? He actually was taken, just like you, on his twenty-fourth birthday, and he returned with tattoos just like yours. His teaching and conversion on the mountain was actually his being trained at the temple of the Volva—our temple. During the time he needed to recharge and return to share himself with us, his followers would sometimes go astray. It was during one of those absences that the Ten Commandments were bestowed on humanity. After forty years he had served his purpose. He returned and lived another eighty years doing other Defender activities. He was a great man."

This revised history was of little surprise to Daniel after all he had already learned. "I picture him a lot differently now. So what do we do next?"

"Well, you can decide where we need to go." She was starting to get more sensual and rolled him over again. "We need a place that can have different kinds weather—hail, wind, and rain. It needs to be near an air force base, be remote, and have long-range visibility. It needs differences in terrain—rocks, hills, trees, and plains. We will need decent camping facilities that are preferably free with few other people around. It also shouldn't be too hot, and of course I'd like it to have no bugs. It should also be in a place where no one will recognize you and where people will ask few questions."

"Is that all?" he said coyly. They both smiled. He had never taken a woman camping before and the thought excited him. "I know just the place. We need a plane for Ellsworth Air Force Base near Rapid City, South Dakota." He reached for her. "And now I need something."

She smiled and gave in to his desires.

* * * * *

Anna thought camping would be a pleasant change of pace. They would take their act on the road, and the new surroundings would refocus Daniel's energy on learning. Besides, she hadn't been camping since she was in school; it would be fun.

She notified the governmental liaison of their need for a plane to Rapid City with a car for an extended backcountry adventure. The liaison was more than happy to get them out of the city and out of her hair for a while. Being a low-level official, she was not unaware of their importance, but neither was she aware of what they truly represented. She just assumed they were from some small micro-republic and were mooching off the United States government. But she had received an order signed by the Secretary of State to give them carte blanche without question or comment, so she suspected that wherever they were from was of some significant strategic importance. She sent her assistant shopping for the list of camping supplies they'd given her. The trip would last at least a month. She figured they would vacation in the Black Hills and she notified her superiors of such.

The evening before their trip, Daniel and Anna took a sauna together, relaxed in the Jacuzzi, and enjoyed a free concert in the mall near the nation's capitol. Tomorrow would be a big day, so after a long mutual meditation, they went to sleep. Daniel had pleasant dreams of campfires and the clear, open skies of his youth. It would be a homecoming of sorts, quite possibly the closest he would get to home for some time.

The plane left early the next morning from Andrews Air Force Base. The weather was clear and the flight went smoothly. Daniel spent most of the two-hour flight sleeping. Anna meditated. The weather in Rapid City was typical for an early July day, clear with cloudless sky and low humidity, the wind picking up out of the south, and the temperature about seventy degrees. It would undoubtedly be over ninety later and thunderstorms would pop up near the mountains in the late afternoon.

The plane was met by a unit of twelve Air Force enlisted men who unpacked the equipment into a waiting black Suburban with U.S. government license plates. The leader, a captain, approached Daniel. "Can you drive?"

Daniel nodded and he and Anna climbed into the Suburban. Once they'd followed a military Humvee through the main gate, they drove south to intersect I-90. From there the couple headed west toward the Black Hills and Daniel set the cruise control at seventy-eight miles per hour, just over the speed limit of seventy-five. He slowed a few minutes later as they approached Rapid City, and Anna laughed.

"I thought you knew this area like the back of your hand."

Daniel sneered but made no other reply.

"Do we go through the Black Hills?" she asked. "I was never out here when I was a kid."

"No, the freeway skirts the northeast side. At Sturgis, we turn north on a two-lane."

"Isn't Sturgis where they have that biker rally thing?"

He used telepathy for the positive reply.

"So where exactly are we going again?"

"Slim Buttes; more specifically, a campground at Reva Gap. We should be there about eleven A.M. It's now just a little after nine NHT."

"What on earth is NHT?" She laughed, thinking she had already read the answer but was still confused.

"Nielstrom Home Time." He laughed too. "The expression just kind of blurted out. I grew up about four hours due south of here. The time zone line really wasn't that far away and we'd have events all over Nebraska, so to avoid confusion we always thought of time as the time on the farm. I went to college in Sioux Falls on the other side of South Dakota and in the earlier time zone."

"It must be a rural thing." Anna was still giggling.

In no time they had made the twenty-seven-mile trip to Sturgis. As the gathering was still over a month away there were no bikers present, so the pair zipped through town and headed back east a bit before connecting with northbound State Highway 79. This road led the couple past one of the area's geological oddities: Bear Butte.

As he drove, Daniel thought about the mountain. Even to the uninformed, it appeared that the imposing forty-four hundred foot, conical mountain was separated somehow from the uplift that had caused the Black Hills. Despite its proximity, its geological history was different. It was the eastern-most volcano located in North America, although it was not quite a volcano. Magma had risen in its core through a subterranean vent. The magma had hardened but never broke the surface, thereby forming the existing cone shape. As to exactly why a vent had formed in the nation's heartland remained unanswered. It was a spiritual mountain to the native peoples, and the mile-and-a-half climb to the summit was a highlight of a visit to the Black Hills.

Most of the traffic on Highway 79 turned into the state park that surrounded the mountain, or the nice park and lake on the other side of the road. Beyond that, the Suburban pretty much had the road to itself. Newell, South Dakota, provided the last civilization before their destination. The next sixty-five miles consisted of open grasslands dotted with an occasional sandstone mesa, antelope intermixed with cattle, usually black angus, and locations with names on a map but without any noticeable town. Daniel could count the number of buildings on the road on one hand.

Twenty miles prior to their destination, without warning, the road climbed out of the open grassland and up a steep grade into an isolated five hundred-foot high, three-mile wide sandstone mesa. The summit was crowned with isolated stands of ponderosa pines and associated flora. The sides of the twenty-mile long mesa were steep and had numerous small shallow canyons cut into the walls. The valley floor on either side was strewn with boulders from rockslides that had tumbled off the walls over the years. The road crossed over the ridge from west to east about one-third of the way up the formation and then followed it to the town of Reva. A brown Custer National Forest sign greeted them. From the summit, the view to the rear was spectacular. Three miles later a sign read You are leaving the Custer National Forest.

Reva itself was just a couple of old buildings at the junction with Highway 20. Except for an odd-looking school with an over abundance of old-style swing sets, the rest of the town lay east of the junction. Daniel turned west. Their destination was the campground at Reva Gap, where Highway 20 crossed the formation.

The area's claim to history happened in 1876. Following the Battle of the Little Bighorn and the death of Custer, the Sioux scattered. Generals Crook and Terry were sent after the Sioux. Their mission was unsuccessful. For over two months, they found not even a trace of the enemy. On September fifth, with his supplies low, Crook and his troops had had enough. He turned them around and headed south toward the Black Hills. He hoped he could get some supplies in the mining town of Deadwood. Then the rain started—not just a little annoying rain, but a full, six-day deluge. Animals dropped and men were collapsing from hunger by the hour. On September ninth, Crook had no choice but to send a smaller force of men ahead to get supplies. As the group of men started up a pass over Slim Buttes near what would become the Reva Gap campground, they accidentally stumbled right into the Sioux camps. Chiefs like Crazy Horse, the Ogallala's Mimmconjous, and many others were present. The small band of cavalry isolated part of the encampment and surrounded the lodges. They drove the survivors into the bluffs and, much to their amazement, found huge supplies of food and ammunition.

The troops were re-supplied and the main force of two thousand men was brought in the next day. The Indian warriors also regrouped and soon numbered around eight hundred. With revenge on their minds, the exhausted troops attacked with extreme emotion, many holding recaptured artifacts from the Battle of Little Bighorn. Indian casualties were high. Slim Buttes was the first victory for the U.S. troops after Custer's defeat. In the twenty-first century, besides the occasional camper or day hiker, a rare geology study, or someone looking for potential oil leases, the area received little attention.

Once back on national forest land, Daniel turned south down the access road into a sparse campground situated between rocky outcrops and scrubby ponderosas. There was no fee to use the campground and by the looks of it, that price might be excessive. The campground road led to a picnic area and a single outhouse. There were two campsites on the right. The first appeared to be in a hole, but the second had a nice view. The road went on past another outhouse and then past a campsite on the opposite side tucked into a fold in the hill. This campsite's access road looked as if it had been unused for some time. The main road bent to the left and soon a small brown Water sign pointed down a steep and dangerous-looking trail that seemed to run straight down the hill. They passed another tucked-in campsite on the left, and then the road appeared to make a loop. At the far side of the loop was a more open camping area that consisted of four makeshift campsites, each with a place for a fire and a picnic table that appeared to have been borrowed from one of the official camping sites. There were no park rangers, and no showers or other modern facilities. Two other couples had set up camp in the loop, and after Daniel consulted with Anna, they decided they would rather stay near the other people and not at the more private locations. Daniel selected the better looking of the two unoccupied sites and pulled in. The site had a few trees that would serve as a buffer to any of the other visitors, but the entire camping area in the loop covered barely two acres and this sparse, tree-lined buffer would be minimal if anything.

Daniel surveyed his fellow campers. The first couple appeared to be in their early sixties. They were sitting on lawn chairs in front of a deluxe Airstream camper. A Suburban sat next to the camper. The couple had a look of permanence about them.

The other couple was making lunch near their pop-up trailer. They were possibly in their mid-thirties. They looked to be on vacation and had Minnesota plates.

Anna took all this in through her mental link with her partner. She was amazed at his perceptions. Obviously this was his element. She wasn't a camper by experience but was looking forward to the experience. As Volva infrequently left the temple and had little time generally for non-purposeful activities, she couldn't comprehend a scenario where she would ever have the opportunity again for such an adventure.

They unpacked the vehicle, and Daniel read a note aloud to Anna that he found attached to the supplies.

I have reviewed your list and took the liberty of adding a few other items for your excursion. I have much experience

camping and my wife and I have had good luck with this equip-
ment. Enjoy your trip. Your travel coordinator, Rodney Sparks

Rodney had included wash-and-wear shorts, his-and-her tank tops, hats, bug spray, fleece towels, all sorts of toiletries, pillows, high-tech mattresses, and a large assortment of freeze-dried and instant food.

Daniel smiled. "The U.S. government does good work considering we're basically a pair of freeloaders. I've never seen such top-notch stuff."

"I'd expect nothing less," Anna said. "This country owes us its very existence after World War II and the Cold War. We kept a lid on all the flare-ups and kept nuclear proliferation in check so they could sit back here and mint money and power. America has been a lucky country. They profited immensely from the First World War by selling arms and raw materials to the warring parties. They never really got their hands dirty, and they entered the actual battle late. That created the boom of the nineteen twenties during which much of Europe struggled under the financial strain of the expense created during the war. And although the U.S. population suffered more during World War II than during the previous World War, the war came at a time that allowed the sagging U.S. economy to prosper and replace manufacturing lost to Europe and Asia while they rebuilt in the late forties and fifties. America was a veritable Utopia until the oil embargo hit in the seventies. All the while we were working hard to keep everyone from destroying each other."

Daniel thought for a moment. "I guess you're right when you look at the total picture. I have to think differently now. I am no longer an American. I am a Defender."

"Daniel, you know, the people here are good people. They actually interest me, and that's saying something. It amazes me that you were so close to the truth of the first couple's story without using your powers. They like keeping to themselves and have chosen this camping spot precisely for that reason. The woman, Jo Anne, is a retired social worker from western Los Angeles. Her husband, John, is a retired financial planner. They both had extremely liberal political beliefs until recently. All the recent hypocrisy, especially in California, along with their interest in amateur archeology and other lifelong experiences, has shown them that what they thought they knew and believed in is largely wrong. They are now on the road trying to find themselves and reform their attitudes about issues, history, and social evolution. Their moving to South Dakota has been a passive-aggressive form of protest.

"The others are Kathy and Steve. They are from rural southwestern Minnesota. They are childless, on a second honeymoon, and trying to determine their future. She's a history teacher and he's a property tax assessor."

"You've been reading their minds?"

"Yes, and so should you. Another important rule of being a Defender is to scout your entire situation up front. You should have examined each of them as I did. In every situation you need to do this. It is not personal intrusion. It is what we do and who we are. You need to change your rules of ethics. Approach every situation the same way. Doing so will save your life and make you a successful Defender. Now, to remember this lesson you need to go back to the highway and read the minds of everybody in the first ten cars that pass. I'll unpack."

Daniel frowned, then turned and walked back toward an overlook just above the picnic area near Highway 20. He knew his Volva would be using her cerebral powers to check his progress, and he hoped that the ten cars wouldn't take all afternoon. There was no cheating with her around. Sometimes he hated being a student. He did learn his lesson, however, and would never encounter outsiders again without doing a preliminary scan of their thoughts.

Anna unpacked their tent and set up the camp. She drew on Daniel's knowledge of camping while he was doing his remedial work. He was only too happy to give her pointers as the first five cars carried people with very dull lives, and the people in three of the cars were still mad at being delayed by road construction forty miles back near the town of Bison. After completing his assignment, he returned to Anna at the campsite, and the couple set off down the trail toward a vantage point Daniel had visited years earlier.

It was a two-mile walk that led down the escarpment, followed a formation called the Castle, meandered through a high prairie, and then led up the next escarpment. Daniel carried a small pack that contained some trail mix, two liters of water, a blanket, and bottle of suntan lotion. The pair was dressed in tan wash-and-wear pants and both wore white tank tops and hiking boots. The trail wound through the ponderosa pines and followed along the steep edge of the bluff. It then turned abruptly toward the center of the butte, but Daniel continued along the edge. One hundred yards later, his makeshift trail ended over a narrow cleft in the rock. He jumped over the four-foot chasm and encouraged Anna to do the same. They followed the structure until it ended a few yards farther in an eight-foot diameter lookout.

From this vantage point they could see the entire plains ahead of them. On each side they could follow the cliff edges for a good half-mile on either side.

"How did you find this spot?" she asked.

"When I was in college, we would watch merlins up here during ornithology trips." He smiled, thinking back to those wild college trips. "This is the favorite place for merlins to nest in North America."

"Merlins?"

"Small falcons." He liked teaching his teacher. "They nest on the cliffs and hunt small birds with blinding speed. Did you see all the pigeons hanging out on top of the Castle? They are a favorite merlin food." He pointed to a lone merlin flying by below him.

Anna looked impressed. "We now have a cover story," she said, always being practical.

Daniel spread out the blanket. Anna was already peeling off her clothes. She smiled at him and he too adopted a more natural appearance. She handed him the lotion, expecting him to apply it to all the nooks and crevasses of her gorgeous body, not just her back. Daniel enjoyed touching his mate.

Next Anna took the bottle and applied lotion on him. "Human beings should not have to apply lotion to their own bodies. We have much too little touching in this world. The sun sure feels good today. You'd think with all the powers we have we could prevent sunburn." She was applying lotion to a now much enlarged male organ. "Do you want me now?" she asked, suspecting the emotions behind the physical presentation.

Although he thought about it fleetingly, he decided it would be good for him to let the feeling pass. There would be time for that later; there always was. He never went to sleep in need of passion. "No, I'll wait. I'm looking forward to my first lesson."

They drank some water and ate some trail mix, then sat cross-legged on the blanket facing the valley. Anna reached for his hand. "I can't really explain this, so just focus on my thoughts and remember what I'm doing and thinking."

Daniel focused and she began. First she made a rain cloud appear on the western horizon. Within a few moments, it had grown in size and ferocity, hovering in front of them. She then undid the process and it went away.

"You've done this before at the temple. Now you try," she ordered. "But don't let it go away."

Although it took longer, Daniel was able to muster the storm cloud. Anna took over and focused a lightning bolt to strike a rock they could both see. She repeated the motion. Daniel tried and failed at first, then after being shown again, he caught on to the technique. He repeated the procedure many times.

"That's cool!" he said. "Can you do this without the cloud?"

"Yes, but not as easy; we'll get to that later. Now let's try hail."

After successfully learning and repeating the creation of hail, wind, and rain, they paused. Daniel made the cloud dissipate and they got up and walked around, finishing off most of the trail mix and drinking a good portion of the remaining water. Daniel was surprised at how draining the mental effort was. They retook their positions.

"Now for something truly special," she said happily. "Everyone gets a charge out of doing this. But be careful until you get good at it. This can easily get out of hand and hurt someone."

Daniel mustered up another storm. Then Anna took control, thinking words in the Old Language that Daniel had never heard before. Daniel felt wind at his side and he looked up to see that the storm cloud had dropped a small tornado. He was both shocked and thrilled at the power before him. Anna released the beast and it quickly went back into the cloud.

Daniel tried to emulate the process but couldn't quite do it. He finally collapsed in sheer exhaustion. The cloud had grown significantly during the exercise, and heavy rain drenched his naked body.

Anna enjoyed the cool shower for a brief moment before she caused the cloudburst to end and the sun to reappear.

"Come on. We'll try it again tomorrow." It had been a long day. After a brief rest, they dressed and headed back to the camp. Despite the early hour, Daniel was starting to show the strain of his exhaustion. At the camp, the warm invitation of sleep was calling loudly to him. He crawled into the tent and Anna followed. He stripped and stretched out on his sleeping bag. Anna started giving him a gentle rubdown and began singing softly to him telepathically. Heavy breathing made it evident that Daniel was asleep. Anna continued her touching exercise for a few more minutes and, with a sense of fulfillment for a good first day, left the tent.

Anna's supper was a glorious mix of reconstituted garlic chicken and rice followed by dates for dessert. She found her first camping food surprisingly good. It had been some time since she'd had to cook for herself, but in general the task went well. She didn't know exactly how to start the camp stove, so she made a fire—an amazing feat because she initially used no firewood. As she ate she could hear snoring from the tent. She chuckled at the sound as she remembered her first time with significant weather making. Her mind hadn't been used to all the energy flowing through it either, and she'd fallen asleep during her training. She was thankful that at least she hadn't had to carry Daniel back from the cliff.

Someone called to Anna from in front of the motor home. "Hey, Hon!" It was Jo Anne. "I see your man has abandoned you. You must've worn him out. Mine is passed out in the Airstream. Do you want to come over? The sunset should be spectacular after all those storm clouds today. I'll supply the wine."

Anna was still dressed in her new camping clothes, so she felt a visit was culturally appropriate. It had also been a long time since she'd had a meaningful conversation with someone who was not a member of the Order. Besides, she had forgotten to order wine on her shopping list, and the thought of some wine after her delightful gourmet dinner seemed perfect. She would indulge the older woman's curiosity and her natural friendliness.

Anna walked over and sat in a vacant director's chair facing west. The declining sun was visible through a large break in the trees. Her host offered her a glass of red wine. "Thanks." She smiled. "My name is Anna." Normal verbal socializing was something she wasn't used to, but her gregarious personality from her youth was coming back to her. She had been all work and no play since leaving the temple. Her male was now worn out, so even a practical woman like her could use the time to relax.

"Glad to meet you, Anna. I'm Jo Anne," the older woman replied. "It's always good to meet someone new. I hope you like red wine; it's all we have."

Anna raised her glass and smiled. "Truly heavenly!"

"Are you staying here a while or just passing through to the hills?"

"We're staying here for a while." She remembered her cover. "We came to watch the merlins, the small falcons. It is such a nice, peaceful spot here. All the hiking wore out Daniel, my . . . ." She paused for a moment, trying to decide what to say. "My mate. I think it was all the fresh air."

Jo Anne laughed at Anna's strategic pause. She passed the couple off for newlyweds and changed the subject. "The mark on your left cheek is very powerful. I have a Brisingamen necklace myself." She pulled out a small, exact copy of Anna's tattoo done in silver and attached to a thin chain. "I don't believe in these New Age religions, you know, but I'm a Swede by ancestry. My mother gave me this when I got married. She said it would enable me to enjoy a powerful sex life." She smiled and blushed. "Norse mythology is very interesting. I'm always amazed when I read about Freyja and Thor and the like. How did you come to decide on that tattoo design? I've rarely seen anyone with a necklace like mine, let alone the symbol used for body art."

Anna now had to determine what level of reply that she should give to the woman. She couldn't just say she was a Priestess of Freyja. What could the woman comprehend and believe? It would be difficult for her to appreciate a mythical figure such as herself. Should she explain that Freyja was actually just one of the first Defenders? Instead she chose to be as vague as possible. "I'm just someone who also has an interest in Norse mythology. It is well that you don't believe in any of the New Age religions, as you call them. Freyja was a powerful, good woman. She had great power without question. She wasn't a god, though. That spirit or life force is far beyond anything attributable to any Norse figure." She looked right at Jo Anne and smiled. "My mate looks at the Brisingamen on my face and makes passionate love to me. I never go to sleep in want."

Jo Anne smiled at her revelation. She loved the honesty and openness of the road. "It will be good to share the campground with you. The few people we see here usually just spend the night and move on. Feel free to use the makeshift shower I set up. I go down with my Suburban every afternoon to fill it up with water. I think it's good to share things you have with others. This site doesn't have water, and a girl needs to keep herself clean if she expects to keep her man happy. I keep the eco-friendly soap on the broken branch behind the shower."

Anna noticed the portable shower bag hanging from a nearby tree. That seemed like a pleasant thought for the morning-after wake-up relations with Daniel. After a beautiful sunset, a second glass of wine, and more small talk, Anna thanked her new friend and went back to the tent. The wine was more powerful than the kind she was used to at the temple, and she was feeling flushed. She disrobed, snuggled next to her naked companion, covered them both with a second sleeping bag and soon followed him into dreamland.

As was their custom, Anna awakened before Daniel. She liked to watch him sleep before her thoughts turned amorous. This morning, however, she had to first go outside the tent to flush the last of the previous night's wine from her body. It was still early and no one was stirring in the campground. No cars could be heard on the highway. Although the sun was up, the morning was still cool. The damp chill caused Anna's exposed nipples to contract and she made quick work of her outdoor visit. Daniel had still failed to stir. He had barely moved in the last twelve hours.

Anna quickly crawled back under the sleeping bag and drew close to her male, looking to warm her chilled torso. But as she gently rubbed Daniel's chest he began to stir, and her amorous thoughts returned. When both had been fulfilled, she again slid next to him for mutual warmth.

Daniel, somewhat light-headed from the marathon slumber, realized that he too had need of the local bush and struggled to his feet. A few minutes later, with a feeling of tremendous relief, he fell back into the tent next to Anna. It took some time for the spinning sensation in his brain to subside, and when it did and his attention again was focused on the soft female next to him.

Daniel liked the fact that he never had to ask his Volva for sexual relations. She seemed to know what he wanted and was always willing to share her body with him. Daniel again drifted off to sleep and into another peaceful dream.

Anna watched Daniel sleep for some time and soon thought about Jo Anne's portable shower. A shower would nicely complement an already fine morning. She was filled with her usual self-assurance and carefree attitude. Nothing could dampen her mood.

Her body tingled in the afterglow of her morning's activities and she wasn't going to ruin the sensation by covering herself up. If her fellow campground mates couldn't handle her nudity this morning, then they just needed to get over it. Besides, they could always leave so she and Daniel could have the campground to themselves. She thought briefly about using her powers to conceal her activities from her neighbors' eyes, but that too would spoil the moment. She and Daniel needed to be here for a while and, although she would try to keep herself covered and appropriate, it was about time the others got used to seeing her in her most comfortable and favorite dress.

She crawled out of the tent, slipped on her German-made sandals, grabbed a towel, threw it over her shoulder, and without an ounce of self-consciousness walked toward the shower.

Jo Anne and John had been up for over an hour. They had just finished making breakfast in their trailer and, as was the ritual, each had brought their food with them to eat at the campsite picnic table. They both sat on the trailer side of the table so neither would have any obstructions in viewing the morning activities in the campground. They typically ate slowly and would sip coffee until everyone else had headed off for their daily activities. People-watching was by far their favorite camping activity. They both smiled slyly as they recognized the sounds originating from the tent in the camping space occupied by the young newlyweds.

Kathy and Steve were also busily preparing their morning meal. Their small pop-up camper didn't have the luxury of a self-contained kitchen, and Steve was frying eggs and bacon on a Coleman stove while Kathy was trying, unsuccessfully, to make coffee over a stubborn campfire. They were focused on these domestic activities and failed to notice anything unusual from their newly arrived campmates—until they saw Anna walking in their general direction. At first, Anna's cloth-like tattoo gave them the impression that she was wearing some sort of wrap, but as she passed out of the shadow and into the full morning light, the illusion was unmasked. Both continued with their cooking tasks, but their attention was focused on the nude woman.

Jo Anne and John also caught sight of Anna. Jo Anne's first thought was that it would be perfectly natural for a woman who had such impressively detailed body art to avoid covering it up. Anna approached the shower and threw her towel around a branch, then took off her sandals and placed them on a nearby rock. Without a care in the world she began her shower in full view of the other campers. Whereas John was noticing Anna's more specific female curves, points, and hair distribution, Jo Anne was observing her intricate tattoos. The tattoos seemed to run in a pattern, not merely a random collage of artwork. Besides the Brisingamen symbol on her cheek, there was also the softly feminine pleated cloth-like garment drawn seductively around her body both to conceal certain anatomical figures and draw attention to others. Jo Anne had never seen anything like it. Then there was the contrasting long dagger that extended from just below her right breast down her leg on the same side. She also had an odd sunburst on her left forearm. The tattoos must have some significant meaning.

When Anna finished scrubbing her body, she leaned back and rinsed off. She was in near ecstasy as the cool water hit her body.

John and Steve were both in heightened emotional states. John pondered whether he should start a new heart medication and was trying to remember where he had left his nitroglycerin. He thought that he might need some soon if the beautiful woman continued her activity. Steve had lived a sheltered life in rural Minnesota and had rarely seen his own wife naked, let alone a strange woman like the beautiful Anna. Neither man even noticed her tattoos.

Like Jo Anne, Kathy also marveled at Anna's body art as well as her brazenness. Although she secretly desired to be more open with her body, she was shy and lacked the courage to bare all even in front of her husband, let alone strangers. She was a beautiful woman, and she had hoped she could open up on this trip. She looked forward to meeting this self-assured woman.

Anna completed her project, toweled off, replaced her shoes, and placed the damp towel over her shoulder. She noticed a clothes-line about six feet from Jo Anne. "Jo Anne, can I use your line to dry my towel?"

"Sure, Anna," she replied. "You seemed to be enjoying your-self."

"It was truly heavenly. Thank you for offering the use of your shower." She hung up her towel, then smiled at John and intro-duced herself. John just waved. She could read his thoughts. Her naked exhibition had nearly caused a coronary event. She focused her energy on the partial obstruction in an artery leading to his heart and the condition was soon corrected. She smiled at Jo Anne and sauntered back toward her sleeping companion.

A great feeling of relief was suddenly present in John's chest. He felt somehow more vigorous, as though the strange morning event had healed him and purified his body. He shared this feeling with his wife. They agreed that the morning encounter had changed them. They soon noticed Kathy walking over in search of coffee. She had finally given up her attempt at brewing her own.

"What was that all about?" she asked the older pair as she poured a cup and sat down on one of the captain's chairs.

"Just a beautiful woman taking a shower," Jo Anne said. "We all should be a little more open than we are. She seems to be no stranger to being nude in front of people. Her intricate tattoos are obviously meant to be displayed. She and I had a pleasant talk last night and I invited her to use my shower." She smiled. "She cer-tainly looked like she enjoyed it."

"Not the sort of thing you usually see, though," Kathy said.

"Maybe if we did, the world would be a better place." Jo Anne paused. "I've been thinking about you and your husband." She pulled out the Brisingamen necklace and gave it to Kathy. "This is a Brisingasmen necklace. My mother gave it to me, and her mother gave it to her. I have no children. I thought maybe you could use it."

"This is the same design the woman had on her cheek!"

Jo Anne nodded. "That's what made me think of it." She went on to discuss the necklace, its history, what her mother had said about it, and everything she knew. At first Kathy was reluctant to take it, but the older woman's insistence changed her mind. She put it around her neck and smiled. Jo Anne winked at her and Kathy headed back toward Steve. Maybe there's something to this Brisingamen thing, she thought. Her heart was racing and she suddenly felt flushed. Is it working already? She could barely control herself as she grabbed Steve by the hand and dragged him, slightly confused, into the camper. He wasn't confused for long. The couple enjoyed each other in ways that had long been absent from their marriage.

John, too, was feeling things he hadn't felt in a long time. His wife looked strangely different. He was seeing her as she had been in her youth. His unblocked artery was giving him energy he hadn't had for a long while. Jo Anne soon followed him into their trailer.

Daniel was still asleep and Anna was lost in thought, detecting all the positive thoughts now present in camp. She laughed quietly, thinking she had forgotten to filter her thoughts as she and Daniel were making love. She had unwittingly spread a little joy into her neighbors' marriages.

Her thoughts turned to the Brisingamen that Jo Anne had produced the night before. It was the same pattern that was tattooed on her left cheek. It was also tattooed on all the Defenders. The symbol had long been believed to be an aphrodisiac, but Anna knew its true history. The symbol, two kissing herons above a heart, was an Old Language symbol for sex, and it was also the symbol for the Defenders' act of sharing their power, their genetic mutation, and their virus, thus empowering a new generation of beings to protect humanity. The symbol informed everyone who she was; it was her identity.

As to how and why people started using it as charm for sexual enhancement, she was unclear. For generations it had been used in certain families of Scandinavian descent for just such a purpose. It was described as Freyja's symbol of lovemaking. The charm was always made of silver and always attached to a chain of the same material. The heart was usually made of amethyst, a common Nordic gemstone. A mother typically gave the necklace, usually a family heirloom, to her daughter on the eve of her wedding. The mother would explain the wondrous powers of lovemaking that the bearer would be able to provide toward her husband. It would also cause the husband of that woman to be faithful and ensure a long marriage of sexual bliss. The mother would instruct her daughter in various positions for the art of lovemaking as it had been taught to her, and she would add knowledge gained from her own experiences. The necklace provided a backdrop for an open sexual discussion between a mother and a daughter.

The symbol had no actual magical ability—neither Jo Anne's necklace nor any charms have any real power. But the necklace did have a tremendous power of suggestion, and since it was accompanied with sexual instruction and continued dialog, bearers of the necklace soon became more aware of and focused in their sexual behavior. The success rate of marriages in the families that possessed a Brisingamen was undoubtedly attributable to the fact that the couples had a lot more sex, spent much more time together, and had a better and more fulfilling bond. Then the happy women shared their happiness with their daughters and the process continued. The men were benefactors in the whole scheme and, due to their wives' sexual ambitions, had little time or desire to stray.

Anna liked thinking about history—real history. She liked knowing what actually happened instead of what scientists thought might have happened. She had been astonished to learn that most mythical people, events, and creatures had at least some factual basis in history. That Thor, Freyja, Venus, and even others like Noah, Adam, and Hercules had existed was hard for her to initially believe. Now she laughed at herself for having been so naïve in her youth.

She'd had enough relaxation and thinking. She put on her hiking clothes and got Daniel out of the tent. They would eat a hearty breakfast and spend what remained of the day in training. It had been a wonderful morning, but he was here to train.

They returned to their place near the cliff. Today's lesson would be levitation, an art that was more difficult than it looked. The technique had been discovered by accident many centuries after the Defenders were created. The process involved distorting the earth's gravitation beneath an object. Once this was performed, upward and lateral movements were accomplished with localized energy bursts, usually of such minor intensity that they were undetectable by any layperson watching the activity. Mastering this activity would be Daniel's preoccupation for many hours during the ensuing days.

After a brief demonstration by Anna, Daniel took to the project with gusto. His target was a softball-sized stone twenty feet away. He had moved small objects at the temple, or so he thought. He later found out the real work being done was by the Volva on duty and he was just sighting the object for her. That process only worked in the temple and close to the Array. So despite his initial enthusiasm, it took him over two hours to effect any significant movement in the stone. From that point, he made gradual progress, and by mid-afternoon he was able to move the rock in all directions.

Anna congratulated him on his progress. "That's good, Daniel. You're starting to master the technique. Moving rocks is good mental training for us. Exercising on boulders will increase your power and ability. This will be a hallmark of your training. Now, see those six large boulders part way down the valley?" Daniel nodded. "After we have a quick bite to eat, you need to practice your technique by first moving them up the incline and then down the incline. It's not too exciting, but the repetition will serve you well in the long run."

Daniel ate some dried apricots and downed about half the remaining water. He was starting to feel fatigued, and he loathed the idea of moving rocks around for the rest of the day. Anna gave him a reassuring pat on the shoulder, and Irena, the Volva on duty, also encouraged him.

He grimaced. "I suspect these rocks and I will become close over the next few days. I'd better get to blow them up before we have to go back to Washington, D.C."

Anna chuckled at his comment.

He named the boulders Allen, Big Boy, Cube, Dog Tooth, E (he couldn't think of an appropriate name that began with E), and Fat One. He concentrated on his task and for the next three hours succeeded in moving each of the multi-ton boulders several times. Initially Anna watched and scanned his thoughts to improve his technique by finding and removing flaws. Once she was satisfied that he was performing up to her standards, she went off to explore her natural surroundings. She found herself watching a chatty songbird with orange-red and black markings for most of an hour. Its song was beautiful and it was very friendly. It didn't seem concerned that she was watching it closely.

The angle of the sun signified early evening when Anna returned from her exploration. Daniel was still moving his stones. Anna again encouraged him, and then instructed him to rest. After a refreshing drink, she sat beside him and they finished the day's training exercises with more weather making. Again Daniel was successful in creating wind, rain, lightning, and hail, but as before, he was unable to create even a small tornado. Following the effort, Daniel was mentally spent and so exhausted that Anna had to help him put his clothes on. With her help, he struggled back to the campsite. Even with Anna's aid, he was only able to eat half his supper. Anna helped him to bed and Daniel was out before she gently kissed him on the forehead.

No pain, no gain, she thought. He'll grow stronger and have more stamina as the days and his training progress. She finished her food alone and afterward decided to make a fire. She gathered some firewood and, using her powers, made a perfectly even fire that was large and warm. The dancing flames lulled her into a trance. Soon, however, she noticed her fire was inviting her neighbors to her camp. Each carried a chair and, as the night before, Jo Anne brought the wine.

"Do you mind if we join you?" Jo Anne asked.

"No, go ahead." Anna replied. She could read their concern about Daniel. "Daniel went to bed early again." She laughed lightly. "I promise you'll meet him one of these days."

Steve introduced himself and Kathy to her. "It must have been a tough day. I hear you're watching the falcons."

Anna noticed how word was traveling about them already. She thought quickly about a better reply, but the truth came spilling out. Being a Volva, she was unaccustomed to anything but the truth. "We were working on the rocks today. The activity is wearing my poor Daniel out."

"You're rock climbers then?" Kathy asked.

"In a manner of speaking," Anna replied cautiously. She felt it prudent to withhold further details. Anna noticed Kathy was now wearing Jo Anne's Brisingamen necklace. She smiled.

Jo Anne passed around the bottle, a fine red wine from Australia. Jo Anne had a trailer full of various vintages and types, and Anna was beginning to like her evenings with the neighbors and topping off the day with a relaxing beverage. The quintet exchanged small talk and enjoyed the warmth of the fire, the wine, and each other. The night wore on until the wine was gone, and after an hour or so the gathering broke up and everyone returned to their own campsites. Anna conversed with Irena, learned nothing distressing, and snuggled next to her nearly comatose partner. Despite his unresponsive condition, she liked his body warmth as it reminded her of the fire and the wine. She too was quickly asleep.

The next day was almost an exact copy of the previous. After her morning shower, Anna crawled back into bed with Daniel to warm up, and he warmed up nicely. Then they ate a big breakfast before heading off to their private location. Daniel spent the entire morning dancing with his stony friends. The afternoon's lessons involved weather making and more levitation exercises. They completed the day's training again with a futile effort to form a tornado and later Anna helped her exhausted mate back to the camp. He made an attempt to eat, then went straight to bed.

Anna shared the company of her neighbors again that evening. They were warming up to each other. Anna liked their company and enjoyed the mix of conversation very much, which amazed her since she had the ability to know what they would say before they said it. Kathy especially was becoming bolder and secretly desired that Anna would remove her top so she could as well. But it was a little too cool. Kathy would have to wait.

The following day turned out to be different. Daniel was becoming easier to arouse, for one thing. Upon getting up to relieve herself, Anna noticed that a fourth camper had arrived during the night, a lone male, and he was sleeping in a cheap, weather-beaten tent. She paid him little notice. She liked the current mix and desired that the intruder would leave. She would deal with him after her morning shower. As she walked to the shower, she realized she had forgotten her towel and casually asked Kathy to lend her one, as she didn't want to wake Daniel. Her naked body filled Kathy's mind with insecurity and self-doubt. The thoughts bothered Anna, and she couldn't keep her thoughts to herself.

Hon, Anna reflected. *You have a natural gift of beauty that exceeds my own. Any man who has difficulty looking at your naked body might as well be blind. Other women should look at you with envy.* Kathy smiled and was immediately filled with self-confidence, not realizing the source of her feelings. Anna completed her shower and walked back to her campsite. She didn't feel like revisiting her mate nor being clothed since the morning was already warm. She started making a breakfast of reconstituted eggs, coffee, and a re-hydrated chicken dish using their camp stove. Much like the temple food, this cuisine took some getting used to.

Anna could sense ugly thoughts originating from her new neighbor. The food would need some time to cook, and this would give her the time she needed to fix a problem. She could see that her nude form had caught the man's attention. He was a dirty man in his mid-thirties, and he wore clothing that needed to be burnt. He drove an older Chevy Impala with Colorado plates. His thoughts were of the most impure nature that she had experienced since she'd left the temple. The man was violent and clearly on the run from the police, ex-girlfriends seeking child support, and maybe even himself. He abused women for fun and he liked to kill animals. He also abused drugs and alcohol. She could tell that he would do nasty things to her if given the chance.

He spoke first. "Bring that naked body of yours over here. I need a little action. You look like you'd be a good fuck."

Anna began walking toward him, and her thoughts became audible. She was no longer just Anna or a mere woman. She was a Volva. He had crossed the line, and he would regret it. "You want a piece of me?" she said in a low voice that was both foreboding and threatening. He wasn't used to forceful women, and he didn't take kindly to threats. That was his final mistake. He would receive no mercy on this day.

A sharp pain suddenly filled his head and he fell to his knees. He looked up at the approaching woman and noticed that her eyes looked as though they were glowing. He felt the sudden sensation of his body moving rapidly backward. He thought he must have been hallucinating or that the speed he had popped yesterday must have been tainted. Then he felt a sudden, sharp thud in his back as his motion stopped. He was pinned to the door of his vehicle, unaware of the seriousness of the events unfolding before him. He felt a sudden crack in the front of his neck. His hyoid bone had snapped; he was now having an extremely difficult time breathing. His confusion turned to panic.

"You should have been more selective of where you camped last night. This campground is full," she said, almost mockingly. "As you sit here dying, I hope you reflect on all the misery you have inflicted during your life." He stared at her, and she seemed to grow in stature. Her voice was quiet, but it thundered in his mind. "I am Anna, sister of Freyja and Volva of the mighty temple of the Defenders. I stand in judgment over you. The penalty for your wicked thoughts is death. Yours is a death for which I will have no remorse." She approached him, then knelt and whispered in his ear, "And by the way, yes, I am, as you put it, a good fuck!"

Death did not come quickly for the man. He struggled for every breath, and he wanted to scream but couldn't. He tried to move but found that he was unable. She backed away and watched him die, her eyes still burning red with fury. He finally breathed his last and died with a gruesome, horrified look on his face. It was as she intended—a miserable end to a miserable life. She cleaned up his campsite, burning his tent with a passing glance. She opened his car door with a thought, and the body hurled itself into the front seat. Then she turned her attention to the car and it started moving, first out of the campsite and then down the entry road toward the main highway. She followed it down the road, climbing a small hill between the campground and the main road to improve her view. Then she guided the car through the rest of the campground, onto the main highway, and finally westbound down the long incline to the bottom of the valley floor, well over a mile away. The car suddenly veered to one side and went over the embankment. "Good riddance," she said out loud and went back to check on her cooking. The whole process had taken less than fifteen minutes.

An article of interest appeared on page five of the following day's *Rapid City Journal*:

A car accident occurred 20 miles east of Buffalo near Reva Gap yesterday morning. An unrestrained driver apparently lost control and suffered a fatal injury when he struck the steering wheel as his 1984 Chevy Impala left the road. The driver, Randy

Martane, a resident of Brighton, Colorado, had outstanding arrest warrants in Colorado and Wyoming for battery, sexual assault, and numerous drug-related charges. Traces of drugs were found in his system and drugs are believed to have contributed to the mishap. The accident is still under investigation.

Anna found Daniel up and about when she returned. "The food's almost done," he said. "Was there another camper here last night?"

"Yes," she said. "He just left."

"Good. We have enough people here already. I'd like to meet some of these friends you have. It seems I'm always sleeping." Daniel saw that Anna had reverted to her clothing-optional status but paid little attention.

They ate, and afterwards she directed him to the shower. He needed a good scrubbing; otherwise he would be sleeping alone. Although he felt awkward taking a shower in full display, he knew from her thoughts that this is what Anna had already done. He was sure the other campers had grown accustomed to her nudity, so he consented and removed his shirt and shorts. The shower was truly heavenly. Anna went to Jo Anne's campsite to retrieve her towel, still drying from earlier. The elderly couple was already taking in the show, watching with keen eyes as Daniel bathed.

"I see you really do have a man with you, Anna," Jo Anne chided. "And his body is decorated as thoroughly as yours."

Anna just smiled and returned to Daniel with her towel.

The three other members of the camp also observed the young naked male at the shower site. They followed every contour of his body to make out all the symbols. They noticed the starburst on his right forearm and the Brisingamen on his face, which were the same as Anna's. The large, perfectly proportioned, attacking wildcat on his back and chest was a stark difference to Anna's tattoo. The dagger on his right side was longer than Anna's and also contained a part of an arm that extended onto his shoulder. His face and neck displayed many small daggers as well.

The tattoos fit together, making a singular statement. It began to dawn on Jo Anne and the others that this was no ordinary couple and that their tattoos were the key to their identification. Jo Anne would look the symbols up when she had access to a computer.

After Daniel's shower, the couple, still unclothed, headed off down the trail. Undoubtedly, they were going to have another long day of rock climbing.

Upon reaching the lookout, Daniel resumed his seat and began moving boulders. The Fat One was definitely going to be trouble today. Anna watched for a time and then decided Daniel needed to learn the art of multi-tasking. She picked up a small rock and threw it at him. It struck him smartly in the lower back.

"Ow!" The boulder fell to earth with a crash as he looked around. "What was that for?"

"A Defender has to be prepared for trouble and on the defensive even during exhibitions of power." A smirk crossed her face. "You need to focus your thoughts in such a way that you can do several things at the same time and still keep your senses on the alert for more trouble. Now, watch me." She sat down. "Throw something at me when you think you can hit me."

Anna raised the boulders. Up and down they went as storm clouds gathered in the valley. The small rock Daniel had first moved was also moving up and down. Daniel found a small stone. After about ten minutes he threw it at Anna. The thrown stone stopped in mid-air even as Anna continued to hold the boulders off the ground. It appeared as though time had slowed down. Anna took the stone from mid-air and threw it back at him, then returned to her concentration, while the stone narrowly missed him.

"What was that?" Daniel asked.

"We can use the earth's energy to temporarily distort time," Anna replied, gently replacing the boulders and dissipating the clouds. "We can slow it down or speed it up. This is all done with only us noticing the change. It is best seen with shooting bullets. We all have a sense of future activities, especially innate danger. If you get that odd sense that something's about to happen, you can slow time down and examine the situation. You can avoid a bullet or a knife. You can even escape explosions. It's a very useful technique, but it takes a lot of energy to hold time still, so you can't keep it frozen for long. This needs to become a reflex action for you. When you need it, you won't have time to think."

Daniel spent the next few weeks learning the arts of multi-tasking and time distortion. After three weeks he could perform it almost as well as Anna. His powers were becoming second nature, and he rarely had to ask the Volva connection for the specific power. Anna frequently would throw things at him or hurl logs in his direction, but after a few days nothing struck him and he was able to avoid all secondary distractions. She literally beat this skill into him, because if Daniel was ever in the firing line he needed to be as well-trained as possible. He and his destiny had been eighty years in the making, and she wanted to give him all the protective skills she could. She was impressed with his quick thinking and learning. The Choosers had selected well. She was also pleased with her own efforts at instruction. All of their hard work was starting to pay off. Daniel was fast becoming a powerful force.

Anna often thought about the whole process of selecting Defenders. Sometimes she wondered about how many were killed or simply died in the desert trying to get to the temple. Was Daniel one in a hundred or one in two? Obviously, there were many failures; there had to be. Upon hearing of Daniel's ordeal, she was left wondering at how lucky he was. It was undoubtedly a survival-of-the-fittest strategy, one that, according to the historical records from the temple, had been going on for thousands of years.

Every day the pair spent at least eight hours training in their sacred arts. The evening was reserved largely for rest and interaction with their fellow campers. Originally Steve and Kathy had planned on staying only a few days at Reva Gap and to be away from home for perhaps two weeks. But the two weeks gradually became three and then four. They were having such a good time at the little campground that they didn't want it to end. Besides, school was out until after Labor Day, and Steve could catch up with his assessing when they finally returned home. While Anna and Daniel were away from the campsite, the other two couples would make day trips into the Black Hills or down to Rapid City, usually to buy supplies and more wine, but by and large they were just enjoying the peace and solitude and each other. Kathy and Steve's search for each other had been their main goal and, oddly enough, soon after Anna and Daniel's arrival, their marriage had improved greatly. Kathy attributed it to her new necklace. Steve attributed it to them actually spending time together.

Toward the end of Anna and Daniel's first week camping, a

significant change started to occur during the evening social hour. It all started shortly after Daniel's arrival to the event. One warm evening when they were all admiring Anna's always-perfect fire, Kathy noticed that Anna looked noticeably uncomfortable in her camping clothes. She actually invited her to take them off. Anna readily agreed and stripped off not only her top but everything else as well. Daniel sensed significant relief in his Volva, and he was working up the energy to follow her so she wouldn't be singled out, but Kathy beat him to the process. She also stripped and resumed her conversation. For the days that followed, the two young women rarely were seen wearing clothing around the camp, and Daniel typically followed suit. It took Steve a few more days, but he too shed his clothing and enjoyed the new carefree attitude. Jo Anne occasionally presented herself topless, but poor old John announced that he would do everyone a favor by keeping his clothes on. "Some things," he said, "are not meant to be seen."

The morning ritual soon changed from everyone watching Anna shower, to people showering and eating with little regard to each other's activities. Kathy and Steve rarely left each other and typically would retreat to a sunny spot with a good overlook and spend most of the day reading, getting a full-body tan, and watching the strange afternoon weather that would suddenly form and then just as suddenly disappear in the valley below.

The evening conversation became much more personal and of a deeper nature after everyone had bared all. Typically, the other four would talk and Anna and Daniel would listen, occasionally interjecting with points of encouragement or wisdom. Everyone marveled at how much common sense Anna had for a woman so young. Of course, only Daniel understood the centuries of Volva wisdom and experience that she carried in her mind. As the days progressed everyone was feeling content and all was well in Reva Gap.

Day twenty-five started with the usual routine as Daniel and Anna shared a long, mutual massage followed shortly by other pleasures. Then they crawled out of their tent and chitchatted with Jo Anne and John while each of them took a cool morning shower. They brewed up whatever dehydrated food looked the best and, after a long morning drink, headed off to their secluded cliff.

Kathy was just coming back from her shower when Anna suddenly smiled and gave her a hug. Daniel was surprised to see the two naked women hugging. He immediately telepathically grasped the significance. Kathy's one goal in life was to conceive and bear a child. She had been trying to get pregnant for so long that she had given up hope; at times she had even stopped trying. She had become as close a friend to Anna during the last few days as any non-Volva could hope to be, and Anna had just sensed that Kathy had conceived. Must be a woman thing, he thought, as he had sensed nothing.

Kathy looked confused. She looked at Anna. "What's up?"

Anna put her hand on Kathy's abdomen and confirmed her diagnosis. "Kathy, congratulations! You're finally going to have a baby!" Both screamed like little schoolgirls.

Kathy caught hold of herself. Yes, she was a day or so late, but that was typical for her. But she hadn't felt anything—no breast tenderness, nothing. "How do you know this?"

Anna's demeanor changed to that of the higher-level being that she was. "I have the ability to tell such things. Without a doubt, you have conceived." She patted her on her shoulder, smiled, and joined up with Daniel for the day's duties. Something in Kathy's mind made her believe that Anna's prophecy was correct. She accepted it as fact and went home to her tent to show Steve her gratitude. She wouldn't let him out of the camper for most of the day.

"Anna, did you get her pregnant or can we do that?" Daniel asked later.

"No, my love, we do not have power over conception," she said without much emotion. "We can heal, encourage, and soothe a restless spirit but we have only been given the power to take life, not create it. We are not gods, you know." She paused. "I suppose I did have some role as she had such a poor body image that she could scarcely even look in the mirror. Understandably, they rarely had sex. Once I corrected her inhibitions and she developed more self-esteem, she and Steve found each other again. It's not surprising that she would become pregnant. She is a very attractive woman, so why would she hide her body or her sexuality from her husband? She was confused. Now she has become what she desired to become.

"But," she added solemnly. "I would not encourage you to try to improve people's lives by and large. On the other hand, there is nothing wrong with helping people. As you read people's minds, I would encourage you to leave them with something positive in return. We are too few to help all that many people, and we need to keep ourselves focused on the big picture, but it's all right to help a few souls along the way."

They resumed their spot and Daniel had a good workout for two hours with Anna's distractions and his usual sextet of boulders. After a break, she taught him a new skill. She first had him focus on her mind as she directed energy deep beneath the earth. Daniel felt a low rumble, its intensity gradually increasing until it subsided fifteen seconds later. Daniel followed her lead and five minutes later a slightly stronger tremor shook the Slim Buttes. He repeated the process twice more until he was sure of the technique. He had created an earthquake.

Anna issued a warning. "Be very careful with quakes. This is a natural earth activity. You are releasing energy that wants to be released. Start slowly and build the intensity to where you want it, and then let nature take over. If you pour too much energy into the process up front, it could quickly get out of control. We've lost two Defenders who got caught up in an earthquake. Volcanoes can also be especially dangerous, but we don't teach the volcano skill anymore. In fact, I'd be shocked if the Volva connection would allow you do anything like that again unless it was the plan of all of us."

Daniel's gaze questioned her.

"The use of volcanism over the centuries had become sort of a favorite way for us to control human activities that we perceived as dangerous to our long-term survival. Take Napoleon in the early 1800s. Our Defender in Europe learned that the French ruler had planned a large invasion of northern Europe. We postulated that if he succeeded he could very well take full control of Europe, Asia, North America, and whatever else he desired. As it has always been our custom to work behind the scenes so as to not make our involvement known if at all possible, a scheme was hatched to use volcanism to change the weather. In early 1815, the Defender in India traveled to Sumatra and selected Tambora as a good candidate for an eruption to affect the global climate. He created a massive eruption, the largest in recorded history. Tons of ash and smoke filled the sky, and the following summer was extremely cold both in North America and Europe. In New England they had frost in every month. Our agent in Europe delayed Napoleon's march long enough so that by the time he got through Austria and into Poland it was already late summer. The Russians, as expected, withdrew toward Moscow, destroying all their supplies and foodstuffs as they retreated home.

"Predictably, Napoleon fell into the trap. The French followed the retreating Russians as they burned their own supplies and avoided confrontation. Absolutely nothing remained over the vast distance from eastern Poland to the gates of Moscow and a decisive battle never happened. In October, Napoleon, overextended, hungry, and cut off from his own supply lines, was forced to retreat on foot toward France. Winter hit with a fury and ninety-five percent of his two hundred fifty thousand-man army froze to death during the retreat in what became the coldest winter of the last two hundred years. Europe was spared his domination and another crisis was averted.

"It was determined that these Indonesian volcanoes were effective tools for affecting global weather patterns, so in 1886, we decided that the same Defender should pass his volcanism skill to a new, younger Defender. They selected Krakatoa for practice since it was on an uninhabited island and far enough away from people. The volcano usually erupted in a slow, stable manner, and the pair could watch the mountain from a safe distance by standing on Java. In May of that year they began the training. The first practice eruption went so smoothly that by late August they attempted a second eruption. That too went smoothly. Unfortunately, a little over a week later their third attempt got out of hand. The momentum of the eruption progressed rapidly and by noon the next day, as the pair tried desperately to quell the explosive force, the entire mountain blew. The ensuing rain of rocks and debris and a monstrous tidal wave killed thirty thousand local people and both Defenders.

"We, however, didn't learn from this mistake. An eruption was brewing on the island of Martinique in the Caribbean, and we sent a Defender to try to learn how to stop it. Whatever he did is still unclear, but a terrible gas flow, called a pyroclastic flow, erupted from the mountain and enveloped the town. Despite a tremendous effort with time distortion, the Defender was also killed. The entire area was denuded of life except for two convicts who were protected from the searing heat by the prison walls. Thousands died. Since then, using volcanoes has been banned. They are just too dangerous and the effects too widespread and too hard to control. Losing three Defenders in twenty years was an intolerable price to pay."

"Did we have anything to do with Mount St. Helens?"

"We are not involved with every natural disaster, Daniel." She was finished with her lesson about volcanoes.

The training progressed and finally it was time for weather practice. Daniel started with rain clouds and, as they built up over the next few minutes, he added some lightning and a light rain for effect. He then bent the wind energy so the whole cloud began a clockwise rotation. The swirling continued until a small finger of energy formed in the middle of the cloud. It was at this location that he concentrated his energy. He focused the wind on the outer reaches of the cloud and then brought it nearer the center. As he shortened the distance, the wind speed picked up, first to twenty miles per hour and then to thirty. Soon it had reached seventy miles per hour and a small finger became visible. As the wind concentrated, the finger became a distinct vortex.

The process soon took on a life of its own. The vortex grew to over three hundred yards long and approached the ground. The imposing giant was soon sucking up helpless prairie grass and dirt, and its color changed from gray to brown, matching the soil color. Although he had seen many twisters in the prairie back home in Nebraska, Daniel was still startled by the awesome spectacle of his creation. He watched it for an instant and, before any damage occurred, he reversed the motion and the storm dissipated as quickly as it formed.

"Whew! That was a rush!" he said, proud of his accomplishment. "I finally succeeded!"

Anna was likewise proud of her student, but her thoughts were also sad. His success meant they would have to move on soon. She was becoming used to the evening social hour. Despite her longing for the company of the Volva and her home in the temple, she had developed a relationship with these people.

This concluded the day's work and Daniel looked more exhilarated than tired. His stamina had steadily grown, and the telepathic exercises rarely drained him as they once had. In fact, as he stood at the edge of the cliff, he never looked better. Having all of the energy transferring through him also had toned and strengthened his body. He was as fit as any twenty-five-year-old man could be. His regal, blond-haired physique was stunning in the declining light; even his abdominal muscles were now rippled. Although he was new to his position, his confidence was growing daily. Anna had herself a truly beautiful man, one she would enjoy for many years to come. The pair walked back to camp holding hands, content with themselves, who they were, and what they had become.

The next day's *Rapid City Journal* stated on the front page:

A series of tremors shook western South Dakota yesterday. The four small earthquakes measured at most 4.5 on the Richter scale and were centered southeast of Buffalo near Slim Buttes. Although no tremors have been felt in this region previously, Dan Larson of the U.S. Geological Survey stated that having small tremors in the Black Hills region is not uncommon. No damage was reported although the tremor was felt from Devil's Tower in Wyoming through Rapid City and as far east as Faith, South Dakota.

An unrelated event occurred in the same region when a small tornado briefly touched down later in the afternoon. A tornado warning was issued for Harding County, but no damage or injuries were reported. The local weather service reported that this tornado continues four weeks of unusual weather for the Buffalo area, with numerous small thunderstorms forming quickly and then dissipating. Local ranchers welcomed the rain.

In the following few days Daniel consolidated his skills. He learned how to increase gravity in certain areas and how to knock over trees. He used the prairie grass to learn how to parch growing plants and make them wither. He also learned simple healing techniques on plants and animals by healing broken stems and branches and later by healing cattle wounded by barbed wire. He also removed ticks and fixed other misfortunes the bovines had encountered. He enjoyed this part of the learning experience most. It had seemed that a Defender was built only to deal death and destruction, so using his energy to heal was a welcome relief.

Both he and Anna knew the instruction period would soon end. Anna announced they would take two days of rest, then say goodbye to their new friends.

Daniel was thankful for the rest. They had worked hard for the past five weeks; he would enjoy the reprieve. Anna too was becoming tired. She loved Daniel but missed her companions at the temple. She yearned to have the awesome power of the Conduction Array flowing again through her body. Once they returned to Washington, D.C., she would have to return to the temple. Daniel could now care for himself, and he would soon need to fly solo. It was a rite of passage. But for now, it was time to rest.

On the first day of rest, the weather was dreary and Jo Anne and John had gone to town early for supplies. They had decided that there was little chance to see the sun so they might as well get their bi-monthly shopping trip out of the way. The Defender pair slept in and, upon awakening, Daniel looked up.

"Not today, rain," he said and held his hand up to the sky. The sun quickly burned through the overcast and the temperature started to warm. Daniel was much happier as he yawned, stretched, and headed for the shower. He met Steve and Kathy as they were leaving for a long walk. Daniel hadn't seen them clothed for quite a few days, so seeing them covered up seemed strange. He was soon lathering under a cold, steady stream from the portable shower and paid the previous observation little further thought. His splendid mate replaced him at the shower. He sat at Jo Anne's campsite and watched her; the view was surprisingly erotic. It had been some time since he had watched a beautiful, wet, wonderful woman; he could feel his heart quicken.

Anna looked at him and smiled mischievously. "Come here; you can wash my back." She had obviously been eavesdropping on his thoughts. She liked being watched, and his interest in her cleanliness had aroused her as well.

Daniel washed her back and soon the washing became caressing. With a little more foreplay she could tell that her mate was anxiously awaiting her. He lathered up parts of her body that weren't typically lathered during a shower. She softly pushed him away and bent over invitingly, resting the palms of her hands on the trunk of the tree that supported the portable shower. He gladly accepted her invitation and soon the passion became intense. For a couple that was used to frequent lovemaking, the new sensation provided by this position and the spontaneity of the moment was extra pleasurable. They telepathically shared their innermost feelings and sensations.

She focused on the intense fire that she was causing him to experience. As the force of his excitement increased so did the fire and her ecstasy. She prayed for him to release, she encouraged him, but the fire grew hotter and hotter. Finally, the moment came and she grasped the tree trunk so hard that she thought her hands would break. Thankfully, finally, she felt her body go into a complete spasm. For Daniel the intense fire turned into a warm glow as she accepted what he had to give her. The warmth encircled her and caused her to feel lightheaded. He wouldn't let her go, holding her to him for a long while so she would accept every drop. These her quivering body willingly accepted, and she enjoyed his tenderness. He would always be the one she loved.

After their passion had waned, they rested to savor the enjoyment for a moment, Anna on one knee and Daniel leaning against the tree. They marveled at the intensity of the passion they shared, and both found today a very good day to be alive. They were thankful to have the campground to themselves.

They ate a hearty breakfast and made plans for the day. They would sunbathe, rest, sunbathe, eat, and finally, after sunbathing, eat again, and later enjoy an evening fire with their friends. They rubbed sun block on each other and headed to a spot not far from Kathy and Steve's campsite that was both flat and sunny. It was already seventy-five degrees and they expected it to reach the nineties before long. After they had relaxed for a while, Kathy and Steve returned.

"I see you two have found the sun," said Kathy as she happily shed her clothes and pulled up a towel next to Anna's. Steve likewise was now used to full body exposure and, wearing only a smile and sunglasses, occupied a flat spot near Daniel. Daniel was sound asleep, but Anna could tell he was still scanning minds and remembering his training.

"How was your walk?" Anna asked, trying her hand at small talk.

"We walked quite a few miles and saw many of those merlins you keep watching," Kathy replied. Steve looked to be taking Daniel's example, becoming more comatose by the minute. "I have to thank you, Anna. You have been such a treasure for me, and this trip has been truly wonderful. I'm pregnant, I look and feel good, and wow, my love life is in a whole new dimension. Look at me!" She caressed her own body. "I haven't looked this good in a long time. I can walk for miles. I think I'm going to be a new woman."

"You're the same woman," Anna said. "You're just looking at yourself differently. Your goal was to find yourself, which you have. You also wanted to feel accepted by your husband. You are also looking for a mother figure to replace the mother you never knew in your childhood, and you have made a lifelong friend with Jo Anne. She needs someone to look out for her and I think you can be that person. Your husband was looking for a woman he could cherish and who would be turned on by him. Your new openness and freedom with your body have gone a long way toward making him the happiest male on earth. He now accepts you more than you could ever know. Finally, you are now with child. I think you've answered a lot of your wishes and needs in the last few weeks."

Kathy hadn't thought about all the fears and anxieties that had melted away recently. She took Anna's hand. "Thanks, Anna, for being here." They held hands for a long time. Both, feeling contented, fell asleep as the warm sun cradled their bodies. Finally Anna awoke much too hot and rolled over. She renewed her grasp with the other hand and felt a contentment she had rarely experienced outside the temple. She had made her friend's life better and knew that Kathy would now have a good, fulfilling life.

"We've decided to name our child either Anna or Daniel after you," Kathy later confided. "You have been a blessing to us, and this is how we'd like to repay your friendship with us."

Anna knew that Kathy would have a girl. It was an innate power of perception the Volva had. She had sensed it when she had touched Kathy's abdomen. She decided to withhold her prophecy from her companion. Anna thought about a namesake living in the farm country of Minnesota. It was a pleasing thought. Finally she replied, "If it's a girl remember to give her Jo Anne's necklace when she is a young woman. Tell her about Jo Anne. Tell her about me, how she was conceived, and about this month we've had together. Tell her about being a woman and truly feeling free in yourself and having the confidence to control your own destiny. Encourage her to accept nothing but the best for herself—education, careers, and men. Finally, tell her about the Brisingamen, what it means and how to use it to satisfy her one true love and to not waste her affection on false hopes and dreams. If you promise to do these things, you can use my name."

Kathy was overwhelmed as she felt Anna's words almost burn into her consciousness. "Thank you, Anna; I will." Kathy smiled and again drifted off to sleep.

Over a late lunch, Anna announced that they would leave in two days. Daniel cooked up one of his rehydrated special surprises for everyone. It wasn't all that special, but the gesture was sincere. The afternoon brought more rest and sun. The women and Daniel had toasted to a golden brown and looked magnificent. Steve seemed to tan only in shades of red, no matter what oil or lotion he tried. He didn't seem to care or to feel any pain, so nobody paid it any further concern.

Jo Anne and John returned in the evening, bearing new wine from Italy. They all agreed that the Australian wine was better. They were saddened but not surprised to learn of the departure plans. They were thankful that the three couples had been able to spend such an extended time together.

The next morning brought more of the same, except the passionate shower interlude was understandably absent since Jo Anne and John were at their stations. Anna and Daniel paused at Jo Anne's invitation for coffee. Kathy and Steve were in their tent making noises that left the quartet with sly smiles. Anna and Daniel planned on spending the day as before, purely in sloth mode. The sun was high, the breeze was mild, and the weather was warm. Kathy and Steve set out on a late morning romp that they expected would last all day. Anna invited the older couple to a sunny spot not far down the trail with a nice view. It was up a cliff but the climb wasn't all that strenuous. Daniel agreed to tote their reclining chairs with him. They all felt that a little sun and exercise along with a great view would be a welcome diversion.

John was feeling extraordinarily spry, as the chronic pain in his knees had left him during the past few weeks. He was feeling younger than ever. The walk actually made him feel good. To be pain-free had been the only hope and dream left in his life. He feared the pain would finally limit his mobility and keep him from enjoying his life on the road. His prayer had somehow been answered and he was thankful.

Anna quietly said, "You are welcome, John," as she walked behind him.

They arranged themselves and the men drifted off to sleep. "Just like men," Jo Anne observed.

Anna was still shiny with lotion as she placed her body in the full sun with nothing on but her sunglasses. Jo Anne looked at her companion's perfect female form. She studied her heavily tattooed skin and her deep, even tan. She realized she was also looking at a woman who was totally unashamed of herself and not concerned with what others thought. She'd almost been that way once. At last she sighed. "What the hell." She took off all of her clothes and revealed a sagging but attractive body. She had all the same features as Anna, except Anna was tighter here and there and naturally blonde. Jo Anne was naturally old and gray.

Anna handed her the bottle of sun block. "That's better. You're beautiful; you should be proud of yourself."

Jo Anne laughed. "I haven't been totally nude in public in such a long time."

They were quiet for a long while but neither fell asleep. Anna was watching a pair of merlins dance in the sky, hunting pigeons that had left their perches on the Castle. "Anna . . . I know who—or what—you and Daniel are."

"I know you know. Is that a problem?" Anna replied.

Jo Anne was obviously troubled. "We went to the library yesterday to print out a history of my necklace for Kathy. I went to a chat room about tattoos and I asked the people on-line about your Brisingamen tattoos and where to get one. As the chat continued, I soon learned that your tattoos are forbidden designs, and could mean death to the artist. In fact, I was warned that a man with a black sword-hand tattoo with an attacking lynx was a supernatural creature. Later I found Daniel's tattoos in a mythology site called Warrior of Vanadis, chosen male of the Seidkona, and Defender of the Earth. It took me a while to find you, Anna. Little is known of the Volva, High Priestesses of the Temple of Freyja."

"Do you really believe all that silly mythology stuff?" Anna asked, still watching the swift falcons above her.

"It just seems astonishing that a pair of mythological creatures would find themselves camping next to me in Nowheresville, South Dakota. But as I have been thinking about it, you two haven't been the normal campers. We've had an earthquake and strange weather, and I swear I've seen rocks moving. The sites I visited on the Internet described a pair of dangerous beings capable of killing mortals. I was warned to fear for my life for even looking at a Volva. To touch her would mean almost certain death." She paused. "To be honest, I'm scared, Anna. I've been afraid to even tell John of my findings. Maybe his innocence will protect him. He spent the whole time at the library reading the *Wall Street Journal*."

"Jo Anne, you can touch me." To reassure her, Anna grabbed her trembling hand. "I'm not here to kill you. You're my friend."

"Are you what they say you are?"

"Would knowing make you feel more at ease with me?" Anna asked. "I will not lie to you. You have been open and kind to me and I would like to be the same with you. I will tell you anything you ask of me. Some say, though, that ignorance is bliss."

"I think I would rest easier knowing." Jo Anne tried a weak smile. "I promise to guard your secret with my life and I do trust you as a friend, but I am just a little confused right now."

"Your description is vague but mostly true," Anna said, grasping her aged friend's hand more tightly. She levitated a small rock at her feet and it flew, much to the astonishment of Jo Anne, over Daniel and into the valley below. Daniel briefly awoke and flipped over; he was uninterested in the female bonding experience. "We aren't monsters; we're basically people just like you and John."

Jo Anne was afraid to speak for a time, but as she relaxed thanks to Anna's warm touch she began to realize this was going to be their only conversation about the matter. "How many are you?"

"Eleven Volva and now nine males."

"Were you born into this or are you selected?"

"Sort of both. I was born and was an orphan. Somehow when I was young, I was selected by some beings called Choosers. They supported me from afar, but I always knew someone was watching out for me and I felt different than other children. When I was fourteen, I was asked if I would be interested in competing to be part of a select fraternity of women. It seemed kind of mysterious and I'd always felt alone, so the thought of a family and togetherness seemed appealing. I received a vague message once a year that sort of loosely guided my way.

"Not knowing what else to do, I worked hard, studied hard, abstained from marriage, and became focused on securing a prize I knew nothing about. I knew even less about my chances of success. I was gifted with a beautiful, fit body, a strong mind, and a competitive spirit. After my twenty-fourth birthday, I awoke at the step of a temple in Africa with the tattoos you see here. I don't know how I got there, and I don't know who or what took me. I was initiated and here, thirteen years later, I lie before you.

"Daniel's process was different. His grandfather pledged him to the Order many years before he was born. The men have a much different path. They have to earn the chance to be with us, and only the strongest survive."

"Are . . . are you a god?"

"No. We are humans, designed to protect our race by using our gifts and powers. The history of humanity is not what it seems. Suffice it to say that it is much more complicated than all those science professors want us to think."

"Did it hurt becoming what you are?"

"No," Anna replied. "The power scared me at first, but it seems to scare everyone initially. The transformation is not without its difficulties."

Jo Anne marveled at Anna's openness. Obviously, she knew vast secrets. "Are you immortal?"

Anna laughed. "No, but we live a very long time, at least two hundred years. Our aging process is slowed way down. Typically, a Volva doesn't die of natural causes. We live very demanding lives and the strain on us is great. As one has finished her usefulness, she chooses a time for her end and is celebrated in a multi-day feast. Good-byes are said, tears are shed, and finally, with songs and many thanks, the Volva is no more. Her replacement brings her death. It is a death by love. We will all know when it is time. Freyja, a very famous Volva, died on the day that bares her name, Friday, and it was a happy and fulfilling celebration. The matriarch trains her replacement. I replaced Fareda, who trained me. I allowed her to pass on to the next life. It was my first independent use of my power after my training. Part of the training is to remember those that we replace. We are given their thoughts and experiences, so part of Fareda lives on in me. I will pass that along to my replacement. In that way we are immortal. Our memories cannot and will not die.

"The men don't live as long, maybe one hundred fifty years. They either die in battle or in old age with us nurturing them. They are solitary creatures. Through us, they protect all of you, keeping you and your offspring from killing each other."

Jo Anne felt the conversation was getting too deep for her to comprehend. She backed off the history lesson and went to the present. "So are you training here?"

Anna nodded.

"Do I need to worry about any ramifications of our time together?"

"No, to the contrary. You have helped me mature as a person. You have given me a mother figure, and Kathy is like the sister I never had. I am truly grateful. You have opened my eyes and reminded me of the kindness of humanity. I will cherish the memories I have made here for the rest of my life. As you have changed my life for the better, I would like to give each of you gifts to better your lives.

"I have given Kathy and Steve their gifts already. Steve just needed a wife that loved him and wanted him as a man. That was easy. Kathy needed to have respect for herself and feel as though she was a woman. She now has self-esteem, she has conceived and will bear a little girl, and she has also found a truly wonderful female friend and companion in her life, you. She will look after you when you grow old and make sure you are not in want.

"You gave her a powerful symbol of the female bond of sister-hood. When you gave her the Brisingamen, you adopted her as your daughter. She is now responsible to return the favor to you. That is what Kathy needed, to feel connected to her womanhood.

"John has a simple fear—pain. He doesn't want to be a burden to you or to suffer. I have healed his arthritic knees and joints and repaired his heart. You have your old husband back." She laughed and squeezed Jo Anne's hand. "He's your problem now." Tears were forming in Jo Anne's eyes. "Now, I have been analyzing what I could give you, my friend, to remember me and to better your life. You have a fear of dying and of the afterlife. I cannot help you with that. I am not God. I have given you comfort in your old age through Kathy, but that is Kathy's gift. I thought about some of your other psychological needs, but nothing I could do seemed appropriate. Your future is already a happy one and you have no concerns about virtually anything. I have finally realized that you have a tremen-dous need for knowledge. You desire to be important and to make a difference in society.

"My gift to you, Jo Anne, is to instill within you a secret, my secret. No living person outside of my Order knows who I am. Daniel has a family that remembers him; they have pictures of him in their house. He is part of their lives and he always has a home. I have no one—no parents, no relatives, nobody. You will be my an-chor in the world. I want you to remember me and be my link with my human roots. When I am sitting in my temple, the power of the world is at my command, and it is nice to know there is someone who knows who I am—not just what I am, but who I am—some-one who cares for me. Would this gift be enough of a thanks for you?"

Jo Anne openly wept. Despite her many years, she had never been touched by anyone like Anna. Her fear of Anna was gone, and the pair sat up and embraced. "Yes, Anna, I will be your an-chor. I will treasure what you've told me. I'm sorry I went to the library and found out about you. I feel I violated your trust."

"Jo Anne," Anna reassured. "You can never disappoint me. Thanks for being you."

They resumed their positions, and Jo Anne resumed the con-versation. "So I'll never see you again?"

"No, I suspect I'll never visit the country of my birth again." Anna sighed. "My home is in the temple in Ethiopia, and I suspect I'll return there soon. You have your memories and I have mine. It is enough for us to know that we are bonded. Rest assured that I will always be thinking of you. I'll think of you, John, Kathy, Steve, and young Anna enjoying this place for many years to come. Just keep inviting young couples over to share our memories each evening as you've done with us. Don't keep your camping circle closed."

"Anna, you will always be in my thoughts and will always be part of our camping experiences."

"See? That's immortality." Anna smiled and re-grasped Jo Anne's hand. "You're immortal now too, Jo Anne." She paused as Jo Anne smiled at her. "Daniel will be around. If you really and truly need me or need anything, I am always with him. We have a telepathic bond, one that probably is too difficult for you to understand. I'd like to know that you're safe and not suffering. Send him a picture of my namesake after she's born. You need only contact the State Department in Washington and they will contact him. He will come as soon as he is able. Oh, and don't be surprised if some summer while you are all sitting around enjoying a nice fire and some good Australian wine, my mate mysteriously shows up for a passing visit."

Jo Anne smiled. "He will always be welcome."

The contented women sat silently for a long while, enjoying each other's company and the bonds that they had formed. Finally, Daniel awoke and announced that he would make lunch. They spent the afternoon in the same way—rest and sun. Finally, as evening was starting to descend, Kathy and Steve returned from their hike. They were extremely satisfied despite their exhaustion. The six spent their last night together as they had most of the previous. Anna made a large fire, and they roasted marshmallows, drank wine, and talked of the future. They also talked of each other and of the good times they'd had. Gradually the sun and drink took effect and everyone retired to their own bed.

Daniel and Anna spent the night in each other's arms but had no further physical intimacy. Both were contented already and the thought of sex was far from their thoughts. Daniel was thinking of the mighty power Anna had shown him. He was now what he was supposed to be. His training was complete and he was truly a happy man. He was comfortable with who he was and what he had become, and he was prepared to face his destiny.

Anna was thinking that this place had caused her to complete her pre-Volva experience. She felt like a complete human being. She was deeply thankful to Daniel for his excellent selection. Slim Buttes would always have a special place in her heart. She felt that she would now be able to grow even closer to her sisters in the temple due to these bonds outside the temple.

CHAPTER 12: A Walk on the Dark Side

Tiger spent the summer researching the strange and powerful beings he had read about. What his research produced disturbed him. The beings were known as the Defenders of the Earth and seemed more mythical than human. They seemed to loosely follow the mythology of several cultures. This scared Tiger because he knew that when several cultures referred to the same event or people in its mythology, the tale was probably based on fact. He also found some sketchy evidence of their presence in modern times.

The literature supported a few basic facts. There were both men and women. The women stayed at a temple while the men roamed the globe trying to keep peace and order for some higher purpose, one that wasn't entirely clear. The temple was located somewhere in Ethiopia, but there were also older references to other temples, so they could possibly have more than one. It appeared to be suicidal to attack a temple or attempt to gain entry. These beings didn't appear to act with the consciousness of the modern world and had no problem with the mass slaughter of their enemies. In fact, they appeared to be undefeated in battle. Obviously, he couldn't just lob a nuclear warhead in their direction.

Their power was poorly understood, but they somehow had the ability to control the elements and to affect one's will and resolve to fight back. Tiger suspected it would be easy to lose hope and morale in a confrontation when a single individual carried more firepower than an entire attacking force. He did, however, locate two references to Defenders being successfully killed. The Nazis had killed one, and another was killed by a surprise volcanic eruption. That was the reference he thought was the most interesting. The death at the hands of the Germans took too long as the Nazis lured the man into a dinner and drugged him after a three-year plot to assassinate him.

He had no idea how many of the powerful creatures existed, but he postulated that they were probably few in number. His agents had identified two, one that was witnessed by Mr. Li himself. The tattooed fellow had just walked by him one day in Macao. Li had put a tail on him and found him living in a local hotel courtesy of the state in Hong Kong. They had started monitoring his every move.

The other one lived in the Middle East. He had been observed a year earlier visiting a mutual associate—the Sultan of Oman. They tracked the man to Istanbul, noting his habits and behavior. Tiger suspected there were others, but as with his biological attacks, he planned on striking quickly. He made a basic plan to attack these two Defenders and any others he could identify in the hopes of distracting them so that right afterwards he could proceed with his own master plan. Once he had unified his people, it would be too late to reverse the process.

He would map their behavior, find a consistency, and take them out with a sudden, large explosion. There would be collateral damage. There always was, but he would make it look like the Moslem extremists were to blame, which would divert everyone's attention.

* * * * *

Anna and Daniel awoke early the next morning and began packing. They quickly loaded up their vehicle and found themselves hot and sweaty. After encouragement from Jo Anne, they used her shower for the last time, covered their bodies with new backcountry outfits, and finished arranging the vehicle. Having already said their good-byes, they gave their final embraces, handshakes, and kisses. The Suburban pulled out of campsite number three, leaving behind a campground of contented people. There were no tears. Anna had seen to that.

"They were certainly good people," Anna reflected to Daniel. They had one final training mission in Sturgis. Their path through the west valley led them over territory that, until today, they had seen only from a distance; places that had recently experienced earthquakes, tornadoes, and freak thunderstorms; places populated only with an occasional herd of antelope.

* * * * *

At Reva Gap, life went on much as it had during the Defenders' presence. Kathy and Steve still celebrated each other. They continued their casual attitude about clothing, made plans for young Daniel or Anna, and decided not to return home until three days prior to the start of the school year. John moved with the body of a man half his age. He had even found new excitement with Jo Anne. Jo Anne treasured Anna's secret revelation in her heart and never told a soul what she knew about Anna and Daniel. She had an important task, and she felt the utmost privilege in doing it.

That first evening, a new couple, Tim and Martha, took Anna and Daniel's former campsite. They were in their early twenties and from Wisconsin. They had been married just a year and were trying to find themselves. Immediately they were invited to share the evening campfire and wine with the other two couples. Although Kathy and Steve's open nudity bothered them at first, they too became friends and spent the rest of August at Reva Gap. Within a few days, they even used Jo Anne's shower. They relaxed and found themselves baring both their souls and their bodies. Every night the wine glasses were raised to toast Anna and Daniel. Although Tim and Martha had never met the couple, as the story of them became nothing short of a legend, they too felt as though they were intimate friends. The trip to Reva Gap would become an annual tradition. The six of them would meet and spend most of the summer at Slim Buttes. It was their link to each other and to themselves as they had found a happiness and contentment seldom experienced in the modern world.

* * * * *

Daniel and Anna walked down Main Street. It wasn't quite bike week in the Black Hills city of Sturgis, but the annual rally was close enough so that bikers had already enveloped the town. The sight of two heavily-tattooed people in such a scene was not unusual. The goal of today's lesson was one of healing, so they were headed for the hospital and the nursing home. First they needed some food, and downtown Sturgis seemed to be the place for it. They'd had enough rehydrated food and needed something new and different.

As they scanned the minds of those around them, they noticed that a lot of alcohol had already been consumed. These guys and gals were by and large hardcore bikers—the casual Harley crowd wouldn't arrive until next week

Suddenly a leathery palm grabbed Anna's shoulder. "Hey, Babe, how about humping a real man?" said the owner of the palm. A massive electrical charge hit his hand full force. "Jesus Christ!" He fell to one knee, holding the offending appendage. Daniel could smell the burnt flesh.

The man grimaced. "You fucking bitch!"

Daniel watched and took up no defense for Anna. When it came to the Volva it was best to stay out of their way. Anna's eyes had taken on the telltale, slightly reddish glow he had seen before when she was angered. The man then decided he was going to slap her around for what she had done to him—he and his buddies would initiate her properly.

The man experienced his final thought as Anna hurled him into an alley where he struck a large green dumpster. As the pair walked away, a sudden stray bolt of lightning struck the very same alleyway. Such was the penalty for the man's transgression. Anna displayed very little tolerance in such encounters. Some people just needed to learn when to cut their losses.

Daniel and Anna ate a fine meal courtesy of a downtown café, then went to the nursing home. Anna felt a deep compassion toward the curses of aging. She had been spared the effects of growing old, and she desired, at least today, to make the lives of the residents of this home a little better. Daniel needed experience in finding pain and healing people, and this was a good place to practice. The bodies of many of the residents had been ravaged by the mines, ranches, and mills of the area. Now that these people served no social purpose, they were locked away here, outcasts of society. The Defenders went from room to room. Most of the residents were happy to have anyone visit, even a kindly pair of strangers. Anna and Daniel made some small talk and quickly went to work.

The most needy were the Alzheimer's patients. They were locked in a world of confusion and fear. Anna showed Daniel how to communicate with them. Daniel had never felt such gratitude in his entire life. The patients thought angels had visited the home. As they passed rooms they had already visited they noticed many residents on their knees in prayer. Daniel and Anna relieved chronic pain and healed lost hearing and eyesight. They fixed cancer, tumors, and chronic breathing problems. Some residents were in such poor shape that they just needed reassurance that it was okay to die.

As they healed the residents, Daniel and Anna instilled a command to not let anyone know what had been done. If they told, they would lose their gift. Anna passed an obviously pregnant nurse who looked puzzled as to what was going on. She read that her baby was terribly deformed and, much moved, touched the woman's abdomen. A blue light enveloped them both. Anna stood up and looked into the eyes of a woman now in shock.

"Your baby is all right now," Anna said with a smile. "I have others to heal."

They finished and then walked to the hospital. It was more of the same, but here, Daniel did all the healing and Anna critiqued. During their visit to both facilities, no one asked what they were doing and no one tried to interfere. The patients and residents were all given a once-in-a-lifetime gift. The whole process took barely two hours, so the couple drove up to Spearfish and repeated the process until Anna was assured of Daniel's mastery.

Satisfied, they resumed their journey back to Ellsworth Air Force Base. The base commander had assumed that the loaned vehicle had been lost or returned to another base, so he was surprised to see them back. They gave their gear to an enlisted man who helped them onto the plane. It was Anna's first, and most likely last, camping experience.

When they arrived back in Washington, D.C., Anna announced that Daniel's progress had been superb and his training was complete. Daniel felt that he could now relax and they could spend some quality time together. He needed a break. The two days off at Reva Gap had been refreshing, but he felt he needed more. Anna had been all business since he'd awakened from his fever. In the thirteen months that had followed he had learned a new language and all the skills of a Defender. It had been a long trip returning from South Dakota, and they were both tired. A military limo dropped them off at their embassy and they headed straight to the bedroom.

Just because they were tired was no reason to refrain from the customary pre-bedtime ritual of male-female relations. Afterward, Daniel fell into a post-coital sleep. Anna watched her man take in steady breaths. She enjoyed watching contented men sleep, and Daniel was the most contented man she had ever met. Anna had just confirmed with Monique, the Volva on watch, that she needed to return. Trouble was in the wind. This was no time for a Volva to be needlessly away from the temple. Daniel could now take care of himself and he needed time to fly solo and gain self-confidence. His powers would soon be needed.

She gently traced the smile on his face with her finger. She had no reason to wonder what he was thinking. She loved to invade the dreams of her sleeping mate, and she deciphered that he was dreaming of her. It was a sweet dream, a dream of a lifetime together. This made Anna content, and she let herself drift off to sleep.

Morning came early. When Daniel awoke, Anna was already up. She had showered and was wearing her white tunic.

"Are we going somewhere?"

Anna smiled. Men always preferred verbal stimuli. Despite her deep love for him, she would enjoy returning to the simplicity of temple life. Why speak when telepathy was so much easier and unmistakable? But she indulged him. "It is time I return home. You're welcome to accompany me to the air base."

"So soon? I had hoped we could spend some more time together." He looked sad.

"Daniel, my love," she scolded. "We will be together for the rest of your life. We Volva fear trouble is brewing and the others need me back at the temple. Connecting with the Conduction Array is a taxing job. The Volva have been short-handed for too long; I need to get back and pull my weight. And you need some time to be alone and complete your journey. You now have the skills to be a very powerful Defender. You just need time to focus on yourself and harness your thoughts. We will always be with you and we are good at keeping you out of trouble."

"Somehow I knew I needed to get used to being alone," he said. "I had a funny feeling last night that we might be uniting for the last time in a while. I guess together in spirit will have to do. Have you made the arrangements?"

"Of course," she replied. "We need to leave in fifteen minutes, so if you're coming you need to get cleaned up."

Daniel started to shower. Thinking about Daniel naked in the shower, rubbing soap all over his lean body and getting clean was more than Anna could take, so she quickly joined him. It began with soap but it soon ended with a more physically taxing affair as Anna almost pinned Daniel to the back of the shower wall and immediately enveloped him. As Daniel recomposed himself he was able to turn her around to a more shower-friendly position to complete his lustful ambitions. It was quick and powerful sex, and it would be their last physical intimacy for some time.

Anna left, allowing Daniel to finish showering and put on a clean tunic. He joined Anna in the diplomatic limousine; she still exhibited a bright sex flush. The pair said little as they soaked up each other's company during the trip to Vandenberg Air Force Base. They zipped through the security checkpoint and stopped behind a jet transport plane, then got out and embraced for one last time. He watched her climb the stairs into the plane. She was filled with a self-confidence and self-assurance rarely found in women, or in anyone for that matter. She had no fear and as Daniel could now appreciate, presented herself with such a force that others gave her as much space as possible.

She stepped through the hatch, looked back at Daniel one last time, and telepathically said *Take care, my love, and trust in yourself. We will be together soon enough.*

Daniel answered her in the same fashion. *Have a safe trip and give a hug to all of the Volva for me.*

The door closed behind Anna. Daniel's mind filled with thoughts of the past year, and he smiled as he watched the plane finish its warm-up, taxi to the runway, and lift off. He paused there for a while to savor the moment, then climbed back into the limo and ordered the driver to drive around for a while. He needed time to think.

Marta was on duty, and Daniel soon enjoyed her ageless wisdom and encouragement. As they drove past the Washington Monument, Daniel ordered the limo driver to stop and he got out to walk. It was a beautiful day. His future lay directly ahead of him, and he needed some time to refocus from his past to the future.

There were surprisingly few tourists at the center of America's government. Daniel quietly strolled past the Washington Monument, wandered past the replica of Monticello, which marked the Jefferson

Monument, and finally sat in front of the imposing statue of Lincoln. The impressive stone figure looked out over the city.

Daniel soon grew tired of the monuments, so he got up and headed north.

At the corner of R Street and fourteenth he paused to people watch. The activity in front of an aging, brown brick, three-story building opposite him caught his attention. Various men, most of them shabbily dressed, loitered outside the building and in the nearby alleys. Three sat under the lone street lamp in front of the building. Others sat on the steps or leaned against the walls, and more just wandered about. He could make out the word Mission on the wall of the building. This was his first visit to a homeless shelter.

An unkempt man approached, unshaven and reeking of alcohol. He asked Daniel for money. Daniel put his hand on his shoulder and looked into his mind. It was largely void and burnt out from a lifetime of drug and alcohol abuse. The man's name was Herbert. Herbert had a family, so Daniel focused on that. Herbert also believed in God. Daniel filled Herbert's mind with thoughts of home, God's love, and avoiding drug use.

Herbert pulled away with his eyes wide open, looking a bit shocked. "Man!" he stammered. "The preacher in the mission is good. I got to get me some religion right now." He stumbled toward the front door and went in.

Marta was always on Daniel's mind, literally. Even now, the ability to continuously share thoughts intrigued him. Although he had learned, after remembering Omar's recommendation, to develop a way to lock the Volva into a recess of his mind, they were always there. It was a pleasant interaction and the Volva never interfered with his day-to-day activities. They would observe and protect if needed and converse when appropriate, but otherwise they remained in the background. He remembered the story of Marco, the Defender who couldn't deal with the voices of the Volva and exiled himself to the Island of Trisdan de Cuhna in the south Atlantic. It seemed to Daniel that ttempting to hide from the women and voices seemed to be futile and self-serving. He considered the Volva his friends and comrades, not tormentors.

It is surely a tragic sight to see such needy people in a land of plenty, Marta contributed to Daniel's observations. *The poverty in places like India or Africa is much more striking, but it is less bothersome because it is in areas with little else to offer.*

I wish we could use our powers more to help people like this, he answered.

Yes. However, we are charged only with the protection of the race. There is too much need in the world for the few of us to make much difference. We can only hope that civilization will solve these other problems without our help. We have to concern ourselves with issues involving nuclear weapons, global conquest, germ warfare, and other evils that threaten our very existence. But remember, there is nothing wrong with helping a few people along the way.

As Daniel and Marta's conversation continued he hadn't noticed that a group of young men had surrounded him. He snapped back to external sensation when a voice was directed at him.

"What's a white boy like you doin' here?" said one of the men. They were all wearing green hats and some wore jackets, which appeared to a novice like Daniel to have gang markings. "You lookin' for drugs?"

Another chimed in. "Dig the robe and the tattoo; he must be some kind of religious psycho."

They waited for Daniel to speak, but he didn't. He felt no fear and it wasn't clear to him whether Marta was blocking his fear response or whether he truly had none. He just stared at the leader and showed no outward sign of emotion.

"He's stoned, man!" one of them said. "He's out of it—must have came up here from the mission."

The leader paused as if for effect and stepped forward while the other members of the gang circled Daniel like predators circling their prey. "Well, I'm a generous man today. I'll trade you your life for all of your money and your drugs." His partners laughed. "So what you got under that dress of yours, Whitey?"

Daniel finally spoke. "You don't know what you're dealing with here, and I'm not really in the mood right now. It would be better for you to just wander off."

Laughter followed and the leader continued. "You're not in the mood? I'm not in the mood for some white trash on my turf." His anger roiled and he pulled a switchblade. "Now, your money!"

Daniel's voice grew in strength. "I don't want to hurt you, so go away!"

"You and what army, shit-for-brains?" said the leader. "The deal for your life is off! Now you die!" As he spoke, three of the young men moved toward Daniel. Daniel stared at the leader and before the men on either side could touch him, the one on the right flew up and over a fence some thirty feet away. He landed with a thud. The second man also went airborne and into the street. All the windows in the cars that lined the streets exploded. The rest of the men froze in place. Their overwhelming urge was to run, but they found themselves unable to move. Daniel never took his gaze from the leader. Suddenly the knife in the leader's hand became bitterly cold, as if all the heat were being sucked out of it. The leader dropped the weapon, and the frozen knife, nearing absolute zero, shattered on impact with the cement.

"I don't need an army," he said quietly. His response had been reflexive and undoubtedly orchestrated by Marta transmitting her power through his thoughts. Daniel gestured and all of the men were pinned to the fence. Fear had replaced the contempt and arrogance of a few seconds earlier. "I don't have money. I never use it." He raised his tunic to reveal his heavily tattooed body. He could sense fear, but he also sensed the men had some good in them. "I'm going to be generous, too." He smiled. "I'm not going to rip you up bit by bit. You gentlemen need to understand that not everything is a power game. You may kick over another rock some-day and again find someone like me hiding underneath. Consider this a warning to change your life."

He pointed to his face. "Remember my markings. These are the markings of death to you. Look in the mirror, watch behind you, and beware of whom you talk to. If you continue in your life of crime, I will return and my revenge will be swift. I will destroy all of you and your families and your friends. Now, go away!" He waved his arm again and they all flew up over the fence. He walked on as the men stumbled to their feet and ran or limped away.

Daniel was happy with his first engagement. Marta complimented him as well. Anna's advice that a Defender always needed to use just enough power to control and defuse a situation, but not so much that it would cause an even bigger problem, worked well. He just as easily could have killed his attackers, but in their case, a strong warning would be better. He hoped the men would start their lives over and become productive citizens, although he realized there was a slim chance of such a conversion in a society that failed to hold the criminal responsible for his own behavior.

Word traveled fast through the neighborhood that some stranger, maybe even a supernatural being, was walking the streets, and everyone stayed well away from Daniel. He was neither accosted nor approached. People crossed the street to avoid him.

As he walked, his thoughts were a mix of his own, Anna's teachings, and Marta's input. He continued to wander along the decay and poverty that is urban Washington, D.C. Despite not hav-ing passed a single human for some time and having no one share the sidewalk with him since the encounter with the local gang, Daniel was growing sleepy and hadn't noticed that he had picked up a tail. The man was middle-aged, black, and wore nondescript clothing. He looked as if he hadn't shaved for at least forty-eight hours. His appearance almost looked designed, and his mannerism and step did not resemble that of the other residents of the neighborhood.

The man originally had no intention of harming the white man, as today was a practice day for him. He had planned to have a little fun with some criminal or some other member of Washington D.C.'s underbelly. He had lust on his mind, blood lust, and now it must be fulfilled. Unfortunately, today was stranger than most. Everyone seemed jittery and nobody was out on the street. After much scout-ing, the only easy target he'd found was some strange, tattooed man in a white tunic.

The stalker was confused as to why a white guy would be in such a bad neighborhood in the first place. The white guy was lucky, the man thought, to have escaped notice by the gangs. The man surmised that the white man was some sort of religious zealot or even a psychotic individual who was looking for the homeless shelter. It was a strange day, and this man would have to do. The stalker knew he would have to hurry, before the white man got too close to Howard University and relative safety.

The stalker was a nurse anesthesiologist by day. He actually lived in Arlington on the west bank of the Potomac, and he liked his job, especially the power it gave him over life and death. He also had a very special private hobby. He killed people. Some he tortured and raped, and some he just killed. Occasionally he would leave a victim alive, in the ancient tradition of sparing a life so that the survivor could tell of the carnage that he alone had wrought.

He wasn't selective. He'd killed prostitutes, truck drivers, children, and drunks, and he'd even killed a young woman who'd turned out to be a legislative intern; the more random the better. He also liked to go on vacations with themes—migrant farm workers in Denver, prostitutes in Vegas, religious people in Oklahoma—and he was having fun planning a tourist theme for this winter's trip to Florida. He had already killed sixty-eight people.

The Romans had punished soldiers after being defeated in battle by making the surviving soldiers beat to death every tenth member. His perversion was to make every tenth death something special. This white religious nut would only be number sixty-nine, so he would keep it simple and make it look like a mugging. He watched as his prey turned down a dead-end alleyway. Some people just deserve to die, and in his judgment, this was an inferior creation. The man picked up his pace, pulled out a large, serrated hunting knife, and closed the gap.

Anna had shown Daniel how to slow the perception of time but Daniel hadn't yet mastered the practice. He thought he'd go back into this alley and work at it as cars passed by on the street. But one thing he had mastered was his perception of danger. Anna had beat this into him so hard that he could perceive bug bites, stubbed toes, or even being hit by raindrops before they happened. Although the Volva could heal most wounds and illnesses, it was better to avoid injury in the first place.

Suddenly, Daniel's internal alarm went off. He turned and saw a man stabbing at him with a knife. Daniel froze the attacker in mid-air. His powers were developed enough to instinctively transfer his thoughts and reflexes into energy. Without touching the man, Daniel telepathically moved him into a prone position opposite a brick wall at his feet. The man could blink his eyes and make some minor facial gestures but was unable to speak or move.

As Daniel began to probe the mind of his assailant, he was shocked and horrified. Unlike the street punks earlier, this man was altogether evil. Daniel could tell immediately that he was no stranger to killing, and that he killed for sport. Most people were terrified when Daniel froze them, but not this man. He seemed to be getting a high out of being controlled. He was still planning how to kill Daniel and now wanted to make the death a special event. The man had no fear as he surmised that Daniel wouldn't have the courage to kill him. He considered himself immortal and believed nobody was smart enough to catch him, let alone hurt him. Besides, humanity didn't have the moral stomach for death. For a moment, Daniel was unsure of his next move.

Marta decided to add her observation. *Remember this man and his thought patterns. He is the definition of evil. No good can ever come of him or any like him. As Defenders, we are like gardeners. We need to watch over the garden and protect it from catastrophic events. He is a weed, and a weed cannot become a bearing crop. If you simply throw a weed out, it will just take root and ruin another crop. It must be destroyed to protect the rest of the garden. Never have doubt or guilt about eliminating men and women such as this. They are rare, but you will encounter them from time to time. You will also find that you have no power of persuasion over this type of person and you cannot affect their actions. Hitler was like this and so was Napoleon.*

Without delay Daniel followed Marta's advice. First he melted the knife the man still held in his hand, the molten steel severely disfiguring his hand. The man relished the great pain. Daniel looked deeply into the man's thoughts and suggested to him that execution was now at hand. Daniel sensed the realization in the man's thoughts that he would not live through this encounter, then closed his eyes and focused on a spot deep in the man's brain. The man's eyes rolled back as the energy coursed through him and his body was lifted two feet off the ground. Then Daniel opened his eyes and released the body. It fell lifeless to the pavement. Daniel shook his head and resumed his walk back out to the main street, where he continued in the direction of Howard University.

Smoke still rose from under the shirt of the dead mass murderer, killed while attempting to ply his craft. Under the intact shirt, etched into his skin was a message:

I am the man who killed the intern before 9/11. I have mur-

dered and tortured many in states and cities far and wide. In my house I have keepsakes from all of my murders.

Please tell the families that judgment has been served and they can now have closure to the demise of their loved ones. An eye for an eye—I was a weed that needed to be destroyed.

The medical examiner had never seen a person die in such a manner. There were no external signs of injury except for the strange note burned into the man's chest and a disfigured right hand. His cerebral cortex had been burned from the inside out, as if in a microwave oven. It had been damaged to such an extent that little remained. It was a puzzling death, one the medical examiner finally determined should be called catastrophic cerebral injury.

Fifty-two victims from twelve states were soon identified as having died at the hands of this man. He was now known as the Potomac Killer. As to his killer, no file was ever made of the crime.

* * * * *

Daniel had decided that the biggest problems facing America were from politicians and terrorists. Either had the ability to cause a nuclear holocaust or to unleash biological weapons which could destroy the planet. He would therefore monitor members of government by finding out where the senators and their aides ate lunch and dinner. He would monitor their thoughts from time to time in an effort to see whether anything was up. He would also monitor newspapers and late night radio for anything suspicious that he would need to check out in person. Although the terrorists would be more difficult to monitor, as they were, by their nature, unpredictable, he would gain access to captured Taliban and al-Qaeda members and probe their minds for more insight. He would need to visit his State Department contacts, then ooze into every rock and crevasse to keep abreast of what was really going on in this country.

Marta thought the plan was a good start and that it would at least keep Daniel proactive in his job. He had to be the eyes and ears in North America for the Order. If something turned up, Daniel's mission could become more focused. It had been a big day, and by the time he reached Howard University, he was ready to relax back at the consulate. His car came around to pick him up and he was dropped off at his door.

Daniel spent the next few days doing background work. He had received news from the Volva of Anna's safe arrival, and she was now undergoing the self-purification ritual. Her twenty-eight days of isolation would be good for his independence, because foremost he needed to get used to working alone. The mundane drudgery of congressional mind-reading would be a good start. He spent his mornings scouting the breakfast hangouts of the powerful and their lackeys. His lunch was more of the same while his evenings were spent learning their bad habits—bars, strip clubs, and the like.

He was soon amazed at what he learned. Although ever since the President Clinton/intern sex scandal his idealized vision of public officials had radically changed for the worse, he still hadn't expected this. The level of debauchery was beyond imagination. It started at the intern level and went all the way up. Interns and junior aides, male or female, would sleep with anyone to get a better job or secure more power. Sexual favors with these underlings were traded for votes or donations, or some were even used as spies. A congressman would send his junior staffers to a congressman from another state for favors. It was like trading baseball cards. Some approached the truly bizarre. If he weren't Swedish, he'd have been shocked by the depravity.

When it wasn't sex, it was money. Washington was the land of the high rollers, and only those with money or who represented money had any real influence. It was a sad system and it didn't matter whether you were a Democrat or a Republican. What bothered Daniel most was the actual contempt most of the politicians and aides had for the common people. He was glad Jefferson, Adams, and the like were no longer around as they would have been suicidal at seeing what had become of their republic.

He was also surprised with the openness that the aides—and in some cases, the legislators themselves—had with national secrets. They shared sensitive details with each other, various reporters, and even their current sexual playthings. The disclosures seemed to have no more purpose than to fortify their feelings of importance. It didn't seem to be difficult for a real spy to get state secrets in this town. These people were morally bankrupt.

Despite his constant vigilance, Daniel discovered no big news or anything of dire consequence that required his attention. His other concern, terrorism, was also of little importance to the aides. They seemed almost oblivious to 9/11, or the Afghan and Iraqi campaigns that seemed to dominate the attention of most Americans. Obviously, there were no hidden terrorism secrets. Nobody knew anything, so Daniel decided it was time to personally interrogate the few prisoners that were being held by the government.

Daniel's arrival at the Deputy Secretary of State's office the next day was without fanfare. The Deputy greeted him with more courtesy this time. Obviously, since their last meeting, he had realized that Daniel was worth listening to. Mr. Andrews started off their meeting with pleasantries. "I hope all was to your satisfaction for your backcountry excursion. Where did you go, Mount Rushmore? Quite a piece of American history."

Daniel smiled. "It was fine. I'm here on official business. I need to interview some of the terrorist subjects you have locked up. I'd like to start with the twentieth hijacker since he is held locally. After that I will see the shoe bomber and the people you've detained from Buffalo, and finally I'd like to go to the detention camp at Guantanamo Bay."

Andrews initially laughed at the request. He still didn't grasp that Daniel was much more than an annoyance. The strangely tattooed man had no country, represented no people, and therefore had no right to see these prisoners. He suspected that even Tony Blair wouldn't be granted an audience with the terrorists. "That's a tall order. I'm not sure how we can approach anything as complex as you actually meeting these people. It is all hush-hush and state secrets, you know."

Daniel could feel his energy welling up within him. Monique was trying to keep him calm and prevent him from doing something dreadful. Mr. Andrews noticed the coffee in his cup was boiling; the mug was too hot to touch. "Mr. Andrews, this is not a request; it is an order. Your car will take me to see the twentieth hijacker at eight o'clock tomorrow morning."

Andrews complied with the request although it didn't seem as though his superiors would approve of this. As the Defender waited, he dialed a person in Justice and without any further effort the meeting was arranged. Daniel went home to prepare. This was his new self-proclaimed day of rest and meditation. For the remainder of the day, he would work on his powers and strengthen his mind.

His car was on schedule the next morning and it transported him directly to a detention facility in northern Virginia. Daniel was given some suspicious looks as he made his way through the various security checkpoints and metal detectors. At the final checkpoint he was asked to sign in. He signed Daniel, and that seemed to be enough for the guard. A member of the U.S. Attorney's office named Mathews escorted him to a prisoner interrogation room.

"I'm not sure how you got access to this guy and I'm not sure what good you'll do," said a rather unhappy Mathews. "He doesn't say anything, generally. He has his attorney present for consultation but is representing himself. He just babbles about being some sort of religious zealot and claims that we have no authority to try him. I don't know who you are or why you're here, but the Attorney General himself said to let you ask whatever you want within the law. You are considered an agent of our government while you're in the prison, so you're governed by our prosecutorial rules of conduct."

"Good," replied Daniel. "I want to observe him for a while first through the one-way mirror."

"Sure." Mathews gave Daniel a chair and removed the opaque covering of the mirrored window. The room on the other side contained two men. The one in orange was balding and had a beard. He was the supposed twentieth hijacker. The other wore a suit, was of Arab descent, and served as legal counsel. Daniel went straight to work, looking into the balding man's mind for nearly an hour. During the ordeal a telepathic connection was made between Daniel, Darna, and Omar. In this way they translated the prisoner's thoughts with only a five-second delay. The Defenders frequently used each other for linguistic translations. Although this prisoner could speak English and French, he thought in his native tongue, which was an Arabic dialect. Omar knew it well and had very little difficulty translating.

As it turned out, the prisoner was a man of insight and more knowledge than Daniel expected.

The guards and Mathews became so bored by Daniel's inaction that they interrupted him. He stared at them and they backed off to let him finish.

"I'll talk to him now," Daniel ordered.

"Johnson, the guard, and I will come in with you. The prisoner has shown violent tendencies toward people without uniforms on."

"I won't need him or you," instructed Daniel. "I would be shocked if he gets violent with me; in fact, it would be the last thing he ever does."

They thought it was just tough talk and laughed silently at the tattooed man's bravery, obviously ignorant of what Daniel was and what he could do. Daniel walked in and removed his tunic, leaving just his loincloth. This was his preferred dress when the weather was warm, and he wanted the prisoner to view the full ramifications of who was visiting him.

The prisoner was having a heated religious discussion with his clearly overwhelmed legal advisor, and his voice died away as Daniel entered the room. The arrogant, self-confident zealot turned deathly pale at the sight of the scantily-clothed man marked with the forbidden tattoos. Daniel sensed extreme fear in the man, and he knew the man had recognized what he was. He read a memory in the man that his grandfather had warned him against any man bearing the forbidden tattoos of an attacking lynx and the black sword hand. They were Defenders, and to confront one usually meant a horrible end.

The lawyer spoke first. "How dare you come in here? Who do you think you are? You have no authority to see this prisoner!"

Daniel stared at him while the prisoner grabbed his lawyer in a desperate attempt to keep him from angering Daniel, finally shouting at him in Arabic.

"You are a Hamat al Omma!" He shouted in a rather fearful tone. Daniel cut him off before he continued.

He replied slowly, but in perfect Arabic with Omar doing the talking. "We both know what I am." As if by magic, Daniel sent one of the chairs slamming against the back wall. The lawyer now also started to tremble at what was before him. "And I know who you are. I know your thoughts. I know your guilt. Hear this: The Homat al Omma have now taken a special interest in you. I do not personally care what is done with you. If I had my way, your entire body would melt away as we are speaking, but I promised the Americans I would not kill you, at least not today. You can be a martyr if you want, but remember, as your grandfather warned, any martyrdom of the sort you planned on 9/11 will not mean an afterlife of virgins, but a harsh retribution from us. We would like to continue being a friend of your people, but if we have to, we will be the end of your people. Tell your lawyer to tell your comrades to beware, as we are watching them."

With that, Daniel turned, opened the door, and left.

Mathews met him. "What was that all about? You did all the talking. I didn't even know you spoke his language."

Daniel put his tunic back on. "I learned what I needed to know. I'll help you with his case by saying this: whatever you think he did or was planning, it was actually much worse. Rest assured that he is a bigger fish than you'll ever prove. Hopefully, justice will be served. By the way, the anthrax thing was related. Now, I need to go to Massachusetts to see the shoe bomber. Will you arrange the meeting for this afternoon? I'm taking my car directly to Vandenberg."

It seemed unusual, but Mathews did as he was told. The whole process was bizarre. How did this tattooed man know anything at all? He'd barely listened to the man. He would report what Daniel told him to the U.S. Attorney, and then he'd be done with it.

A plane was waiting for Daniel when he arrived at the base. Three hours later he was at another detention facility many states away and studying another man in a similar fashion. This man, however, was much less useful. He was just a nut who'd patterned his life after his heroes of 9/11. The story of his acquisition of plastic explosives alerted Daniel to how easy it was to obtain such material. Daniel didn't waste time meeting him face-to-face.

The same was true of the Buffalo Terror cell. Although they had been terrorists and had some major plans, they were just lackeys for others of whom they had no knowledge. They didn't know their superior in the terrorist network by name because he was just a voice on a phone. Daniel got little useful information from the men. He interviewed two other terrorists with the same results. He figured Cuba would be his next best source of information.

Nothing new was being shared from the temple except that

Anna would be back with her comrades in another three days. He looked forward to hearing her mind directly when she returned to her position on the Array. Xu Li was running the conduit today, and she mockingly teased Daniel at this thought. "My body seemed good enough for you when you were here, lover boy."

She was correct in this observation, as Xu Li was good at her craft. She had been a dancer in her previous life. She had excellent leg strength and was extremely energetic in bed. She was a Chinese woman of unquestioned intellect and beauty, but despite her physical attributes, she was no Anna. Xu Li was the humorist of the Volva and since she was on duty, he shared with her two weeks of funny stories he had overheard. She enjoyed a good laugh.

He arrived twenty-four hours later at the naval base in Guantanamo Bay. The detention camp being used for the Taliban and al-Qaeda captives was a dreadful place. It was hot, sultry, and buggy. Each detainee was basically a persona non grata. Daniel could tell that the military didn't know what to do with them. They were not prisoners, but they were not going to be allowed to leave since they were too dangerous. To Daniel, they had minds full of thoughts that he wanted to discover.

Marine Colonel Max Tewell was a big man. He had a silver bird on his collar and he took no guff from anyone. He wasn't about to take orders from any goofball tattooed civilian that Washington was trying to push down his throat. This tattooed man didn't even respect his body, so how could he respect him in return? However, when he met Daniel, his mood softened.

Tewell was a mighty fisherman. Daniel filled his mind with thoughts of smallmouth bass fishing on the glacial lakes of northeastern South Dakota. Tewell didn't know quite where he remembered seeing a television episode about South Dakota fishing, but the images were pleasant enough. Mysteriously, Daniel was afforded quick access to the all the dirty, orange-clad former fighters from Asia. The whole process took all day and lasted into the night. Most were just simple people with very little knowledge of where they were, let alone of any terrorist activities. A few, however, gave Daniel valuable information. Darna was most useful in talking with these men as she was fluent in most of the languages of the sub-continent and was able to translate the thoughts of the Afghanis and Pakistanis without much difficulty. Only two men had thought patterns that nobody could discern.

The picture was becoming clearer for Daniel; these terrorists were not just religious zealots and martyrs looking to purify their religion and ultimately the world. They were part of a larger, more sinister plan. It was becoming obvious that someone had been plotting something for a long time. From the detainees and the twentieth hijacker, he deduced several facts:

First, the 9/11 terrorists received aid and training from an organization or country that was far removed from Osama bin Laden or any Moslem nation. Iraq and Hussein had little connection with al-Qaeda. The whole war with Iraq had been a bit of a ruse to divert America's attention from something else. The Americans had been fed misinformation to quell their political appetite. The al-Qaeda involved with the project actually knew very little. They were religious idealists who had been whipped into a frenzy by the planners and religious teachers. The whole process was supported by a secret enterprise that was pervasive and deeply entrenched. Daniel immediately suspected China, but it could have been any number of sponsors.

Second, despite claims to the contrary, most of the recent terrorist activities—including some activities that hadn't yet been attributed to terrorist activities—had all been planned by this unknown underground organization. The anthrax attacks, 9/11, most of the Israeli bombings, the TWA crash, and many more had been centrally organized. The men Daniel probed revealed that there were many other unsuccessful projects aimed at destabilizing America and their allies. One of these events involved a FedEx truck explosion in Missouri, which was actually a terrorist bomb that went off too soon. Another involved an explosion of a fuel barge in New Jersey that was not accidental but was not officially linked to terrorists.

Daniel wondered how widespread the group's activities were. Was the recent appearance of monkeypox a terrorist plot designed to look like smallpox? It seemed nothing was out of the reach of these people. It also seemed that his little fact-finding trip was leading somewhere. Exactly where, he wasn't sure. The only lead that wasn't speculation was gleaned from a single detainee and confirmed by the twentieth hijacker. Both had referred to an unknown front company in Belize. It was a source of money for terrorist activities and served as a meeting place to plan those activities. The former al-Qaeda leader Daniel had met today had supplied one more helpful detail: a Lebanese restaurant in San Pedro, Belize, was the front for the operation, but he didn't know the name of the contact person. Now he knew his next destination.

The Volva decided to organize a group update that evening, during which all the Volva would attach themselves to the conduit. This would connect all the members of the Order. The process would start in three hours. It would be Daniel's first contact with Anna in over a month; unfortunately it was not an appropriate social situation. The meeting took less than fifty minutes. Daniel prepared for it by meditation, and during the discussion he relaxed in a darkened room. This was his first group connection since leaving the temple, and he was greeted warmly by all of his comrades.

Daniel shared the information he had uncovered. The group determined that he should continue his pursuit, while the remainder of the Order would start fact-finding activities independently to determine who was orchestrating the potential disaster unfolding for humankind. Nothing else seemed as urgent at this time. Daniel was congratulated on his initial work. Then Anna briefly said hello and the connection was terminated.

Despite Tewell providing Daniel with VIP accommodations, Daniel got little sleep. He linked up with Anna after the meeting and they shared their thoughts for most of the hot, sultry night. Having her thoughts in him made him feel more connected again. She was anxious to be with him, which he appreciated since he was growing lonely and yearned for her company. He remembered Tanoka's message: Anna will be a blessing for you during those lonely days on the road. Daniel was beginning to understand what that meant. He stared out into the darkness of southern Cuba, listening to the constant hum of mosquitoes through the netting that lined his bed. This would be his fate, living on the road, going from place to place, and protecting humankind from destruction. He lay down again on his bed and resumed his link with his woman.

Thank you, Anna, for being with me, he said.

She decided he needed some rest. She telepathically hummed

a sweet song, the same one she had hummed several times during his reaction to the virus. The music had a calming effect and he was soon asleep, content in all he was and especially content with his relationship with Anna.

CHAPTER 13: The Aracari Lives

The flight into the San Pedro airport was relatively smooth. Daniel was aboard a small British Air Force transport plane that was on its way from the British base in Bermuda to Belize City. It had stopped in Cuba along the way to pick up Daniel at the behest of the U.S. State Department. The plane, not counting the flight crew, held three junior officers, a civilian military contractor, and Daniel. The plane descended along the long, straight beach that formed the southeastern shore of Ambergris Cay. Daniel looked out the window as the plane flew over scattered resorts and then over the small town of San Pedro, the only village on the island. The opposite shore of the narrow island was made up of man-groves and what looked like extremely shallow water. No buildings faced this direction.

The Belize mainland was still fifteen miles away and from this distance it looked like untamed jungle. Landing on the short run-way, the plane stopped at the end where a small building served as both arrival and departure terminals. The airport was used for fre-quent tourist hops from the main international airport thirty-five miles away in Belize City. The single-engine props made flights every thirty minutes or so. Daniel's arrival stirred more interest than most, as the locals rarely saw a military plane in this secluded corner of the world.

The side door opened, and Daniel made the thirty-yard walk toward a large sign marked Car Rental as he heard the military plane power up for its final leg to the mainland. It was early after-noon and the palm trees swayed in the constant sea breeze that blessed this piece of paradise. It was humid and the temperature was a balmy eighty-eight degrees. The deep blue sky was inter-rupted with frequent popcorn clouds that signaled a good chance of evening rain. This was Daniel's second trip to Belize but his first to this island.

The main road was more like an alley and was covered by dirt with a little gravel. The first strange thing he noticed was that all the vehicles traversing the main road were carts better suited to doing eighteen holes of golf than commuting. He laughed. He had landed in a place without the internal combustion engine.

Daniel approached the rental agency and used his gifts of thought transference to convince the rental agency attendant to lend him a cart for a while. The cart was green and had a single bench seat. Some of the carts on the island were two-seaters and some even had flat beds and resembled miniature trucks. The attendant described the approximate location of the Lebanese restaurant, about a mile south. Daniel followed the runway in his cart and then the road started to wind south. Along the route he passed small hotels and brightly colored Caribbean buildings. This was one of the few places where purple with yellow trim was an acceptable color scheme for a house. He passed a school, a crab shack, and a pair of grocery stores.

The road then turned right into a beach resort called Banyan Bay before taking another sharp right. Soon the buildings were becoming more spread out. At the reverse osmosis water plant he stopped and turned around. He had passed through town and had apparently missed his target. He worked his way back. This time he proceeded more slowly, and just two buildings up from the turn in the road at the resort, he saw the restaurant; it was a nondescript, white flat-roofed building with a sliding glass patio door for a main entrance.

The sign, in both Arabic and English, proclaimed Lebanese Restaurant. It was a simple name, almost too simple, and it looked deserted. He checked a sign on the door: Open 5 to 9, closed Mondays. Today was Monday so he would have to wait. Now he had nothing better to do than enjoy this location. He saw a sign pointing to the beach. He pulled the cart over, grabbed his small bag, and followed the sign for sand and surf.

The beach was just a hundred yards away along a small, narrow trail of foliage and overgrown trees. Once there, he noticed the allure of the place—a beautiful, coconut palm-lined beach next to gentle waves. The water was dark turquoise and the surf was gentle due to the barrier reef about a third of a mile off shore. He sat on the beach and noted that he was in a wild, undeveloped spot between two large condominium projects.

Even with the developments, the beach was surprisingly abandoned; there were only a few people in either direction. In front of him, however, was a steady stream of boats. Some were ferrying people to the reef from resorts or the main dock at the city center, and others were apparently ferries to Cay Caulker or Belize City. He had been on a similar boat to Caulker when he'd visited the country during his college years. Caulker was a much smaller island and had left him feeling claustrophobic. He was now having no such feelings as he stretched out in the sand and fell asleep.

Daniel awoke later, sweating under the direct sunlight. Digging into his pack, he pulled out some shorts and quickly slipped them on. The water was a nice temperature, but due to the lush sea grass, he was disappointed with the swim. He enjoyed the cooling effects nonetheless, and as he sat in the water, he began to think. Daniel concluded that it would best be able to gather information by quietly observing everyone who entered the restaurant. He could read the mind of each person and possibly find out who was orchestrating things. It would be helpful to gather as much information as possible before confronting anyone.

While he was drying himself off, a pair of blonde European women approached. He was still thinking about needing somewhere to stay when one of the women spoke to him in Swedish. "Vill du följa med oss?" They were asking him to join them.

At first he didn't know what to say, and then he replied, "Hej, Talar ni Svenska?" The women smiled. "Mitt namn är Daniel. Har ni ett en extra sang?" Still smiling, the women nodded. Daniel was surprised to have found two Swedish-speaking women in Belize. He put on a shirt and followed them to a small condo nearby. They passed out some Cokes and sat on the deck overlooking the beach.

Daniel learned that they had gone to Belize on a whim for a month-long vacation, or semester, as it is called in Sweden. They had rented a condominium from a surgeon in Wisconsin and were enjoying themselves immensely. However, unlike most Swedes, neither spoke English well enough to understand the Caribbean accent. After two weeks they had begun to feel socially isolated since most of the tourists were middle-aged Americans.

The women were students and lifelong friends from Linköpping in central Sweden. They attended the university in Uppsala and were surprised to find a Swedish-speaking American. They confided that they had approached him because somehow they felt he knew their language.

Daniel's thought projection was at work again. He had become used to thinking in Swedish so his thoughts wouldn't affect the Americans around him as almost nobody in the States spoke his favored tongue. The Volva also couldn't understand some of his personal thoughts as none of them fully understood Swedish. Marta could understand him somewhat, but her knowledge of his language was based on her fluency in German and some familiarity with Baltic languages from growing up on the opposite side of the sea from the Swedes.

He confided to the women that his family was from Falun and that he had been to Linköpping with his cousins and his dad during one of their Swedish visits. Linköpping was the home of Saab Motors, and his father had wanted to see Swedish craftsmanship in person. Because of this side trip, Daniel was always confused as to why his dad continued to buy Volvos. He also confided that he was a dual citizen of both Sweden and America. Mostly, he listened, as the women were eager to talk to somebody in their native tongue.

The women had rented a two-bedroom condo but had been sleeping together in the same room, so they offered the second bedroom to Daniel without charge. It would be a pleasure for them to have someone around to talk to and share their vacation with. He scanned their minds and found nothing unusual in their thoughts, so he accepted their invitation.

Daniel found that their motives were truly honorable. During most of his stay on the island their relationship remained platonic, and Daniel spent his evenings alone in bed. It was a change to spend time with women without having sexual relations with them. The women never commented about his strange body markings and Daniel never told them what the markings represented. They just enjoyed each other's company.

Late the next afternoon, Daniel found a place on the roof of a nearby condo that gave him an unobstructed view of the Lebanese establishment. At about five P.M., the owner arrived. He was a big man and looked to be from the Middle East. He sat on a white plastic chair outside the establishment and waited. Later he rose and turned on the grill out back, but put nothing on it. He casually walked across the street into the small grocery store and brought out a whole cooked chicken and a Coke. He took his time, wrapping pieces of the chicken in aluminum foil and drinking the Coke. He again sat on his chair and waited.

One by one, other Arabic-looking-men arrived. Some came on foot and others came by golf cart. To most of them, he gave a piece of chicken and another foil-wrapped package that he took out of a gym bag. Some of the men stopped and talked for a while. A few gave him a package, and sometimes he gave these packages to other men. It was clear that this was no simple eating establishment, but a hub that functioned as an exchange point for a larger network.

Through Omar, Daniel was able to read most of their minds. He learned that the aluminum-covered packages usually contained money, but sometimes the men didn't know what was inside and acted only as middlemen in the process. For the men who received money, it was for them to live on or to pay operational expenses. Daniel soon concluded that the Lebanese Restaurant was a worldwide hub for financing terrorist activities.

The next morning he decided to take the chance to find out more information. He remembered his old e-mail contact at the Bank of Belize that he had spoken with earlier trying to get information about the investment scam he had uncovered back at the bank in Watertown. Maybe old Altorini would be useful to him after all. He had almost forgotten about this scamster who was stealing old people's money. A lot had happened since his days in Watertown. He hadn't thought about Altorini since Omar had found him in the desert. He dialed the number for the main branch of the bank in Belize City. His contact there would have no reason to suspect that he wasn't at his former post.

Daniel introduced himself. "Good morning, Ms. Windsor. This is Daniel Nielstrom from the Far Western National Bank in Watertown, South Dakota, U.S.A. You probably don't remember me but we had a brief e-mail discussion regarding an offshore bank one of my clients was looking at that turned out to be less than reputable."

"Yes!" Ms. Windsor exclaimed. "I remember that e-mail. We are always on the prowl to rout out fraudulent competition since that kind of thing hurts our whole industry. How can I help you today?"

"I have another client looking into Belizean real estate and off-shore businesses. He was visiting your country and fell in love with a restaurant that he felt wasn't being fully utilized. He instructed me to try to determine its owner and purchase the property. I must admit that he didn't give me much information. He'd also like me to try to arrange some local financing for the operation. He's paying me a fee to facilitate the whole arrangement. As I haven't any regular Belizean contacts, I thought you'd be a good place to start."

"Sure, we do things like this all the time," she said. "Where is the property?"

Daniel relayed the property's general description on Ambergris Cay and what he knew about it. She put him on hold for quite a while.

"Mr. Nielstrom, I have access to all the property ownership information on computer," she said. "San Pedro's property ownership has been recently computerized." Daniel could hear her punching keys on her keyboard. He wished his telepathic skills worked over the phone. Now he understood why Defenders didn't like using phones. He no longer had an advantage. "This is unusual . . . . Are you sure that property is a restaurant?"

"Yes, I'm looking at a picture of it. It is definitely a restaurant. I can see a small grocery across the street in another shot. Why do you ask?"

"Well, the owner of that property is a company known as Western Caribbean Agricultural Pharmaceuticals, S. A. It's a Belizean corporation." She paused. "In fact, they actually have an account with our bank. I don't have a contact person for you, which may seem odd . . . . In fact, considering the size of their business, it is odd. I'll do some more research and see what I can learn."

Daniel agreed to call back in a few days. He thanked the woman for her help and hung up. Although he had hoped to get lucky with whatever the woman found out for him, he had discovered enough to realize that whatever was going on was very complex. He suspected its complexity meant it must be far-reaching. Nobody would go through the process of creating layers of red tape to mask something insignificant.

That evening he resumed his lookout to observe the comings and goings at the restaurant. The evening started out with a humorous surprise as he watched a family of six—one teenager, two seven-year-olds, a toddler, and two parents—walk past the restaurant and hesitate. They were obviously Americans. Daniel had watched them come from a condo next door at Banyan Bay. He read the thoughts of the father. It turned out the teenager was his sister and they were from northeastern South Dakota. They even had a house on Enemy Swim Lake, a place Daniel knew well.

The family was building a new house and they'd gone to Belize for a break from the cool weather and the messy construction. They were getting a new floor installed while they vacationed. The father was concerned that the floor was too expensive and was also worried that the construction crew might make a mistake while he wasn't home watching them. He had seen the Lebanese Restaurant sign and both parents were curious about it. Having never experienced Middle Eastern cuisine before, they thought it might be an interesting culinary diversion. Apparently they'd had enough of the local fare of rice and beans and everything chicken.

The wife observed that the door was locked despite the fact that the establishment was supposed to be open. Apparently it wasn't, but in a truly American fashion, she persisted in trying to open the door. Finally she approached the loitering Middle Eastern man on the side of the building and asked him when the restaurant opened. The man was in fact a notorious member of Hamas, a terrorist group from Palestine, and by his thoughts Daniel confirmed that he had killed at least ten Israelis with a car bomb. He was currently waiting for his special package. The man went back and found the manager, the big man named Husam.

Husam stormed around the corner to confront the woman. Daniel was afraid for her and prepared to defend the innocent woman and her family with his powers. But what happened next confused him. Instead of causing trouble, Husam unlocked the door and welcomed them inside. The interior of the restaurant was unbearably hot and Daniel could feel the American patrons' anguish while the window air conditioning unit kicked in. The Americans were offered no menus as Husam carried in extra chairs from the outside. The only fare he offered them was barbequed chicken and rice. They ordered it as well as beverages all around.

While the tourists sweated it out, Husam walked across the

street and got supplies. The intense heat in the enclosed building made the family irritable, and they squabbled while they were left alone. Daniel laughed. They must be of Scandinavian descent to endure such a setting instead of just getting up and leaving. The tourist family suspected that the food must be good since they'd seen several men come by to pick up food packages.

The American family suffered through the food, the temperature, and each other and left without incident. Daniel could tell that Husam's "home cooking" was less than optimal. Hopefully, the tourists wouldn't get sick. It took Husam quite a while to produce a bill, and he finally agreed that thirty Belizean dollars, about fifteen U.S. dollars, would cover the tab. The group felt guilty and left a small tip. The whole scenario was amusing for Daniel, and of all the many days that he observed the restaurant, these were the only real customers who ever dared to dine there.

Daniel continued to watch men come and go. Finally, he climbed down from his perch and approached the restaurant. He saw a short man of Middle Eastern descent pick up a package from Husam and throw it into a backpack he was carrying. Then the man turned and walked back toward the airport. Daniel decided to pursue the man for a more intimate interview. He was in constant contact with Ushenna, and she cloaked Daniel's presence to the man and Husam.

When the man was far enough up the road to be out of view from the restaurant, Daniel used his powers of persuasion to coerce the man to turn into a beach property that was vacant. The man walked as instructed toward the beach. Daniel caught up with him and paralyzed him. He then put his hand on the man's head to get a complete picture of all his thoughts and memories. During the whole episode, the man was terrified and had no idea who or what Daniel was.

The man's thoughts scared Daniel. The man was a Jordanian who trained Middle Eastern suicide bombers. The package of money he had received was payment to the families of two potential new suicide bombers attempting to cause chaos in Israel and Palestine. The man used false religious teaching to persuade the otherwise hopeless and unfocused Palestinian youth to commit such acts, and he sifted through his world to find potential individuals for this type of martyrdom. Each family was paid twenty-five thousand dollars cash for their son's act of bravery, and they were convinced that it was for a greater purpose. This recruiter's purpose was not religious zealotry. He was paid ten thousand dollars for each bomber he recruited who completed the act. He personally didn't even believe the Palestinians deserved a home state. He recruited bombers only for the money; he was a true mercenary. He received his orders from Husam about general targets and goals. Where those orders originated, the mercenary had no idea.

Daniel was disgusted by the man's callousness toward life. By the time Daniel was finished with the man, it had become completely dark. Unsure of what to do with his prisoner, Daniel thought initially of letting him go. That however, didn't seem like a good idea since the man might remember his ordeal and continue his mission to kill more innocent Israelis. If Daniel killed him, then he would have the problem of what to do with the body. How could Daniel make it look like an accident?

Daniel smiled as he came up with a solution. "This is your reward for all the death and destruction you have caused," he said, anger spicing his voice. With a flick of Daniel's hand, the terrified man flew out over the open ocean until he was just over the reef. When Daniel released him, he hit the water hard. The impact knocked the man unconscious and the sea enveloped him.

Daniel picked up the bag containing the money—seventy thousand dollars. He counted out twenty one-hundred-dollar bills and returned the rest to the bag, then incinerated it.

He removed his sandals and followed the beach back toward his condo, happy that he had at least saved a few innocent victims. He planned to give a thousand dollars to the Swedish women for his share of the condo rent; he was sure they would appreciate the gesture. He figured the other thousand would come in handy at some time in the future.

It was late; his roommates had already gone to bed and the main room was quiet. There was little activity outside, so he too went to bed. It was easy to fall asleep in this part of the tropics with the constant sound of wind rustling through the coconut palms outside his window. He chatted telepathically for a short while with Ushenna and, after finding out that nothing was new, he drifted off to sleep.

Olaf Danielson

It was mid-morning when he wandered sleepily out to the kitchen. He was met by one of his young Swedish chums in the kitchen, still topless from her morning sunbath. Daniel suspected the deck was the place to be today. The restaurant was closed on Mondays, so he suspended his surveillance activity. After a relaxing soak in the hot tub, he wandered out to the deck wearing only his towel. He preferred to let his damp hair dry in the morning breeze. He found his women friends just as he'd imagined them. One topless and reading a book, her black-thonged-bottom providing little protection from the elements or his gaze. The other woman lay on her stomach wearing nothing but suntan lotion, and her tan lines were barely visible. As Daniel walked by his topless friend, she playfully grabbed his towel.

She smiled. "I was just checking for tan lines," she said in Swedish. She'd noticed that Daniel was bronzed, and he had neither tan lines nor any shame at his nakedness. Now freed from his towel, he laid it on the lounge chair and relaxed, face up. He donned his sunglasses, planning on a morning nap. His nude friend rolled over to look at his golden features, long blond hair, and exotic tattoos. She smiled and handed him a Coke.

After a brief interlude he drifted off into a warm slumber. He instinctively rolled over when his skin warmed so as to bake evenly in the sun. The gentle rubbing of suntan lotion into his hot back awakened him. He enjoyed the all-over application and returned the favor. Although he could tell that the pair would be amenable to more than just sharing their condo and suntan lotion with him, he wanted friendship more than sex. For the moment, he just wanted to enjoy their company. The continued warmth of the sun caused them all to doze until something being hammered to their front door awakened them.

Daniel replaced his towel and walked down the stairs to see what had caused the commotion. He returned with a flier from the Ministry for Civil Defense:

Warning: A mandatory evacuation of the barrier islands including Ambergris Cay has been declared for tomorrow morning. Hurricane Ramon is due to make landfall in San Pedro within 36 hours. You are to report to the main city center be-

fore 7 A.M. Boats will be present to shuttle you to Belize City, and from there buses will take you to shelters in Belmopan. There will be no exceptions.

Daniel looked out into the ocean. It was early fall and still hurricane season. He saw some larger-than-expected waves and squalls in the distance, but nothing immediately threatening. He went to the television and turned on the Weather Channel. Hurricane Ramon was small and compact, but was a fast-growing Category Four hurricane with winds nearing one hundred forty-five miles per hour. It had blossomed just twenty-four hours earlier, and some of the forecasts called for it to intensify, with winds possibly nearing one hundred seventy-five miles per hour. It could quite possibly be the storm of the century. Daniel consulted with Monique and decided he would deal with Ramon later.

"What was that about?" asked his two friends. Anja had now agreed that a thong bikini bottom was of no need here on the balcony with her otherwise-nude friends. She was in the process of taking it off when Daniel returned.

"Nothing much," he replied in Swedish. "It was just somebody inviting us to a party on the mainland."

They all enjoyed a day of full sun together, but by evening the sky had become too overcast for tanning. At dusk, Daniel left his associates in the hot tub and went out to the beach. He had work to do. He just didn't have time for Ramon; it would have to go.

Daniel walked naked into the surf up to his navel and outstretched his arms, using the full power of the link with the Volva. He felt the energy from Marta flow through his body. Remembering his training, he made a competing storm of a magnitude similar to Ramon's. He then created a tremendous upper level wind to move his storm out into the ocean, where the two systems would collide. That collision and the great wind shear he'd created would end the cyclone.

His long hair suddenly pointed straight out to sea as he changed the wind direction, and lightning flickered out over the open ocean. Daniel's storm pulled all the low-hanging clouds around him out to sea.

Daniel remained at his post for over an hour until the ocean had become strangely calm. He was hot and sweaty after the tremendous mental ordeal, so he submerged to cool off. After a brief swim he climbed back onto the beach and walked to the condo. His room-mates had already gone off to bed and he followed suit.

The morning sun awakened the sleeping Defender. He rolled over to find he was not alone in the bed—both of his roommates had joined him during the night. He patted a naked back of some-one, not sure whether it belonged to Therese or Anja, as he climbed over her heading for the bathroom. Apparently, they had expected him to climb into their bed when he'd returned from the ocean. No matter, he hadn't violated anyone yet and he was enjoying playing hard to get; he knew it was turning them on. When he left the bathroom, he wandered out to the living room and turned on the Weather Channel.

It was a surprising night in the tropics last night as Hurri-cane Ramon quickly dissipated. Hurricane warnings and man-datory evacuations for the area from the Yucatan Peninsula to Belize were canceled after midnight. As you can see by the satellite images, the hurricane was suddenly ravished by a de-veloping offshore storm that disrupted the cyclonic activity of Ramon. You can see the eye wall here on this image; it was gone fifteen minutes later. A strong, upper-level wind formed, creating a wind shear that broke up the storm. This was a com-bination of events never before seen. But with weather, noth-ing seems impossible.

Now Daniel could go on with his business. However, he was soon to learn that life on the island was slow to go back to normal. Almost everyone had left when the evacuation notice had been announced, including the owner of the Lebanese Restaurant. The trio had the beach to themselves as most of the tourists had left and new arrivals had been canceled. After forty-eight hours of inactiv-ity, Daniel decided he'd keep a promise to a friend.

The next morning he surprised his two Swedish companions by treating them to a trip to see some Mayan ruins. He still had the thousand dollars he had kept after his visit with the Lebanese man from the restaurant, and he decided this would be a good way to use it.

The plane was twenty minutes late. Daniel bought three tickets. The price, including the tour of the Mayan ruins of Tikal, was only two hundred and forty-eight dollars each. While the girls waited in the air-conditioned departure lounge, Daniel wandered across the street to one of the many gift shops. With some difficulty he found a t-shirt with enough red and yellow so he could make his marker. Outside the store he ripped the shirt into a square, half red and half yellow. He walked back to the departure lounge and rejoined his friends.

The plane carried only two other passengers on the bouncy flight. Looking out the window, Daniel saw below him a few mostly-empty boats and a few manatees, feeding and swimming in the shallows that marked the majority of the water between the cays and the mainland. The plane crossed the Belize River, started its descent over a large salt-collection project, and landed smoothly at the country's main airport. The connection to Flores was already waiting due to the delay, and they immediately transferred, then took off and headed northwest across jungles, rivers, and a few houses. Soon they descended into Flores.

Flores, Guatemala, was located on an island on Lake Petén Itza fifty miles northwest of the Belize border. It was the last stronghold of the Mayan people before finally falling to the Spanish conquistadors over four hundred years ago. The original inhabitants either died by the sword or from the effects of smallpox or measles. Now the area was in the middle of an ever-festering civil war. Due to the bandits and rebels on the road connecting San Ignacio, Belize, and Flores, Daniel had been unable to come to the area when he was visiting the region during a college trip. His college didn't want to risk casualties, so they went to another smaller ruin, Altun Ha, instead.

A late-model Toyota nine-passenger van was waiting for them. Two elderly males, a young couple, Therese, Anja, and Daniel climbed aboard. Obviously not everyone had left the country. The trip to Tikal was rough, jarring, and sparingly quick. Guatemalan roads reminded Daniel of some he had seen in other third-world locations. The majesty and immensity of Tikal brought gasps of awe from everyone in the car and made them quickly forget about the roads.

The Mayans had built Tikal, according to the current scholars, around seventeen hundred years ago. At its height, the city reportedly contained over a hundred thousand citizens. Mysteriously, however, it was abandoned before the Spanish ever saw it and was formally discovered by modern scholars in 1848. Some of what the learned modern archeologists theorized was correct, but a lot was woefully wrong. Daniel kept the truth to himself and admired the impressive ruins for being a memorial to human achievement.

He started out with the tour group, but after half an hour he left his fellow tourists to admire the one hundred foot high Temple of the Giant Jaguar, the Temple of the Masks, the Temple of the Jaguar Priest, the north and central Acropolis, and the numerous associated courts. These were not their real names, but rather, the names assigned them by the modern researchers. He continued from the Great Plaza up along the Tozzer Causeway to the base of a mighty gray and black stone structure. This mighty temple had the misfortunate and unimpressive designation of Temple IV but was by and large the most impressive structure of the lot. He climbed the stairs. The pyramid had carried the distinction of being the tallest man-made structure in North America at two hundred and twelve feet until it had been surpassed some thirteen hundred years after its creation by a non-descript skyscraper in New York City. For this reason it was selected eons ago by the Choosers as a location for communications between themselves and the Defenders.

Daniel was short of breath as he reached the top. From his elevated vantage point he could see the Great Plaza and the north Acropolis in the distance, and he could also gaze over the canopy tops from the jungle trees in the surrounding Petén Jungle. It was a stunning view, and he sat down to fully absorb the experience.

Although Maria was on duty he had little trouble consulting with Marta. *Do you really want me to do this, Marta?* he asked telepathically.

Daniel could feel that Marta was hesitant, but soon she reaffirmed her position. *Yes, Daniel, it is what I want to do. Thanks for consulting with me one last time, but it is for the better.*

Without further discussion Daniel removed the makeshift signal cloth from a pocket and carefully unfolded it, anchoring it with a loose rock on the summit. Then he turned and moved down the pyramid. He wondered at Marta's decision but would not question her. After all, he had no idea of what living two hundred years was like, but obviously it wasn't all Nirvana. Besides, she was old enough to determine her own fate.

About halfway down the steep steps, a sudden movement in a nearby tree caught Daniel's attention. Just twenty feet away was a beautiful Central American avian beauty. The bird was about a foot tall. It had a large, four-inch bill that was black with a dark red spot near the tip. The bird's body was colorful, a yellow belly with red stripes and a dark back with red highlights. It had a red eye ring and a medium-length tail multicolored with red, yellow, and black plumage. This bird was in the toucan family. Daniel instantly knew it was a collared aracari.

He was fascinated with birds. He had been given a field guide while in the fifth grade, and he had started a lifetime bird list while still in high school. Nebraska had always been a good place to spot many species on their migration paths. He'd also seen many species during his desert and Swedish travels. His lifetime bird list had contained nearly six hundred species when he'd gone on his college trip to Belize. He had decided to make toucans his main focus. Eventually, he saw all of his goal species save one. That elusive bird, the collared aracari, had remained hidden until this moment.

As he studied the gorgeous bird, it seemed sort of an omen. Somehow, seeing this bird was telling Daniel something. It sat a mere twenty feet away for over fifteen minutes as Daniel patiently enjoyed its presence. Somehow though, he kept returning to his suspicion that the bird was serving as a signal.

Most likely, any potential signal had something to do with the message to the Choosers he had just left. Daniel didn't know what mechanism he had just set in motion by leaving the red and yellow fabric, but he suspected that soon a great selection process would unfold. Secret men would be scheming and selecting the best candidates to protect his species. The chosen woman would someday join the sisterhood and be linked mentally with Daniel, and later she would also share herself with him in the Volva manner. He was part of a big process and as he sat there watching his avian friend, his part in the larger scheme suddenly hit him; he felt burdened with a load of responsibility.

This lull of thought lasted a short while until Daniel remembered his tour and hurried down the rest of the steps of the pyramid and returned to the Great Plaza. Other tourists were also milling around the structures. He soon spotted his group near a structure now called the Temple of the Masks. As he hurried to rejoin the group, Daniel failed to notice a dark, elderly Latino man in sunglasses walking slowly in the opposite direction. In his rush, Daniel failed to notice that the man's right arm was covered as if to conceal a tattoo.

The Latino man slowly ambled to the tall structure, flushing out the colorful bird, and ascended to see what the young Defender had left for him. He picked up the bi-colored cloth and put it in his pocket. He looked neither sad nor joyous. The meaning of the message was clear to him and plans needed to be made, so he moved back down the pyramid and disappeared into the jungle.

Daniel rejoined the six-member group and finished the tour. Nobody seemed to have missed him, and in their minds he had never been absent. Later, Daniel and his two Swedish acquaintances returned to Ambergris and their condo. The excursion had been a wonderful experience for the women and they thanked Daniel for the opportunity. He was ambivalent about the trip, both sad and excited about Marta's decision. Even the aracari sighting left him unsure. Everything seemed to have a deeper meaning than whatever appeared on the surface.

* * * * *

Mr. Li was just leaving one of the casinos in Macao when he saw the tattooed man across the crowded street. The man was walking nonchalantly and was marked exactly as Tiger had described. He had an unmistakable tattoo on his face and also had visible markings on his right arm. The strange man was heading off in a direction that would be difficult for Li to follow, but this was his turf and he had ways to keep tabs on people. Using his cell phone, he alerted others to follow the man but warned them to stay back and remain unnoticed at all costs. He just wanted the tattooed man under casual surveillance for now.

The man was observed from windows, rooftops, and passing

cars. Finally he turned into a well-known international hotel. Li was notified of this development right away. He sped to the location, a mere eight blocks from where he was currently keeping vigil. The man was staying in room 824. Unfortunately, the owner of the hotel was from a different syndicate than Li, and his men could keep only a cursory watch from the outside. Li wasn't about to upset the delicate balance of power in the underground of the former Chinese colony. He was just happy he'd accidentally found the man. He returned to his room in the casino to alert Tiger of his discovery.

Tiger was very pleased with Li's discovery and wanted him to use whatever he had at his disposal to keep track of the man. Nothing would be done at the hotel. Since the hotel was not affiliated with associates of Tiger or Li, an untoward event could raise more suspicion and investigation than Tiger wanted. They would be patient. The tattooed man was obviously a significant force; for now, Tiger just wanted to learn the man's habits and weaknesses. Everyone had patterns and everyone eventually made a mistake. During one of those mistakes, Tiger would strike.

Reports were also coming in from another source in a land far away. Another of his regional terrorist organizations had sighted a similar strangely marked man. His habits were also being observed and documented, and he too would make a mistake. The time was nearing for Tiger to move forward with his master plan. These Defenders had to be controlled. Although he couldn't understand their power or their significance, he deeply feared what they represented, and he rarely feared anyone. But this was a fear of the unknown, as he couldn't imagine how a single man could wipe out fifty thousand elite German and Italian troops. Since he doubted that he could control their power, he concluded that he needed to eliminate it.

Two weeks later, he assembled a meeting of his entire top overseas agents, including Mr. Li, who was now back in good graces with him, thanks in no small part to his discovery of the man in Macao. The small group discussed the information they had learned and compared notes with their leader. Finally, after much discussion, they developed a plan for the termination of the two men.

Tiger didn't like these distractions. He was readying his new nuclear arsenal for mass production, had orchestrated the removal of UN arms inspectors from his country, and was busily producing plutonium. His Pakistani scientific team was designing small- to medium-sized nuclear devices, and his rocket team was scheduling another test flight over a neighboring country. He was seeing how far he could push things; it amazed him how far he could go. The Americans had done as he wished and had invaded invaded Iraq. He was even having his own agents stir up Baghdad so as to look like the pro-Saddam crowd was organizing a guerrilla war. So far, it was working perfectly. The Americans were too busy to worry about Tiger. All he needed now was to watch and wait for the two Defenders to reach an early demise.

* * * * *

Daniel's life in Belize began to slowly return to the pre-hurricane pace. He went from sunning in the morning to stakeouts in the afternoon and early evening to social time with his two women friends at night. It wasn't a bad experience, but he needed to stay on task. Soon the restaurant became a hub of illicit activity again. Also, he remembered that he needed to get back in contact with Ms. Windsor at the bank. Maybe she had more information for him.

The next morning he checked in with his contact. She had done some research and learned some interesting facts. The corporate information for Western Caribbean Agricultural Pharmaceuticals S. A. was a matter of public record, but since the corporation had only local nominee directors, they would be of no help. The company was set up with bearer shares, so the exact owner of the company was unclear as well. Although the bank account of Western Caribbean Agricultural Pharmaceuticals S. A. had a name of record for authorization of transfers and withdrawals, it was apparently a Hong Kong-based attorney who had paid a local attorney to set up the corporation. She had seen this before and suspected that neither man knew anything about the actual functions of the company and that neither man would know the actual owner of the property. She wouldn't divulge their names, but said she did have a name that might help. A man named Clive Edwards had called her a year or so back representing International Pharma Research Limited. Mr. Edwards had claimed that Western Caribbean was a long-standing client of his firm and he was checking to confirm that they had received a wire transfer. Since he knew the amount and the originating bank, she had given him the verbal confirmation. As neither Mr. Edwards nor his firm were clients of her bank, she felt no obligation to withhold his identity and gave Daniel the man's callback number in Road Town, Tortola, British Virgin Islands. Ms. Windsor prided herself in keeping detailed notes of every phone conversation. She hoped this man would lead Daniel to the restaurant's true owner and wished him good luck in his pursuits. Daniel promised to run the financing through her bank if he were able to strike a deal.

As Daniel hung up, he postulated that the next location of this adventure would be Tortola. He needed to pay Mr. Edwards a visit, but first he had a lot to wrap up here in sleepy little San Pedro. That afternoon, he sent the girls off to Captain Morgan's, a fancy resort across the canal and north of San Pedro, to go scuba diving. He loaned them his golf cart for the three-mile ride. He had no time for another day of fun.

At the usual time he took up his position on the rooftop. Husam showed up as expected, as did his customers. The men today were of even less use than those previously as they all seemed to be mules and knew nothing of their contacts, cargo, or purpose. The mental tedium, warmth, and humidity of the early evening caused Daniel to doze off. Suddenly, his mind stirred to life. The inner alarm that Anna had beaten into his subconscious was signaling danger.

He instinctively froze time, then opened his eyes to see a man six feet away pointing a handgun at him. The man was about to pull the trigger of the Glock. Still holding time, he got out of his chair and walked behind the big man. As he let time go back to normal, he hit the man from behind. Whether it was from his adrenaline rush or his powers Daniel was unsure, but the force of his blow snapped Husam's neck. He crumpled dead in front of him and was now useless to Daniel as a source of information. Luckily the weapon had not fired during the exchange, and no one in the street below paid any mind to the events on the nearby roof.

Daniel sat down next to the lifeless body, happy for Anna's

good training and his survival of the attack, but unhappy for his dumb luck of killing his only real witness. Anna, on duty, consoled her pupil. He thought he was bungling his investigation, but she only cared about his safety. He took the gun and threw it far out into the surf. Husam suffered a similar fate as the gun and was found four days later, washed up on shore of nearby Cay Caulker. He was believed to have been the victim of an accidental drowning. He'd obviously slipped, struck his neck on the side of the boat, and fell overboard. It was a common occurrence, and the local dive operators never reported missing men or women since it might affect tourism. Unreported missing bodies washed up all the time.

After levitating Husam out to sea, Daniel walked to the restaurant to see whether he could find anything of interest. He first inspected the gym bag. It contained a whole chicken, fourteen bags of money, and three aluminum canisters. Each canister was labeled Biohazard and carried the inscription Property of International Pharma Research Limited. He put them in plain view next to the barbeque, then went to the grocery store opposite to watch and wait. He wanted to meet the men who came for this package.

Daniel thought, International Pharma Research Limited—that was the same name I heard from Ms. Windsor. Tortola seemed less of a wild goose chase than he had first believed. He continued to think about his next move as he leaned against an electric pole advertising everything from restaurants to exciting day trips.

Soon three confident men walked down the street toward the restaurant. Daniel could easily pick up their thoughts in Arabic, and Omar was soon patched in. The men were here for a pickup and then were off for Canada. They were laughing at the ease with which they would be granted refugee status. They stopped at the restaurant and immediately noticed the canisters. That was what they were after, and the absence of Husam didn't cause them alarm.

They talked about the aluminum canisters but did not discuss how they would get them into Canada. As they looked them over, they referenced some words that Omar had difficulty translating. Literally they described a "blistering disease of cows." Despite the fact that he'd grown up on a cattle ranch, the exact name of the disease didn't immediately hit Daniel. He thought of anthrax but the little he knew about that disease didn't seem to fit this description. He listened to their thoughts more intently. They would move to Winnipeg, Manitoba, and after some time, when the word was given, they would cross the border to spread the contents of the canisters around cattle ranches in the Midwest. They were certain they wouldn't be affected as the disease only sickened animals. Daniel picked up a constant theme in their thought: *Down with the Infidel! Down with America! Praise be to Allah!*

Omar recognized the name of the disease before Daniel did, identifying it as hoof and mouth disease. Daniel remembered concerns of it from his father. Even a suspicion of it in a herd would lead to the culling of the whole herd, possibly even millions of animals. He remembered pictures of a recent outbreak in England, or was it France? The news carried graphic details of truckloads of dead cattle being dumped and burned. He concluded that he needed to deal with those canisters.

Daniel walked toward the men, and as his gaze caught theirs, they tried to run but found to their amazement that they couldn't move. Daniel approached them and casually removed the cylinders from their possession. One by one he put his hands on their heads to probe their thoughts more deeply. As before, none of them knew much more than their mission as they had all been contacted over the phone. All were members of Hezbollah, and they had been recommended by one of their leaders for this mission. Each had worked aboard a freighter until reaching port in Belize. From there, they had caught the shuttle flight. Once they had received their packages, they would travel aboard another ship bound for Thunder Bay, Ontario, from Belize City. While this ship was taking on grain, they would disembark and file for refugee status, then disappear into the bureaucracy that was the Canadian immigration law. Daniel already knew the rest of the story.

He made short work of the men. His anger at their cruel disrespect for life aided his judgment of them, but their deaths caused him no joy, nor did the ultimate combustion of their bodies, as it was such a waste of human life and talent. Had they been better guided they could have helped their people instead of trying to destroy others. Daniel next concentrated his energy on the three cylinders. It took a lot of heat to melt the aluminum, but he was reassured that at that temperature, the terrible virus would also be destroyed.

Melting the cylinders was overkill, but Daniel's goal was accomplished. Frustrated at the evening's events and the minimal knowledge he had gleaned from the men, Daniel wandered back to the Swedish women's condo.

Anna telepathically consoled Daniel as best she could and realized that he physically needed her most when his confidence was shaken. Unfortunately, that wasn't possible in their current situation. Anna knew just what he needed—a diversion—and in Volva fashion, she found two wonderful diversions: one named Anja and another named Therese. Anna had learned a bit of Swedish from Daniel's mind, especially words that would turn on adventuresome women. She was soon to learn that Swedish women do not need much encouragement.

Daniel had barely made it through the door when Therese attacked him. Her playfulness soon turned hot. Three weeks of his playing hard to get had driven her past her breaking point, and with a little encouragement from Anna, she'd decided she wanted Daniel and wanted him bad.

Daniel was soon filled with all sorts of passionate thoughts. Some were from him and others were from Anna as she assisted him from afar. To his delight, Therese removed her top. He was past the point of no return. He hadn't been with a woman since Anna had left and, despite being a Defender, he was still a young male. He was inside of Therese on the couch in no time, but this wasn't good enough for her. She squirmed out only to replace her embrace on his manhood from above. In this fashion they released themselves. Following their mutual passion, they slipped into the Jacuzzi together for a relaxing soak. Anja joined them. She had heard everything but had politely waited her turn. It would come later that evening.

After he had spent himself, Daniel felt slightly guilty. He still was not accustomed to casual sex, and he was mad at himself for giving in to the temptations of romance with his two Swedish friends. Anna reassured him that it was normal for him to have such relationships. It would be rare for them to be together, and it was normal for Defenders to have relations with women besides the Volva. In fact, casual sex was generally encouraged.

The trio spent the next day as they had spent many days previously except for the one added activity. They swam, sunned themselves, talked freely about life, and intermittently shared themselves sexually with each other. Daniel learned that the women were leaving Belize the next morning. He confided that he also had to leave. As the evening drew near they talked of plans to meet the following summer. Although they officially decided nothing, Daniel knew their friendship would last for quite a while to come. He finally agreed to meet them the following summer back in Sweden. They would camp at Böda Sand on the island of Öland in Anja's father's Kabe husvagn, a Swedish-built camper trailer. They planned on spending the entire month of July at the beach.

Daniel had never been to Öland before. "Är stranden stenig?" He asked about the beach, thinking it must be rocky like the ones he had experienced east of Stockholm.

"Nej, det är sandig." Therese replied that the beach was sandy. "Vi trivs utomordentligt. Kan jag få din address?"

Daniel too had had a wonderful time with the women but since he didn't really have a home, it was hard for him to give them an address. He just instructed them to contact him through the U.S. State Department. They could even send letters to him through this liaison. They could call the liaison on the number he gave them, and she would give them the address. They spent their last night together after a relaxing soak in the tub. Daniel felt comfortable with them, but he was also glad tonight would be their last together, at least for many months. Exhausted by the day in the sun and comforted by the warmth of their bodies, Daniel was soon fast asleep. It was as sound a sleep as he had experienced for some time, and deeper than he would experience for many days to come. He had become used to sleeping with one eye open to watch for trouble. San Pedro, at least temporarily, had been rid of trouble.

Daniel awoke to giggles from his bed partners. They were still unclothed and had been watching him for some time. Anja was tracing his lynx tattoo with her finger.

"Vad skratter du åt?" asked Daniel playfully about the giggling.

"Vad du ser vacker ut!" Therese said with a seductive gleam in her eye. Daniel was already up for one more round and apparently so were the women. An hour later, Therese announced, "Vi måste tyvärr gå nu."

Daniel needed to get going too, and all three hurriedly cleaned up and packed. After Therese had checked out of the room, Daniel escorted them to the airport. With a parting embrace to both, his final Swedish words to his friends were simple. "Hoppas vi ses snart!" See you soon.

*****

Chang had been a Defender since his initiation in 1912. Although he had been with the Order some ninety years, his life of service had been mostly one of observation. He had been involved peripherally in preventing the Korean conflict from escalating, but the lion's share of the work in bringing the conflict to a stalemate was of Tanoka's doing. Even during World War II, Chang had been mostly in Tanoka's shadow. Such was the problem of being from the same area and time of a great man.

Chang had been the guest of one of the world's wealthiest men and had been staying in his casino in Macao for the last few weeks. From the time of the group communication from Daniel alerting him to a potential worldwide conspiracy, Chang had seen nothing odd nor uncovered any suspicious behavior on the crowded island. After staying in Macao an extra week, he had become restless and decided to move his center of observation back to Beijing. Typically Chang alternated his observation post from Hong Kong to Beijing with occasional stops in the middle for a change in pace. He had initially headed south from Beijing to Hong Kong to personally observe the threat caused by SARS, the new deadly virus that had swept through the former British colony in the spring, but as summer started the disease quieted down. Despite its lethality, SARS drew only cursory notice from the ever-vigilant Volva; up to this point it had only claimed five hundred victims. Chang made his way from his eighth-floor room at the Macao casino and headed toward the ferry docks. Despite his great powers of perception, he was unaware that associates of Mr. Li were continually observing him. The ferry to Hong Kong was crowded as usual; crowds were the way of life in China. Even though Macao had been part of Portugal and Hong Kong had been British, the one commonality between them and China proper, and even Taipei for that matter, were the crowds. Now, again united with the motherland, not even the political differences were obvious.

Chang failed to notice two businessmen that, even though sitting far away from him, were monitoring his every move. Their frequent discussions on their cell phones also went unregistered. Chang left the dock area and coerced a taxi to take him to a train station. The train to the Chinese capital would take two days, but Chang was not in a hurry. He had all the time in the world.

A peasant and two other passengers were also on the train. Their ultimate destination, however, would not be Beijing. They had other plans, as did Mr. Li, and had no intention of staying on the train to its terminus.

CHAPTER 14: Revenge in Macao

The military transport landed on the island of St. Thomas. Daniel was unable to arrange a flight from Belize to Tortola due to the State Department rule that a U.S. possession had to be on at least one end of the flight. The U.S. Virgin Islands were as close as he could get. From the airport he secured a taxi ride into the city of Charlotte Amalie. It had a Caribbean flavor but not the usual charm. Three large cruise ships were plainly visible to Daniel, and he suspected more were on the way.

He soon learned that the easiest way to get to the British Virgin Islands was to take a water taxi to Tortola, one of which was available from the simple dock in the harbor opposite a small group of jewelry outlets. The tourists usually took a larger, scheduled boat from the ferry terminal in Red Hook, but since money was no object and because he preferred the private charter to a boatload of tourists, he climbed aboard.

The captain seemed to understand his special passenger's travel needs and soon cast off without even a verbal confirmation. The boat, powered with two large Mercury outboards, sped out of the harbor, cruised past a gorgeous hotel situated on an almost sheer cliff, then hung a sharp left. They followed the shore until they arrived in the channel between St. Thomas and St. John, passed two large ferryboats taking cars between the two islands, then headed toward St. John. As his guide pointed them out, the sharp volcanic peaks of Tortola came plainly into view. Daniel sat back and relaxed. He closed his eyes, and the drone of the twin Mercs lulled him to sleep.

* * * * *

Chang was also asleep. His train was making slow, steady progress through the Chinese mainland. The men with cell phones had disembarked at the last station. They had been given one-word instructions from Li—Leave—and being good soldiers, they had obeyed.

Had Chang remembered his training, undoubtedly his internal alarm would have been blaring at that moment, but he was lost in a world of his own dreams. Likewise, the Volva on watch was not aware of anything suspicious with Chang's surroundings. All she picked up from the constant link was his peaceful dreams of childhood. He was a child of Chinese peasantry. He had grown up near a rice paddy and, until he had been selected to participate in the Chinese system of higher education, he was more at home with cattle and being ankle deep in water than he was with a book. He never knew why his grandfather had pledged his life to the service of the Order, but soon after his twenty-fourth birthday, he awoke tattooed and alone in a desert. His special Volva was Xu Li, and they had spent many intimate moments together over the years. She was constantly in his thoughts and her sense of humor amused him even during the dullest times. It had been four years since his last return to the temple, and he was overdue. Unfortunately, it would never happen.

While he slept, the train approached a large bridge over a canyon. The bridge was in desperate need of replacement, but the Chinese had spent a good portion of their capital infrastructure budget on the mighty Yangtze Gorge Dam project. They had no money to repair a simple bridge on a secondary railway line. The engineer of the train couldn't have known that explosive charges had been laid under the main support of the structure, and he failed to notice ten regular army soldiers with shoulder-mounted antitank missiles aimed at one of the sleeping cars. Tiger believed in overkill, and he always made sure that when he did something he did it right. Multiple explosions soon were visible in front of, below, behind, and in the train. The old bridge gave way, allowing the entire structure, train included, to fall to the valley below. The valley filled with fire, small explosions, and twisted steel.

* * * * *

Daniel awoke to a sharp pain in the side of his head, a pain like he had never experienced before. The severity of it knocked him to the floor of the boat. He grabbed his head with both hands and moaned audibly. The driver stopped the boat in an attempt to help him, but Daniel motioned him away. The pain was followed by a tremendous sense of sorrow and loss. He was unable to determine its meaning until Irena shared with him the news of the tragedy.

Chang has been killed, she communicated in an almost emotionless tone. *The pain was his mental link being torn from our network.*

Why did I not experience that with Tanoka?

As he died, Minh gradually pulled his mind away from ours. This lessened the severity of the broken link. Chang's death was not controlled. You will have some dizziness and nausea from this event for at least a few days.

Marta joined the link. She explained to all the Defenders what she suspected had happened. While he was sleeping, an explosion had ended Chang's life. Nothing more was known. He had just left Macao, Hong Kong, and was traveling by train to Beijing. Nothing unusual had occurred before the explosion and no other suspicious activity had been observed. Just to be safe, the Volva would begin double duty. Marta's intuition suggested that somebody was targeting the Order. She warned all the Defenders to be extra careful and avoid unnecessary travel. She also noted the whereabouts of all the men.

The water taxi pulled into Road Town harbor and carefully negotiated a path between all the beautiful sailboats anchored at the dock. Daniel observed an especially sprite-looking fifteen-meter boat with a Swedish flag flying at the stern. The boat was appropriately named *Freyja's Revenge*. Even at this dark hour, the irony of the boat's name made Daniel smile. If the sisters of Freyja discovered the perpetrator of Chang's death, they would exact significant revenge. Murdering a Defender would result in the severest retribution that Daniel could imagine. He suspected he was closer to the answer than anyone; he might even be the instrument of the ultimate revenge.

The boat dropped him off at the main pier and Daniel walked cautiously through the restaurants and shops, looking for a public phone with a phone book. He watched numerous people, mostly Anglo-Saxon, walk into the myriad banks near the harbor. He read their minds as they passed him. They came from everywhere: New Zealand, America, Canada, and all over Europe. As the procession went on, Daniel discovered that they had one thing in common: all were concealing money.

Some were harboring more suspicious thoughts, like worrying about the IRS, a soon-to-be-ex-wife, or even a nosy business partner. Offshore banking was one of the British Virgin Islands' largest industries. Daniel observed that Road Town had a different look to it than San Pedro; it had the look of money. The buildings were better and all of the homes looked more stately and sturdier than their Belize counterparts. They looked almost American.

When Daniel located a pay phone, he removed the attached phone book, took it to an inviting sea wall, and sat down. Sitting down quelled his vertigo at least enough to notice that, just as in America, a phone with an undamaged phone book was a rare occurrence. Most of the business section had been ripped out, so the book was of no aid in his search.

Looking around, Daniel observed a large map on a sign near his sea wall. He walked over to the map—it was a guide to all the best shopping. He found what he was looking for and wandered toward Main Street by walking through some bushes that were strategically placed to separate it from the main coastal highway leading away from the city center.

* * * * *

Clive Edwards was just heading off to lunch when he remembered that it was time to switch the business signs. He was tired of seeing the Aracari Ltd. sign in the window anyway, so he exchanged it for the International Pharma Research Limited sign that had been gathering dust in the closet. He smiled at the change as he locked the door. His partner, Williams, had already gone home for a long weekend.

It had been a slow day; in fact, the entire week had been slow. Edwards had expected to receive an invoice from Western Caribbean for the previous month of outsourcing activities, but no fax had arrived. He knew from experience that if a fax wasn't in from Belize by lunch, it wasn't coming. He dreaded another afternoon of tedium. So as he locked the door, he decided to have lunch at home and also start the weekend early. He was planning on taking his family shopping over on St. Thomas in the morning. It was just a week before the Christmas holiday and they had bought no presents. He reopened the door and placed a Closed: Be Back on Monday sign on the door. They'd had no walk-in traffic since the departure of the American tax official, but since Tortola was very British, and therefore, a very polite society, he stuck to protocol and left the sign for the world to see. The practice made him somehow feel more honest. Undoubtedly he would also charge himself a half-day of vacation. He was always the honest cheat.

Mr. Edwards casually descended the stairs to the street below. As he turned the corner, he almost ran over Tom Jenkins, the office landlord. Jenkins was also heading home for the weekend and the pair exchanged pleasantries. As they talked, they failed to notice a strange, tattooed man ambling down Main Street below their elevated sidewalk. The man avoided the throng of tourists and walked into a small grocery just three doors away. Edwards finished with Jenkins, walked across the street, climbed into his Range Rover and sped home.

* * * * *

Daniel was not pleased with his lack of progress in locating the pharmaceutical company and was beginning to think the company was just another sham. The grocery store he entered was not only devoid of a phone book but the clerk knew nothing about the company. Daniel left the grocery, after having been given a Coke and a candy bar, and reversed course. He walked a little bit and then stopped to eat his lunch. He'd just taken a big swig from his liter bottle of Coke when a word in the distance caught his eye: Pharma. He stopped drinking and moved closer for a better look. The sign on the second story office just over the street read International Pharma Research Limited.

Figuring it was better to be lucky than good, he laughed as he climbed the stairs to the office. His chuckle turned to disappointment as he read the message on the locked door. Some luck, he thought.

Daniel climbed back down, crossed the hedge bordering Main and Waterfront Streets, and hailed a cab. He enjoined the driver to take him to someplace nice for the weekend. As he now had nothing to do until Monday, he concluded that he might as well wait in style and comfort at a nice resort on a beach. Three more nights at a beach hotel—life wasn't all that bad in his new occupation. The driver took him down the coast, then over the mountain to the opposite shore, and drove into a place called the Long Bay Beach Resort. The major difference between Tortola and Belize, it seemed to Daniel, was the ubiquitous speed bumps that were strewn along even the main roads here. He had never experienced anything so annoying. Obviously the road commissioner had an interest in a car alignment shop somewhere on the island.

Long Beach was a nice place with individual condos, a pool, and a hot tub located on a bridge overlooking the pool. It also had a strange little golf course that looked more like an overgrown lawn with flagpoles sticking up. The road was steep and the ascent reminded Daniel of his climb up the pyramid at Tikal. He wondered whether the Choosers had received his message yet, and Marta, ever present in his mind, assured him they probably had. Daniel settled into his room, stretched out on the bed, and planned for a long weekend of inactivity mixed with frequent naps.

* * * * *

Although nothing significant was going on in Omar's sphere of influence, the Middle East, he had been busy of late providing translation for Daniel as he surveyed the thoughts and ambitions of men half a world away in Belize. Omar had never been anywhere near Belize in Central America. He also wasn't exactly sure why Belize had been chosen as an international hub of Moslem terrorist activity, but strange things happen in strange places. Omar checked in with Daniel and found out through the Volva that Daniel would be inactive over the weekend because the next lead was unavailable until Monday. Omar wasn't sure whether Tortola was a country, an island, or a town, but when he received a visual image of the island's azure-blue waters, its lofty green peaks, and its immense, sandy beaches, he jealously inquired when it was going to be his turn to be on duty in paradise.

Omar decided he would use the break to catch up on some of his own business. Hopefully, his Arabic translation skills wouldn't be needed in the tranquil paradise, but he would be ready for whatever was needed when Monday came around. He was half a world away and he needed some rest. His days were Daniel's nights, so Daniel's use of his translation skills had significantly interrupted his sleep. He would rest after he had finished his errands.

First he needed to go to the bathhouse district in Istanbul and see whether he could pick up anything from the latest gossip. Men had a way of baring both their bodies and thoughts at the Turkish baths, and Omar had learned a lot there over the years. Many a secret deal or a nefarious plot had been contrived or discussed under the porous cover of steam.

Omar had been given a new Toyota Land Cruiser by the Turkish government for his use. It was two-toned, dark blue with tan trim. He'd had little time to drive it recently, due to all the translation work, so he still wasn't sure he liked it. He would put it through its paces today, and if he didn't like it he would send it back to the government official who gave it to him and receive something else.

He pulled away from his apartment and headed downtown just as he had done many times before. Istanbul was a maze of traffic jams, congestion, and narrow streets. Omar was a practical man. Once he had found the most efficient route, he kept to it. As he had demonstrated to Daniel, he had become a very good driver. He shifted, honked his horn, steered the wheel, and made hand gestures out the window all without slowing or looking bothered in the least. He was even singing an Elvis tune as he drove. He wasn't sure why he was singing "Hound Dog," but coupled with his all-appendage driving style, the song seemed to fit.

As he was starting to pass a broken-down delivery van parked along the road, his internal alarm went off. Without even a thought he immediately paused the time frame. With the added power of both the Volva on the Array, he had a little more time than usual to examine the situation.

He opened his door, got out of the Toyota, and walked the three meters to the van. Nobody appeared to be anywhere near it. He needed to hurry, as the women were straining at their task of funneling the massive energy he was now using. He opened the back of the van and saw the cause for his alarm. It was packed with explosives, and detonation had already begun. Sparks were shooting from a single brick of plastic explosives surrounded by what looked like fertilizer that was most likely drenched in diesel fuel. He turned and ran for all he was worth.

A pretty young woman was standing motionless in his path, and as he came near he grabbed her, threw her over his shoulder, and continued running as fast as he could. He was barely one hundred meters away when Monique signaled that she couldn't hold back time any longer. Omar threw himself to the pavement, covering the woman with his body as the scene shifted back into real time. His SUV was caught up in the massive explosion. The woman Omar had pinned to the ground had just begun to struggle when the percussion from the van engulfed them. The explosion was massive; pieces of Omar's Land Cruiser and the van flew over his head. Windows in the surrounding buildings were shattered and blood and carnage were everywhere.

CNN Headline News:

A massive truck bomb, believed to be similar in size and construction to the one used in the Oklahoma City bombing, went off this afternoon in Istanbul, the capital of Turkey. Police fear at least 25 deaths and many more wounded. Some bodies in passing vehicles may never be found or identified. The exact target of the bombing hasn't been determined. No terrorist group has claimed responsibility. Turkey has recently been free of terrorist activity, and the Prime Minister was at a loss to explain the sudden return of this terrorism in his country. Witnesses say the bomb left a crater 12 feet deep and 40 feet across. Buildings as far as a block away sustained heavy damage.

Omar, however, was only wounded and found that he could move all of his extremities. He dusted off the debris and sat up. The woman he had saved was in shock but appeared uninjured. Omar had suffered cuts to his legs and buttocks, and half of his shirt was missing, exposing most of his lynx tattoo.

The woman's name was Myra. She was an Orthodox Christian and had spent her life as a persecuted minority, despite Istanbul being the former center of the Orthodox faith. She was nineteen, single, and on her way to the market. She was at a loss to explain how she had been moved backward in a split second and subsequently avoided the explosion and certain death. All she could do was hug the strange man who was responsible for saving her. She noticed her benefactor was hurt and invited him to follow her through the smoke to her place. The least she could do was dress the wounds of her hero. Undoubtedly the man was an angel and she was being tested for her hospitality and generosity.

Omar assumed that the scene was being watched for his survival and that he'd better sneak off before the smoke cleared. He followed the woman, limping slightly as he struggled the ten blocks to her parents' home. They weaved through onlookers who had heard the explosion and were rushing to see what was happening. No one noticed Omar because he was cloaking his presence.

In Myra's house he stretched out on his stomach while she patiently cleaned his wounds and applied bandages. His body was filled with the loving warmth of the healing powers of the Volva and the healing started immediately. Omar knew it would take him only twenty-four hours to completely heal. He had learned from previous experience that while this happened, it was best to lie still. It was also important for him to drink fluids during this time, and he needed to refrain from medications that could adversely affect the process. The warmth he experienced from the accelerated healing process caused him to sweat. To the inexperienced it appeared he had a fever.

Omar decided that it would be good to lay low for a while anyway. His assassins would be easier to expose if they thought he was dead. He was sure his apartment was being watched, and before he returned he needed to be fully healed. Myra's house was as good a place as any to hide out. Omar announced to his host that the shock had left him with some dizziness and that he would need to rest. She offered him whatever he needed and made up her own bed for him. He wasn't lying; his ears were still ringing from the percussion. He chugged some water and moved off to his host's bed. Soon the warmth he was feeling put him to sleep.

Marta was immediately in all the Defender's thoughts after the attempt on Omar, and she had her associates transmit a mental re-creation of the events to the Order.

* * * * *

Daniel was in the middle of a dream involving his two Swedish friends in compromising situations when he suddenly awakened. It was two in morning, and all hints of sleepiness were gone. He was experiencing Omar's assassination attempt as if he were actually there. The vivid details shocked and horrified him. When the vision was over, he was happy that his old friend had been left with only scratches.

Monique instructed Daniel to lay low for a while, and Tortola seemed as out-of-the-way as any place. He decided he would vary his routine and suspected that his sudden, unannounced trip to Tortola was a good way for him to avoid any assassins. After his full briefing, he walked out to the deck that was attached to his condo and watched the lights of the island below him. The resort was mostly quiet except for the sounds of the gentle trade winds. Now fully awake and without fatigue, he decided he would try the hot tub on the bridge over the pool. The refreshing soak allowed him to converse with his Order and relax enough to go back to bed. Christina enjoyed the company. With two Volva on duty, sometimes there wasn't much to do.

Christina, is this always the type of life that we live? I mean, I have only been linked for a year and it seems to me that we live a life of constant action.

No, Daniel. These events are quite rare. Typically we lead a life of monotony. The big wars kept us busy, but typically nothing of consequence happens for years. I guess it was good that you came along when you did. The Choosers have a way of having good timing. The last assassination attempt before Chang was over sixty years ago, when the Germans tried to infiltrate us. Now we have had two attempts within a few days. Obviously something is afoot, and I suspect you are hot on its trail. It was good that you left no evidence in Belize. The perpetrator of all this probably does not know that you are coming. Stealth is always the best attack. We suspect they believe they killed Omar.

Will he be all right? Daniel knew the answer but he needed reassurance.

He will be fine. She was laughing in her thoughts. *He will probably get a woman out of all this if he wants one. The Florence Nightingale effect will take over. She will keep him out of trouble for a while. Omar has never been known to pass up a free meal, if you know what I mean.*

Omar is ever the opportunist, I agree. Daniel laughed at his old buddy, remembering the dual marriage back in Uber, Oman.

Rest now, Daniel, Christina ordered. *I will help you fall asleep.*

Daniel followed her suggestion, climbed the stairs, entered his room, and fell back in the middle of the very same dream with Anja and Therese. Soon the events of the day were forgotten, at least temporarily.

Christina liked both Anja and Therese. Their thoughts were simple and they were women of good nature. They were nurturing to Daniel and provided a good diversion from his responsibilities. She and the other Volva had no problem with Defenders associating with common people. The men needed some companionship, since being a male Defender was physically a lonely business. She suspected Daniel would see them again after the current crisis was over.

Without anything better to do the following morning, Daniel went to the beach. He headed off early in the morning and stopped for his complimentary breakfast, which was described by the resort as a buffet—fruit, day-old pastries, eggs, cold bacon, and cereal. The food was edible but nothing special. He grazed until he was satisfied and wandered out of the restaurant onto the beach.

The beach had soft sand and the shore fell at a considerable angle into the surf. The hotel clerk had warned Daniel that there were some rocks immediately in front of the resort but these gradually disappeared if he veered to the left past a large rock called Black Rock. It was the only outcrop of any sort on the beach and it marked the point where, although it was technically illegal, clothing-optional status had been known to occur. Daniel figured that the hotel clerk had just warned him because it was a requirement, so he paid the warning no attention.

But as he inspected the water, he noticed that the jagged rocks were so close and the break of the waves was so strong that swimming here would be dangerous. He continued up the beach a few hundred meters with more of the same until he passed Black Rock, where he noticed a change to gradual, sandy shallows where he could actually swim. The nudists knew their stuff. Daniel looked around and saw no one on the beach. Figuring the rock would obstruct any notice from the condominiums, he shed everything and dove into the azure blue water. He prefered this mode of bathing anyway, so he was glad he had the water all to himself.

After a refreshing dip, he sat in the mid-morning sun, his golden-brown body air-drying in the tropical warmth and gentle breeze. He marveled at his new physique. He had ripples where he'd never had ripples before. He still had his tan from Reva Gap and his month in Belize. He was becoming a regular Adonis.

Marta piped in. *You should not be so vain.* She was kidding since he wasn't a man who had previously noticed such things. While he was admiring himself, he didn't see a young couple walking up the beach. They sat only ten meters away. They were Australian, and the woman smiled at Daniel's beautiful body. Without shame, he smiled back. Her boyfriend poked her and she quietly removed her top and stretched out on her back. The boyfriend kept his pants on.

Daniel decided to remain as he was until the sun grew so extreme that he was forced to retire to his condo for lunch. The rest of the weekend was more of the same—rest, sun, and an occasional swim. He ate when he was hungry, napped when he was tired, and all the while scanned the thoughts of everyone around him for any suspicious activity. He was amazed by the lack of Americans at Tortola. The tourists consisted of mostly Brits, Germans, Canadians, Kiwis, and Aussies. There were very few from his home country. Apparently they all stopped at St. Thomas or St. John and never made the trip over to these islands.

Monday finally arrived and, after breakfast, Daniel caught a ride into town. He found a suitable spot from which to observe the comings and goings of visitors to International Pharma Research Ltd.

He watched as two men, both black Carabineers, entered the building. He also saw a man enter the barrister's office below. He filled the man with concerns over his house and soon watched him leave for home. Daniel felt it would be better for him to have as few witnesses as possible to his conversation with the men of International Pharma. As far as Daniel could tell, no one else could see the front door, so he headed up the stairs and entered the office. He pulled up the only vacant chair and sat with his back to the door. The two startled men looked up.

Williams began with, "Can I help—" Daniel silenced him. Neither man could move or speak.

He scouted their minds and was somewhat confused by their thoughts. These were not the same kinds of men he had observed in Belize. John Williams and Clive Edwards were family men, and as far as he could tell, neither knew exactly what they were a part of. He learned that they were providing legitimate fronts for the huge financial engine of international terrorism. Williams ran a company called Aracari Holdings Ltd., and Edwards ran International Pharma Research Ltd. Neither man knew the relation of the two businesses.

Aracari was involved in international shipping. Through it, the men booked charters from various companies to other companies and ports. International Pharma Research received payments from government sources for research, then subbed it out to various intermediaries like Western Caribbean, a company both men knew well, or at least thought they knew. Their upper-level contact for Aracari was a certain Mr. Li, and their contact for International Pharma Research was a Professor Khan. They knew nothing of Khan's whereabouts, but both men knew Mr. Li was a big businessman from Macao, a former Portuguese colony located off the coast of China near Hong Kong.

Marta told him that Chang had spent the last few weeks of his life in Macao. Daniel knew there was no such thing as coincidence, especially in his new line of work. If it looked like a duck and walked like a duck, it was a duck. Li was ultimately responsible for Chang's death, and he would have to pay for his crime.

While the men were frozen, Daniel looked through the paperwork in the office. Both companies comprised a maze of subsidiaries from all over the world. Most were in Barbados and the British Virgin Islands, but there were others in Iceland, Bermuda, Switzerland, and Cyprus. Their financial books showed that hundreds of millions of dollars were being passed through the companies. With

Iran, Libya, Iraq, Sudan, Yemen, North Korea, and others involved, this office played a central role in the big business of state-sponsored terrorism. As he had suspected, both Aracari and International Pharma Research funneled most of their profits into research for other firms. They were not designed for profit. He concluded that as long as he followed the chain, he would eventually come to the head of the organization. That person would answer for Chang's death. He suspected Li wasn't the head of the snake but just an important intermediary. But Li needed to be culled as well.

Daniel would have to go to Macao, but first he had two very frightened men to deal with. He regained his chair and sat. With a flick of his hand both men were flung out of their chairs and against the back wall of the office. He made a chopping motion with his hand and both desks were cut in two.

"Williams and Edwards, my name is Daniel," he said sternly as a reddish hue overtook his otherwise blue eyes. "I am from the Order of the Defenders, a follower of Freyja and a Protector of the people. You have been involved in something you should have stayed away from—very far away. Li and probably Khan have conspired to kill another of my kind. The penalty for that was long ago written—death for all. Their families, their pets, their livestock—everything that bears their mark—will be destroyed so that even their memory is blotted from the earth.

"You two are just as bad. You have financed terrorism, death, and destruction beyond what you can imagine. I have read your thoughts, and I know your knowledge of these events is limited. Because you have financed your personal lives with this blood money, judgment for you will be severe. I will give each of you two choices so you will have determined your own destiny.

"First, you can choose death, here and now. It will be neither painless nor quick. Many have suffered for your greed and you too will suffer. But I promise you this—your family will know nothing of your whereabouts. They will live on as before, and they will never know whether you died or just left them. In time your wife will know other lovers and your children will know other men as their fathers.

"Your second choice is one of change. You will leave this place. You will take your families and catch the next boat out of Tortola.

You will go with nothing but the shirt on your back and the money in your pockets. If you go, you will go now. This island will be as a bitter pill for you. You will never return and you will have no contact with this land or anyone here, ever. You will never utter or other-wise communicate the word Tortola or the name of this country. If you so much as step ashore here ever again, I will return and track down every member of your family, every contact, and anyone who knows you—and they will die a horrific death while you watch. You, however, will not die but will be forced to live with your trans-gression. Finally, from this moment on, banking, computers, and money are your enemy. It will not be an easy life, but you will have your life and your family.

"Now, each of you must choose." He first looked at Williams. "Williams, what is your choice?"

Williams could now feel he was able to speak, but he hesitated to try to determine his options. Although he knew it would be hard, his wife was from poor stock and could handle the life change. He hoped she would someday understand what had happened. He looked into the eyes of the strangely marked man. "I choose to leave."

Daniel looked at Edwards. The man had urinated on himself and was sweating. "Edwards, what say you?"

Edwards was having other thoughts. He had chosen his spouse badly. His wife was used to the finer things of life. She would leave him as soon as he said they had to leave. When she wouldn't leave with him he feared the wrath of this man would destroy his children as well. He didn't care about his wife, but his children were dear to him. His only option seemed to be death. They could live on without him. Hopefully, someday someone would tell his children about him. Stuttering, he said, "I guess I'll have to choose death. The first option."

Daniel was harsh. "You'll guess nothing."

Edwards's final words were an emphatic restatement of his choice. "I will take the first choice. Death with my family being spared."

Immediately smoke started rising from his body. The searing flesh required him to scream, but he could not. The spontaneous combustion of his body progressed slowly and steadily until only his head was left unaffected. Daniel's eyes glowed red with the anger of the Volva as they took some revenge on this man for the death of Chang. But the choice had been his.

Soon nothing was left but a small bit of carbon on the floor of the office. Daniel picked up the black dust and wiped it on Williams' pants. "Remember what you've seen here, and remember your choice. I will not be so nice the next time. Now fire up these computers. Move all the money to the account of any charity, so neither you nor Li will ever use it. It must be made available to do some good in this world."

Williams leapt for the computer and worked feverishly, finally moving a nine-figure amount into his main business account. He then transferred some to the hospital in Tortola and moved the rest to two charitable organizations. One was a medical school in Kenya; the other was the parent church of his faith. Tomorrow they would have a pleasant surprise in their bank accounts. Next he reformatted the hard drive as well as the one on Edwards' computer, then changed his answering machine to state the office was closed for a month-long holiday. He left a message on Jenkins' phone to allow him to rent the space to someone else at the end of the next month. All the while Daniel was destroying the office files and equipment.

When all was ready, Daniel led Williams down the stairs and ordered him to double-park his Daewoo. It would eventually be towed. The pair took Edwards' larger vehicle. Daniel climbed in beside Williams. "Now, let's go pick up your family. The ferry to St. Thomas leaves soon."

Williams stopped at two different schools and soon three confused children dressed in the local school uniform of Road Town were bouncing in the back seat. It was his wife's day off, so he hoped she was home. He drove up the hill to his house and was relieved to see her beating a rug on the front step. He jumped out and ran to her. She looked confused at first but soon understood that life had just taken an unexpected turn. She ran inside and grabbed a satchel of important papers, then climbed into the back with her children. No one said a word as they drove toward West End and the ferry terminal.

They parked in the small lot next to the simple, one-story building that served as customs, the ticket booth, immigration, and a taxi station. Their boat had just arrived.

As Williams headed for the ticket booth, Daniel stopped him. "You won't need tickets."

They walked without complaint through the doorway and aboard the boat. Mysteriously, nobody else got on the boat. This was a private voyage. They continued to St. John where the customs officer met the boat and waved them to go on. At Red Hook they transferred to a van marked as a taxi for a twenty-five-minute trip to the airport.

The confusion that was St. Thomas's link to the outside world seemed orderly today. No cruise ship passengers had yet arrived for their airline trips home. Daniel stopped the family in front of the numerous check-in stands. "Now you must choose your destination."

Daniel watched the children as their parents considered their options. Finally, they returned with an answer. "We'll go to Trinidad. We've read that they have some decent job openings and the population is large enough so that their society is not closed to us." Daniel booked five one-way tickets on Liat. No money changed hands. Daniel watched them board the plane that would eventually take them to Port-of-Spain, Trinidad, where they would continue the rest of their lives.

Daniel too was done with Tortola and the tropics. He walked out and met a waiting military transport. The Gulfstream jet was the pride of the U.S. military. It was first class all the way to Hong Kong. He watched as the Caribbean slowly sank beneath his view. He was off to find a man he knew little about. He ordered a meal and drank a Coke. Tomorrow would bring more of the unknown.

When the plane landed in Hong Kong, he made his way onto the crowded ferry to the island of Macao. During his visit, he planned to keep a low profile and use his powers to mask his presence. Obviously, the walls here had eyes and undoubtedly the people who were watching Chang would be watching him as well if they knew he was present. He went into a casino-hotel and walked right into a sixth-floor room.

He would spend the next several weeks peering out of the window and examining the thoughts of men below. Xu Li's translation ability was the mainstay of Daniel's surveillance. Nobody, however, seemed to be thinking of the mysterious Mr. Li. Daniel observed thoughts that made reference to many things, like pickpockets, drug trafficking, and subversive activity, but nothing pertaining to his investigation. It was as if the entire Macao connection had vanished. But he was patient. He knew eventually he would find a lead.

* * * * *

Li was back in Pyongyang. He'd been ordered to present himself again to Tiger and explain his failure. Things weren't going quite as planned. They had attacked two tattooed men successfully, but Li was still at a loss to explain their importance. Other plans he was involved in were also having snags. The money hub in Belize had stopped operations for some reason. The man Li knew as Husam had vanished, as well as most of the money used to fund that side of the operation. For that matter, his financial arm had recently gone on vacation. Williams had left for the month, as had Edwards.

He entered Tiger's office. Tiger was his usual self, coming straight to the point. "Li, my man for answers! I need some updates from you. Did the mules get the canisters to the pickup spot?"

At least it wasn't all bad news. "Yes, they did."

"Did your agents make it to Belize to pick them up?"

"I know they got to the island, but the pickup was delayed due to the hurricane," Li answered. "I have flight manifests in, but none out. The ship they were supposed to be on has gone out to sea. I assume they disappeared into the background like they were trained to do and have by now reached Canada and gone underground. The plan was for them to have no contact after Belize. They are some of my best men. I know they will deliver the cargo as expected."

"Good. Now, the financing has slowed and I have been receiving complaints. I do not like complaints, Li. What is going on with that?"

"My operative in Belize disappeared soon after the canister drop," Li answered honestly. It wasn't good to lie to Tiger. "He is nowhere to be found. I have sent my own number two man to check the restaurant, and there are no signs of anything. It looks just like it always did. My contact, Husam, is missing and so is some of the money."

"And your solution will be . . . ?"

"As I cannot set things up again quickly in Belize with a new man, I will move the money transfer hub to Macao immediately." Li feared he would leave the office a dead man if he held back anything. "I will make up for the monetary shortfall with my own money until it is found. The thief will be caught. My number two is searching the Caribbean for Husam. He will be found."

Tiger paused and got up to look out the window. "For some reason I suspect that I should kill you right now. Your unwitting incompetence is jeopardizing all that we have worked for. I cannot explain this feeling, however, so I will accept your backup plan. Mark my words though—your days are numbered if you screw up again." He indicated the door. "Go."

Li literally ran to the door and didn't stop running until he was back in Hong Kong. There, he met with his men and told them he would use one of his hotels as the new money drop. The men passed the word to all the field agents. Then Li called his number two man. The number two man still knew nothing of Husam or the money. Li sent him off to Tortola to look for Williams or Edwards. He needed answers. After the call he took a cab to the ferry and headed back to his modest apartment for some rest.

* * * * *

Daniel soon observed a plain-looking man talking on a cell phone and tuned in to his thoughts. The word Belize sparked his interest before Xu Li had even provided translation. The man was telling someone that Belize was finished as a hub and that the Colonial Hotel and Casino was the new drop. The man hung up and Daniel froze time so he could hurry down the stairs and tail his new lead. If this man weren't one of Li's men, he would at least cross paths with one of them.

It took two days of following other contacts before Daniel happened across his elusive quarry in the lobby of the Colonial Hotel. Li was unassuming and looked weak. Daniel saw that he was just another hired hand. Daniel watched as he went upstairs, discovering from his thoughts that he was going to room 411 for a nap. He had a woman up there as well and hoped she could help him get some much-needed rest. He had developed a case of insomnia.

Daniel spent the next few minutes erasing the memories of Li's men at the casino. He'd identified thirty men as part of the Macao connection. Twenty-eight of the thirty had no useful information except that something big was in the works, and after each mental interrogation, Daniel wiped their memories clean. He removed even their own self-awareness, sending each on a singular purpose to opposite corners of the metropolis. Once each man finished his task, he would be totally confused and of no use to anyone. As their penalty for their minimal involvement with Chang's death, they would either have to start over, like a stroke victim, or end up in an asylum for the mentally ill.

The other two men he identified had tailed Chang through the city. Their memories of the tattooed man were clearly evident. They would receive a much harsher judgment. Both men, like the others, were cleared of thought, but their mission was to walk to the ferry pier and jump in. Neither could swim, and Daniel instructed them to grab nothing thrown to them. He hadn't the time to waste on these minor players; besides, their suicides wouldn't raise suspicion.

He climbed the stairs to the fourth floor. Room 411 was just down the hall. Two men stood guard at the door. He made quick work of them. As he had with the man back in Washington, D.C., he focused on a point in each man's brain and let heat energy do the rest. Neither made a sound as they departed life.

He found the door unlocked. It opened into a suite. A nude woman was sitting on a towel watching the television. Daniel could hear the shower. The naked woman was of no use to him; she was just a whore from the casino. He erased her memory of the present and filled her with self-confidence that he hoped would give her a fresh start in life. She left the room unclad, just as Daniel had found her. Li was still in the shower.

Daniel noticed a gun and cell phone on the nightstand as he slipped through the half-closed bathroom door. He pulled back the shower curtain to find a naked, very startled man.

Li found himself staring into fiery red eyes. He watched as Daniel took off his shirt to reveal the full extent of his markings. Li quickly surmised that Daniel was not a man of this world and real-ized that killing the other tattooed man had been a big mistake.

"I see by your thoughts that you don't understand our impor-tance," Daniel said in a stern voice. "You ordered the death of one of my own. How can that be? You have brought a great wrath down upon yourself. Was the murder at the bequest of another?" Daniel paused, as the visualization of the man Li knew as Tiger flashed into his mind. *So this was his true enemy!* He siphoned Li's thoughts into his link with Marta on the Array. Xu Li would provide the primary deciphering of them. Daniel was being sprayed with water from the showerhead, so he melted it with a glance. The flow stopped.

This confirmed to Li that his association with the Chang affair was definitely not good. He deduced correctly that he would soon breathe his last. "The penalty, Li, for the death of a Defender is signified by my tattoos. You have disturbed an ancient tradition, and all of you—your seed and your father's seed—shall be destroyed. I see by your thoughts that your worst fear is of falling to your death. I guess we need to go to the roof." Daniel turned and headed toward the elevator with his captive. They were let out on the top floor. No door to the roof was available so Daniel opened one of the guest rooms. Room 3507 was empty. He dissolved the full-length window in an instant and the room filled with wind.

"Tiger will be the next man I visit. It saddens me to have to do this to you, but you chose this end when you became his partner in this whole episode. I will allow you the ability to scream." Without warning, he levitated Li out the window and over the street. Then he looked into Li's eyes and filled his mind with a thought. *You can always beg for me to end your life quickly.*

Li was too tough for that, at least right now, but Daniel wanted to break him. Suddenly, Li was plummeting face-first toward the pavement. He screamed in terror. A mere foot above the ground, he stopped and was raised back to the top of the building. On the fourth trip, he passed out from sheer terror. Daniel waited for him to wake up. A lack of consciousness would not be an option. Li begged for mercy. The Defender had tired of the activity, so on the fifth occasion, having made the event as miserable as possible for this killer of a Defender, he mercifully allowed Li to fully partake of the power of gravity. Li's body was unrecognizable after the fall.

Daniel returned to Li's room just as the cell phone rang. Daniel picked it up and, using Li's voice, spoke Chinese to the man on the other end. It was Li's number two man.

"Talk!" Daniel said using Li's usual greeting.

"I'm in Tortola. Williams and his family are not here. Edwards' car is at the ferry terminal and he's gone too. His wife has no knowledge of his whereabouts. She refused to talk even when I pulled the trigger. Their office is a shambles—looks like a typhoon hit it. Everything is in ruins, the computer destroyed, the records burned. I searched everywhere, but nobody knows anything. The two men just disappeared into thin air. The bank accounts are frozen, and even the lawyer downstairs is gone.

"But I have other news. I overheard a tourist talking about a man with beautiful tattoos, like those on the man we hit in China. He was on the beach sunning himself just a few weeks ago. I do not think it was a coincidence. What shall I do now?"

Daniel, still using Li's voice, rambled, "We have failed Tiger. He will order all of our families destroyed. I will go to Korea tomorrow and report the facts. I will tell him that you have taken your own life, and I will take a cyanide capsule in front of him as a gesture of my loyalty. You will not make a liar of me, will you? At least our families will live."

The man understood his orders, however harsh; he knew Tiger's word was law. He would watch the sun set, then swim out into the ocean and be no more. Tortola was an out-of-the-way hell hole for him, an urban city person, but his remains would be buried in the azure blue waters forever.

Daniel hung up. He knew the man would do as ordered. He needed all the loose ends tied up. A few remnants of Li's gang showed up minutes later. They received the same fate as their brethren. Daniel spent two days searching the colony for the remnants of the Macao cell.

After eliminating the loose ends, he was off to North Korea. He would pay a visit to Tiger and his operation. Tanoka was right to be wary of North Korea, and he was glad that Tanoka had shared his knowledge of their language with him. Having completed the Volva's revenge in Macao, he boarded a ferry for Hong Kong's airport. It was surprisingly quiet. SARS had restarted its scourge and was a larger epidemic than the one the previous spring. The few people he saw were wearing masks. Most airline flights had been canceled, and even his contacts in the U.S. government refused to lend him a plane. He obviously had some work to do in Hong Kong before he left. He could feel in his gut that this Tiger was behind SARS, so he went to the hospitals to cure the sick and control the spread of the disease. Besides, the only flight out was to India. From there he could catch a flight to Tokyo and then to Seoul, South Korea. Nobody flew to North Korea.

He healed whomever he could during his delay in Hong Kong, and after four days of travel he found himself on the Korean Peninsula. He knew nothing of his enemy or who or what Tiger was, so he started his search at the university library. He would immerse himself in a sixteen-hour-a-day study of the two Koreas. He had much to learn, but he had become a quick learner.

CHAPTER 15: A Tiger Hunt

Daniel made good use of his time at the excellent library at the university in Seoul. Because South Korea had been run by a dictator and subject to governmental censorship, Daniel was surprised at the amount of information that was available to him. Every day he crossed lines of protesters at various places in the university complex. The protestors occasionally rallied against specific issues, but most of the demonstrations were anti-American. Infiltrators from the North were instigating a lot of these protests.

By and large, the sentiment he perceived from the population was favorable toward the United States, but he also perceived variations that made sense to his understanding of the situation. The older people who remembered that the West had come to the aid of the South and stopped the rape and pillage brought on by the North, the Chinese, and the Japanese, thought only good things about the United States. The students, however, were disillusioned about their current economic situation and blamed the West for their troubles.

The South Korean government had been hopelessly corrupt and worthy of the young citizens' complaints. Unfortunately, by supporting this government, the West appeared to be causing their hardships. Most of the young people seemed to ignore all the success their small country had achieved in the fifty years since the armistice. It was the typical short sightedness of youth to focus on the acorns and ignore the trees. There were foreign agents who had long ago infiltrated the student associations and were stirring up trouble on the peninsula.

Daniel's knowledge of both spoken and written Korean made available to him a wide range of resources that typically would have been avoided by Westerners. He never had to think about using Korean, as it was almost as entrenched in him as English, Swedish, or the Old Language. Even the strange Korean writing system, unlike Chinese or Japanese, made instant sense.

Daniel studied material as he found it. The current leader of North Korea was a man named Kim Jong Il. The population referred to him as Dear Leader. He was the oldest son of the previous leader, Kim Il Sung, a man still referred to as the Great Leader.

Kim Il Sung was an ordinary junior military officer until the

Russian occupiers unexpectedly appointed him as the leader of the state in the aftermath of World War II. He led the country through an ill-fated attempt at unification, the Korean War, and remained the absolute ruler until his death. From all accounts of unbiased reports, the elder ruler was a man of vision. It seemed to Daniel, however, that these praises held little substance. As far as he could tell, somewhere after the mid-sixties, nothing in North Korea seemed outwardly successful. Kim Il Sung, for all his successes in the post World War II period, just seemed to put the country on cruise control. He looked in charge and he acted in charge, but the country went backward in every sense. Yet his people did nothing and they praise him even to this day. Even the South Koreans seemed to revere the former leader of their archenemy to the North.

This didn't seem to make sense. If North Korea was so bad and his people so repressed, there should have been demonstrations or defections, or someone would have tried to remove their leader from power. Daniel suspected that even though the documented sources seemed knowledgeable, something was going on that kept the people from acknowledging their suffering. In the mid-nineties, the Republic of Korea had captured two malnourished soldiers from the North. Those soldiers seemed to be the main reason everyone believed the people of North Korea were starving. Could they have been operatives who were put on a starvation diet before being conveniently found by the South? It seemed odd to Daniel that a country able to put satellites into space was unable to feed its military.

On July 7, 1994, while inspecting a guest villa in the mountains with the temperature nearly one hundred degrees, the eighty-two-year-old-leader had complained of unexplained tiredness. Later that afternoon, he collapsed from a massive heart attack. He died at two A.M. the next morning. His death was mysteriously kept a state secret for thirty-four hours. At eight a.m. the word went out that all the children in schools and adult citizenry should watch state television at noon for an important announcement. When it came, the people were in shock. Tens of thousands of people amassed below his statue in the main square in Pyongyang, and hospitals were overflowing with heart attack victims. This was not a response of people who were starving and suffering.

Without so much as a whimper of a challenge to his new power, the eldest son, a moon-faced man with weird hair, took charge of the country. Everyone from the South Koreans to the Russians suspected that the North was on its last leg, that it would survive maybe a year. The new leader, from all the reports Daniel could gather, hadn't led anything in the country, yet North Korea chugged along without missing a beat. In the years since his father's death, the Dear Leader had made only one public speech, yet nobody seemed to care. The military, by all accounts, seemed as strong as always. They had even restarted their nuclear program and had fired rockets over Japan. Every source but one seemed to think the new leader was a fool.

That one source, Lim Dong Won, was a close advisor to the President of South Korea. He'd visited Pyongyang and met with the Dear Leader. He was one of the few outsiders ever to have met him. He wrote that the man was a strong dictator, possibly even stronger than his father. He was open-minded, decisive, and listened to his advisors. Despite this, Daniel kept getting the feeling that the ruling family wasn't really pulling the strings in the North. There was no reason for him to believe that this dictator was the man referred to as Tiger by the men in Macao.

Daniel thought a secret society must be present in both republics, and that the men of these societies ran the politics of both countries. Could these secret societies be one and the same? Daniel read the accounts of the Hyundai founder, who had committed suicide after funneling money from his country to the North. Why was a South Korean businessman giving money to his enemies? Daniel began to suspect the secret society was behind everything of significance that happened on the peninsula.

He was just finishing his third day of research when he picked up on a stray thought in the library. A man was thinking of what name to write. He chose the name Khan. Why would he use a Moslem name in this part of the world? Unfortunately, it was too late for Daniel to make himself disappear. The native students in the library had become used to the oddly tattooed, blond-haired, Korean-speaking man at their table, so making himself invisible now would be impossible. He moved to a hidden corner of the study section where he was partially obscured by a pile of books.

He watched the man check out some books at the desk in the opposite corner of the building. The man looked as out of place as Daniel was. He definitely was not Korean.

Daniel got up to see better, but something had spooked the man and he'd left. Daniel ran into the square outside the library, but it was a maze of people. He froze everybody, trying to pick out a thought that seemed out of place. It was like listening for a specific voice in a sea of conversation. Suddenly, he noticed a vehicle with government plates driving away. He focused on the man in the back seat. The man thought in a language other than one Daniel understood. He surmised it must be the man called Khan.

Daniel was soon forced to let time go back to normal. He couldn't keep up with the government car on foot so he summoned the Volva to transmit their power to the car. It was a technique discovered by Omar. They could focus their energy to make things break down. It worked well, and the Hyundai in which Khan was riding suddenly lost power. Before Daniel caught up with him, though, a side door opened and the man darted off to the left.

Daniel continued his pursuit until he got a good view of the man; then he was able to freeze the man in his tracks. Out of breath, Daniel walked up to the frightened, exhausted man. They were still in a crowded location, so Daniel put his arm on the man's shoulder and together they moved to a sidewalk table where both sat down, one to rest, the other because of an unexplained power that controlled his movement. Daniel ordered a Coke and looked at the stranger. He delayed further activity due to the fact that Omar was in the middle of something. Daniel would require Omar's translation skills. Daniel suspected correctly that the delay was due to a woman. But there was no hurry—Khan wasn't going anywhere. Daniel enjoyed his soda.

A few minutes later, Daniel began the mental interrogation. This was the man who had been behind the planned hoof and mouth disease outbreak. He was one of the world's eminent microbiologists, and he was on the payroll of the man named Tiger. He was on his way to an important, high-level planning meeting before the master plan was to be initiated. Khan was cooperative enough to give Daniel the address to his boss, something Li had been unable to do.

Daniel also learned all about Khan's disease-making activities. They seemed a severe threat to humanity, so Daniel took careful note of the locations of the various labs and the names of the intermediaries Khan used for his nefarious activities. After they had learned everything, Omar agreed to go on a mission to start eliminating these labs.

Following his full disclosure, Daniel spoke to the man for the first time. "Mr. Khan, I will speak to you in English. It is a language I know you understand. I am a member of a secret order. We protect humanity from itself. It is an ancient order, some twelve thousand years in existence. I have been granted special powers to enforce our goals. You are determined to destroy this world, although I cannot understand why. It is apparently more than a quest for money or power. Even by your own thoughts, I cannot truly understand your motives.

"I think you are truly an evil person, if that is the correct term for you. You have lost touch with your humanity. Of all the people on whom I have passed judgment, you make me the saddest. You have much power to help save people's lives, but you have chosen to ruin lives. You have created much suffering and misery. Therefore, you shall die as did those people you killed with the SARS virus. I am no medical person but I understand the pathology of that disease. You will ultimately die of suffocation. I hope you spend your last few moments of life praying to your God for forgiveness. You will be judged by a higher power than I. Quite possibly the suffering you will soon endure will be only the beginning of the suffering of your spirit."

Daniel touched the man's neck as he got up to leave, then he casually walked away. Khan, now able to move, grabbed his own neck. He was experiencing increased difficulty getting his breath. Bystanders tried in vain to remove the suspected obstruction from his trachea, but there was no obstruction. Daniel's touch had shattered Khan's hyoid bone and fused his vocal cords. Khan died a terrible death of fear and suffocation. Khan was no more, and soon the terror he'd levied on humanity would end.

Daniel now had all the information he needed. He picked up a vacated bicycle and headed for the Demilitarized Zone on the border with the North. Demilitarized Zone was a misnomer as the area was the most heavily armed, mined, and watched place in the world. Daniel headed for a small farming village called Panmunjom. It was officially devoid of all military except for a token force of soldiers from each side. In a small building that sits astride the border, a meeting table marked with a line divided the two nations. This was the only place to safely cross on foot.

Daniel walked past the final American guard checkpoint and down the hill into town. He crossed the imaginary border to the North without even disturbing a local cow. Soon he passed the opposing checkpoint in the North and, without notice, slipped into the back of a jeep. The driver suddenly had an overwhelming desire to drive to the capital, Pyongyang. By evening, Daniel was in the middle of the most closed capital on earth. The nice spring day had turned cool, and Daniel wasn't dressed for cold.

His presence cloaked, Daniel walked into a building that looked like a hotel. It was nothing like any hotel he had ever seen before, but he found a bed. He'd had a long day and needed to rest; then he would locate Tiger's office before the big meeting.

He woke up late. It was nearly noon as he wandered in search of food. There were no open-air restaurants, though he did find a place that offered cabbage and rice. He ate, then wandered out, still cloaked, and searched the town. It took half of the rest of the day, but he finally found the building Kahn had described. It was tall, but otherwise of no significance. Tiger did not operate from an opulent mansion or palace as did the leader of the country.

Daniel listened as people came and went the rest of the day. He actually heard very little of use because the people were focused on the completion of their various assigned tasks. There was no unhappiness and no jealousy, no one thought of sexual conquests, and nobody thought about their home lives. Work was their defining objective. North Korea was a society with a singular purpose—the desire to serve and please the state.

Daniel went back to his room and waited for the big meeting. He meditated and consulted with his Volva. A big day was at hand and a battle loomed with the mighty Tiger. He finally enjoyed a few hours of restless slumber, but morning came early. After another early meal of the same fare as the day before, he arrived at the building just after the scheduled start time of the meeting. He was pleased to learn that the North Koreans started everything promptly.

As he casually made his way through the hallway of the administration building solely devoted to Tiger's use, he began to focus his concentration on the three women dressed in plain clothes sitting at desks that stood directly ahead of him. They were secretaries and might possess valuable information. He was as surprised by their thoughts as he had been with the thoughts of the people on the street. They were focused beings, and as far as he could tell, they possessed no passion, no dreams, and no aspirations. Their lives were wholly devoted to the state. It was as if they had no initiative; as such, their minds were difficult to read. They thought very little about anything other than the task at hand.

Daniel shook his head. *Humanity is much more than this. These people lead a terrible existence. It is a life devoid of creativity, expression, art, literature, and spontaneity. They have no free will at all. They are what they are, and that is it. They have no chance to improve their lot and everything is dictated centrally. I do not like this way of life at all.*

Marta and Astria agreed with Daniel. They thought the most important quality of life was individuality, and that meant a lot coming from two women who thought about things with a collective consciousness. Daniel needed to remain focused on his task. His chief adversary was behind the large wooden door only forty feet ahead of him.

One free thought Daniel picked up was of utmost importance. The Tiger was having a meeting with his chief lieutenants. They were all present except Li and Khan. Daniel waited outside the meeting room. One by one he would drain each of the lieutenant's thoughts so he could find out what they were up to. He would then eliminate them. After he'd intercepted Khan, Daniel had fully realized the truly sinister methods these men were using. He knew the SARS epidemic would eventually die out, as would the West Nile Virus, but he was more concerned with the prospects of the nuclear weapons program and the other evils Tiger was planning along the way to reuniting his homeland.

Unfortunately, if the Americans had delayed the end of the Second World War, the Soviet Union would have finished their drive through this peninsula. In an odd way, the problems of North and

South Korea would have ended just like the problems of Poland or Hungary had ended at least ten years ago. Korea would have been unified, a potential hot spot would have been eliminated, and a war that had resulted in over a million casualties would have been avoided.

One by one, Daniel watched as the men left the meeting room. From each he extracted essential information, passing it along to the Volva so they could decipher it later. He learned of hidden nuclear facilities, underground production plants, oil stores, food warehouses, and stashes of top-of-the-line military aircraft, tanks, missiles, and other hardware. He learned of secret arms deals with numerous countries, some involved with terrorism and some trying to fuel civil wars. He also learned of a massive network of international spies. One of the men even knew the whereabouts of bin Laden and other chief terrorists. In ten minutes, Daniel had learned enough information to keep his associates busy for weeks. It had become clear to all the Defenders that this organization was as well formed as the one Hitler had put together.

Hitler had an advantage in that the Nazis were from a larger, more-endowed country. However, Hitler did not operate in secret, and so his quest for world domination countered that advantage. He lacked focus, wanting to be everywhere and do everything. Tiger was focused on his goal to recreate a united Korea and have Japan as a puppet state. Daniel was amazed that it had been hidden from the Order before he'd luckily stumbled onto it in Belize after the lead from the American detainees.

Finally, Daniel learned that he had arrived just in time. The attack on the South was set to begin in nine days. Hopefully, all of Tiger's planned distractions for the world could still be found and eliminated. Stumbling onto the hoof and mouth disease plot was lucky, and all the Defenders now needed to be on full alert. Astria assured him that his associates were already moving to eliminate the men associated with that plot.

Fifteen men passed before Daniel. They were soon fifteen dead men. They all decided to walk down the many flights of stairs instead of taking an elevator. None realized that this choice had been telepathically instilled in them by Daniel. One by one they opened the door, walked down a few steps, and died. Their deaths were unremarkable. Daniel had no time for theatrics. Tiger, however, was in for something special.

Like Hitler, Tiger would meet a similar, very painful end. Hitler was found in his bunker by one of Daniel's associates in April of 1945. Hitler knew the penalty for Heinrich's death and he'd just sneered at his judge as he slowly burned alive. He also watched without emotion as his new wife was killed before his eyes. Finally, due to extreme pain, he passed out and the Defender put a bullet in his brain and left enough of him recognizable so his Nazi followers and the Russians could identify him. His death was written off as a suicide. Suicide better described the truly evil man as a coward.

Daniel passed the female secretaries and cleared their minds of Tiger, this office, and their soon-to-be-former jobs. Their past lives were now vaporized from their consciousness. He paused, then opened the door. An unremarkable man sat at his desk. No one else was present. The office was plainer than Daniel had expected. Was this the office of one of the most powerful men in the world? Daniel saw numerous mementos around the room. The models and pictures looked like something from a teenager's bedroom, except that each model illustrated a tragedy that Daniel remembered from world events. He recognized the numerous model planes, ships, and scale models of buildings.

Tiger was just finishing jotting notes from his meeting when he heard the door open. He wrongly assumed that it was just one of his secretaries coming in to see if he needed anything or if he wanted her for an early lunch. His gaze caught something totally unexpected, and he wasn't used to the unexpected. A man had entered his office, a strange man, but one that Tiger quickly recognized. He looked up at the muscular blond man in front of him and watched as Daniel removed his white tunic.

Tiger studied the lynx tattoo, the black broadsword, the strange combination design of a heron and heart on the man's cheek, and the numerous other tattoos. This man also had one truly unusual feature—his eyes glowed bright red. The color reminded Tiger of fury and made Daniel look something other than human. But Tiger showed no fear. Fear was for the weak, which he wasn't, and besides, this man was on his turf. He had developed a mechanism for dealing with unwelcome guests.

"You would do well to fear me," Daniel said in perfect Korean.

"Son, I fear no man," replied the cocky Korean.

"That would be appropriate if I were just a man. I am Daniel, a messenger from the Order of Freyja, Defender of the People. Some call me a Homat al Omma, others the Modafea Danya. In the mythology of my people, I am called one of the Vanir. We are a race of god-like people who protect the world from destruction and people like you.

"The women of my race, the daughters of Freyja, the Volva, sit as your jury. Their verdict is death. As your judge, I am here to execute this sentence. You have killed one of us, the Chinese Defender named Chang. You have attempted to kill another, Omar, my teacher and friend. Rest assured, unlike you, the great Omar will awaken tomorrow morning and break bread with humanity. You have eaten your last meal."

Tiger paid little attention to the diatribe. Homat al Omma or whatever, he had no time for some naked, tattooed fool threatening him. "Yet I see that you are alone in this mission." He laughed. "As has been said before, you and what army?" He laughed again. "And a jury of women. Where is this jury of women? I would wish them present so I could rape them in plain view of your dying body."

Daniel didn't move and continued his narrative. "I am an army." He flicked a finger and Tiger's desk shattered in front of him. He then gestured with his arms, causing all the plate-glass windows behind him to shatter and fall to the ground, many stories below. The office filled with wind. "I found your accomplice, Li. He died an unpleasant death. His followers have also been neutralized. I melted the canisters in Belize. The hoof and mouth disease plot has been averted.

"Khan was intriguing, but he did not use his knowledge for the greater good. His mind was informative. He died a choking death, as did those he infected with SARS. Your own top henchmen are all dead in the stairwell of this building." He wandered to the window and looked out, watching a presidential motorcade pass below. He stopped the vehicle and transferred the Dear Leader into the now windowless office to serve as a witness. He pinned the frightened man in a vacant chair. "One should always be left behind to serve as a warning to others.

"I see by your thoughts that you have read the account of the ill-conceived Nazi plan to infiltrate and attack my Order. Somehow, though, you do not believe what you have read."

Tiger still wasn't frightened, nor did he believe he was in a grave situation. "Mr. Defender, I do not believe in fantasy. The mere thought of a few people stopping and destroying three divisions including air support and Panzers is beyond any realm of possibility. I do not believe the impossible. You are just a man, as I am."

Daniel laughed. "And what do you think you could do that fifty thousand men could not? The desert is still littered with the melted debris of their battle tanks. It is just as real as the air that we breathe. We left one man alive so he could tell the world about it, so the world would learn from Hitler's folly. You, however, did not take heed of this warning even after reading the man's own diary. You doubted what you could not comprehend." Daniel walked to the window.

Tiger tried to move but couldn't. He was trying to reach for a gun under his chair. His thought of it gave him away, and Daniel redirected his attention to the chair. He levitated the weapon, an old German Luger, into his hand. "I see you still like Nazi weaponry."

Tiger was still cocky. "That pistol was used by Hitler to execute one his rivals from the old SA before he assumed power. It was a treasured possession of one of his followers, who died recently in exile in Paraguay. I have used it for just such a purpose many times since."

"I see you are beginning to experience fear." The Modafea Danya continued looking out the window. "Your mind is giving me a picture of the real you. My Order has the power to experience your thoughts and fears. As you can see, I can also easily control your movement.

"I see your military headquarters, your chief military complex, and the seat of your secret society over there." Tiger and the Dear Leader watched as the whole complex was hit with a tremendous earthquake. Fires and explosions leveled the building as a relatively limited eight magnitude earthquake extended out from just in front of the building. Using lightning bolts, one by one Daniel set the remaining military buildings on fire. "That is how one person can win a battle." He held up the German pistol in front of Tiger. Molten steel dripped from the tip until all that remained was a steaming puddle of rapidly hardening steel on the floor. "This Nazi execution pistol shall never be used by you or anyone again."

Tiger tried to speak but was unable. At some level he still felt the exhibition was mere trickery; magician's nonsense. The Dear Leader, dumbstruck, with urine dripping down his leg, was too scared to attempt anything.

Daniel did the rest of the talking. "It has been written that Freyja and her followers had such power that they were invincible in battle. The nature of the power has never been fully described, but as you can see, it is real and worth remembering. It is written also of Freyja that she was usually called upon to bring order and make things right by passing her power on to men and empowering them to restore order. I am one of her men.

"I will share with you a Norse prayer that I studied as a student. It is a typical prayer to Freyja: Queen of the warrior-women, Freyja of the black sword hand, mistress of magic, enchantments deep, you who beckon to fallen heroes, hearken this, your child. I would weave strong magic for protection, deep magic to bind and chasten. I lift up my sword to repel all attackers. Beware, foul troublemakers, for Freyja whispers her spells into my ear! Freyja, Queen of the Valkyries, stands at my side!

"As I stand here, the sisters of Freyja whisper in my ear. No mere mortal can possess or control us. Beware of any who wear the mark of the black sword hand." Daniel looked at the Korean dictator. "Any trouble from you, Dear Leader, and we will be back to incinerate this land. We will sterilize it to such a degree that even weeds will struggle to grow. It will be devoid of life. The dreams of the Great Leader will be fulfilled and Korea will be a land united, but it will not be the unification of his dreams. The North will be extinguished of its flame forever and only a ghoulish nightmare will remain. Do you understand, Dear Leader? You are my witness." The man nodded vigorously.

"Study your mythology, Dear Leader, and you will find us. You will see the warnings given long ago to justify our fury and retribution. All great societies have known us, but some have grown headstrong and forgotten the warnings. It is now on your head to make things right so I do not have to return and eliminate you as a people."

Daniel turned and ripped off Tiger's shirt to expose the tattoo of the tiger on his shoulder. Then he ripped the tattoo off, skin and all, and handed it to the Dear Leader. "See that my order is implemented." Tiger writhed in pain.

Daniel allowed Tiger to use his voice again, and the first reply was a scream. Numerous Korean swear words followed as blood dripped down his arm and onto the floor. "My organization is too big and too well organized for you to stop us, Defender! We will prevail!" Tiger spit in Daniel's general direction. Tiger thought of the sleeping gas that was at his disposal in the room, but he was unable to move and reach the button to trigger its release. He was also unable to reach any of the many firearms strategically hidden throughout the office. *Why can't I move?*

"You still do not understand. You are the master of your people but you have no capacity to understand. At least the Dear Leader comprehends the situation. Somehow you still believe this is all some magic trick. Your skin sitting on his leg did not come from trickery. And your organization? We are already dealing with that." Daniel transmitted the real-time views through Omar's eyes into Tiger's mind as Omar destroyed a nerve gas factory somewhere in the deserts of Arabia. "Do you see what we are doing?"

"You will never defeat me, Defender!"

Daniel levitated a model from the undisturbed table, made the model red hot, and used it to brand places on Tiger's skin. One model at a time, Tiger was forced to experience a little piece of all the hells he had imposed on innocent victims. Daniel used models of planes that had crashed, buildings that had been destroyed, and ships that had been sunk. He heated each one to a searing red heat before grinding them into Tiger's raw body. Tiger's screams were deafening, and the Dear Leader turned away in horror, fearing he was next.

Finally, only two models remained. One was a model of a bird very familiar to Daniel—a brilliantly carved and painted aracari. Daniel kept this one aside. The other was a model of the World Trade Center. It was long and square and made of metal. Daniel heated it until it was glowing red, and flung it at Tiger's chest. The projectile entered easily, severing the aorta.

Showers of blood spurted around the room as a horrified look flashed across Tiger's face. *I am not supposed to die! I'm too powerful for that! Who the hell is this nude man? It must be a magician's trick! I cannot die! It is all an illusion!*

Tiger felt a weird sensation as his brain, now starved of oxygen, began to die. His mind raced, but it focused on an alien emotion, something he struggled to recognize. The blood had slowed its mass exodus. A horrific grimace crossed his face.

Daniel smiled. "That was fear, Tiger. You were right to fear us." The last vestiges of life passed from the man. Satisfied with the revenge, Daniel picked up the colorful bird and glanced at Kim Jong Il as he walked past. "Remember this day. You do not want to see me again." Kim was too shocked to reply.

* * * * *

Daniel was off to tidy up the rest of the country. He neutralized nuclear weapons, poison gas, nuclear power plants, and all other nefarious instruments of mass destruction. He worked slowly and carefully, like a surgeon removing a cancer. He performed his duties unmolested while the country tried to cope with the massive earthquake damage it had suffered. *BBC News* reported the tragedy the following day:

Today a powerful earthquake rocked central North Korea. The massive quake, over eight on the Richter scale, did incredible damage to the capital. Although President Kim Jong Il is safe, appearing on both local and international broadcasts, the visibly shaken leader narrowly survived a building collapse near his car. Numerous key leaders are dead, including most of the senior military leadership.

The nuclear reactor, the center of so much controversy lately, was destroyed and the radiation has been contained. No death toll has been given, but losses are expected to be large. Red Cross teams are on the way as requested through the U.N. This was the largest quake to hit Asia in quite some time. Due to geography, the quake's effects were limited to a relatively local area. It was barely noticed in Seoul, South Korea.

Daniel was mentally and physically exhausted after his ordeal. He had finished cleaning up the country, so he decided to take a rest. It had been two weeks since he had executed Tiger. He had crisscrossed the country, catching rides on whatever mode of transportation available. He destroyed much and killed many who had been part of Tiger's sinister plot.

It was now a pleasant, late spring day and Daniel was near the Demilitarized Zone. He had been so focused on his mission for the past few months that he had barely taken time to think of what he had become or what he had done. He had been a man on a mission.

He leaned back against a tree to think and share his thoughts with his Volva contact. Ever since the destruction of Tiger, the Volva had reduced their watch to one woman. Anna was on duty today. Daniel needed her wisdom, as she knew him better than anyone and he trusted her judgment and advice.

As he began to replay in his mind the emotional strain of the events that had unfolded, Daniel began to sob, thinking he'd become some sort of monster. He had killed many bad men, but he had also killed many civilians who were not part of the master plan. These were generally innocent people. Daniel worried that he had let the power of his position get the better of him.

Anna tried to reassure him. *Life is not perfect, Daniel. You may not have saved humanity if these men were not stopped.*

He shook his head. *I feel ashamed. I think I may have become some sort of monster. In retrospect, I do not feel that I was any better than those terrible men. Who am I to judge them? Why was I chosen? Did I use methods that killed too many innocent victims?*

Anna smiled in his mind. *First of all, Daniel, nobody is innocent. All the members of the North Korean society had choices, to serve and follow or to rebel and disrupt. The easy choice was to continue to promote their nationalism and their reunification plans, thus maybe inadvertently supporting Tiger. They all wanted to destroy the South and its allies. You killed no innocent victims.*

Second, the Choosers picked you because you are the best for this job. Nobody else could have solved this situation as quickly as you did, and you had been on your own for only a few weeks before you started on the trail of these global terrorists. I will turn it around. If you had not been chosen, the virus attacks that Khan had planned would have been more widespread. SARS killed many people, but because of you, it will never threaten our whole species. If Khan would have lived, then something else he might have developed later on might have been worse than even SARS.

Tiger was a threat, but his concerns were narrow. He wanted reunification, world recognition, and maybe to control Japan. Khan, on the other hand, was truly evil. He wanted to use the innocents of the world for disease transmission. He was by far the real threat. I do not think even Tiger would have actually used his nuclear weapons.

Daniel was regaining his composure. *I guess you are right, Anna.* It was obvious the strain had taken its toll. His emotions were as much a by-product of fatigue as they were of his actual feelings. *Khan and Tiger had to go. I just hope we killed enough of them so their organization cannot be rebuilt.*

Anna sent kind thoughts to him. *There will always be others, if not from this organization, then from another we do not know about. Bad men come, they go, and then more bad men replace them. This process will repeat until the final days, until Ragnarök is upon us. We will all be destroyed in that final calamity. It cannot be helped. As Defenders, we are here to give the world a little more time and maybe during that time humanity can cure itself of its evil traits.*

Anna reminded him of their first conversation about the beginnings of the Order and how humans had been designed with a flaw. They were bent on self-destruction. She relayed her hopes that mankind could prevent its inevitable doom but that so far, religion, differing forms of government, and social evolution hadn't provided a fix and that everyone, including Defenders, were doomed.

The humanists believe man is essentially good and that if we search for a higher meaning and purpose, good will prevail. But finding higher meaning and purpose will not solve our basic problems. Even we in the Order are mortals, not gods. Despite our great powers, at some point we will fail and we will all pay the ultimate price. At some point, perhaps very soon, we may need to throw humanity into another Dark Age in order to protect our race. Choosing such an extreme option is one of the most difficult choices our Order has had to consider. But doing so will give all of our children at least some chance at life. Even our Volva-Defender society works only because of the extensive checks and balances that have been put in place. I had to give up most of my individuality to subscribe to the collective consciousness that makes me a Volva.

Daniel nodded in agreement instinctively, even though he was communicating telepathically and wasn't visible to Anna. *I imagine that the loss of your independence was hard to accept at first.*

Yes, but the Choosers picked me because I had a strong need to feel as though I belonged. I think that is why they choose orphaned women. You, Daniel, you had to give up more. You had to give up your family and any hope of leading a normal life. You had to accept the rules of our existence. You have had to share yourself equally with all of my sisters. You may love me as truly as I love you, but you know I must share myself with other men. You have great powers, but you have to spend most of your life alone.

He tried to correct her. *But, Anna, I did not choose my lot in life. Gunnar, my grandfather, did by his decision to live.*

She sighed. *Daniel, have you learned nothing from your adventures or your experiences so far? We all choose. You had the choice in the desert. You had the choice to die or live. You chose life. That life was not what you expected. It was life as one of us. If you had not pushed yourself in Oman, if you had just curled up and died, you would have made a different choice. As has been said before, some choices are hard and painful. Sometimes the painful-looking choices turn out to be the better ones. Sometimes, both choices are very bad. In those cases you have limited options from earlier decisions. Nobody said life was easy or fair, but we do make our own destinies.*

Daniel appreciated the way she looked at life. *You are always the pragmatic one, Anna. I guess I will just go on and prepare myself for the next time I am needed.*

Yes, that is your job. A Defender should always be happy

with who and what he is. You have accepted your position and who you have become quite well. Do what you have to do and move on. We will never let you do things you should not do. Never worry about that. It is very rare that we have to refuse a request for power. As you learn the limits of the Order, it becomes innate knowledge. Our job is at times difficult. We pass judgment frequently and make decisions that affect life and death, and we usually have no room for error.

Omar and the others report that they have cleaned up the loose ends worldwide. You would be surprised at Khan's setup. He even had vials of smallpox. He had three labs and they have all been destroyed. There was a lead about a possible fourth lab in Africa someplace, but we believe it closed long ago. The Congo and Zaire are now in disarray, so we doubt any meaningful trouble could originate there, but we will keep our eyes open.

Good. I do not like loose ends, Daniel thought to Anna. *I suppose it is like World War II. It will take some time for everything to settle down. So what should I do now?*

You need a break. It would be good to tie up some of your own loose ends. You should go back and visit your family. Let them know you are alive. I suspect that they do not believe you are dead. There is nothing wrong with using your power and position for your own enjoyment and satisfaction. I solved some of my own internal problems with our trip to Reva Gap. You need to find yourself and let go. You will always be a Swede from Nebraska. That is who you were and still are. But now, you are a Swede from Nebraska who is marked, can read minds, and use earth energy for dramatic feats of power.

He agreed. *I would like to give my family some closure. I never liked thinking they believed I was dead. I thought I could never visit them again.*

There is no rule against it. The Volva do not have families, so we do not think about you Defenders having them. Go take a sauna or—what do you call it in Swedish—a bastu with them.

Anna, are you learning Swedish?

It will not do for you to think in Swedish on the belief that we cannot understand your thoughts, Daniel. He could tell she was laughing at him. *That will just mean that as we perceive Swedish words for things, we will learn the language. I would encourage you to try something else, like rotating what language you think in. That is what Omar does. We do not know what he is thinking sometimes.*

You should also spend time with those two Swedish women friends of yours from Belize. Anna really liked the two women. *You need something to make you forget about your troubles and they would be a healthy distraction. They understand that they can never have you, and they enjoy being with you. You are different than anyone they have met before; you can even tell them more about yourself if you want. They have a remarkable ability for tolerance and understanding. It must be a Swedish thing. That camping trip sounds like fun. Do not be afraid of them as women. You need not worry about ethics and values. Yours are different than the majority of society and that is okay. I think it is also okay with them. It appears that the Swedes have a much different attitude about sex than just about any Western people. You are harming no one if you choose to be with them. So go ahead and do what you want and enjoy yourself.*

Thanks Anna, he thought, knowing it would soon be time for the Volva on duty to change. Anna had other worries to attend to. *Or should I say, Tack!*

Versagod. She laughed, giving him the Swedish version of, "You are welcome."

The warmth of the sun was making him sleepy. He decided to nap under the tree for a while before starting his next project. He would tie up all of his personal loose ends and then, if he felt like it, he would head to Sweden.

It made him laugh to think that the Volva were learning Swedish. He was getting used to them sharing his mind. In fact, he kind of liked them keeping him company. How many people who were not MPD could actually use "we" all the time? He laughed out loud.

CHAPTER 16: Tidying Up Loose Ends

Having now saved humanity from itself and feeling refreshed from what must have been a three-hour nap under the tree, Daniel wandered back to the border with the South and crossed the Demilitarized Zone. It still amazed him how little notice he generated as he passed the numerous military checkpoints. Most people were stopped, searched, questioned, searched again, and told to wait, sometimes for hours. He was waved through as if they didn't notice him at all.

His telepathic link to the temple was strong. Monique was now on duty. He bid her a happy day. His mind wandered back to the first time they had united. They both smiled at the lustful thought.

Telepathy was such a strange experience. Omar was right; these Volva knew every nook and cranny of his mind, and nothing was sacred. This was especially odd for a young man brought up in the Swedish tradition of reserved speech, thinking before talking, and only saying what was necessary.

Monique was having a slow day; only Daniel was doing anything that would require her services. Daniel was going to spend a little time in South Korea before heading back to the States. Something might turn up in the turmoil that he had caused that would require his services. Besides, he enjoyed his command of the Korean language and looked forward to continuing using it. Then he would visit Sweden.

When Daniel asked if Anna would be able to go with him on the trip to Sweden, he perceived something in Monique's mind that he hadn't noticed earlier. Anna would be unable to accompany him. She had conceived when they were camping at Reva Gap and was expecting his child—a girl.

Monique, why was I not told? Why was I unable to see this telepathically?

Simply put, you were too busy, she said without emotion. *There was nothing you could do. We could not allow you to be distracted from your mission.*

Can I come visit? Daniel asked. *I would like to see her and the baby. I honestly cannot believe I'm going to be a father!*

According to tradition, you must enter the temple at the

second full moon after the birth, Monique instructed. *That will be mid-August. You will have plenty of time to spend with them after that. We will have a naming feast the night after you have completed the purification ritual. You will see your child for the first time and give her a name. We expect a good Scandinavian name, Daniel, so start thinking. It is your choice alone. It will be nice to have a child at the temple.*

Wow! Now he understood Anna's instructions for him to clear up his family business. He would have a busy and joyous summer.

By the way, Daniel, you did a good job with the terrorist-Tiger ordeal. We are all proud that you made the choice to join us. I hope we all have a nice break before the next crisis.

Daniel announced that he had some unfinished business back in the States. The Choosers had kidnapped him before he had settled a problem. His Swedish sense of fairness was now starting to cause him unrest. It wasn't a problem that was going to affect humanity, but it was impacting a lot of innocent people.

Monique thought, *You should dispatch that Altorini fellow and then go and visit your parents. Remember that to them, you have been buried for nearly two years, so you must take care how you present yourself. People have trouble with ghosts showing up in their lives.*

Daniel agreed to be careful and thanked her for being so kind to him.

We are all in this together, Daniel. We are humans first and Defenders second. We need to continue caring for our fellow man or we would not be any better than the Hitlers and Kims of the world. She told him she would contact Serge, a Defender in Europe, and that proper arrangements would be made. After three more weeks in Korea, a plane would pick him up for the trip to America.

* * * * *

During the next three weeks, Daniel perfected his Korean and slept up to sixteen hours a day. The plane came as scheduled, but it went west instead of east and Daniel woke up in Reykjavik, Iceland. He was at a U.S. Air Force base and his plane was refueling.

He decided to take the opportunity to spend a few days in this strange land.

It was ten degrees Celsius and overcast, yet it was a wonderful early summer day, one that would never end here above the Arctic Circle. He caught a ride to the international airport to find some information to plan his mini-adventure on the island. He had stopped at that airport a few times previously, but neither he nor his family had ever ventured into the countryside. He walked around until he saw what he was after, an advertisement for the Blue Lagoon, a spa based on a deep blue geothermal spring. He planned to wallow in the hot bath for hours.

The Blue Lagoon was excellent. After a soak that was starting to make him dizzy due to the heat, he stripped off his trunks and donned a towel for a soothing massage, his first since his Swedish friends had left Belize. The woman with the kind hands was Hildur Björndötter. Iceland was still using the Old Norse way of naming. Daniel had always thought it quaint, but it was difficult to use for tracking the family surname. He had hoped his knowledge of Swedish and Norwegian would allow him to communicate with the Icelandic people, but they basically spoke Old Norse, which was too far removed from his adopted native tongue. But Hildur and everyone else spoke English and many spoke Swedish as well in this international society.

Iceland was a small country—even smaller than Daniel had realized—and Hildur was a friend of the Prime Minister's daughter. This man knew of the Defenders, and having such a powerful being in his country was an honor for him and his people. Daniel was requested to attend a state dinner and his stay at the Blue Lagoon was courtesy of the state. Then, after three days of soaking in the unnaturally blue briny water, he made plans to depart before any more official government functions demanded his attendance.

Daniel went to back to the air force base where a C-130 cargo plane was waiting for him. Except for a refueling stop in Maine where Daniel walked around the base and found some food, he slept for most of the long flight. C-130s are not known for their luxuries, so sleep was his only entertainment.

The airport in Sioux Falls, South Dakota, was quiet when he

landed at about ten A.M.. The morning planes from Minneapolis, Denver, and Chicago had already come and gone along with their passengers; it would be noon before the second rush would hit the airport. On the morning of June 12, the sky was clear and the weather was warm. Summer was just beginning, but Daniel suspected thunderstorms would arrive in the late afternoon. Weather was always just about to change on the prairie.

He arrived at the rental car counter to find he was the only customer present. A young, pretty, blue-eyed woman approached. She was of northern European descent and she was wearing her uniform with an Augustana emblem on a necklace. He smiled. He hadn't met a fellow college alumnus in a long while. He knew he could seduce her, but kept to his task. "I need to borrow a car for a few days."

Rachel had just started at the rental counter. She was between her third and fourth year of college, and it had so far been a wonderful summer job. The job didn't keep her too busy and she got to meet a lot of people. She was gregarious by nature and disliked the long waits between rushes of customers. This blond-haired man fascinated her. He had the deepest blue eyes she had ever seen. He seemed full of self-confidence. She hadn't seen that in any of the men she had been with. She never noticed the strange markings on his face. She just kept looking at his eyes. "I need a driver's license and a major credit card," came the rote request. She could almost feel that he was in her mind, probing her every whim and fancy.

"I hate to admit it, but I don't have either. I don't even have money. I'm not really fussy about which car to take. I'll take good care of the car, though."

This seemed unusual to her. He had no credit card, no money, and no license. His eyes were so kind, though, that she couldn't say no. She felt she had to give him a car. He would take good care of it. "Do you want to sign anything?"

"No, not really. You have my word that I will return it unhurt." Daniel kept probing her mind and was shocked at the demeaning attitude and abuse she had taken from her boyfriend. She had so little self-respect left, he felt sorry for her. "I see you're at Augustana and that you're going to be a senior next year. You should take the

Swedish foreign studies course at Darlarna University. You need to get away from certain people and certain things. You will come back with a new attitude and maybe even with a new man." She listened intently, and his suggestions were persuasive. "I think they have an opening for you. You're a nice person, Rachel. You deserve better. You've been so kind to me, I just wanted to help you out."

She suddenly found her mind filled with Swedish words and phrases. She didn't remember learning any Swedish, but she did have Swedish ancestors. Maybe they were words her parents had said to her when she was a child. She was filled with self-confidence and her most overwhelming thoughts focused on her going to Sweden to study. Rachel would be off work in a few hours and would go to the college and apply for the program. Her boyfriend would not approve, but she suddenly she didn't care. She would move out of his apartment this afternoon as well.

Rachel would go back to Wells, Minnesota, and visit her parents, then fly to Sweden a few weeks early to settle in and work on the language. She was so happy that she barely remembered whether she had given him the correct keys. She couldn't even remember how long he wanted the car for, but since he was gone, she marked Open Ended on the computer. A license and credit card number were on the screen, but she didn't remember seeing one. Her mind was filled with pleasant thoughts of Sweden, beautiful blond men, a new culture and no more abuse. She was having a wonderful day.

Daniel quickly found the new Dodge Neon and drove out of the airport and down I-29 southbound, heading toward Yankton to settle his former problem. About thirty miles south, near the town of Beresford, he was passed by a young man driving wildly in a fancy BMW convertible. He gave Daniel the bird as he passed by. Daniel just shook his head. He looked at the BMW speeding away at ninety-five miles per hour and it suddenly slowed and stopped. Daniel waved as he passed. The man was cursing at his stricken chariot. "Should have bought a Volvo." Daniel laughed out loud.

He was in Yankton an hour later. The Far Western National Bank building was a converted fast-food restaurant on the strip of the major highway in town and was much smaller than the Watertown branch he was used to. He walked through the front door filled with his new self-confidence. He was a new man since he'd left South Dakota, a new man with new powers. He had saved the world from harm and he wasn't even twenty-six years old. Altorini would be his dessert.

The man was not only still employed; he was now the branch manager. Apparently Daniel's e-mail had gone unnoticed. The receptionist ushered Daniel into Altorini's office where he waited while Altorini finished a phone call.

Altorini was a middle-aged man with dark hair and brown eyes. He also had an air of self-assurance, obviously due to his family connections. The photos on the wall showed a man of leisure and privilege. They pictured him with politicians, prized fish, blondes with surgically enhanced breasts, large mountains, and Caribbean tropical vacations.

"Can I help you?" Altorini asked, hanging up the phone. The man before him looked strange. Tattoos covered most of his face and neck, and he was dressed in Middle Eastern garb. He probably was from the university in Vermillion, but he had an ominous look in his eyes.

"I have become aware of a small matter of securities fraud involving a certain fictitious Belize bank. You have been stealing millions from the old folks around here," Daniel began. "You are going to give it back today, then go to the FBI and turn in yourself and all of your partners."

Joseph Altorini was a cool man. He had been under the spotlight of authorities since he was a teenager. No tattooed man was going to scare him. But he needed to find out just how much the man knew and whom he'd told. Then he would call his uncle's men in Omaha to tie up a few loose ends. "You didn't give me your name. Who is going to make me do all of this, then?"

"No, I didn't give you my name. I'm your nightmare. And I personally am going to enforce these terms."

Altorini laughed as he lifted his coffee mug to his lips. It exploded and hot coffee sprayed everywhere. He yelped and grabbed for the napkin on his desk. He had been mildly burned and his Armani suit was probably ruined. His smugness turned to anger. "Do you know who I am? I have some powerful and influential friends, sort of the Italian Mutual Assistance League, if you get my drift. I could make life for you and your family very, let's say, life threatening."

Daniel showed not even the slightest concern. His army was ever-present and it was not an army to be messed with. "I'm already dead to my family, Altorini, and I'm not liking your attitude here. Let's see . . . how can I demonstrate?" He remembered the Mercedes he'd seen outside with the Altorini plates. "I really don't think it's prudent for a good Italian such as you to own a German car. The Germans did some despicable things to your Sicilian and Italian relatives after Italy collapsed during the war." A large lightning bolt pierced the air, and the silver Mercedes was engulfed in flames.

Altorini reached into a drawer that contained a Glock 8 mm handgun. The drawer closed on his wrist, preventing him from grabbing the gun or wresting his arm loose from the tight grip.

"That would be an unwise choice," Daniel scolded. "And you do have a choice here. Everyone needs to have choices. We can do this the easy way or the hard way. Security fraud is what, three to five years in the federal pen? If you plea-bargain the sentence I will not be pleased, and I might have to mete out my own punishment—or you can choose my punishment directly. You have not treated me with the respect I deserve. In some cultures, that would mean me wiping you, your family, and all that you have out of existence. That seems a little extreme, of course, but it is your choice." The pictures all fell from the wall in unison and the coffee maker melted on the table into an amorphous blob. "Give me an excuse, Altorini. Going on an Altorini extermination crusade would be an enjoyable exercise." He pointed at the computer screen. "Now, I think a buyout of the First National Bank of Belize stock for one hundred twenty-five percent of the original investment would be appropriate."

Altorini started typing. "I don't have enough to cover it."

"I'm sure you have some accounts from your Italian friends," Daniel said. "They should contribute as well. After all, it is an Italian Mutual Assistance League, isn't it? You need all the assistance you can get right about now."

"They'll kill me, you know."

"Maybe, but I'd make yours a more terrible death," he said, looking directly into Altorini's eyes. "You'll watch your family die one by one, and then you will melt from your feet up to your neck."

Altorini realized he wasn't kidding. He had never felt such terror before, and he believed the tattooed man meant what he said. He dutifully repaid all that was due, some sixteen million dollars. He also repaid a newer scam involving a different offshore bogus bank for another eleven million dollars. Most of the money came from a Mafia slush account in the Cayman Islands.

"Now, who else was in on this?" Daniel probed further.

"A branch manager from the Watertown branch—he figured it out a couple of years back," Altorini explained. "We had to give him a six-figure loan from the bank. Of course, he never made any payments on the loan. Two men at the main bank in Sioux Falls were also involved."

"You will testify against all of them or our deal is off. You will personally plead guilty and ask for five years. I'm sure you'll get the country club prison anyway."

After all the transfers were complete, they headed to the FBI office. Daniel offered to drive since Altorini's car was now a smoldering ruin in the parking lot. Altorini felt he had no choice. The pair got into the Neon, cleverly avoiding the fire trucks that had assembled in the parking lot. Nobody seemed to know where Joseph Altorini was, and the authorities needed to tell him that a freakish bolt of lightning had mysteriously destroyed his car, a weather anomaly that seemed especially odd on a cloudless day.

The nearest FBI office was in Sioux Falls. Twice Altorini made sudden movements, and each time his seat belt tightened. After the second event, the belt was so tight he could scarcely breathe. During the rest of the ride, he sat motionless and afraid to speak. He felt that any chitchat might lead to the strange man pulling over and leaving him dead in a cornfield. In any event, Daniel appreciated the silence.

Daniel stopped in front of the Federal building in downtown Sioux Falls. When Altorini was let out of the car, he never looked back, and ran up the stairs. He would heed Daniel's warning. In his hand he held a CD containing all the evidence the FBI would require to convict him and his associates. Altorini especially disliked

345

the manager from Watertown who two years earlier had tried to blackmail him, saying he had a secret witness and demanding a five hundred thousand dollar bribe in the form of a loan. Nobody black-mails the Mafia and lives, but they could never find the secret wit-ness, so they paid the man. The manager was a fool and had left his money in a personal account at the bank. He was stupid not to spend it, so Altorini used this money for part of the restitution as well. He remembered paying off a woman named Martha Johnson with that money.

Having tied up this loose end, Daniel drove to the park at the falls. He had been enjoying the cascade over the red rock since he was in college. Sitting on the bench at the top of the cascade, he could think for hours about nearly anything. He'd always thought it odd that such a sizable falls existed in the middle of the prairie. He also marveled at the nearby Devil's Gulch in Garretson. That red rock canyon was another geological oddity that was also made famous as an escape route by Jesse James when he jumped his horse across the twenty-foot narrows to the other side. The posse from Northfield, Minnesota, was reluctant to be so daring, so they'd halted the pursuit.

Daniel would not have time to revisit Devil's Gulch and sus-pected that he would never lay eyes on the falls again. His new activities with the Order would keep him away from this sleepy heartland of the United States. This was a perfect place to raise crops and children. It had virtually no crime, good morals, and hardworking, honest people. Unfortunately, he would not be a fam-ily man; his destiny was now much different. There would be other falls to gaze into at more exotic locations. This, however, was an important sight to him and he wanted to fully absorb it for the last time. He thought about his future and his family for a long time. He wanted to see his family, but was afraid. What would he say? What could he say?

* * * * *

It was morning in the Ethiopian valley, and Anna was again on duty. She reassured Daniel and apologized about keeping her preg-nancy from him. Her thoughts warmed his heart and filled him with happiness. He was about to tell her of his choices for names but realized that she already knew them and also knew that it was his choice alone. She also knew of his conversation with Monique. Anna was looking forward to them being together again and yearned for his return.

He spent the night in a suite in the local hotel. The attendant not only had a complimentary room for Daniel, but she also delivered take-out food from next door. He was too tired for any other male-female activities, so he tried to keep his mind clear.

Anna kept trying to break his concentration. She remembered his tutoring with the Swiss woman back in Washington, D.C. So did Daniel, and he seemed unable to avoid his mental persecution. It was her form of entertainment. The poor woman from the hotel kept coming and going. Anna enjoyed teasing her lover and knew the male mind very well. Daniel was happy when she allowed him to eat and let the poor woman from the front desk escape back to her job. The blonde Volva rewarded her young love by filling him with sweet dreams. He had one of the most peaceful nights that he could remember.

The following morning, Daniel pointed the Neon south in the direction of Ogallala, Nebraska. It had rained overnight but the roads were not bad and the drive was pleasant. Around noon he tuned in to one of his favorite AM stations out of Yankton. The station had been a fixture of his youth on the ranch. Its powerful signal beamed the weather, ag reports, news, and sports into six states. He enjoyed the country music they played. At noon it was time for the news:

In world news, North Korea has reached an agreement with the United Nations to surrender its entire nuclear program to UN authorities. They also agreed to UN-monitored total disarmament and planned to stand down their military by September. The UN agreed to provide food for the Korean people and help develop new industries in conjunction with the South Korean government.

The leader of the Arab terrorist group, Hamas, who turned in a nuclear device earlier this month to Swiss authorities, without preamble today, called off the Jihad against the West. He

*stated that it was time that the Arabic people learned to live
with their neighbors and added that he hoped the Moslem world
would return to their roots of education, arts, invention, and
literature. In a related story, the king of Saudi Arabia has do-
nated one billion dollars to help start mandatory female education in his country. They are targeting a goal of ninety-eight
percent male and female literacy within ten years.*

*In local news, Joseph Altorini, nephew of the suspected
Omaha leader of the organized crime syndicate, pled guilty at
a preliminary hearing this morning to multiple counts of securities fraud and was sentenced to five years in Federal prison.
Indictments were issued for three other executives of the Far
Western National Bank on the same charges; their names have
not been released. The bank, Altorini, and the U.S. Attorney's
office were unavailable for comment.*

Now for the interstate weather....

Daniel continued his drive into Nebraska. He needed gas and
stopped at a convenience store in the central part of the state. It
had a pay-at-the-pump option. Daniel easily turned the machine on
and filled the tank. He sometimes felt guilty about getting something for nothing, but he knew this was the price society had to pay.
He typically liked to help people who gave him things. He would
encourage people to change their lives just as he had for the woman
at the car rental site. Most of the time people just needed encouragement and confidence. People all too often felt that they had no
options when they actually had many. Daniel would just point out
the obvious and the people would be the better for it.

* * * * *

Mashira was having a good day in Uber, Oman. She had just
received some beautiful cloth from which she would make herself
a new outfit. It would be an enjoyable week of sewing. Ever since
Daniel had left, her stature had improved dramatically. She and her
two sisters now ate meals with the men. This had never before
occurred for women in her region. It was a mark of her status. She
hoped to eventually use her status to uplift all her fellow females.

348

She was happy being the wife of Daniel, the all-powerful Homat al Omma. She had hoped to conceive his child. However, if she never had a child, there would still be local children for her to help raise. Her status in the community was no longer judged by whether she had children, and it was no longer judged or controlled by her father, the local sheik. She was now her own woman and she could do as she pleased, wear what she liked, and eat when she was hungry. No one would ever dare to put her in her place. No one would dare invoke the wrath of her husband. She and everyone else were now well aware of the legends. All had seen with their own eyes the Homat al Omma's execution of his captor in front of her home.

It was a sunny day in the desert. Most days in Uber were sunny and unbearably hot. Mashira would take a long bath in the men's communal bath with her sisters. Of course the men would immediately leave—to see another man's wife naked was the same as adultery, and retribution by the Homat al Omma was the penalty. Mashira liked to push the envelope and she yearned for a more Western society. She strived for a culture that allowed both sexes to eat, bathe, sleep, and worship the almighty Allah together. It would happen, but probably not during her lifetime.

She hoped Daniel would someday return, but she had no illusions. He was a very busy, important man. Undoubtedly he was off somewhere saving the world from destruction. He was a very gentle husband to her, and that was something she truly appreciated. He had treated her as an equal. She was glad he'd picked her to spare the life of her father. If he did come home, she would present herself to him as she had on her wedding night and make him a happy man. That was the duty of a good wife and it was the least she could do for the man that had given her so much in her society.

Tonight Mashira would eat goat. It was a big community celebration. She would have the best cuts and would choose her food before her father or any of the city elders were allowed to choose theirs. There would be much song, dancing, and eating, and she would be in the center of it all.

* * * * *

In mid-afternoon, Daniel approached North Platte. Since he was going to get up early tomorrow, he decided to call it a day. He checked into a nice family motel with a wonderful pool. He yearned for a dip in the pool and hot tub, but the only clothing he had was the white tunic that had become his trademark garb. He preferred to be au-natural, but he wasn't in Europe and this wasn't a freluftbad, a Swedish place where clothing was optional. He decided to relax by the pool on a beach chair anyway. The sun was warm and a younger couple was swimming, an older couple was sitting in a chair opposite him, a family and two children were splashing in the shallow end, and two middle-aged women were sunning themselves next to him. He enjoyed watching everyone having a good time and soon the warmth put him to sleep. Daniel thought of Sweden, of a more European attitude about one's body, of the freedom of being clothing optional, and of cool water enveloping his hot, naked skin.

He awoke from the daydream as, to his surprise, the young couple emerged from the pool totally nude. The older couple was removing their clothes and giggling, the mother in the pool was topless, and the two women were now sunning au-naturel, face up, next to him on a beach chair. Daniel could read by their thoughts the freshness, relaxation, and acceptance everyone now possessed of their new-found freedom.

Today's Volva of record was Darna, the Indian woman. She was amused with what had happened. Daniel realized he had to watch out for vivid daydreaming. He had a lot of power and could cause problems with thought transference. It was typical for Defenders to exclude themselves from society, and he was beginning to understand why. In this case, the people were having a good time splashing around together, so nobody seemed the worse for it.

The couple in the pool encouraged him so he pulled off his tunic and jumped in. The water was excellent and he enjoyed himself immensely. Everyone asked about his tattoos. They all felt his body art was tastefully done and marveled at the detail of the lynx on his left breast and back. He agreed that experts had applied them. The older woman even correctly identified the Brisingamen design on his right cheek. He told her it was the symbol of the goddess Freyja. Everyone liked his beautiful body. He, in turn, felt they all had beautiful bodies and instilled in them the confidence of accepting themselves as they were. Others who came to the pool joined in the relaxed atmosphere and everyone, he was sure, would long remember their trip through North Platte, Nebraska.

On June fourteenth, Daniel awoke early, as was his custom on his birthday. He was now twenty-six years old. He drove out early into the prairie to watch the sunrise. Meadowlarks were singing and the breeze was light but slowly stiffening. He enjoyed watching the wind run through the prairie grass in waves. It was going to be a happy day. Every day now seemed happy to Daniel, especially since he had met Anna and discovered he would soon be the father of a healthy daughter. Both mother and daughter were doing well. Maria, the Latino Volva, was on duty. Nothing new needed his attention, so he headed west toward Ogallala.

* * * * *

The Nielstrom house was busy on this particular Thursday. Erika Nielstrom had returned late the previous evening from Sweden. Her plane into Denver had been delayed, and even with the jet lag and the excitement of returning home, she was still up early, talking to her family. She was a student at Darlarna University in Falun and had just finished her first year of study.

Hanna had also returned from abroad; she had met a man and was living with him. Although she planned on getting married, the Swedish custom was to live together first. He was a young doctor and he would come to visit the family in a month. Dag, Daniel's father, suspected the couple would return to Sweden happily married. He liked the old Swedish customs better than the new ones.

Daniel's mom, Ingrid, was busy preparing lunch. It was her son's birthday. In the Nielstrom family, Mom always made your favorite food on your birthday. Even though she didn't expect to see him again, she would remember him with her family by eating his favorite food this day. She suspected her daughters had returned for the same reason. Especially after Dag had shared old Gunnar's strange letter in the sauna, she felt that Daniel was still alive, somewhere. She still missed him and yearned to see his smile.

Today, lunch would be *husmanskost*, consisting of pea soup and pancakes. In the Old World it would be traditionally served on

Thursdays. Today was, coincidentally, Thursday. This combination was also served to Dag's father, Gunnar, when he'd met his wife, Erika, and fell in love. Her own lovely younger daughter, Erika, all grown up and reunited with the family, was Grandma Erika's namesake. She was glad she had chosen such a pretty name for such a pretty child. Maybe she would have a granddaughter someday by that name as well. It would be a special meal for a special family. She even placed a spot on the table for Daniel since it was his birthday.

Dag could see that the kitchen, filled as it was with women, was no place for him so he headed down the long driveway to get the mail. The doctor had advised him to get as much exercise as possible, and this lengthy stroll was his main non-farming-related activity. As he reached the mailbox he noticed a green Dodge Neon approaching on the dirt road. It was definitely not the sort of car a Nielstrom would drive. As it got closer he noticed the red, white, and blue South Dakota plates. *Not somebody lost again!* he thought. The car slowed and Dag still supposed it was a lost tourist. Despising giving directions, he decided that he would speak only Swedish to the man in the car. Being lost was a punishment for being unprepared. His dad had taught him to never leave home without knowing exactly where he was going. It would serve the man right to be ignored.

The window rolled down and a familiar Swedish voice called out to him. "Hej Hej!"

Now confused, Dag approached for closer identification. This strange yet familiar voice had disrupted his plans. A Swedish-speaking tourist lost in Nebraska? It was almost incomprehensible. A tattooed, blond-haired man wearing a white tunic emerged from the car. It had been over two full years, but Dag immediately knew his own flesh and blood and hugged his son tightly. They left the car and walked back to the house just as they had many times before.

The three women were turned away talking as the men entered by the back door near the kitchen. Daniel's mother didn't look up. "What did we get in the mail, dear?"

"Nothing but a wayward traveler desiring a good Swedish meal on his birthday," replied Dag.

Daniel also replied in Swedish. "Hej Hej, Mama!" For a moment, the room went totally silent. Nobody dared turn around for fear it was some kind of mass hallucination. "I could smell the pea soup from so far away it brought me home."

Hanna was the first to speak. "My God! Is that you?"

Daniel hugged her, then his mother. Erika had backed away from the table in disbelief. She had never believed the tale Grandpa Nielstrom had sent from the grave. Her brother had to be dead. When she reached out and he grabbed her hand, she finally gave in and cried joyously, louder than everyone. Daniel knew their thoughts and asked Darna to help keep his powers away from his family. The Volva agreed to help out.

"Erika, because you seem to be the most in need of something to remember me by, I have brought you a present," Daniel began. "It is a memento from my travels." He gave her the beautifully carved statue he had taken from Tiger's office. "This is an aracari, a bird I saw in Belize. It gave me hope and served me as an omen of good fortune. But it represents my past. I have grown, and I want you to know that even though you may see me rarely, by having this bird, you will know that I live and am part of you and our family."

She accepted the statue as a treasure to be cherished and thanked her brother with another big hug. The family sat and talked about life, family, and relationships. Daniel was soon caught up-to-date with all of the family events. They never asked what had become of him. They were glad he was back and they were relishing the moment.

As typical to the home, lunch was comfortably quiet. Each person enjoyed every bite of the delicious meal. Daniel had forgotten how good a cook his mother was, or maybe it was just Swedish food or the memory of the North Korean cabbage and rice, but it was so flavorful to Daniel that he ate it in very small mouthfuls and took his time.

After lunch, Dag hinted that he should fire up the sauna. Everyone agreed with so much enthusiasm that he ran to the pile of firewood. The bastu in the Nielstrom house was, without a doubt, the shared family experience. Daniel enjoyed the quiet smiles of his family at his return. He was filled with happiness. His spirit was renewed as he appreciated a wonderful sense of belonging.

They walked to the sauna and everyone disrobed. Typically, Daniel had been the most self-conscious of all the family members so everyone covered most of their essential anatomy as they walked in. Daniel, having long ago lost this restricted attitude, just put his towel over his shoulder and walked in and jumped into the cold shower next to the bastu. His two sisters, having just returned from Europe, followed suit and everyone, now very relaxed with each other, sat and enjoyed the heat.

Daniel noticed that his two sisters had grown to be beautiful young women. The Swedish doctor would be a lucky man, and he was sure Erika would also find someone special. Daniel smiled at his parents, sitting nude beside each other, holding hands. He felt comfortable knowing he had parents who loved each other so deeply.

The Nielstrom family marveled at the handsome man that was their brother and son. Each, in turn, observed the ornate markings on his body. The markings obviously meant something, but they were afraid to ask.

"I have a necklace exactly like the symbol on your face." Erika was always the first to state the obvious. "I think it was Grandma's. She left a note with it to be careful wearing it, so I've been scared to wear it at all. I figured it was a Norse symbol and I've been meaning to do research on it but haven't gotten around to it."

"It's a Brisingamen, Erika," he replied. "It's a symbol of Freyja, the Norse goddess of love and sexuality. She was a powerful figure, some say the most powerful of the Norse gods, and she was undefeated in battle. Maybe she wasn't really one person. Maybe she was a whole bunch of people, men and women. The myth that got condensed over the centuries blended them into her. In her Order, the women were called Volva and were very powerful and tended the temple. They would transfer their energy to the men, the Defenders, who would use that power to protect humanity and balance man's evil nature. They traditionally kept cats as pets, powerful cats like this lynx." He pointed to his chest. "See? They have pointier tufts on their ears than our bobcats. They were good people, an ancient race. Some believe they still exist today. I don't know, though; I've always found it hard to believe in myths.

"But you do need to be careful with that necklace. If it is worn on someone Nordic who truly believes in its power, it could lead you to enamor some young male. Use it only with the one you want forever. He will never leave you or think about another." He whispered the rest of the legend of its power in her ear, and then said, "I think it's a family tradition. Remember what they said about Grandma and Grandpa Nielstrom." They all laughed and Erika blushed, turning red from more than just the heat of the bastu. "It is the curse of happiness, something we Nielstroms have a lot of these days."

They all suspected that this would be their last sauna together, and they wanted to savor it to the end. After the sauna, they all went into the pool for a refreshing dip. Then they wandered inside and sat on towels in the living room. They all seemed to understand what Daniel had become and who he was. They had to share him with the world and that would be fine. Knowing that he was alive was all they wanted. He would always be part of the family. They all savored the moment and no one spoke. The smiles were enough.

Dag had raised a wonderful family and was proud of all of them. He could now grow old with his wonderful wife and die a happy man. He loved his daughters and his son. He knew both Erika and Hanna would raise wonderful families themselves. He marveled at the thought of being a grandfather. Ogallala needed a doctor, and a Swedish son-in-law doctor would do just fine. He was sad that the Nielstrom name would die out, but he didn't care. He'd done his job as a father. He knew his own father would be proud of what he had done.

He went to the special chilled-liquor cabinet. He had saved a new bottle of O. P. Anderson schnapps for just such an occasion. He wanted to have the honor of toasting his beloved son in person, both as a hello and a good-bye. When all the glasses were filled, he lifted his and looked at Daniel. Together with his wife, they said "To our beloved son."

Erika and Hanna added their own toast before anyone drank. "To our wonderful brother, may the world be his."

Together they all replied, "Sköl!" and the family drank in unison.

Other Savage Press Books

CHILDREN'S BOOKS

Out of the Rainbow by Jay Ford Thurston (Due in 2007)
Pond Frog by Dennis Sears (Due in 2007)

OUTDOORS, SPORTS & RECREATION

Curling Superiority! by John Gidley
Packers "verses" Vikings by Carl W. Nelson
The Duluth Tour Book by Jeff Cornelius
The Final Buzzer by Chris Russell

ESSAY

Awakening of the Heart, Second Printing by Jill Downs
Battle Notes: Music of the Vietnam War by Lee Andresen
Color on the Land by Irene I. Luethge
Following in the Footsteps of Ernest Hemingway
                    by Jay Ford Thurston
Hint of Frost, Essays on the Earth by Rusty King
Hometown Wisconsin by Marshall J. Cook
Potpourri From Kettle Land by Irene I. Luethge

FICTION

Burn Baby Burn by Mike Savage
Capitol Reflections by Jonathan Javitt
Charleston Red by Sarah Galchus
Keeper of the Town short stories by Don Cameron
Lake Effect by Mike Savage
Lord of the Rinks by Mike Savage
Northern Lights Magic by Lori J. Glad
Off Season by Marshall J. Cook
Sailing Home by Lori J. Glad
Something in the Water by Mike Savage
Spirit of The Shadows by Rebel Sinclair
Summer Storm by Lori J. Glad
The Devil of Charleston by Rebel Sinclair
The Year of the Buffalo by Marshall J. Cook
Voices From the North Edge by St. Croix Writers

REGIONAL HISTORY, MEMOIR

Beyond the Freeway by Peter J. Benzoni
Crocodile Tears and Lipstick Smears by Fran Gabino
Dakotaland by Howard Jones
Echoes from the Past by Nan Wisherd
Fair Game by Fran Gabino
Memories of Iron River by Bev Thivierge
Stop in the Name of the Law by Alex O'Kash
Superior Catholics by Cheney and Meronek
Pathways, Early History of Brule Wisconsin by Nan Wisherd
Widow of the Waves by Bev Jamison

BUSINESS

Dare to Kiss the Frog by vanHauen, Kastberg & Soden
SoundBites Second Edition by Kathy Kerchner

POETRY

A Woman for all Time by Evelyn Gathman Haines
Eraser's Edge by Phil Sneve
Gleanings from the Hillsides by E.M. Johnson
I Was Night by Bekah Bevins
Pathways by Mary B. Wadzinski
Philosophical Poems by E.M. Johnson
Poems of Faith and Inspiration by E.M. Johnson
Portrait of the Mississippi by Howard Jones
The Morning After the Night She Fell Into the Gorge
                                        by Heidi Howes
Thicker Than Water by Hazel Sangster
Treasures from the Beginning of the World by Jeff Lewis

HUMOR

Baloney on Wry by Frank Larson
Jackpine Savages by Frank Larson
With Malice Toward Some by Georgia Z. Post

OTHER BOOKS AVAILABLE FROM SP

Blueberry Summers by Lawrence Berube
Dakota Brave by Howard Jones
Spindrift Anthology by The Tarpon Springs Writer's Group

To order additional copies of

Marks of the Forbidden

call

1-800-732-3867

or

purchase copies on-line at:

www.savpress.com

Visa/MC/Discover/American Express/
ECheck/accepted via PayPal

All Savage Press books are available through all chain and
independent bookstores nationwide. Just ask them to special
order if the title is not in stock.

Coming Soon. The exciting Defenders of the Earth sequel:

No Peace in Exile

Recovering from his battle with Tiger, Daniel hopes
to find peace and relief in the form of his newborn daughter. It is not to be however, as, after a joyful reunion at the
Volva temple, a maverick Defender who has been in hiding for over thirty years becomes the world's greatest
threat and Daniel's next great challenge.

In this second book, Olaf Danielson introduces the
Aesir, or Choosers, the mysterious men who search the
world for those special enough to become *Defenders of
the Earth.*